Chords of Infinity

Dimensional Alliance series, Volume 5
Bonnie K.T. Dillabough

Cover art by Richard McKenzie

Acknowledgements:

To my amazing team: Lynette M. Smith, my copy-editor; Richard McKenzie, my cover artist; George C. Dillabough, my alpha reader: and beta readers, Carolyn Hardy Greiner, Maria Gurriere, Angela Bryner and Delia D. Michael. And I would be remiss not to mention all of my readers who continue to support and encourage me. There will yet be at least 4 more books in this series and I couldn't have done it without you. Thank you from the depths of my soul.

Table of Contents

Prologue:

The kiss on her forehead woke Jenny with a start. Burt grinned down at her. "Wake up, sleepyhead. We have company and you have breakfast. Get dressed and we'll see you out on the patio. It's a gorgeous day and Tidbit, Chidwi, BaaGah, and Lolly are entertaining our guests at the moment. Bob and Merv wanted to brief you in person."

Jenny stretched and yawned as she watched him turn and leave out of the bedroom door. She had read into the night to finish the first of Lizzie's journals and was anxious to start the second one, as she only had these few weeks to finish them before she went back to full duty.

She had spent a large part of her sleeping time interacting in cross-dimensional mindspeech with various members of the Dimensional Alliance regarding the ongoing efforts to prepare to liberate the various dimensions potentially enslaved and ravaged by the Insenium. As Gatekeeper, it was part of her responsibility to manage the various gate guardians and keep up to date with the ongoing operations and then report to the Alliance Council.

Fortunately, due to her expanding mental abilities, she had learned to do something no one else, including Liliath (the dragon who currently headed the Alliance Council) had known could be done. She could contact people mentally even across dimensions, as long as she knew the person well. She had discovered she could do this while sleeping, although it did affect the quality of her sleep.

While on light duty, due to doctor's orders, she had to limit her nighttime work. But during the day, her time was her own for the next couple of weeks. She had spent the first week of her recuperation delving into her aunt Lizzie's journals.

She hadn't had the opportunity to get to know her aunt while she was alive and had been so surprised to find herself the heir to her estates. She had no idea the impact this would have on her life.

As she had discovered while reading that first journal, Lizzie had been given a similar opportunity that had taken her off of her planned path into a lot more than she thought she had bargained for.

The difference was that Lizzie had actually been given the opportunity to go through the entire training process available to agents and gate guardians. Jenny, contrary to anyone's expectations, had been given almost no time to train as a gate guardian and had been thrust untimely into the role of the Gatekeeper, in charge of all other gate guardians.

Fortunately, Jenny had been given a guide, Tarafau Bane, a shape-changer whose persona while on Earth, except in special circumstances, was normally seen as a big black cat named Tidbit, of all things. Without him, she might have been even more overwhelmed than she was.

As she dressed, she continued to marvel at the chain of events that had pressed her into this position and taught her so much about the multiverse and, even more importantly, about herself. Little did any of them know the hidden abilities she had been born with, abilities she would have never discovered if she had continued as a well-paid ghostwriter, hanging out with her hiking club and living a quiet but satisfying life.

For now, she dashed through her morning routine. Her hair was so short and curly now that after a quick shower, she simply towel-dried it, fluffed it, and let it do what it would. She didn't bother with makeup—she almost never wore it—so, practically jumping into some sweatpants and a t-shirt, she was ready in almost no time.

Sure enough, when she headed out the french doors to the patio, Bob and Mervin (aka Merlin) were seated in lawn chairs under the covered patio, leaving another lawn chair and the chaise lounge for Jenny.

They rose and gave her gentle hugs. "You're looking better than I expected," Merv said by way of greeting, his eyes twinkling.

Jenny imagined him with a long grey beard in wizard's robes, but for now he wore his favorite uniform, jeans and a t-shirt with the emblem of a famous '80s rock band.

Bob just said, "Hey, kiddo, how's it going?" The concern on his face touched her. His salt-and-pepper mustache twitched into a crooked smile.

"I'm doing better every day, you two. Don't look so grim. Yes, the whole 'shout' thing took a bit out of me, but I'll be ready to go by the time the doctors clear me for duty. You folks are doing all of the heavy lifting, so I'm just keeping track and staying up to speed. Speaking of which, I think Burt said something about a briefing?"

At that point Burt came out holding a tray with breakfast for all. After Bob and Mervin took their plates, he handed one to Jenny that had scrambled eggs, hash browns, and buttered toast.

"I'll be right back with some juice and utensils. Don't start without me," he called back over his shoulder after setting his own plate on his chair.

Jenny laughed as she noticed that strawberry jam had been dribbled onto her toast in a smiley face. And Burt was right back out, sharing forks and glasses of orange juice for all.

Seating himself, he turned to Merv. "Okay, so let's hear it. I understand you two have been up to some interesting stuff."

Merv, who had just taken a big bite of his scrambled eggs, chewed hurriedly and said, "Well, we got to thinking about the situation we find ourselves in. While it is true, we have disrupted the Insenium in a major way, we still have to deal with the implications that there are many dimensions still struggling under Inseni tyranny, as those involved probably haven't gotten the memo yet that their boss is extinct and there will be no more help coming from that quarter again.

"However, until we get enough information from the remaining captured Inseni agents, we don't know enough yet to pinpoint which dimensions are affected. Generally, these are dimensions that are not members of the Alliance and may not even have gate guardians. The Insenium was careful, most of the time, not to get on our radar, as they would have done if they had attacked a member dimension.

"In the meantime, it occurred to us that we probably didn't locate all of the Inseni agents currently on Earth. Although we have located and closed one of their portals on the planet, we can't be sure there isn't another one.

"On that note, we are developing the tech to locate the signal or resonance created by one of those portals, but there is another concern.

"Now that the L.A. gate has become the Gatekeeper's gate, we need to up security. We don't want another recurrence of what happened at Miriha's gate."

Jenny shuddered at the thought. She imagined this lovely quiet neighborhood ravaged and its people captured and enslaved and shook her head.

"No," she almost whispered, "not here."

"Exactly," Bob chimed in. His house was across the street from hers on Infinity Loop, and these neighbors had been his friends for many years.

"So, we realized we needed to create a system to guard this gate," Merv continued, "and give you instantaneous support for any threat we could imagine. Therefore, we took Burt's idea of a 'net' and extended it with a new piece of tech that Bob came up with." Merv nodded to Bob appreciatively and Bob grinned.

"We have installed a kind of pulse generator in your backyard. You can't see it, nor can anyone else. It is microscopic and is installed in the yew tree. Your gardener, Ted, won't even notice it. It is embedded under the bark of the trunk, and the bark has been repaired in a way that looks natural.

"The pulse generator scans constantly for certain types of DNA, specifically alien DNA. There have been certain exclusions. For instance, Tidbit aka Tarafau, BaaGah or any Mookookie, and Chidwi, not to mention I, myself. As need arises, we can add to those exclusions. In the meantime, any DNA that enters a one-mile radius of this net will automatically set off an alarm that will notify you and any of the occupants of this house if there is an issue.

"The alarm will also trigger the opening of a gateway that leads to an Alliance trooper barracks whose troops are on standby to answer that alarm immediately. Within less than a minute, troopers will pour out of the gateroom into the house, prepared to defend the entire area.

"These are non-uniformed troopers, all humanoid and dressed appropriately for the area. I guess you would call them guerrilla fighters. They will be able to infiltrate the area without alarming the residents and will be armed in such a way as to be unobtrusive. Any questions?"

He turned to Jenny, who sat there, her breakfast forgotten and her mouth open.

"Wow," was all she could think to say. "What are the chances we'll find ourselves attacked?"

"Better than I'd like to think," said Burt solemnly. He looked into her eyes more seriously than she had seen before. "We have no way of knowing how many agents were planted here that were not a part of our earlier issues with Sam's plots. We also don't know how many might have escaped our assaults on their bases in Louisiana and the Amazon.

"Quite frankly, after the attack on Earth, shutting down all electrical devices, we don't know there aren't more threads to that plan, even after completely disrupting the Insenium. There are way more questions than answers here, and we simply can't take any chances."

Jenny sighed. She had known there was still a lot to do if they were going to clean up the mess made by the Insenium, but she had thought that at least Earth was safe.

"We wanted to take some of your stress away," Bob said, his eyes reflecting his concern. "You have enough on your plate to be going on with. This will work. We have tested it off planet, using some Inseni agent prisoners and other DNA samples from various cultures."

"Thank you," Jenny said, and she meant it. She appreciated the fact that they hadn't brought this up before they had come up with a solution. It would have definitely haunted her to think of the danger they might have been in. Even after all she had been through and seen since taking on the Gatekeeper's post, it hadn't occurred to her that the threat was still there for the Gatekeeper and what that represented.

They finished breakfast while watching their various companions frolicking among the flowers, chasing butterflies, or watching the koi in the little pond under the yew tree. It was good to have company, Jenny thought, but her mind continued to stray to the box that contained the next of Lizzie's journals.

Reading the journals had been such a great distraction from her current concerns. She could hardly wait to go back to Lizzie's account of her training, especially since Lizzie had been about to begin her internship as an agent of the Alliance with Tarafau.

Mervin stood after handing Burt his empty plate. "Great breakfast, Burt. Maybe we need to hire you as the lab cook?"

Burt shook his head and chuckled. "I had help. Lizziebot is very good at cooking, among other things. By the way, Jenny, we may have forgotten to mention that Lizziebot has had an upgrade to coincide with your defense net. She will get the first notification if the boundary is breached. And you may not realize it, but she has some defense capabilities of her own that Bob included in her originally, before we went into the Amazon venture, which has since been upgraded with 'diabolical alien tech.'

"Needless to say, you are as protected as we are able to make you. In a couple of weeks, we'll take you through some of the other discoveries we've made, but for now we need to get back to it. Do you need anything else before we skedaddle?"

"I'm fine. Thank you, all three of you, for taking such good care of me." She stood and hugged Merv and Bob and kissed Burt. With an arm around him, she escorted them to the gate office and saw them through the door to the gateroom and out the door that led to Alliance headquarters.

In the dining room, she invoked the box of Lizzie's journals out of her MDP. Placing it on the dining room table, she extracted the second journal. The cover bore no date. It simply said, in Lizzie's hand, "Agent Training."

She decided it was such a lovely day that she would read out on the patio in her chaise lounge. She noticed Lizziebot had already cleared away the detritus of their morning meal and was standing by the chaise, waiting for her.

"Lizziebot, could you please take the first journal from the box and scan it into your database in two formats? I'd like one in her original handwriting and one set in type for ease of reading. I'd like to preserve her writing if we can. I'd hate to lose her history if something happened to the house or the box for any reason."

"Indeed. Would you also like me to scan in the photo albums?"

Jenny knew there were several of these and nodded. "That would be great, Lizziebot. Thank you."

Lizzie strode off through the doors to the dining room, and Jenny settled herself on her chaise. Burt had taken BaaGah with him and Bob had taken Lolly, even though she was bonded to Jenny. Lolly and BaaGah were helping Merv and Bob with their research, and evidently there were a number of Mookookie who had joined the Alliance science team.

Jenny sighed contentedly. She knew she had only a short time to finish these journals, but somehow she felt it was important, that there might be something in these journals that would make a difference as she went forward with her duties as the Gatekeeper, especially since she had never had the full training that an agent or guardian would normally have had.

She opened the journal written in the clear hand of her aunt that had now become so familiar and read....

Chapter 1: Inklings and Linklings

Lizzie ran in the sunshine, the amazing sky filled with the pale echoes of the rings that orbited the Daringi planet. At night the view was spectacular. You could barely see the stars for the brilliant light show of the colorful rings around the planet. Beside her, running at her pace, was Tarafau.

The large Daringi man was her "guide," there to steer her through her internship as an Alliance Agent. He had been Gaston's guide before her. They had replaced Gaston's guide with a "gardener," a humanoid agent of the Alliance. Why they had felt Lizzie specifically needed Tarafau to be her guide, she had no idea, although she had some vague suspicions.

Each of her podmates in agent training had been assigned a guide for this stage of their instruction. It had been a bit sad for Lizzie to be separated from her podmates. She especially missed Minth and Gi, with whom she had been so close.

Every time she sat in the quiet of the huge back yard of Tarafau's home playing her mbira, she found her mind drifting back to those impromptu concerts between the pods at the agent training center.

All of these things ran through her mind as she jogged along the road that led from a wooded area beyond Tarafau's home and the dome-like house he lived in. By now the path was familiar, and it was easy for her mind to drift as she ran. It was quite different from the grueling pace that Lall had put her pod through on the Alliance training grounds.

From time to time, they nodded to others walking past on various errands.

Suddenly, she felt more than heard the swish behind her. Without thinking, her quarterstaff was in her hands, meeting the intended blow with a loud clack. As she whirled to face her attacker, Tarafau grinned at her, swinging again, low this time, towards her shins. She caught the blow with her staff, connecting lightly and pivoting to swing a blow towards his stomach. He met her counter easily, which did not surprise her. She almost never got in a tap on Tarafau.

Back and forth they went, Lizzie oblivious of their surroundings and now completely focused on the task at hand, keeping Tarafau from adding to her current collection of bruises from these defense sessions.

She never knew when he might attack. It wasn't malicious on his part, she knew. It was simply that part of his job was to see to it that she could hold her own in any situation. And it wasn't just physical defense. He and his wife, Amenia, had been also working with her on mental defenses, not only to prevent someone from being able to overwhelm her with a mental attack but to also control her reactions to pain and to be able to control basic bodily functions such as slowing breathing and even maintaining or adjusting body temperature.

This was only the smallest part of what she had come here to learn. She had sat in on countless meetings with various groups of beings on this planet, which was home to five sentient species that all lived in relative harmony.

Council meetings, various cultural events, even classes in the local university were just a few of the things she had been exposed to over time in this part of her training. And all of this was just a warmup to the actual internship that was yet to come. When Lizzie had completed this part of the internship with Tarafau, she would return to the Alliance training center for an orientation with her podmates that would officially launch them into actual assignments, each accompanied by their assigned guide, that would take them to dimensions as yet unknown to them.

Finally, Tarafau got a tap in on what her dad called "the funny bone." Not so funny, actually. Ruefully, she bowed to him as was proper, acknowledging his triumph. He grinned.

"Better this time," he sent in mind speech. *"But it might have been better yet if your mind hadn't been drifting from the start. Generally, in most assignments for the Alliance you won't be in mortal danger, but you need to be ready. However, you did seem to sense the first blow coming, so that is a definite improvement."*

Lizzie couldn't help but groan. She was pretty sure she would never measure up to the majority of her podmates in this particular skill. Her elbow hurt, but not as much as it could have. Tarafau had exquisite control of his blows and could pull them as easily as he could direct a powerful killing stroke.

She, on the other hand, had only once been in a desperate conflict, and it was the adrenalin and fright that had given her blows the power to inflict serious injury. The staff she had used in that conflict had had to be replaced, as it had been shattered to a splinter by repeated blows with a heavy club. But, in that desperate battle for survival, she had killed a being who would have gladly killed her. Nevertheless, it still hurt her heart to think about it.

As she came to herself, she realized their exhibition had collected a small crowd of onlookers. She smiled and nodded at them. She hadn't noticed that they had arrived just in front of Tarafau's home, and these were his neighbors for the most part. These occasional staff fights had become a source of entertainment for them, evidently, since they applauded in Daringi fashion, snapping their fingers vigorously and smiling.

At that moment, Amelia emerged from the house at a run. *"Quickly! It is time! They are coming!"*

"Time? Coming?" Lizzie sent back, confused.

"Ynni! The babes! It is time! Come!" Amelia sent again.

They all ran into the backyard, skirting the little dome structure that hid a much more generous underground home. In the few months Lizzie had lived with them, this backyard had become her favorite place on the property. It was large, bordered by very old, towering trees of various types in which Ynni and her two companions had established a little colony of linklings.

Initially It had just been Lizzie and Ynni, but on one of her visits to Miriha's planet, where she had initially encountered the linklings, Ynni had visited with her friends who lived in the grove outside Miriha's little village. The result was that Ynni had become pregnant and, at her request, the "sireling" of her babies (she said it was twins), as well as her sister, had agreed to move to Tarafau's grove to help care for Ynni and the younglings when they came.

They arrived to the soft crooning of Sympha and Rinn. It was a joyous sound, and in Lizzie's excitement of the impending birth her elbow was forgotten. Linklings were not very big, less than two feet tall, not counting their tails, and she was sure the little ones would be tiny indeed. They had created a nest of sorts, low in the nook between branches of one of the trees closest to the yard, and Lizzie could just see the two heads on either side of Ynni. The bond between her and Ynni had become closer over the months since their first linking, and now she felt calm emanating from the three of them that surprised her.

She had heard that human births often came in the midst of a lot of huffing and panting and often even yells from the mother giving birth, but this was nothing like that. It was almost like the linklings were calling to the babies, encouraging them to emerge.

And then, there was suddenly another presence among them. Sympha and Rinn set to work carefully cleaning the new linkling and holding it as a second one was delivered. They gently laid the first next to Ynni in the nest. The infant linkling was already crooning softly in harmony with Ynni, who radiated calm satisfaction.

The entire miraculous process seemed peaceful, and the crooning never paused. Ynni sent to Lizzie, *"They are Mina and Gil. A girl and a boy. Our tribe is now five. Rejoice with us!"*

Lizzie almost danced with excitement, looking up into the faces of the linklings peering over the edge of the nest. Early on, when the nest was first built, the linklings had agreed that Tarafau could add a ladder leading up to it. It was a simple thing of wooden dowels lashed together, but it was sturdy. Lizzie had often climbed up to visit with the three of them as they tidied the area, preparing it for the advent of the younglings.

Now she asked, almost shyly, *"Can I come up and see them?"* She knew that newborns were delicate and mothers often very protective of them in the first several weeks.

"Of course! Lizzie must greet them! You are one with our tribe." Ynni's warm enthusiasm almost vibrated in Lizzie's mind.

As she climbed the several steps up the ladder, she thought about how far her journey had led her beyond anything she had expected or even wanted. She would have never imagined any scenario where she would be bonded to an alien creature for life or would have such a strong resonance with another lifeform.

As she peered over the edge of the nest, she was flooded with such awe that her feelings overwhelmed her. Tears were streaming down her cheeks. She not only felt joy for her little linkling friends but received through the link the maternal feelings of a new mother for her offspring.

The tiny linklings were about the size of the palm of her hand. Like their mother, they had huge blue eyes surrounded by a halo of white fur. Every tiny finger and toe was perfect. Unlike the adult linklings, the dark-green long eyebrows that blended into the trailing mustaches were not yet evident. Their nearly chartreuse fur was still somewhat damp from the birthing.

They blinked up at Lizzie, almost in unison and then from Ynni...

"Mina, Gil, this is Lizzie. She is ours. We are hers."

"Lizzie is ours," they repeated, agreeing in mental unison.

Lizzie was shocked. There was no doubt. These tiny newborns had just spoken to her in the common language of all linklings. How was this possible?

"Lizzie is surprised," Ynni sent, a smile on her face, her nose and eyes crinkling in amusement. *"As linklings are quickened in the womb, they are already speaking with the mother. It is not so with Earth babies?"*

"No, Ynni, it is not so. Humans generally do not learn to communicate vocally until they are well past nine months old. They do not usually communicate mentally at all. I had to receive this ability from the Gatekeeper to be able to do it myself. It is not a common gift among humankind."

Ynni appeared thoughtful. *"I had not thought it would be so different. Perhaps, because Lizzie can mindspeak now, it will be different for you when you have your own younglings."*

"Maybe... we'll see." Privately, Lizzie didn't' think she would ever find out. Marriage, children, neither of these were in her plans. In the meantime, it was enough for her to continue on the path she had begun.

"Do you have everything you need, Ynni? Can I get you anything?"

"Sympha and Rinn will take care of us, Lizzie. It is why they have come. When you can, we would like for you to play for us more. It is soothing to the babies and we like making music with you."

Lizzie had taken to bringing her mbira out with her into the grove on her breaks and playing it under the trees. It had delighted her that the three linklings had joined in with their soft harmonic crooning. It reminded her of the little impromptu concerts they had done at the training center, and it calmed her mind.

"I would be happy to do that, Ynni." Lizzie reached out her hand and Ynni gently wrapped her fingers around one of Lizzie's fingers.

"Ynni will be with Lizzie more soon," she assured her. *"Ynni has help with younglings. You and I still have many things to do together. You will see."*

Lizzie's face was again wet with joyous tears. She nodded and climbed down the ladder. She wished she could have taken a photo of the mother linkling and her babies, but she knew it was an image that would never fade from her heart.

Chapter 2: Cha-Cha-Cha

(Jenny wiped tears from her own face, hoping they wouldn't drip onto the pages of the journal. She knew her aunt had never married, and she wondered herself, if she had a child, how she would balance the duties of the Gatekeeper with the responsibilities of motherhood.

She knew that there were gate guardians with children, but her duties were multiplied far beyond those of most guardians. She hadn't had this conversation with Burt yet and wasn't sure how she felt about it. On the one hand, she had always assumed she would have children someday, but so far her life had been consumed by other things.

She also hadn't considered that perhaps Chidwi might want to have her own linkling babies and what that might entail, as far as introducing a new species to Earth was concerned. So many things to think about.

She turned the page...)

Lizzie woke and dressed hurriedly. She had slept a little later than she had intended and, from the smells wafting in down the hallway from the kitchen, she realized the others were already breakfasting. She didn't bother to shower, just jumped into her workout clothes and ran a brush through her short auburn hair.

Amenia had been amused that she wished to keep it so short. Her own hair was long and luxuriant, falling in tight waves to her waist when it wasn't braided or coiled on top of her head. But she had willingly found someone who would keep Lizzie's hair in its usual pixie style. This was a quick and easy and looked neat and professional.

As she strode into the kitchen, they all looked up and smiled. Lizzie had to admit that Tarafau's family had been very welcoming. Amenia didn't "mother" her exactly, just treated her like part of the family—when she wasn't instructing her in mental control, that is.

Today they would be working on her mental shielding, an ongoing process. Lizzie knew she was progressing, but so far it had been slow going. It often felt like what her mom had called the cha-cha-cha of life, "one step forward, two steps back." However, Amenia had mentioned the day before that she thought she might have a way to get past the blocks Lizzie was encountering during her training sessions.

One thing every agent needed to learn was the ability to shield their mind from two things: actual mental attacks from others, and pain that could be inflicted either intentionally or by accident in the performance of their duties.

Lizzie had a hard time imagining what kind of situation she might encounter that would require this. And from time to time, she wondered anew what Gaston had seen in her that told him she might be up to the task.

However, this morning she sat down with the rest, gulped down one of Amenia's high nutrition breakfast drinks, and followed her and Tarafau to the workout room.

Amenia was a counselor, a kind of mental therapist, but unlike any Lizzie had heard about on Earth. Her clients came to her here in her home; and instead of an office and a couch or comfortable chair, they engaged in physical and mental exercises similar to what she was doing with Lizzie.

Like Lizzie had done in Sanglarka and the Alliance training center, they started each session with advanced breathing and relaxation techniques, which then transitioned into exploring

Lizzie's mental environment to teach her how to have more complete control over her physicality.

These sessions were followed by a physical workout. In addition to the morning sessions, Tarafau also took her out on a run. Add to that the fact that they walked everywhere they went, and she could see why she seldom saw anyone on this planet who was not fit and healthy.

Lizzie, Amenia and Tarafau began by seating themselves on mats placed on the floor. These looked somewhat worn, if in good condition. As they sat there, they began the complex breathing and relaxation patterns that required complete attention and intention to achieve, even though they had become routine to a certain extent.

Learning to breathe in a specific pattern as you relaxed some muscles in the body while tensing others was almost like a dance. It had taken Lizzie many hours of practice to make it all work correctly, and the focus it required had the added benefit of taking her mind off of any worries or concerns that might otherwise have been on her mind.

Early on in her mental training, Lizzie had discovered how she pictured the place where her mind lived. The entrance was a bank vault, and one of the most important places within that vault was a seemingly endless library with one special area that was her "quiet place." It looked much like a little alcove in her favorite library on earth, surrounded by shelves of reference books and equipped with a comfortable office chair, a desk with writing supplies, and great lighting for reading.

However, as she continued to explore the space with Amenia, she discovered she could actually exit out of the library through the double oak doors into what might have been a city park with expansive lawns, shade trees, and paved paths that wound through it and beyond to what might have been thought of as a village.

The neat village square was surrounded by shops and offices of various types. In the shops were goods of the kind that most interested Lizzie, so none of them were boutiques or salons. A few specialty bookstores, gadget shops, a music store, and even a bicycle shop represented her mindset.

On one side of the square was a medical clinic and a law office, which baffled Lizzie as to why she had included them here.

Today, she and Amenia strolled out of the library doors into a beautiful spring day. Lizzie had noticed that the seasons outside seemed to change depending on her mood at the time. Sometimes the area was buried in snow; other times, rain pelted them from glowering skies.

Today, however, with the younglings doing so well and the imminent return to the Alliance training center, she felt buoyant. They were going to the music store today. Amenia had commented on how connected Lizzie had become with the mbira and the music she was able to create with it. So, this might be the place in her mind where she might find the key to breaking her resistance to the complete relaxation that was vital to improve pain control and to strengthen her mental shielding.

As they entered the little shop, there was a tinkling sound. Immediately a woman emerged from the back of the shop. To Lizzie's surprise and delight, it was the same woman she had met in the shop in Los Angeles where she had bought her first instruction booklet on the use and care of her mbira.

"How can I help you today?" she asked brightly. "Are you enjoying your mbira? Does it need tuning?"

"I'm enjoying it very much." Lizzie glanced at Amenia, not sure what to say next.

Amenia smiled, placing an arm around Lizzie's shoulder. "Lizzie needs to relax, and we think the joy she receives from her mbira might be vital to helping her do that. She has not yet learned to trust herself enough to give in to complete relaxation. Can you help?"

"Ah yes," the shopkeeper said with a smile. "A retuning, then. Come with me."

She led the way to the counter on one side of the shop and got out a little hammer and a pitch pipe from a drawer underneath. "Lizzie, give me your mbira, please."

In this purely mental environment Lizzie knew that none of this was real in any physical way, but Amenia had explained to her that the symbolism of clear imagery was necessary to increasing her mental abilities.

She invoked her mbira from her MDP and handed it to the woman behind the counter.

She examined it carefully and plucked each of the keys, listening intently. "It is obvious this instrument has been well cared for. It is, however, slightly out of tune. We can fix this. I will show you how, and in the future you will be able to do it for yourself."

She blew a note on the pitch pipe. "This note is a "C" on the scale. The "C" is the center tab on your mbira, and if it is out of pitch everything else is thrown off."

She played the "C" note again on the pitch pipe and then thumbed the "C" tab. It was ever so slightly lower than the pitch she had played. She tapped the tab gently upward with the hammer. She played the pitch again and plucked the tab again. It was closer, but not quite there. Twice more she repeated the process until the tones matched as perfectly as the ear could determine.

She repeated this process with all seventeen tabs on the instrument and handed it to Lizzie. "If you don't have a pitch pipe and a hammer, you will want to get them, but for now your mbira will play perfectly.

"You should realize, however, that as the instrument is used, the tuning will drift over time. This is why it is important to tune the instrument on a regular basis. No instrument stays eternally in tune, so regular maintenance is necessary."

Lizzie took the mbira back with thanks for her help. Humming, the shopkeeper went back to her work at the back of the shop.

She and Amenia exited out of the shop into the sunlight of that perfect spring day. In the park across the street, they found a park bench and sat, Lizzie still clutching the mbira in her hand.

She turned to Amenia. "So, what was that about? How does that help me? It isn't like this is my real mbira. If it is out of tune in the real world, it is still out of tune."

"Think about what she said and what she did. Remember that all of this is symbolic of something. You have often said yourself that science is useless without imagination. What does the mbira represent? Why was tuning it important? How does this apply to the reason we are in this session today? It is important that you answer these questions yourself. If I do it for you, the exercise is instructive but useless to accomplish the purpose of why we are here."

"Why are you here?" That was the question Gaston had asked her what seemed long ago in his office at the university. It was the question that had launched her into this adventure, and it still seemed to come up over and over again.

So, what did the experience in the music shop have to do with all of this?

Amenia waited patiently and Lizzie sighed. These mental exercises often took more out of her than any of the physical training had done.

And what about the tuning thing? Why was that important? If the mbira represented enjoyment, companionship, and relaxation to her, how did that relate?

Finally, she looked up. Amenia's face had not changed. She was one of the most patient people Lizzie had ever met.

"I think it has to do with the idea that, first of all, even though I trust that the mbira will make the music I want it to make when I pluck the right tabs, it isn't perfect, at least not all the time.

"Perhaps one of the reasons I need to continue these exercises to learn to control my mental responses is to symbolically keep myself in tune with who I am. When I do this, I can trust that I will be able to access the music or abilities within myself.

"The pitch pipe and the hammer represent the tools I have available to me. In this case, the breathing and relaxation exercises and the counsel and encouragement of my mentors.

"The fact that the music shop is one of the permanent structures on my village square means that somehow music might be one of the important keys to my success."

Amenia beamed at Lizzie when she paused as if to say, "Is that right?"

"Very good. Since we know that your mbira is a symbolic key to your success, every night from now on, I want you to come here after your breathing exercises and just play your mbira anywhere in your mental village that seems most appropriate. Once Ynni is able to leave her younglings into the care of her tribe, you should begin to include her in these sessions as well.

"As you play, I want you to imprint on your mind that this is your safe place. You have a peaceful place inside your library, but playing your mental mbira will become your shield to anything that isn't well with you. If you experience pain or feel the impingement of another mind on yours, you can instantly recall this, and you will be protected. Play your mbira now. I want you to notice something."

Obediently, Lizzie began to play, remembering those times when she was accompanied by her friends. As she did so, she began to notice a glow that began around her thumbs as she plucked the tabs from her perfectly tuned instrument. The glow expanded slowly at first and finally rested in a protective sphere that surrounded her and Amenia, much like a snow globe she had been given in her childhood.

When she stopped playing, after a few minutes, the globe shrank again almost as if it was sucked into the resonant chamber of her instrument.

"Wow! What was that?"

"It is a representation of the mental shield you are now able to produce. Over time, it will become nearly impenetrable; but, like playing an instrument, this will require practice. You have done well. By the way, if you wish to practice this with Ynni, you can do it in the grove during your usual break time with her and the tribe. That link will strengthen your shield and your bond with your friend."

At that they faded back to the workout room where she, Amenia and Tarafau sat on the workout mats. It always felt a little unreal to Lizzie when they first returned from these mental excursions. It was almost as if the mental world was more real than the physical one.

Amenia grinned and hugged her fiercely. *"You are amazing, Lizzie Japhet. By the way, I thought you might want to be the first to know. I am expecting a child. It will be a girl. I am going to name her Elizabeth, after you. I can only hope she is as strong and delightful as her namesake."*

Lizzie was overcome. She looked up at Amenia and Tarafau, tears of joy once again sparkling in her eyes.

Chapter 3: On a New Note

(Jenny had known, of course, that Elizabeth had been named after her aunt, but sharing that revelatory moment had been precious indeed.

Absently, she nibbled on the pickle Lizziebot had included with her sandwich. After lunch she would get up and take a walk around the neighborhood. She had noticed a "For Sale" sign on Elias Mensch's lawn just yesterday and had wondered about it. As she thought about it, she realized she hadn't seen him out walking Cinder (or Cinder walking him) for quite a while.

Jenny resonated with Lizzie's experience with Amenia in her mental village. Amenia had been the one who had gotten Jenny past her own mental barriers to become the first, to anyone's knowledge in recent Alliance history, to be able to project mental communications beyond dimensional barriers.

She had never heard anyone in the Alliance discuss her aunt's mental abilities, and now she wondered where this breakthrough might take her.

Putting the rest of the pickle back on the plate, she turned pages...)

Over the next few weeks, Lizzie continued to immerse herself in the culture of Tarafau's planet. Five different intelligent species and cultures on one planet was unusual and allowed her to experience diversity in a way that wouldn't otherwise have been possible in such a short time.

The baby linklings, unlike human infants, had become active surprisingly quickly. Within two weeks, they were scampering about, transported from the nest in the tree to the ground by clinging to the backs of either Ynni or their father or aunt. They were playful and interactive.

Amenia and her family loved spending evenings watching them play and even dance when Lizzie brought out her mbira and the adult linklings joined in crooning with her musical doodlings. Any time Lizzie came out for her usual break in the grove, she was soon surrounded by linklings, to her ongoing delight.

Mina and Gil would clamber up onto the chaise with Lizzie, each of them snuggling arm in arm and mind-chattering about bugs and flowers and their view of the amazing lightshow the sky put on during the day and even more spectacularly each night of the colorful rings that surrounded the planet.

Lizzie had to admit that she would miss this intensely when she embarked on the next stage of her training. She was sure Ynni would need to stay here with her babies, and she already had noticed a difference when she went about her duties here without her linkling companion perched in her usual place on her shoulder.

She remembered it was not that long ago when Gaston had introduced her to Thumble, and her reticence about having a "pet," Up to that point, she had never had any responsibility for anyone but herself, nor had she aspired to. Now, on the other hand, she not only had Ynni, but had grown fond of her entire little tribe.

On top of that, she now had friends who were more than just people she spent time with. She had become close with Tarafau, Amenia, and their family in a way that was surprisingly, and somewhat to her shame, closer and more intense than her relationship with her own family.

Once she had begun her life in college, it was as if she had somehow disconnected herself from her brothers and parents. Not that she didn't love them or that she had any disagreement with them. She just didn't see them more than just for an occasional visit for a holiday or celebration. Even in the summer, when she was off of school, she was working two jobs to pay for her tuition, and she was so focused on her studies during the school term that she almost never even wrote a letter or made a phone call.

She was finally taking advantage of the technology the Alliance had made available to her, so that occasional letters, birthday cards, and postcards were being sent to her family and she would definitely take the time on her next holiday break to make some phone calls and perhaps even visit her parents.

Her time with Amenia and Tarafau had begun to impress on her the value of family ties; and even the linklings, with their joyful little tribe, made her realize she was missing out on something precious if she didn't make some changes in her priorities.

In another week she would return to the Alliance training center to participate in her first assignment debriefing. This required her to report on her activities in a more focused summary than the weekly reports she currently submitted via the tablet that had been issued to her as part of her agent status.

Because Tarafau's planet and dimension didn't actually have a gateway, Tarafau had been using his amazing dimensional-travel talent to make a weekly trip to Alliance Headquarters to submit her reports. This usually meant he was gone for only an hour, since his commute was only seconds long. He always returned with her tablet and the remarks by her various instructors.

In addition to that debriefing, she would also get to hear the reports from her podmates and vicariously enjoy their adventures during their first experiences in their pre-internship.

She was really looking forward to that. They would then get a short holiday to visit family and return to the training complex to get their final agent training before beginning the real internship.

At the end of that time, they would become official agents of the Alliance, with full privileges and authority to act as a representative of the Dimensional Alliance.

Originally, when she had made the one-year commitment with Gaston, it had been because she had wanted to escape the restrictions placed upon her in the university. In college she had strained against the pace of instruction, which to her felt like trying to run a race dragging a wagonload of lead bars.

Her experience as an agent in training, however, had been so very different than anything she had imagined or wished for, that in the beginning she had only been going through the motions, doing what was necessary because she had committed to the process and wasn't one to go back on her word or break a contract.

But slowly things had begun to change, not the least of which was within her own heart. Linking with Ynni seemed to be a big hinge point for her. Add to that the ultimate confrontation between her and her pod against a group of rebels who were against non-member dimensions' being included in Alliance business, and she had come to understand she finally had a cause worth her time and attention.

Now many weeks into her first assignment attached to her guide, Tarafau Bane, she continued to gain more and more respect for the process of agent training and how it tied into her constant hunger for learning. The exposure to varying disciplines over and above the sciences she most craved to understand were opening her mind to more possibilities than she had previously considered. That, in and of itself, was a huge change for her.

She began to realize her viewpoint had been narrow and shortsighted. New ideas, new worlds, and indeed new dimensions were literally opening to her that were beyond anything she could have previously imagined for herself, and she felt like maybe she could make a difference with her own contributions, however small or inconspicuous they might be.

She found herself looking forward to the next stage of training, even though from time to time she had to wonder why she had been paired with Tarafau. She did like him, most of the time. He was intelligent, and it was obvious as he moved in the political circles of his planet that he was respected by everyone who knew him.

Nevertheless, they still butted heads, mostly when he would try to slow her down and make her think. Although her irritation rose when this happened, she had to admit he was right most of the time, and that definitely chafed.

Today the plan was to go to the Apex, a huge pyramidal structure that housed what almost seemed like an indoor city. At the ground floor was a marketplace that could have easily held several large football stadiums. It was edged all the way around with various shops and then concentric aisles of even more shops. These eventually gave way to a center area where people could sit and either eat some of the delicacies offered in the food stalls or just chat and enjoy the various entertainments offered—jugglers, musicians, and more. There were even storytellers declaiming everything from histories to Daringi fables.

The building was taller than any skyscraper Lizzie had ever heard about, and each level had different functions. One level was devoted entirely to crafters and various small manufacturers who created much of the merchandise available on the main floor.

To Lizzie's delight, the university inhabited one of the lower floors. Melek, Tarafau's oldest son, was one of the instructors there. He was a scientist of some renown among the Daringi. His main focus was the study of energy in all its forms. The top level of the pyramid was one of his many breakthroughs. It had begun as a basic solar collector, but Melek's work had expanded it to so much more.

Lizzie had been fascinated by the different ways they were able to harness the power of the sun and thermal energy from within the planet to create enough energy to fully power every home in the nearby area, including the suburbs surrounding the city.

Because the Daringi led fairly simple lives and each home had its own solar power, the cumulative needs of the city were actually fairly small. Nevertheless, Lizzie yearned to take these technological advances to her own planet.

However, part of the agreement she had made when she began this journey as a representative of the Alliance was that she would not bring alien technology to Earth. It was the belief of the Alliance that all cultures should be allowed to progress at their own speed. Their experiences of the past had shown that when technology was artificially advanced when the culture wasn't ready for it, there were often severe consequences.

Today they would be going to one of the levels in the Apex devoted to government. It housed not only the council rooms but the vast main council chamber, more like a gigantic auditorium than anything else. It was larger than either the house or senate assembly rooms in Washington, DC; and when the representatives were assembled there, the chamber was filled with beings so diverse as to amaze Lizzie every time she thought about it.

This time they would be going to the private council room to meet with the upper level Daringi representatives. These were chosen by a kind of lottery, not by a vote. Every Daringi was trained from a young age to be prepared to participate as a representative of their area, and each was expected to accept the call when it came to serve, unless there was a medical reason to be excused.

During their service, the needs of the representatives and their families were provided for; and when their time was finished, they returned to their trade, whatever it had been before they had been called.

According to Tarafau, it had not always been so, but over time, when the Daringi had finally realized they wanted peace more than any other priority, they had developed this system.

Lizzie had learned that, although not all representatives agreed on every issue, jockeying for power or riches was not in the equation. Money or fiat currency, as Lizzie understood it, no longer existed in the Daringi economy.

Every transaction was completed based on hour credits. The hour of a homemaker or a delivery person was valued equal to the hour of a scientist, a doctor, or a statesman. Lizzie knew that many ancient cultures had done business on a barter system, but to her this system seemed so logical that she wondered why it hadn't occurred to anyone on her own planet.

For now, she wasn't really all that excited about sitting in on another meeting of the council, but Tarafau had emphasized more than once, when she complained about more meetings, that this would be an intrinsic part of her agent duties, and it was important to learn to listen carefully, not only to what was said, but to the subtext or unspoken part of the conversation.

After each of these sessions, they had gone back to his house into the grove while they discussed what had been said, as well as what it meant and what it might portend for the Daringi people. In the course of these conversations, Lizzie had learned much about the Daringi people and the other beings that coexisted on this planet.

One of the good things about today's meeting was that Ynni would be coming along, perched, as usual, on Lizzie's shoulder. The little ones were being happily tended by Sympha and Rinn until they returned. She could barely feel Ynni's little arm encircling her neck as they entered the council chamber, but she noticed that the councilors sat up a little straighter when they entered.

They had been somewhat surprised when Tarafau had originally introduced Lizzie and Ynni as a linked pair. Linklings had previously been unknown on their planet, and there were now discussions about introducing a new intelligent species where there were already five.

It had come down to a vote by the entire assembly for them to agree that not only could Ynni live there but she and her family could establish their small tribe in the grove behind Tarafau's house. What had been in their favor was that they were not a predatory species, they were peaceful in nature, and they agreed to have no say in planetary policies.

All of this had been impressive to Lizzie. She couldn't help but wonder how many species on her home planet might have more intelligence than humans had considered. The incredible diversity of lifeforms represented on Earth made her realize that this study alone would take many lifetimes and a vast concentrated effort in the scientific community to accomplish.

She bit down on the thought. *"Focus,"* she told herself forcefully. She was striving not to be overwhelmed by her unquenchable thirst to know everything, but it was hard.

The Daringi delegation, gathered around a long table, greeted her with quiet enthusiasm. They were a somewhat reserved group with the exception of one of the younger among them, Verl. She was only 90 years old, practically a youngling compared to the long lives generally lived by the Daringi. Some of those on this council were nearly at their millennial mark. Lizzie often found herself wishing for that kind of lifespan. How much more could she accomplish?

"We meet here today to celebrate the advancement of our guest, Lizzie Japhet. It is our understanding that she leaves us soon to continue her training with the Dimensional Alliance. It is our hope that she will return frequently to us. Lizzie, your contributions to our discussions have been a delight, and we look forward to hearing from you again as your assignments permit."

Lizzie was at a loss for words. *"Thank you, councilor,"* she sent simply. *"I have enjoyed my time here and have learned so much. I appreciate your patience with my learning process. I will return when I am able."* This was all she could think to say. Tarafau had evidently thought this would be a nice surprise for her.

"Tarafau says he will continue to be your guide as you move forward in your journey. He will update us on your progress. We have enjoyed your different perspective, and your questions always give us something to think about," sent Verl, her brown eyes twinkling. *"We wish to give you a parting gift."*

She handed Lizzie a small wooden box. Like most things crafted by the Daringi, this was elegantly made. Because things were valued more by the hours put into making them than by a brand name or a commercial valuation, Daringi creations tended to be carefully and beautifully fashioned.

Inside the box, which opened on small brassy hinges, was a simple piece of cloth. It was skillfully finished on the edges, and the weave was more complex than anything Lizzie would have been able to weave on her simple frame loom and with her limited knowledge.

She remembered her visit to the weaver's craft hall in the Apex in the beginning of her time here. Tarafau, knowing her fascination with weaving, thanks to her first project for Gaston, had thought she might enjoy seeing where the fine cloth that produced their colorful native clothing was produced.

Unlike her very basic loom, the looms here had been huge and much more complex, but they could weave very wide pieces of cloth with extremely fine warp and weft threads, and there was more to the weaving patterns than the simple over-and-under she had produced or even known about. Each loom had been set up for a specific type of cloth.

The small piece of cloth delicately placed in this finely crafted wooden box, however, was a bit of a mystery to her. It didn't appear to be a scarf or anything she recognized. For one thing, the green cloth was oval in shape, and she was trying to imagine the loom that might have created such a finely finished shape. She didn't want to ask, "What is it?" for fear of insulting them or showing her ignorance, but Verl continued, *"We knew of your fascination for music, and the unusual instrument you play. We thought you might be interested in expanding your understanding and increasing your ability. This is not what it seems."* To demonstrate, Verl pulled another almost identical cloth, except in some shade of violet, from a pouch at the waist of her skirt.

Verl laid the cloth onto the table before her and began to stroke it gently. For a moment, it slithered and squirmed and began to inflate into a shape somewhat like a flattened beach ball. When it stopped expanding, Verl picked it up and held it with her arms around the widest part of the oval. She began to stroke it gently with her fingers, as if there were invisible strings on its surface.

Incredibly, soft musical tones began to emanate from it, similar to the sounds of a viola. The voice of this instrument was so different from the mbira, but similarly calming. Lizzie was entranced.

"How do you know where to put your fingers?" was all she could think to ask.

"This is called a kareena. It responds to your mind. You project the notes from your mind through mental energy generated by your fingertips. It takes a little practice, but Amenia tells us that you have progressed far in extending your mental abilities. The fibers woven into the instrument are psychokinetic. They respond to mental musical input. The voice of each kareena differs from one player to the next, like the mental voice of each person sounds different from every other voice."

"I am in awe of such a gift. This is a treasure beyond anything I could have imagined. And when you are finished playing it, how do you deflate it to store it again as if it were a piece of cloth?" Lizzie asked, finally finding her mental voice.

Verl demonstrated. *"Simply stroke it again, across the widest part of the oval, side to side, instead of top to bottom as you do to inflate it. As I said, this takes practice, and we won't ask you to try it in front of a group of people, but Amenia has told us she will be happy to work with you on it during your next training session.*

"We understand you only have a few days left with us. One of the reasons we asked you to come today is to invite you to a traditional gathering that fortuitously will be celebrated tomorrow in the gathering square in the center of the city.

"There will be entertainment, many crafts, and excellent food. We call it the Choice Festival. It is intended to celebrate the time of choosing when we decided, many centuries ago, to forsake the culture of greed and oppression. We would love to have you there as a special guest before you leave to attend to your duties for the Alliance."

All of the councilors nodded in agreement. It had surprised Lizzie that Verl was often the spokesperson for the group whenever they were communicating with her. She guessed that they may have considered Lizzie little more than a child in some ways, based on her age, so that she might identify more with Verl.

Regardless, their kindness and acceptance during this part of her internship had touched her heart, and she gently closed the lid of the little wooden box.

"Thank you, so very much. I would be delighted to come. This time with you has been such an inspiration for me. I have learned so much from the Daringi and other beings on your planet. Your acceptance has meant so much to me. You have taught me that there may yet be hope for the beings on my own planet and to not be so impatient with the apparent failings of others. This alone was worth everything I have gone through so far."

They all stood. *"We have another meeting yet to attend,"* Verl told her. *"We just wanted to make sure we set aside some time for this meeting with you first. We will see you at the Choosing Festival."*

Lizzie and Tarafau stood also and, surprisingly, each of the councilors stopped to hug her and pat Ynni's head before leaving the chamber.

Lizzie stowed the little box into her MDP, and Tarafau led the way down to the main floor of the Apex, stopping only to purchase some bud-crawler buds for their lunch. These would be delivered to his house by the time they could make the walk back. Amenia was expecting them and would have buds roasting out on their grill by the time they returned.

Lizzie could hardly wait for their session that evening. As they ate, she told Amenia of all that had happened at the Apex, and she pulled the little wooden box out of her MDP to show it to her. Ynni had scampered off to tend to her babies after telling Amenia, *"Our Lizzie has great honor with your people, Amenia. Ynni could see this in their faces today. Lizzie will make much music. Much, much, much!"*

Amenia had laughed that tinkling laugh of hers and had greatly admired Lizzie's gift. She went back into the house for a moment and returned with a similar box. Inside was a yellow version of the kareena.

"Why didn't you tell me you had this? We could have played together during my breaks."

"I didn't want to interrupt your meditations or distract you from our other sessions. You weren't ready for this at the time. Now we can get you started. We have four sessions between now and the time you leave. More than enough time to give you the basics.

"And from now on, Ynni will be attending your sessions. She tells me that the little ones are now strong and healthy enough to begin eating regular food and that she can trust her sireling and sister to care for them, so she will be returning with you to your training. Also, Tarafau, with the permission of the council and Miriha, has agreed to transport two more pairs of linklings to our little grove.

"The council has decided that the linklings are a worthwhile addition to our world and that we can donate our grove to them. It is as large as the grove near Miriha's village and can sustain a fairly large tribe. At some point there may even be additional linkling colonies at various places surrounding the city."

One surprise after another, Lizzie thought. She had worried about returning to her training without Ynni. Not only had she become accustomed to having Ynni with her, but she knew that she would have felt like a part of her was missing without Ynni's comforting and useful presence.

Chapter 4: Reunions

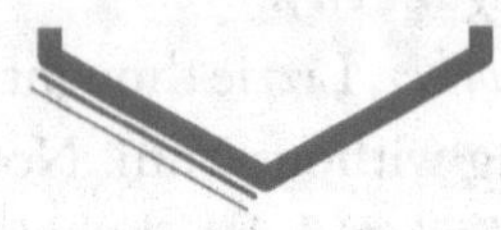

(Jenny spent most of her time on her promised walk thinking about Lizzie's revelations. Jenny had spent a short time with Tarafau, visiting his home, but this was so much more than anything she had experienced.

The musical bent that her aunt had acquired during her training was a complete surprise to Jenny. To her knowledge, though she had heard a lot about her aunt's being a bit eccentric, no one had ever mentioned her inclination to play music.

More than likely, although Lizzie had expressed a desire to connect more fully with her family, she had still experienced long stretches between meetings and the whole music thing had possibly never come up. The Japhets weren't especially musically inclined.

The other thing that came to her as she walked was that her own link to Chidwi was a direct result of the chain of events that linked Lizzie to Ynni. She was seeing that history unwind before her eyes.

She paused before Elias Mensch's house, the 'For Sale' sign making her wonder. She knew she was out of touch with her neighbors. Once things settled down, she made a pledge, much like Lizzie's, to get more closely involved with friends and family. Maybe she and Burt could go on some hikes with her hiking club? It was an interesting idea, since the last time she had seen any of them was before Sam's betrayal, and that felt like eons ago.

Entering under the wrought iron arch covered in bright scarlet bougainvillea, she noticed Tidbit's amber eyes peering out at her through the window-seat curtains. She wondered if he had news or whether he was just surveying the neighborhood.

Entering the sunny living room, she was delighted to see Burt sprawled indolently on the loveseat next to the cat.

'Hello beautiful," he greeted her, and he stood to grasp her tightly into a hug, followed by a fervent kiss. "I've got a little bit of time to hang out. I ordered in Chinese, if you don't mind." All this was said with his usual cocky grin. "I thought I could catch you up on 'all the news that's fit to print' and maybe get in a cuddle before I have to get out of here."

"Chinese sounds great and so does the cuddle," she murmured into his chest. She was feeling so comfortable just standing there, breathing in the scent that meant love to her, that she jumped when the doorbell rang.

Burt laughed and greeted the delivery person at the door, gave her a generous tip, and took the carry out bag over to the table. "Sit. Sit. I'll get the plates and you can lay out the goodies. I made sure they included chopsticks. It just doesn't taste right if you eat Chinese with a fork.

It was delightful to enjoy what would have passed as a very normal newlywed activity that didn't involve making any decision more important than whether she wanted sweet and sour sauce for her wonton or not.

The news Burt had to tell wasn't anything really new. The council was working assiduously with all of the member dimensions to secure gates with the new tech that Merv and Bob were developing. Elizabeth had been enrolled as a new agent trainee. The Mookookie had all finally gotten the word that they could pause their multiplying frenzy, to the relief of some of those who had accidentally transported them to their home planets.

This was especially interesting to Jenny in view of the entries of Lizzie's journals she had recently read, about the introduction of the linklings to Tarafau's planet.

Mookookie could be problematic. They were literally omnivorous, consuming pretty much anything with a solid atomic structure. If they were properly directed and managed, they might serve any community well by eating those things that might have simply been waste in a dump somewhere.

Mookookie were fairly submissive on the whole, but Jenny found herself wondering what the outcome would be of the proliferation of Mookookie to multiple dimensions, and whether they would once again find themselves classified as pests rather than looked upon as the delightful companions they were capable of being.

After a lovely meal and the promised cuddle time, Burt rose reluctantly from the loveseat with a sigh. "I have to go. Meeting with Bob and Merv on the next stages of security and then with Brendan in Australia regarding the space fleet. I hear Lova may have vetted a couple of guardian candidates for you to choose from, for that and the India gate, as soon as your recuperation leave is finished."

He kissed her gently on the forehead as he loved to do. "I'm guessing you're anxious to get back to your reading. I'll leave you to it. I may actually be back before bedtime. See you then."

She nodded and decided she would read indoors today. She noticed Lizziebot had discreetly placed a glass of iced mint tea on the little table next to her favorite reading chair. She opened the weathered journal, carefully turning the yellowed pages, anticipating the next stage of Lizzie's training...)

Tarafau removed his hand from her shoulder and Lizzie was delighted to find herself on the grove path that led to the little village square near the large building that housed Miriha's gate office.

Linklings swarmed down the trunks of the huge trees to greet Ynni and Lizzie with enthusiasm. *"Ynni's younglings are well?"* one of them asked, the rest nodding.

"They are well. Mina and Gil are staying with Sympha, and Rinn sends greetings," Ynni sent happily. *"We are invited to create a larger*

linkling family tribe at Tarafau's grove. We would like two pairings to go with Tarafau after Lizzie leaves to visit her tribe family. Please decide among yourselves who will come.

"There is plenty to eat and no things to fear there. It will be a safe and pleasant place. Much love. Much joy."

"We will consider until Tarafau returns to speak with us. You will go with Lizzie?" the first linkling responded, nodding solemnly.

"Indeed, she is my link to happiness and life. I will not worry for my younglings. They are safe and much loved."

Soft crooning ensued with much gentle patting of faces, including Lizzie and Tarafau. Cheek patting was the equivalent of a human hug in the linkling culture.

As they continued down the path towards the town square, they were accompanied by the crooning and delighted hooting of the linklings saying a fond farewell to Ynni and company.

The square was filled with people. It appeared to be well into the market day and shoppers filled the square, perusing the goods on display and engaging in mindspeech conversations with animated gestures and facial expressions.

Lizzie really enjoyed the atmosphere of the little town. She had never been beyond the boundaries of the square, but she was fairly sure the town had a considerable population, based on what she had seen in the square when the market was in full swing.

The large green building at the head of the square was the home of Miriha's gate office and also contained other offices relegated to local government through doors on the main floor. Miriha's dimension was an Alliance member, and the citizens in this small town were all aware of what she did, to a certain extent, which was why unusual visitors were not even a curiosity for most of them.

At the top of the curving staircase, the door to Miriha's office opened as soon as they approached. She rose from behind her desk, extending both hands in greeting. Clasping both of Lizzie's hands, she looked deep into her eyes. *"Welcome Lizzie. I hear good things about your progress. And congratulations, Ynni, on the birth of your twins. Are you both ready for a holiday?"*

"We definitely can use a break, but I am excited to move into the next stage of training and I miss my podmates. I am very curious about what comes next."

"Curious is a good word for you, Lizzie Japhet. You have developed curiosity as a fine art, I think," her eyes twinkled in amusement. *"However, something tells me you have found a little more balance between your search for answers and the acquisition of wisdom. I can see growth in you that bodes well.*

"And now," she said, releasing Lizzie's hands and turning to Tarafau, *"I understand you will be migrating some of our linklings to your world. I needn't say that this is both encouraging and a little sad."* At this, Miriha's linkling appeared on her shoulder. He tended to keep his reflection turned off, making him invisible in the presence of visitors. He nodded and reached across the space between Lizzie and Miriha to pat Ynni's cheek.

"Your tribe will be magnified and will be a light among your new peoples," his soft mind voice crooned. *"Perhaps someday I will come to see what you have begun."*

Ynni reached to pat his cheeks in return. *"You and all of our tribe will always be welcome in my new home."*

Miriha's tender smile lit her face, and a tear glimmered in the light as it trailed down her cheek. Her linkling wiped it away with a tiny gentle hand.

Miriha continued, *"Now come, we must not hold our travelers for any longer. Gaston awaits you at the L.A. gate, and then you will return here before going to the Sanglarka gate and then on to the Alliance training center. Enjoy your holiday, Lizzie and Ynni."*

She led them through the office door that went into the gateroom. From there, she opened the door that led into the now familiar gateroom outside the guardian's office in the little house on Infinity Loop. Gaston stood there grinning like a schoolboy anticipating a special treat.

"Lizzie! Ynni! So good to see you! I understand Tidbit won't be showing his whiskers on this trip. Thumble misses him. Come! Come! Nita has lunch prepared, and then we will discuss your agenda and make arrangements for you both."

Lizzie couldn't help but chuckle. Gaston's enthusiasm was one of the things she loved about him.

Ynni patted her cheek. *"I will turn off my reflection now and go to visit the outside place here. I will return when we are ready to leave this place or when you call me."*

She felt the slight weight of Ynni shift and knew that she had scampered out of the office door.

As they exited the gate office into the hallway, Lizzie could hear Nita humming to herself as she set the table for guests.

As they entered the dining room, a man not quite five feet tall, with a close-cropped graying beard, came through the french doors. He was dressed in what you might expect from someone who had been working in the yard: jeans and a blue cotton shirt with an open collar. He swept a straw hat from his head and nodded to them.

"You must be Lizzie," he said cheerfully. *"My name is Arvid Stronghammer. I am Gaston's new guide, also known simply as 'the gardener,'"* he sent with a chuckle at her surprised look when he shifted from vocal to mindspeech.

He laughed out loud. "I'll need to wash up for lunch," he said, still chuckling at Lizzie's reaction. "Nita is very particular about that."

And with a grin he strode down the hall to the bathroom.

Gaston laughed. "Arvid's a bit of a character, but he's actually a very experienced bond canny agent. He speaks English and several other Earth languages. If I can't have Tidbit, he'll do nicely. You should see that man wield a staff." He shook his head. "I've seen him take down folks twice his size without even breaking a sweat. He used to be one of the trainers at the agent training center. Obviously, even though he's humanoid, he isn't from around here."

At that moment, Nita bustled in with a tray of various sandwich and salad ingredients and began to lay them out along the center of the dining room table. "Let me put this down, to greet you properly, Lizzie," she said, propping the now-empty tray onto one of the chairs.

She offered a grandmotherly hug and a smile. "The professor tells me you are doing very well in your studies and that you're moving on nicely."

She said that as if she was speaking of just another college student, but Lizzie knew she was very well aware of what "the professor" was really up to. She took in stride the mysterious comings and goings through the gateway, including Thumble, the little six-legged furry companion Gaston had brought home at one point.

"Come, come! Sit and rest yourself. Arvid will be out in a minute, and I have almost everything ready for our lunch."

She bustled back out and returned with a couple of pitchers, one filled with iced mint tea and another with pink lemonade.

Once they had all seated themselves and bowed their head for a blessing on the food, Gaston opened the conversation. "So, Lizzie, what's first in your priorities? You have a little over a week, by my reckoning, before you go to Sanglarka and then back to the agent training center."

As they discussed her options, they helped themselves to the various sandwich fixings, each of them building a unique sandwich to their taste.

Lizzie explained to Gaston her priorities to visit with her family after shopping for some appropriate gifts, both for giving during her visit and to be mailed out at specified times for birthdays and other family events, a service Gaston had volunteered to do for her. She also planned to buy some special things to take back to her podmates at the training center.

The lessons she had learned in the first stage of her training had taught her that, although she knew she wouldn't have the opportunity to spend much time with her family due to her duties as an agent, she never wanted to take her family ties for granted again.

She had begun to appreciate the importance of familial connections, especially after watching Ynni and her little tribe and their tender interactions. She knew her parents cared for her and her siblings, and she wanted to continue to be a part of their lives in whatever way she was capable.

The technology made available to her through the Alliance had given her the ability to stay in touch via the regular mail system, with exotic postmarks that gave them the feeling that she was traveling through isolated areas and gave her the cover story of doing foreign studies on scholarship with an exclusive private foreign university.

By the time she completed her agent training, the cover story would shift to doing hush-hush private research that required constant travel to out-of-the-way places. But for now, she really needed to spend time with her family.

Gaston agreed that she could make the necessary phone calls right after lunch and that he would be happy to take her to her parents' home in San Diego. He said he'd take time to visit the zoo there and perhaps do some whale watching.

The meal passed pleasantly as they listened to some of Lizzie's recent experiences, and both she and Gaston related some of their own particular memories of their time in training.

At one point, Thumble had hopped up on the table, chirping. "Lizzie's back! Thumble is happy!" Lizzie petted the top of his tiny head with an outstretched finger which Thumble in turn hugged with fervor. She gave him a slice of apple off of her plate, and he munched happily as they finished up their meal.

As in most households, the telephone was situated on an end table in the living room, and Arvid, Gaston, and Nita all excused themselves to do other tasks so Lizzie could have some privacy for her phone calls. As she dialed her parents' number, she found herself a bit nervous, as she knew she couldn't tell them the whole truth about what was going on in her life.

Her mom's voice, when she answered the phone, actually brought tears to her eyes. It had been a long time. "Hello, Mom, it's Lizzie," she said and jumped when her mother squeaked and called out, "Henry! It's Lizzie!"

"It's okay, Mom. I had a break from my studies, and Professor Cormier is letting me use his phone. I was wondering if I could come for a visit? I only have a few days, and I didn't want to miss the chance."

"Of course! When can you come? Your room is still as you left it. Your brothers are both working in our area, so I am sure they will want to come too. We can make a real party out of it. Oh, Lizzie, we've missed you so...."

She trailed off, and Lizzie got the feeling she wasn't the only one tearing up. Then her dad came onto the phone. "Your mother is having a moment," he said wryly. "She has kept every single letter you've sent and has nearly worn them out, reading them over and over again," which seemed to imply that perhaps she should write more often.

"I'm sure you're busy with all of the things you're learning," he assured her, "and I understand you don't have access to phone service during your internship. But even a postcard now and then would help. Did I understand you're coming to visit?"

"Yes, Professor Cormier said he will be happy to take me down to see you. He has some things he wants to do down there anyway, and it will save me a long bus trip."

"That will be very good. Well, since we'll be seeing you soon—tomorrow maybe?—we can catch up when you get here. Don't want to run up his long-distance bill."

"Yes, Dad, we'll be there tomorrow afternoon. We'll be leaving in the morning. Please give Mom a hug for me, and I'll return the favor when I get there."

As she hung up the phone, she broke down. One of the things that seemed to be changing for her was this newly acquired emotional sensitivity. She wasn't sure she liked it and resolved to get a handle on it. It wouldn't do to get weepy like this all the time.

Wiping the tears from her face and straightening up, she walked out to the garden, where everyone had gathered on the patio. In the past when she had visited here, the backyard had been mostly lawn with an eight-foot fence, an edging of flower beds, and a few small trees.

It was a comparatively large yard for a Los Angeles suburb; but this was a pretty high-end neighborhood, as neighborhoods went. However, she could see that some changes were in process.

For one thing, a slab of concrete had been laid just outside of the french doors that exited into the yard. It was a new trend to create "patios" where folks could sit and talk. To one side on the concreted area sat a round cedar table, with a hole in the center for a shade umbrella and four individual curved benches around it.

Gaston was seated on one of them, a book in hand. He looked up from his book as she came out.

"All set? We can leave in the morning, but in the meantime, do you have any errands to do? We've got the rest of the day to do whatever you need to."

Ynni scampered up and hopped up onto one of the benches. *"Ynni comes too?"* she asked, looking up expectantly.

"Yes, Gaston, I do have some things on my list. And Ynni wishes to come along, with her reflection turned off, of course."

"Very good. Then, we'll be off." He called over his shoulder to Nita, who was hanging clothing on clotheslines behind the garage. "We'll be heading out, Nita. Do you need anything?"

Nita turned and smiled, shaking her head. "We're good. I have everything I need for supper. I'm doing a roast with all the fixings to celebrate. Should I pack a lunch for your trip tomorrow?"

Lizzie spoke up before he could reply. "Mom would be very upset if she didn't get to feed us both when we arrive, Nita. With one of your wonderful breakfasts in us before we leave, we should be good until we get there."

Nita nodded happily and returned to her clothes-hanging. Ynni hopped up to Lizzie's shoulder. Even after all this time, Lizzie was still surprised at how light she was and what a comfort it was to have her there.

They stopped first at her bank into which her Alliance funds were deposited. She wasn't entirely sure how that worked, something about a dummy corporation established by the Alliance and converting precious metals and gems that were plentiful in many member dimensions. She would have to inquire about that when she got back into training.

There was a surprising accumulation in the account, as she had not had many reasons to spend any of her allowance as a trainee. She had never even ordered checks when she had established the account, being accustomed to using cash for any transactions she needed to make, so she withdrew a large amount of cash that hardly made a dent in the balance.

She had a shopping list and made sure to get something for each member of her family. She knew that since the family had transplanted from Missouri to California soon after the first world war, there would likely be no cousins, aunts, or uncles to see on this trip; just her parents, her brothers, and perhaps their wives and children. She couldn't remember all of the kids' names or ages, so she got some generic toys. *After all, an almost never-seen aunt should come bearing gifts,* she mused.

And she couldn't leave out her podmates, either. She had some fun ideas for gifts for each of them, considering that they might soon be going their separate ways, and she wanted each of them to have something to remember her by.

Ynni was enthralled by the experience of riding in a car and confused by the traffic patterns. She kept up a constant mental chatter about the vast numbers of people and buildings as they went about getting the things Lizzie wanted.

Of course, they stopped at one of Thumble's favorite places, the farmer's market. Lizzie thought Thumble would be sad he missed their little jaunt, so she made sure to get him a pineapple, one of his all-time favorite treats. While she was there, she stocked up on a number of her own favorite treats, such as strawberry jam and beef jerky. She kept a stash of favorite things in her MDP to supplement all of the interesting and varied foods she was offered in her training situations.

They would also go to a grocery store before she left for Sanglarka, but the farmer's market was more of an expedition than a common shopping trip. Lizzie loved the environment of shopping in the various stalls. It was especially fun to sample some of the more unusual offerings, and Lizzie was even able to sneak Ynni an occasional treat, checking to be sure no one saw her holding a bite of something up to what would have appeared to be thin air and have it disappear.

The various packages for her family were put into the trunk of Gaston's car as they went, with the things Lizzie bought for herself and her podmates going into the MDP. They chatted off and on about Lizzie's experience on Tarafau's planet and speculated about whether or when Earthlings might develop similar systems and technologies at some future point.

Gaston encouraged her to stay focused on the work she was doing for the Alliance. In the long run, he told her, when Earth was ready, they would potentially catch up faster than she might think. In the meantime, what she was doing would protect the Earth and its inhabitants more than pretty much anything she could do in a lab on the planet and allow its ongoing development to proceed in some kind of safety.

The drive from L.A. to San Diego was a pleasant one. The Pacific Coast Highway was a delight, with its view of the ocean and the many little towns with hundreds of unique and colorful little shops selling everything from fish bait and tackle to antiques, souvenirs, and novelties.

As they meandered down the coast, they drifted between animated conversation about agent training and Gaston's new guide and Nita's latest grandchild into occasional companionable silence, which allowed Lizzie to contemplate the coming reunion with her parents and siblings. She had been considering how best to present her new situation without blatantly lying to them.

Gaston had been helpful in that regard. "Treat this as if you were working for a lab with a government contract requiring secrecy. The official 'corporation' we are contracted to, that pays our paychecks, represents itself as a research facility. We are registered in Switzerland, and all of your 'paychecks' come from a Swiss bank, so secrecy is guaranteed.

"You can tell them that the work you do in this internship is highly confidential and you are under contract not to reveal the nature of your work. This is all true. You can also say that the research we do is and will continue to be for the benefit of all mankind and does not represent any government on the planet."

Lizzie nodded. Everything he had said was entirely true, and yet she regretted she couldn't share any of her adventures or any of the things she was learning from them. Ynni would be present with her reflection turned off and had been advised that, since she could still be felt even with her reflection turned off, she would probably not be on Lizzie's shoulder.

Lizzie knew that Ynni was agile enough to not get herself stepped on unknowingly by any of her family, and it would be interesting to experience her family from Ynni's perspective.

Her parents lived in a small suburb north of the main city, and with Lizzie's directions they were finally parking in the driveway of the three-bedroom home. It was obvious her parents had been watching for her, because before they could get the bag of presents and Lizzie's overnight bag out of the trunk, they were already rushing out to greet them.

Her mother and father hurried to her and put her in what they called "a Lizzie sandwich," surrounding her with linked arms in a warm and fervent hug.

"Let me look at you," her mother said, stepping back to gaze with hungry eyes. Lizzie couldn't help but notice that her parents had aged more than she had expected. It had only been two years since she had been home, but there was noticeable gray on their temples, and the smile lines around her mother's eyes were more pronounced. "We've missed you so much! And this must be Professor Cormier! Welcome!" And she held out her hand to shake his as he shifted Lizzie's overnight case to his other hand.

Her dad also shook his hand enthusiastically. "Lizzie tells us you are the one who gave her the opportunity for this internship. I understand she will be getting college credits for her work?"

"Indeed," Gaston replied cheerfully. "Lizzie's work and enthusiasm for the sciences suited her perfectly for this position. It's a rare opportunity, and she is showing herself worthy of the trust they have put in her. It is satisfying to see a student succeed in their field. We expect great things from her in the future."

"That does a father's heart proud," her dad responded. He was as stocky as ever, his plaid shirt tucked into his jeans showing just a bit of a pot belly. Lizzie had been surprised as a teen when she finally realized she could look directly into his eyes without having to look up. That had never changed his stature in her opinion. She would never stop looking up to him.

"Will you be joining us for lunch?" her mom cut in. "Let's not stand out here in the sun. Everything is ready, and you can just set all of your things on the couch in the living room."

Gaston agreed with enthusiasm. They entered the house through a mirrored entryway that led into the living room. Per her request, they deposited their bundles on the large sofa and followed her into the dining room.

The table was already laid with mom's best china, and a floral centerpiece with a little hand-lettered banner that read, "Welcome Home, Lizzie!"

Lizzie and Gaston sat at her mom's direction, and she and her dad left into the swinging kitchen door and returned nearly immediately with trays containing her mom's famous tuna casserole, fresh baked rolls, and a large salad bowl. Already on the table were several choices of salad dressing and a large pitcher of ice water.

They sat, and her dad led them in a blessing on the food, thanking God for a safe trip and the blessing of having their daughter once again in their midst. Lizzie felt the familiar calm she had always felt when listening to her father pray. He was never flowery, but his sincerity often made her want to look up from her bowed head and closed eyes to see if there was actually Someone standing there listening to him.

Lizzie realized as she ate what people meant by "comfort food." Mom's tuna casserole had been a staple growing up, and she wished she could just freeze a bunch of it and take it with her to eat whenever she felt homesick. Unfortunately, as far as she knew there were no freezer units in her MDP, and no way to power them if there were.

After the meal, Gaston excused himself jovially. "Lizzie should get as much family time in as she can. Hopefully she will be able to visit more frequently in future, but for now, I have to get to my motel and on to the zoo. I have an appointment with one of those famous gorillas! I'll be back in three days to pick her up for the return trip.

"Enjoy your holiday, Lizzie." And with that, he turned with a cheerful wave to all and left.

"Such a nice man," her mother commented as she began to clear the table. Lizzie gladly pitched in, and they chatted as if Lizzie had never left as they put away the leftovers and did the dishes together, her mom washing and Lizzie drying and putting away.

"Yes, I always enjoyed his classes. I can't tell you how surprised I was when he offered me this position. I knew it meant I wouldn't see you all as often as I'd like..." she trailed off.

"Even when you were just in the university in L.A., we didn't see much of you," her mom mused. "I can understand when you are working out of the country that it will be difficult. I'm just glad you've taken to writing more often."

Lizzie blushed at that. While she had been at college, she had seldom written and, due to the cost of long-distance phone calls, she had hardly ever called.

"I'm trying to get better at that," she admitted. "It's hard when I can't tell you much about what I do, but I don't want to make you worry."

"Gene and George will be by in just a bit," her mom said, changing the subject gently. "George and Lisa are expecting a little one soon. They're hoping for a boy, but so far his two girls are betting on another sister. Gene and his wife are still hoping, but so far, no luck in that department."

Lizzie felt this was more than just news. She knew her mom had been disappointed that Lizzie had put off marriage and motherhood in pursuit of her education, but her mom tried really hard not to be too pushy about it. She had acquaintances in college who often complained about their mothers' nagging them for grandchildren. Once again, she was grateful her mom was at least subtle about it.

Her mom laughed. "Of course, I'll be happy to see that, but I know how you are when you get focused on something important. Just don't stop. In the meantime, I think I hear a car...."

Sure enough, moments later her older brother, Gene, opened the door and called out, "Is that wandering sister of mine here yet?"

He was as tall as she remembered, his curly red hair trimmed short and his blue-green eyes twinkling with the mischief she always associated with him. She had always envied him his curls, but he was embarrassed by them. His wife, Lorraine, was close behind him. Her silky straight blonde hair and brown eyes were quite a contrast.

They both hugged her with enthusiasm. "Mom briefed us that your job is confidential, but we spent the entire thirty-minute commute here speculating what you could possibly be doing that could require you to keep secrets from family," Lorraine said with a mischievous grin. "I'm guessing rocket science or some such thing. Gene seems to think it's more like a cure for the common cold."

"Nothing so monumental," Lizzie replied offhandedly, ducking her head. "It's interesting to me, and it's stretching me more than I expected, but I doubt it will ever make the papers." This, she thought wryly, was true enough.

They had no sooner seated themselves in the living room than the front door opened again, letting in George, his two girls, and his wife, Lisa, her pregnant tummy nearly preceding her into the room. George could have been Lizzie's twin, although a bit older. They were of a height, and his wife and girls had long, honey-colored, wavy hair and large brown eyes.

Hugs again ensued and, amid some giggling by the girls, Lizzie congratulated them on the imminent new addition to their family.

"I've missed a few birthdays and holidays," she said as they all settled themselves again, the girls sitting cross-legged on the floor, "so I brought a few gifts to make up for that."

She opened the large bag she had placed in front of her to make room on the couch. Each of the gifts she had bought the day before brought appropriate *oohs* and *aahs* and *thank-yous* from each of them. There was even a shower gift for the new little one, Lizzie having been warned ahead of time of the impending birth.

As Lizzie watched the faces of these people she loved, she realized that things were shifting inside her. She had always felt somewhat detached from the other human beings in her life, but now she saw them through new eyes. She recognized that her values were changing and that she would never feel the same way about her family again.

She had often heard the old saw, "Absence makes the heart grow fonder," but she never understood it until now.

All that evening they talked about their lives and laughed and even cried with one another. Mom had prepared a buffet table to allow them to get up and eat as they chose with no formal dining, each of them eating from a plate in their laps as they continued.

Dad told some funny stories from his youth, and George told some tales on the girls that made them roll their eyes. Gene talked about his work in city planning; and as Lizzie listened to that, she regretted she couldn't tell him about her experiences on other worlds or recommend some ideas that might make the cities he worked with better and more advanced than they were.

She enjoyed getting to know more about her brothers' lives, each of them with differing personalities and interests. The time flew by, and it was late when they regrettably agreed it was time to stop for the night. Evidently a picnic was planned for the following day, as well as a trip to the famous San Diego Zoo, and they all needed to get some sleep before starting out in the morning.

Lizzie went to bed in her old room. As her mom had promised, nothing had changed since she had left. To Lizzie it represented her mom's determination that Lizzie would always have a place to come and would keep a place in her heart. Feeling warm and loved, she went to sleep grateful for this opportunity to come home, even if only for a few days.

Chapter 5: Without Missing a Beat

(Jenny hadn't known much about her great grandparents or her great uncles, but she enjoyed the descriptions of the picnic and the zoo trip that had followed and sympathized with Lizzie's frustration of not being able to share her own adventures with her family.

In Jenny's case, her dad actually did know a little bit about what she was doing, but he was the only one of her family who realized even the smallest part of what she did.

She almost sighed when she got to the part where Gaston picked up Lizzie at the end of her visit, feeling Lizzie's sadness at parting again so soon. And she even felt as if she were present at Sanglarka when Lizzie returned there before setting off through the gate with Tarafau and Ynni to the training center.

Jenny was most curious about what would happen there, living vicariously through Lizzie's experiences in her training. Every page seemed like adding a new layer to her own understanding of what it meant to be an agent of the Dimensional Alliance...)

As Lizzie, Ynni, and Tarafau exited the gate in the basement of the training center, Lizzie exhaled almost in relief. This seemed more like coming home than going back to Los Angeles or San Diego had been. Lall was there greeting all of his trainees as they exited the gate.

"We'll be meeting formally at the pod in about an hour," he told her as soon as they stepped forward out of the gate. He was all business at the moment. Warmer greetings would come later, she knew, so with a

friendly nod they left, going up the stairs and down the now familiar hallways to the huge exit doors that led onto the training grounds.

Lizzie stopped, looking up at the two suns and the cloudless sky. Before her on either side of a stretch of grass larger than a football field were the pod buildings, much like the barracks on a military base. They were spaced slightly apart; leafy trees in the gaps between each that led to the paths on the other side. These paths ran between the dining halls, the outfitters' buildings, and the dispensary, as well as other training areas and equipment.

Lizzie's pod was the last building on the right, so she and Tarafau walked down the paved path side by side, Ynni with her reflection turned on, sitting blithely crooning on Lizzie's shoulder. Just outside, under a tree, sat several of her podmates, including Gi and Minth, her two closest podmates. Reanni and Negoth were also there, Negoth holding forth with expansive gestures, evidently about his internship or his holiday. All of the others were listening attentively.

Gi was the first to look up and notice them. She jumped up and tootled a melodic sound which Lizzie could remember was a greeting by her people. Gi had begun teaching her some of her melodic language before they had parted to go their separate ways for the first part of their individual internships.

Lizzie replicated the sounds as best she could. Gi insisted she spoke with "an accent." Regardless, Gi's expression was of delight and welcome. They threw their arms around one another, wobbling Ynni still perched on Lizzie's shoulder.

"We're catching up," she sent when they broke apart. *"Come and join us. Have a seat. Maybe we can do a short concert later, but I have a feeling Lall has something in store for us in just a bit. Otherwise, one of the other instructors would have been greeting us at the gate, I think."*

"I'll bet you're right," Lizzie replied, ruefully shaking her head. *"I'm guessing he's wondering if we've been keeping in shape since we left."*

She sat and they chatted cheerfully as more and more of them gathered under "our tree," as they had come to call it.

"I have something special to show you, when we get some time," she confided to Gi. *"I think you'll like it. I can hardly wait for one of our concerts."*

Her friends were all congratulatory to Ynni when Lizzie told them about her babies, and all agreed that it would be fun to visit the grove in another ten years when the little tribe would be more established. None of them had forgotten the valiant run Ynni had made that one horrible night to bring Liliath, the instructors, and the troopers to their aid during their battle with the rebels.

Eventually, the two remaining Geln strode up with Lall in their wake. To Lizzie's relief, they were smiling and seemed healthy. She was sure the loss of the third part of their mind-joined trio had impacted them in many ways, but for now they seemed happy to see their podmates.

They all stood and followed Lall into the pod building, curious to see what he had to say and what came next. Lizzie was surprised to see that Tarafau stayed with her. None of the other "guides" had accompanied her podmates.

"Welcome back to the next stage of your training. I would like to introduce you to my assistant, Tarafau Bane. He will be supervising the majority of your physical training for this term. I will be supervising a new pod this term and, although I will be checking in on you from time to time, Tarafau will be stretching you, I promise."

Lizzie thanked Professor Baird for his training in not showing emotions on her face. She almost groaned. Not Tarafau! She knew how demanding he could be. She had actually been looking forward to a break from him while she completed this next stage in her training before she was finally certified to begin her final internship requirements.

She had known that Tarafau was a permanent assignment to her, at least until such a time as she was a certified agent, but she almost rolled her eyes at this news.

The rest of her podmates seemed to take it in stride except Mang, who raised a skeptical eyebrow. The contrast between Lall and Tarafau was striking. Lall was short, stocky, densely muscled, and humanoid. He had no discernable ears, and his hands looked a bit odd, with only three fingers and a thumb, but she had gotten used to him.

Tarafau was tall and also muscled. His amber eyes nearly blazed out of his face, which was blue-black like Tidbit's fur, and his ears came to points at the bottom. He towered over all of the trainees. His mental voice was deep and soft, belying the fierceness Lizzie knew he could display.

"I am looking forward to working with your pod. I have heard good things about you all from Liliath and also Lizzie Japhet, your fellow podmate. For this term, we will be continuing to work on teamwork, but also individual stamina, and we will take your defense skills to the next best level any of you may be capable of.

"I expect you to achieve the potential that is within each of you and will uphold that standard with every workout. Liliath will continue to shore up your mental defenses, and we will be combining both to increase your abilities even more."

The pod nodded a silent assent. Lizzie wondered if they, like she, were groaning inside. She had a feeling that Tarafau's idea of what her potential was might be more than she could actually produce. Gone were the days when she could confidently assume she would excel beyond any of her classmates in whatever class she took.

Not until she had come to the agent training center had she ever felt consistently challenged. The only comfort was that her podmates had also struggled to keep up with the coursework. She imagined that most of them were on par with her intellectually, obviously one of the requirements for agent training.

Tarafau and Lall waited silently for a moment, perhaps waiting for questions or comments. When there were none, Lall sent, *"You have until second lunch to yourselves, to catch up before your first classes. You will meet here the hour preceding the supper meal to work the forms and do your first defense lesson of the term. Two hours after the supper meal, you will assemble as usual for the evening stretch and run. Starting tomorrow, you will resume your regular workout schedule. We will leave you to it then."* And nodding to Tarafau, he preceded him out the door onto the training grounds.

"Well, that was interesting," Linlin sent, her face expressionless as usual, but her hair was writhing as it often did when she was agitated. *"Lizzie, you know this Tarafau. Will he be as hard as he sounds?"*

Lizzie squirmed a little inside. This was one of the things that worried her. She was a link to Tarafau. Would this distance her from her podmates? *"Tarafau is fair, and he is very good at what he does, but yes, he is also strict and can be demanding. I imagine the word 'stretch' will take on a new meaning this term."*

Linlin sighed. *"I guess you got a guide like mine. Juien is strict, but kind most of the time. She doesn't allow much in the way of slacking though, and she is as picky as Baird about telegraphing emotions. She is constantly on my case about the reactions of my hair."* And as she said this, she rolled her eyes and her hair calmed to its usually subtle movement.

And this opened up the floodgates. Each of them had stories about their guides and their experiences with the "away" part of their term as a fledgling intern. Lizzie joined in happily. She had missed this interaction and was gratified to learn that her discomforts were not as unique as she had feared.

"You said you had something to show us," Gi sent at one point. *"Can we see it now?"*

Lizzie grinned. She pulled the little wooden box from her MDP. *"Another mbira?"* Gi asked, but when Lizzie opened the box, she cocked her head in puzzlement.

"A scarf?"

Lizzie grinned and stroked the oval cloth, and it swelled. Amenia had loved helping her learn to use her mind to play this instrument. It turned out to be able to play in multiple voices, depending on Lizzie's intent, and she had caught on quicker than she had anticipated. Amenia had made a comment that summed up the experience: *"Music is more about the heart than an arrangement of notes and tempos."*

Lizzie enjoyed the puzzled looks of her podmates. She began to tap and stroke the kareena, her eyes closed in bliss. Ynni joined in, and she heard gasps and oohs. She opened her eyes to see Geln swaying to the music and noticed Gi had pulled out her harp. *"Can we go out under our tree?"* Geln asked hopefully. *"This should be shared."*

They all nodded in agreement and trooped out to gather under "our tree." This was something Lizzie had missed so much, and once again she and Ynni and Gi made glorious music in the circle of the podmates that had become her family as much as her family on Earth. It was good to be back.

Later, true to his word, working out with Tarafau was stretching more than just their muscles. The defense lesson was now expanded to bouts with one against two. He told them that by the end of the term they would be doing bouts of one against four as well as teams of three against three.

By the end of the first session, even Mang was panting with stress. The pod agreed that if the rest of the lessons were this intense, they were in for a wild ride this term. Hopefully it wouldn't include any actual conflict like last term.

Each of their professors began their classes by asking about how their perspectives had changed on the particular topic at hand as a result of their first internship outing. The consensus seemed to be that it was beginning to dawn on them the true purpose of their various courses of study. Many expressed surprise that they had actually used much of what they had learned during their different intern journeys.

Lulindu's class had transitioned from studying the member charter agreements of the Dimensional Alliance to beginning to talk about the workings of the council and how the various dimensional council members represented their dimensions. They would be attending some live council sessions and discussing the issues on the table, as well as how they were dealt with.

In Fin's class, they would be working on the concept of diplomacy and how that played into their role as an agent. This, of course, included things like addressing various systems of rank in different cultures and how to deal with the differences in cultural and political attitudes on various topics.

Meta would continue to teach dimensional travel theory and how to deal with differing levels of technology without creating "technology pollution" of a culture, as well as instructing them in the newest technology that allowed them to communicate with the Alliance under stressful situations.

They had been more than a little shocked to see the mirrors gone from Baird's classroom and not a cubes game in sight. Instead, the chairs had been placed in a circle again. This term they would be practicing how to guide a discussion in the direction they wished, especially when it seemed to be headed into something that could be disastrous for the Alliance. The idea was to guide without pushing and to keep their balance and temper even when the discussion seemed to go astray despite their best efforts.

At the beginning of each class, they would be given a topic for discussion. Two of them, unbeknownst to the rest, would be given a specific direction into which they would be expected to take the conversation. The tricky part is that each of those assigned to guide the dialog would be given opposite points of view, and they got extra points if no one realized that they were the "discussion guides."

Leave it to Baird to give them seemingly impossible objectives, Lizzie thought; and she could imagine, although her podmates' faces gave no hint of it, that they were as befuddled by this task as she was. However, like the ability to control their facial expressions, she was sure that with constant application and exercise (there was that word again) they would eventually get better at it.

Lizzie was painfully aware that gentle persuasion was not one of her strong points, and she had a sinking feeling in the pit of her stomach that this term was once again definitely going to deflate her former pride in being top of her class as she had been in the university.

Her initial session with Liliath was enjoyable, at least at first. Evidently, Tarafau had told her about the kareena, and she asked for a demonstration, then took her into her mental exercises, where she also had Lizzie play the kareena for a while.

Liliath had her consider how she could multiply the sound in her mind to create an entire orchestra. Then she brought her back out to the workout room, where she once again had Lizzie play.

This time Lizzie found that she could add additional voices in the conscious world, making each of her fingers a different instrument, tuned to a different harmony.

When she asked Liliath how this pertained to her agent training, Liliath simply replied, "It's all a part of who you are. You may find that this new gift you have discovered, thanks to your time with Tarafau's people, may allow you to impact many more than you may ever do with simple logic or reasoning."

"Does the kareena count as alien technology? Will I be able to share it anywhere I go?"

Liliath gave a mental sigh. *"Unfortunately, on planets with little to no technology, you will have to keep it in your MDP, especially if they are in non-member dimensions. That being said, your simple mbira will allow you to touch many, even without the kareena. Don't neglect the simple mbira, even though the music the kareena makes is so very impressive. Both have their place.*

"Oftentimes you will find yourself in situations where, although you have the technology to resolve something easily, using that technology will be proscribed and simpler methods will be necessary. In Fin's and Lulindu's classes, you will be hearing that over and over again, and Meta will be emphasizing it throughout your instruction this term.

"It may be a struggle sometimes to restrain yourself, but you must remember that our purpose is not to necessarily resolve every problem of every culture we encounter, and that using technology or teaching scientific principles that are yet unknown to them can have disastrous results."

Lizzie just nodded. She had expected this would be the answer.

Liliath continued, *"In the meantime, I will be introducing you to a new private instructor in addition to your other lessons. I know you are being stretched this term and it already seems to you that the challenge is more than you can handle. However, in your case I not only believe you can handle it but think it will magnify your usefulness to the Alliance and will achieve more of your own goals than if we neglected it until later.*

"Come to me tomorrow morning with Ynni after breakfast, and I will introduce you. I believe that this may eventually even make your studies more enjoyable and expand your understanding in new ways."

Lizzie's head spun like a top at this. More coursework? A new instructor? She was already feeling more than a little overwhelmed. However, she had committed to follow the course of instruction and do whatever she needed to do to become a certified agent, so the following morning, already loaded down with more coursework than she had ever experienced at the university, not to mention the physical requirements, she presented herself in Liliath's office.

There, beside the chaise where Liliath reclined, was a hoverchair with its back to her. She had used such a chair last term, after she had been released from the hospital and was recuperating from her violent encounter with the rebels. As she entered the room, the chair turned to face her. Seated in the chair was a man with something on his shoulder. Not a linkling, and she couldn't tell if the man was humanoid or not.

"Ah, Lizzie, you are prompt. Allow me to introduce you to Reloi, an agent of the Alliance, and Tanata. It can be said that Reloi has an interesting perspective about symbiotic relationships. Tanata is an emerin, a distant relation to dragonkind. Reloi and Tanata found one another during one of Reloi's assignments, and they are bonded together in a similar way as you are to Ynni.

"They have been together for many years and have found new ways to use the bond in strengthening Reloi's mental abilities and using their mental bond to increase his effectiveness as an agent."

Lizzie really looked at the two, trying to take in what Liliath had said. Reloi was bald with silvery spiky eyebrows and large, nearly violet eyes both of which were striking enough, but the reason for the use of the power chair was evident: he had no arms or legs. Lizzie didn't think she could ask without embarrassing both her and him as to whether this was normal for his species or if he had lost his limbs in an accident or if this was a congenital abnormality.

Perched like Ynni on his shoulder was what might have been a gecko, but unlike those tiny lizards, Tanata was about a foot tall, his head level with the top of Reloi's head.

"It is good to meet you, Lizzie," Reloi sent. His mind voice was a mellow baritone. *"Tanata and I will be working with you and Ynni*

every day in Liliath's workout room, in the evening between supper and your physical workout. I understand you play some musical instruments, and we will be melding that into our sessions."

Lizzie nodded, unsure what to say.

"It isn't surprising for you to be a little hesitant, so I will answer the questions I already know that you have. I was born on the planet Grild, where all of my people have arms and legs and hands and feet, just as you do. Our species are very similar. I am a singular mutation, born this way. I had loving parents who chose to raise me as if I were undamaged and never let me feel like I was unusual in any important way.

"Because of their strength and their willingness to help me figure out how to be me, I can do much more than most people would think, and I won't take offense if you have any questions for me about my unique challenges as we go along. And I promise if I have any questions about your own, I will not hesitate to ask you, with the understanding that you too will not take offense. Does that sound like a fair bargain?" He smiled mischievously, his spiky silver eyebrows raised with the question.

"Yes, Reloi. I think that is fair enough. It's good to meet you and Tanata. Ynni, say hello."

"Hello, Reloi and Tanata. Lizzie and Ynni will enjoy learning more about how we can work together. Tanata, do you sing?"

Tanata's mind voice was surprisingly similar to Liliath's, soft and calming and yet strong. *"Tanata greets Ynni and Lizzie. Yes, I sing when I can. My people sing across long distances, calling for gatherings or warnings or sometimes for the joy of being. I look forward to joining voices as we learn together."*

"I can see Ynni and Tanata have things in common that will make our instruction together very profitable for all of us. I know you need to get to your next class. We will see you this evening?" Reloi asked, his eyebrows raised with the question.

"Yes, for sure. Thank you, Reloi."

"Lizzie, don't forget our meeting today. I think there may be some interesting outcomes based on our last session. I will see you then," Liliath said with a nod of dismissal.

When Lizzie got to Meta's lab and sat down between Gi and Minth and waited for Meta to start the class, Gi leaned over, looking into her eyes as she sent, *"What was that about? Are you in trouble?"*

"No, just extra coursework because of Ynni's link. I'm learning from someone else who is linked to a symbiote. They are going to teach Ynni and me how to work as a team."

"That sounds exciting! With all of this extra coursework, are we still going to be able to do our daily music breaks?"

"I think so. We'll just have to do them between first and second lunch instead of in the evening. I think I'm going to need it more than ever. Is it just me, or is the pace and pressure increasing way more than expected?"

"You aren't alone. You should hear Geln. They are having extra coursework too, learning how to make their plurality work for them. They're complaining, and you know they never complain about anything."

Minth nodded emphatically. *"I'm getting extra time with Meta because she thinks she may have a tech solution to my electric charge that may mean I can go without the gloves or boots. We're going to be working on the tech together with one of the scientists from my dimension. If it works, it may mean we can interact more fully and frequently with other dimensions.*

"But that means a bigger load for me as well. And Mang is working with Lall on a new defense training program for the new trainees that will move them along faster. It's possible he may actually end up as an instructor after his internship."

At that point, they had to interrupt their conversation as Meta came into the lab. However, Lizzie found it a little harder to concentrate as she considered how each of them was being directed into differing paths at this point of their training.

Would they be able to continue these strong bonds of friendship over seemingly unimaginable distances and indeterminate amounts of time spent apart in their various assignments? Even with the few months they had spent apart during their first experiences with their intern guides, Lizzie had missed them more than she had expected, more than she had ever missed any of the students she had attended college with.

Chapter 6: Beyond Imagining

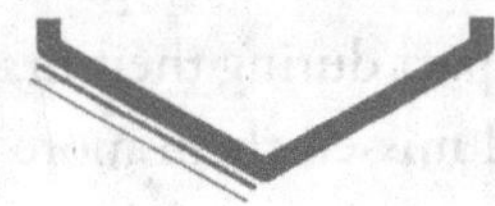

(Jenny had a lot to think about on her walk that day. Every time she finished reading in the journal even for a short time, she found herself contemplating how Lizzie's journey had affected her own life.

She also realized she would definitely need to add more training to her to-do list. For instance, she and Chidwi had only had a limited time with Amenia to learn how to work together. It seemed evident at this point how much more she still had to do, beyond her other duties as the Gatekeeper for the Alliance.

It was ironic that the one person fully trained as a gatekeeper was still ensconced on a planet eons away from here. Anela lived on the dragon planet, Liliath's home world, in a castle on a mountaintop. She was the "alternate gatekeeper," whose sole duty was to be available to take over the gatekeeper's duties should Jenny be unexpectedly killed.

Had it not been for the circumstances where Jenny was present at the death of Miriha, the former gatekeeper, and that Miriha had judged Jenny worthy of the task, when Miriha passed, Anela's key would have activated, and the central gate would have transferred to the main gate on her planet.

But for now, she still waited, evidently patiently and happily. She, much like Jenny's aunt Lizzie, was more focused on learning new things than anything else. Her continuing work with Cornelium, Merv, and Bob was proving to be extremely useful in the current conflict, and that seemed to satisfy her.

Jenny consulted with her from time to time via her special gift for interdimensional mindspeech, the ability to communicate over unimaginable distances once Jenny knew that person and could recognize their mind. Jenny herself wasn't entirely sure how it worked, but Amenia had given her the key to it, almost by accident, on one of their sessions intended to expand Jenny's mental abilities.

As far as anyone knew, this was a unique ability, and all, including Liliath, were intrigued by the possibilities. It had been hinted that when the current crisis was over, several of those most mentally gifted would be studying with Jenny and Amenia to see if this was unique to her or whether someone else, with proper guidance, could also learn to do it. This was especially necessary since communicating this way was much more timely and convenient than the usual methods of using the Alliance communications network.

Jenny hoped so, for it would take a lot of the burden of coordinating all of the needs of the Dimensional Alliance via interdimensional communication off of her.

As she finished her walk, she noticed that the "For Sale" sign had changed to "Sold," and she found herself wondering who her new neighbor might be... a question for another time. For now, she had reading to do while she still could...)

Lizzie entered Liliath's workout room with a kind of squirming anticipation. On the one hand, she was sure this new kind of instruction would be helpful; and on the other hand, this instructor was new to her and so unusual that she was having trouble deciding how she felt about any of it.

Reloi was seated on the mat with Tanata beside him. At first it was almost like they were two interesting sculptures. Both were staring straight ahead of them, their faces slack. Lizzie cleared her throat, and their eyes immediately came into focus, looking up at her.

"Come in and be seated," Reloi sent with a smile, gesturing with his eyes at the mat.

His smile was pleasant and warm, and Lizzie sat and assumed a cross-legged position. Ynni hopped down beside her, settling on her heels, imitating Tanata's attentive position.

"Today we will get to know one another better, and we will start with the basics pertaining to the correlation between a reciprocal relationship and how we can expand the benefits of being joined not only mentally but on a deeper, heartfelt level.

"Since bonding with Tanata, I have learned more about myself, because each of us can see deeper into one another than we could have seen into ourselves without the bond. At first it was just pleasant. I enjoyed Tanata's presence in my life, but I didn't realize how intense and deep the bond went until a tragedy in my life caused me to turn to him on a much more personal level.

"We met almost casually. I was touring one of the newest Alliance member dimensions, and while on his planet we stopped to eat a packed lunch on a field trip through one of the jungles that led to a lagoon that was an important local landmark.

"As we ate, seated on a blanket on the ground, my local guide was explaining some of the local wildlife, and I had laid my plate on the blanket beside me with the remains of my lunch on it. As I turned away from where my guide had pointed, I saw Tanata, calmly sitting and eating a partially finished piece of fruit off of my plate.

"He looked up at me and when our eyes met, I felt something I had never felt before. A connection had been made instantly. Suddenly I knew him, and he knew me in a way I had never known anyone before.

"Does that sound familiar?"

Lizzie nodded. *"It was similar for me and Ynni. She sought me out. When she first touched my hand, it was like we were tied together with an invisible line that ran, not from my mind, but into my heart."*

Reloi smiled in agreement. *"Yes, that sounds right. It turns out that Tanata's kind make these connections seldom, but when they do, the bond is for life. He has been a great help for me, and together we can do so much more than apart. He also has helped me learn a lot about myself and what I can do that I never suspected. This is why Liliath believes that Tanata and I can be of assistance for you and Ynni. For example."*

Reloi looked past Lizzie, and suddenly a glass of water floated between her and Ynni to Reloi and tipped itself gently towards his mouth as he took a few sips. The glass righted itself and then floated back to the small table it had rested on before.

Lizzie's eyes nearly popped from her head. Magic? Really?

Reloi grinned at her, cocking his head. *"No, it isn't a magic trick, and no, I can't read your mind. Everyone always thinks that, so I figured I'd make it clear from the beginning.*

A few years after I bonded with Tanata, I found myself in a life-or-death situation. We were in a rocky area with a group of other agents, being attacked by creatures we hadn't expected. I had been on the ground, out of my chair, looking at some of the interesting stones our guides were pointing out.

"The attackers were larger than most of us, and I had no weapons I could manipulate without hands or limbs. My companions were struggling, each with their own battle; and although I was behind them, I could see that a few of the fanged and clawed creatures had broken off their attacks on my fellows to focus on me. As they approached, I knew myself for a dead man.

"Suddenly, Tanata simply sent, 'Rocks! Use them!' And, without thinking I pictured the rocks rising up and pelting the angry creatures approaching me. And they did! From all around me, rocks were rising from the ground, some of them closer to boulders than simple stones.

"I think the creatures fled more from fright of seeing the rocks arise, seemingly from nowhere, to attack them, than for fear of being hit by them. It saved not only me and Tanata that day but my companions as well.

"Afterwards, when Tanata and I were alone and I could calm my mind, we searched inside of me for the ability I had discovered that day. We practiced lifting and manipulating the things around me in my room at the local Dimensional Alliance admin building.

"It took me some time to learn to control it, but you can imagine what that ability means to someone with my physical limitations. Even though my parents taught me from birth to be as self-sufficient as possible, this mental gift has expanded my capacity to do more and to live a more conventional life. Not that there really is such a thing."

Lizzie's mind was racing. *"So, are you saying I can learn to do this?"*

"Not particularly, but Liliath seems to think that you and your linkling have potential to unlock some hidden abilities when you team up. For now, our goal is to explore what will work for the two of you, without necessarily patterning it after anything that Tanata and I can do. We will begin by the four of us visiting your mental space and see what we find there that might hint at what we are looking for or what might be possible.

"Assume your REM state and we will proceed. I need you to take us into your mind. We cannot trespass otherwise."

Lizzie began her breathing and relaxation. It took her almost no time these days to fade into the dream state, and in only a few seconds she was standing in front of the bank vault door that led into a vast library which in turn led out into the town square with shops and various brick buildings with white trim and shutters, much like a photo she had once seen of Georgetown in Maryland.

She led them through the library and out the large maple wooden doors with their ornate doorknobs, down the stone steps between two large lion statues.

"Impressive," Reloi remarked, taking it all in with a sweeping glance. Startled, Lizzie realized that here in her mental world, Reloi was no longer in a hover chair. Instead, he had arms and legs, hands and feet, and strode along beside her at her normal long-legged pace; and as usual in her mind space, they appeared to be no longer using mindspeech but could speak to one another as if they both spoke the same language.

"It appears to me that tradition and order are both very important to you, but," he said, turning his back on the neat town square to view the huge library, "even more important is knowledge and learning. Let's see what else you value."

They walked by a large bookstore and a small café, then coming upon the music store, which had grown in size since her last visit there with Liliath. The small sign had been replaced with gilt lettering in the large picture window, which now featured not only the mbira but also a kareena, whereas most music stores would have displayed a grand piano or other large instrument.

"Ah yes, Liliath told me about your musical inclinations. Two unique instrumental choices, I would say. I think we will explore this side of you in a future session for sure."

They came next to an apothecary shop, designated with a representation of a typical mortar and pestle on a sign over the door.

"Hmm. Why this, I wonder? Do you feel the need for medical assistance? But not a formal doctor-patient relationship. Interesting..."

They walked on, past the ice cream shoppe and the five and dime with its jumble of assorted dry goods. He paused, however, in front of the tiny toy store. It was about a fourth the size of any of the other shops.

"Not much for fun and games? I notice there is a cubes game in the display window and a bicycle. Such disparate choices."

Lizzie didn't reply. She hadn't even realized all of these shops were here, other than the music store. It was a mystery to her how she could have all of these things in her head and not know it or even understand the reasoning behind it.

They crossed over into the park at the center of the large square surrounded by buildings. There were all the usual features of a city park: a small pond, paths that wound through the trees, a playground with swings, a slide and a sandbox, and park benches spaced around the edges of the path.

"There is comfort here, a place for contemplation. Let us sit." And putting words to action, he sat on the next bench they came to. Lizzie did the same. As they did so, Tanata and Ynni sat between the two of them on the bench, eyeing one another curiously. To Lizzie's surprise, Ynni put one furry arm around the shoulders of the little lizard, looking into his eyes.

"Ynni likes Tanata. We can be friends, I think," she said.

"Yes... friends," Tanata agreed.

"That's a good start," Reloi said with a fond smile at the two of them. "How long have you and Ynni been linked?"

"Not very long, several months. The bond was instant, but we're still learning about one another."

"How far away can you be from one another and still communicate mentally?"

"Hmm, I'm not sure. I've never really checked."

"Then this is a good place for us to start. I need time to consider the surroundings of your mental village, and it will take continued observation by me and Tanata to see where we need to take this next.

"So, here is your first assignment. I want you to take some time in the next couple of days to get away from each other physically while continuing to communicate with one another mentally. Go as far as you can. Kind of like a game I hear you play on Earth. I think they call it "Marco Polo." You send to her, and she sends back to you until the return send doesn't happen anymore.

"Preferably you should do it when you can't actually see one another. When you have measured this a few times, we will see what we can do to stretch that. For Tanata and me, we can get as far as several miles away, not that this happens often. For us, and I am guessing also for you two, we don't like to spend any more time apart than we can help."

Lizzie nodded. It made sense to test the limits of their ability to communicate with one another; based on some of their earlier experiences, this might have come in handy.

"Sure, Reloi. I think that's a very good idea. What else will we be doing?"

"We need to find out in what ways Ynni can boost your mental abilities. Different pairings have different limitations, but your bond seems to be very strong for the short time you've been together. And now, as pleasant as these surroundings are, let us return to the physical world, shall we?"

And as quick as that, the little park faded from Lizzie's view and she was back in the workout room, facing the man and his lizard friend, with Ynni's arm actually around the shoulders of Tanata. Was the little lizard smiling?

"That was an excellent first session, Lizzie. I am sure you noticed that in the mental state I appear to be quite different than I am in the physical world, and I'm also sure you would be embarrassed to ask me about it, so I want to explain.

"We all have a picture in our minds of who we are that doesn't necessarily correspond to what we can see in a mirror. In my dreams and in my thoughts, I appear to myself like everyone else, a healthy and usual humanoid body with all the right appendages. As you just experienced, in the mental state, I have no limitations.

"You need to understand this because a lot more happens in our minds than we think. You've probably heard the saying 'It's all in his mind.' But when it comes down to it, it really always is. Everything we do, every action we take, all begins with a thought of one kind or another. This is why, as we train our minds, we find out that we can move beyond what we picture as our physical limitations."

He pivoted onto one shoulder and, pushing up hard from the ground, actually sprang into his hover chair, landing neatly and swiveling to face her. His grin lit up his bald face and his eyes were merry.

"It will take some time for you to get used to me and my... shall we say... eccentricities, but I think, like our little friends have done, we can decide to be friends and companions in discovery. I know you have a lot to do yet today. Are you coming, Tanata?"

He nodded at Tanata and Tanata also leapt up into the chair and scrambled up Reloi's shirt to perch on his shoulder.

Ynni mirrored the action, jumping to Lizzie's shoulder before she rose from her seat on the mat.

"Thank you, Reloi and Tanata," Lizzie sent with a smile. *"I think I'm going to look forward to these lessons most of all."* And to her surprise, she realized she meant it.

Chapter 7: Harmonizing

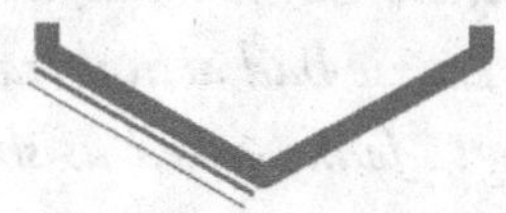

(Jenny didn't even notice Burt bustling around in her little kitchen or that he had even come out of the gate office door until he called out, "Anybody besides me hungry?"

She had been so absorbed in these most recent revelations that someone could have put a bomb under her chair, and she wouldn't' have noticed.

Jenny had been surprised to learn that her new husband was actually quite a good cook. The smells wafting into the living room were heavenly. She had only gotten to cook for him a few times before he told her that slaving over a hot stove wasn't his idea of resting and recuperating and she was either to let Lizziebot cook, or he would cook for her when he was home.

"I'm not a complete invalid..." she had protested, but he had waved that away.

"Nope, nope, the only duty the doc wants you doing is your daily walk and your nightly mental visits with a limited number of dignitaries. We need you well and whole and ready to take charge when your recovery is complete. I promised the healer I would make sure that happened."

He placed a beautiful chef's salad at her place on the dining room table and some fluffy rolls on a bread plate beside it.

"Rolls courtesy of Arvid," he said when he noticed her look of surprise. "I'm no baker. Anything interesting in your reading today?"

He pulled out her chair and kissed her forehead when she sat down at the table.

"Yes, so much I didn't know about Lizzie, about the Alliance, and about the linkling bond. When I am finally allowed to do so, I intend to apply some of these things to Chidwi and me.

"Did you know that Lizzie had actual training concerning how to interact with her linkling?" Jenny asked as she buttered the fat, flaky roll.

"No. I didn't get to spend a lot of time with her either. Remember that after she found me, I had to go through my own agent training and internship. After you finish Lizzie's journals, we'll have to compare notes."

"What are you and Bob and Merv up to these days?" she asked around a mouthful of salad.

"Just the usual, I guess. They are obsessed with figuring out the puzzle of the Inseni portals and how to detect them. They believe the Mookookie might be able to help them posit a way, but so far they just keep getting closer and closer without actually arriving at their destination. If anyone can figure it out, they will.

"In the meantime, I'm working with Cornelium on a new, non-lethal weapon to use during our first assault of one of the dimensions compromised by the Inseni. Anela has been very helpful. I think she has a crush on Cornelium. Imagine that...."

By the time they finished their supper, Burt had to leave again, but he told her that tonight he would pop in for a bit before bedtime. He still had some significant work to do, and the day/night cycle on the planet he was working from was exactly opposite of Earth.

She had known this would be an issue when she married him. Like her, Burt was committed to doing his duty for the Alliance; and this meant that, like her dad, he wouldn't always be able to be around as often as she would like.

After a kiss and a cuddle, he left through the gate office door. There were yet a few good reading hours between now and bedtime. She sat back in her reading chair with a sigh, picked up her aunt Lizzie's journal, flipped through, and began to read...)

It was amazing to Lizzie how the time seemed to fly by as she and her pod began to work on their new, expanded schedule. There had never been a lot of time to relax in their previous term, and now it was even more intense for each of them.

In addition to the classes they attended together, each of them had personalized lessons in various disciplines tailored specifically to their needs and talents. Add to that the rigorous physical requirements under Tarafau, and this translated to little leisure time, except on the two days of break each week.

In Lizzie's case, both she and Ynni were feeling the intensity of the training. At the end of each day, sometimes even before the usual lights-out, they would collapse on their bed, not even noticing the stirrings of their podmates around them before the silence shield dropped at the official lights-out.

Of all the training, probably the most satisfying and enjoyable was their time with Reloi and Tanata. Sometimes even on their breaks Reloi and Tanata would come to visit, interacting easily with her podmates at whatever they were engaged in at the time.

Cubes tournaments were a traditional breaktime activity, and it turned out that Reloi was quite good at it, maneuvering the cubes easily with his kinetic abilities.

The one thing her podmates absolutely insisted on was the daily inclusion of the impromptu concerts under "our tree," regardless of the stresses of any given day. This tradition had become a trademark of their pod, and many other trainees attended every afternoon, surrounding the tree from both sides. Over time, some of the more musically inclined brought their own instruments and participated in their little "jam session" with enthusiasm. Sometimes this was a cacophonic disaster until new participants got a feel for the musical "doodling" of Lizzie, Gi, and Ynni.

Nevertheless, it was interesting for Lizzie to discover that Reloi also had a musical talent. He played an unusual wind instrument, similar to a harmonica, that was strapped from behind his head to hold it in place. The tones from his "nuno" harp harmonized well with the mbira or kareena and Gi's lap harp. Before they knew it, there was a regular orchestra and chorus interweaving melodically.

Lizzie thought that part of the reason they could do this successfully had a lot to do with the fact that they were used to communicating mentally with one another. It was one of the advantages of mindspeech that when one communicated with a particular person over time, you got to a point where you could anticipate and react much more quickly than through vocal speech and there was a connection that developed with specific people that seemed to translate into the music they were making as well.

All of this enhanced her sessions with Reloi and Tanata. She was learning a lot about how her mind connected with the music and her physical instruments, but also how she was able to increase her skill in composing music spontaneously. She wasn't quite sure how this related to future agent duties, but she was grateful for it.

Unlike her other instructors, she found that she looked forward to spending time with Reloi outside of the classroom. He no longer felt strange or unusual to her. Rather, she thought of him as unique and unexpectedly engaging. They often had long discussions on scientific principles and theories and laughed at a lot of the same "inside jokes" related to science and math.

One of the things she was learning was how much her relationship with Ynni colored her attitudes and how she thought about herself and others. It had dawned on her one day that she had previously been extremely judgmental and critical of others, relying on snap decisions about who they were and what they stood for without really knowing anything about them.

Ynni had been a major influence in that area. Ynni saw people differently than she did. Because of the unique gifts of the linklings, Ynni could read the minds of those around her. She often gently corrected Lizzie when she jumped to conclusions about others. However, she generally didn't reveal other people's thoughts to Lizzie. She would never do this unless the person meant Lizzie harm or represented a danger to those around them.

Instead, Ynni would nudge her gently. "Didn't you notice that this person is sad?" or "Did you see this person might not understand what you just said?"

Usually Ynni was right, and Reloi had pointed out that this would be invaluable as she began to work in assignments that required diplomacy and insight.

When he looked at her with those amazing violet eyes, Lizzie forgot to see the rest of him. His body reminded her of a large rectangular pillow, but despite his lack of limbs he could do surprising things. His MDP was around his neck, just above his agent necklace with its gold infinity symbol. He could invoke and manipulate anything that came out of it with surprising dexterity.

But his mind and heart were what intrigued her. Over time, as they spent more time together, she realized that this was someone she could respect and that he was just as strong, intelligent, and engaging as anyone she had ever known. She often found her mind wandering to their last conversation when she should have been paying attention to what another instructor was saying. And she had more than one bruise from letting her mind wander in that direction while in a sparring match.

She knew that at the end of this term there would be an evaluation by each of her instructors, as well as Liliath and Tarafau, he being her guide; and, assuming she passed the evaluation, she would get her first guided agent assignment. Each assignment would be made based on the recommendations of her guide and the results of her evaluation. Once she had completed her initial intern assignment, she and her podmates would finally be certified as fully qualified agents.

In Tarafau's case, she expected he would likely be reassigned to Gaston at the L.A. gate. All gate guardians had a guide assigned to them. In this role, guides were almost a backup guardian in case of accident, illness, or catastrophe where that gate was concerned.

But Lizzie wasn't given a lot of time to dwell on this. If anything, they were picking up the pace in every single one of her courses.

It was becoming more and more apparent that she was getting more than she had ever expected in her bargain with Gaston. She still wasn't completely sure where this was all leading, but for the first time in her life she felt like she was heading for something meaningful, which would fulfill her need to learn something that really mattered.

One day, she received a note from Reloi before she went to her session with him to leave Ynni at the pod. Unexpectedly, he wasn't seated on the mat, but in his hover chair without Tanata on his shoulder, and she noticed he was dressed differently. Instead of his usual abbreviated pants and tunic-like shirt in the muted forest colors he favored, he wore what she immediately recognized as a one-piece bathing suit.

"Get your bathing suit out of your MDP and go into the changing room, Lizzie. We're doing something new today. See you in a minute."

Lizzie wasn't sure she trusted his mischievous smile, but she did as instructed.

Her one-piece navy blue swimsuit hadn't gotten much use over the past year, and she hadn't had any idea there was a pool in the training complex. She donned it and pulled a towel from her MDP, wondering if she needed her bathing cap. She added that to her towel and returned to find that Reloi had put on what looked like an abbreviated lifejacket while she had been changing.

"Follow me," he sent, and headed out through one of several doors in the back of the workout room. It led into an Olympic sized swimming pool, which also appeared to be uniformly deep, as far as she could tell when viewing it from the surface.

He maneuvered his chair to the edge of the pool and without comment, leapt from the chair into the water with a splash. As he bobbed to the surface he sent, *"The water is just the right temperature to be relaxing. Come on in. You do swim, am I right? I thought it might be the case, since you have that beautiful pond in the park in your mind space."*

Lizzie didn't reply but dropped her bathing cap and towel where she stood and dove into the water beside him, barely causing a ripple. It felt marvelous. The water was warm, not quite bath temperature. She had once swum in the ocean in a bay in Hawaii, and this felt a lot like that.

As she came up out of the water, he was grinning at her, bobbing up and down, his violet eyes sparkling. *"Amazing! Obviously, you are more than proficient. This will make today's session much easier. We are going to take you to a higher level of meditation, requiring the release of gravity. I know there are swimmers who swim well but aren't very good at passively floating. How are your floating skills?"*

In reply Lizzie allowed her feet to float to the surface. Floating was actually something she did naturally. She couldn't take any credit for it; but unlike her father, who often said he was sure his heels were made of lead, she was a lot like a cork. The hard part for her was keeping her feet from floating to the top.

"Excellent. This will be better than I had expected, then. What I want you to do right now is to listen and breathe. What will you listen to, you might ask? I want you to listen to you. To start with, listen to your breathing and your heart, but then I want you to listen to your

music. Don't strain for it; it will come to you. It is there. I have heard it in you almost from the beginning.

"In your mind is constant background music. You are so used to it that you almost never notice it. You seem to be oblivious to the fact that every time we enter your mental sanctuary, music plays constantly in the background. This is a part of yourself you are only beginning to explore.

"When Yaw gave you the mbira, it opened up something in you that has always been there but needed an egress to escape.

"Listen. Just listen. I am here, no fear or worry. The water embraces you and gravity is released. Listen..."

His voice faded from her mind, and she focused diligently on her breathing, individually relaxing and tensing each muscle which now happened almost instinctively. As she did so, she listened to the soft "whoosh, whoosh, whoosh" of her lungs. With her ears under the water, this was amplified somehow. She then began to notice the "kathump-kathump-kathump" of her heart, doing its job with efficient timing. Over time, she wasn't sure if it was minutes or hours, the sounds resolved into a rhythmic cadence that had more to it.

It wasn't quite a march, but there were chords pulsing along with those beats. Before she knew it, she was not only hearing it, but directing it. In her mind she saw herself before an orchestra of wind instruments, strings and percussion, a baton in her hand. She was in charge of the music. She was directing each ebb and swell, each emphasized passage, each softening of the mood.

As she viewed herself as if from above, she noticed there was no audience. It was just her, the musicians, and the music in a space where every tone and note resonated and vibrated exactly as it was, without distortion or distraction. It was pure sound, each instrument contributing to the overall feel of the music, lifting, swelling, driving to the ultimate climax of uninterrupted silence.

And then she was floating again, hearing her breathing and her heartbeat, the water lapping gently at her sides. But the water on her face was not from the pool.

She opened her eyes to see Reloi's large violet eyes looking intently at her, his face a transport of joy.

"You took me with you," he sent. *"That was glorious. I knew it would be."*

"How? I'm just an average person. I never had a music lesson in my life. I know nothing about composition or meter or any of the things people talk about when they speak of music. My one music appreciation class only happened because it was required. I would have never opted for it otherwise.

"I do love music, and learning to play the mbira has been a joy, even though I couldn't play a known tune from sheet music to save my life. I'm just a music doodler. The kareena allows me to play music I already know in my head, but not because I have any understanding of how it works.

"But is this me? And if it is, how does that tie into me being an agent for the Alliance? How does that help prepare me for what is coming, whatever it is? I feel like I am falling short, and I dread the time when they turn me loose on the multiverse without a guide.

"Seriously, Reloi. I just don't know how I can learn quickly enough or if I will ever be enough to make a difference, no matter how many classes I take, no matter how many books I read, no matter how hard I try to be what I think I need to be."

Reloi shook his head, the radiance from the skylights above them glinting off of his shiny bald pate. Tears glistened in his eyes, but he was smiling.

"Lizzie, if you have one flaw, it is that you see so much potential in pretty much everything around you, but never notice your own.

"There are an infinite number of intelligences in the multiverse. Each plays its part, and each is in the inevitable process of change. Not

that their identity changes—that is outside of time and space—but they are in the process of becoming the purest form of self, the ultimate expression of who and what they are.

"We tend to think in linear time, but the multiverse is not as linear as it appears. Yes, there is order here. Yes, there is a certain amount of timing, but neither you nor I have the perspective at this stage of our existence to clearly see the incredible design that makes it all work.

"That includes our understanding of self. We are so much more than we appear to be. The spark within us that we identify as "me" is neither the beginning nor the end of our existence. When we transition from this dimension to the next, we are simply becoming more of that "me-ness."

"Probably the most amazing thing about all of this is that we get to choose how, to what end, and how fast we progress in our becoming. This is why who you are is precious to me, Lizzie. This is why how you see yourself matters. Don't give up. You are in the process of becoming more, but who you are right now, at this very minute, is enough."

Lizzie raised herself to a standing position in the water, treading beside him. She had never met anyone quite like this man. True, she had spent months with Tarafau and Gaston, two men she admired for their wisdom, kindness, and attainments. But Reloi was different in so many ways.

For all of his soft-spoken kindness and good nature, there was a strength in him that went beyond anything in anyone she had ever met. How he managed to be so much bigger than his physical presence was almost magical to her.

"Do you really think so? The multiverse is vast, and I am just a speck of a speck of an even smaller speck in the sum of things."

Reloi smiled. *"It is a conundrum, perhaps, that without you, the multiverse might not even exist at all. Matter and intelligence are eternal, and all is dependent on everything else. Matter and intelligence aren't created, nor can they be destroyed; but they are in constant flux and movement. What we call 'creation' is simply taking matter and reorganizing it for a particular function.*

"Eventually, you may come to understand this. The important thing is to realize that until you decide to be you and recognize your own worth, you will never get as far as you wish.

"You don't have to settle for mediocrity. You get to choose to move beyond that, and striving for excellence is not only commendable but necessary. Just be the best you that you can. That is the key to moving forward to become what you were intended to be."

This was a lot to take in. *"Can I quote you on that?"* she joked weakly.

He laughed, and she heard the music in that sound with new ears.

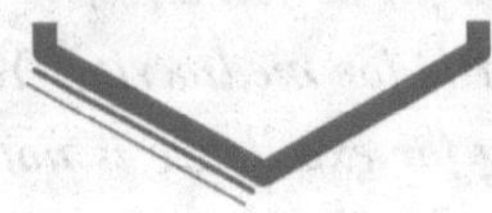

Chapter 8: Soloist

(Jenny rose early the next morning. She had closed the journal reluctantly. She had suspicions where things were leading, and she was anxious to move forward.

After she had done her mental rounds through her dreams, meeting with various individuals in the Alliance, hearing reports and forwarding them along the chain of command, her regular dreams had been full of music, played by Lizzie's amazing orchestra.

She had never heard even a hint in anything anyone had ever told her about her aunt that Lizzie was so engaged with music. This one revelation alone made Jenny wonder how much anyone ever really knew the people around them.

It seemed to her, however, that there was more to any of this than she had imagined. It was obvious to her that Lizzie's training had been unique, and she couldn't help but wonder what her own would have been like, had she been given the opportunity to do the full training.

How would she measure up to the task she had been given? Reloi's advice applied as much to her as it did to Lizzie. Jenny had often felt inadequate to the tasks she had been given, and she continued to be puzzled at the events that had led to her role as the Alliance Gatekeeper—a title she had never aspired to or would have, even if she had known what that actually meant.

If she was honest with herself, she had to admit she still didn't completely understand. She knew her duties so far, but the actual scope was beyond her. She was no figurehead, sitting placidly in an office *somewhere issuing orders. She was a part of a vast mechanism meant to manage the fine balance between allowing all dimensions to order their own affairs and keeping the "bullies" of the multiverse from pillaging and enslaving their less sophisticated or more pacific dimensional neighbors.*

Of course, she couldn't do this alone. The Alliance Council and all of the diverse member dimensions who were in agreement about these principles, did most of the "heavy lifting," as her dad would call it.

Nevertheless, her responsibilities were definitely

"enough to be going on with," which is why she was so grateful for this short break, allowing her to read from Lizzie's journals.

After breakfasting with Burt, he went off through the gate office to work on his current project and let her know he might not make it back until the next day. They didn't talk much about the Alliance in the little bit of time they got to spend together at home. Both had their roles to play; and although they sometimes overlapped, their time together as a couple was rare enough to be too precious to "talk shop."

Lizziebot cleared up afterward, and Jenny picked up the large heavy journal next to her reading chair. She was less than halfway through this one and had less than a week and a half before she would have to go on full-time duty.

She noticed that the entries seemed to be spaced farther apart in this journal. Doubtless, Lizzie's studies gave her much less time to write. As she turned the page, she realized that a few weeks may have passed at this point...)

"200 yards!" Lizzie sent to Ynni, peering past the barracks. Ynni had deliberately turned her reflection off and they were playing what amounted to a mental hide-and-seek game.

"I hear you."

"We need to go to the admin building. Meet me there. The course schedule is changing, and I don't want to miss anything or hold up the works."

"Ynni will meet you on the steps, as I am nearly there already."

This was true. Lizzie was clear at the far end of the training ground, past the pods. It wasn't a terribly long walk, but she could run and so she did. It wasn't an unusual thing to see trainees running around on the campus. Of course, every being had their own way of "running," but regardless, physical training was as important as any of their other coursework.

So far, their training schedule had been what had become familiar in the last term, but the one thing she knew was that as soon as any of them became comfortable with something, it changed.

She ran the 200 yards to the steps of the admin building and, as promised, Ynni was waiting patiently with her reflection turned back on. She hopped lightly up to Lizzie's shoulder without waiting for Lizzie to stoop down.

"Ynni thinks our podmates are excited. All of them have already arrived and are waiting in Liliath's office."

Sure enough, as she entered the office, she saw her podmates already ranged along one wall, to all appearances standing patiently. They were all becoming more and more proficient in keeping their faces and body postures neutral.

Gi smiled at her as she entered but didn't speak as Liliath and the other teachers entered from the conference room door on the opposite side of the room at the same moment. Lizzie was sure they had timed it that way and felt chagrined that she had held up the proceeds.

Of course, she hadn't been messing around. She was fulfilling her assignment, even though it had admittedly been fun. But she shushed her mental roiling and waited patiently as the entire staff, including Tarafau and Reloi and Tanata, lined up next to Liliath facing the assembled interns.

"Intern agents," Liliath began in her soft, gentle mind voice, *"Today things will be shifting to an even more individualized*

instruction. Each of you have shown specific inclinations towards various disciplines as well as unique talents that will apply to your specific future assignments as agents. To this end, you will no longer be attending classes as a pod.

"Each of you now have a new schedule loaded to your tablet. You will still be getting a two-day break at the end of each week of instruction, which is yours to use as you choose. Not all of your instruction will take place on campus and little of it in the classrooms.

"Physical training will continue with the idea of maintaining your current physical abilities, but for most of you it will not escalate. My reports indicate that, generally, you have reached the peak of your abilities in that area."

Lizzie mentally sighed in relief. The physical part of the training was definitely her least favorite.

"To that end," Liliath continued, *"Lall will resume his duties as your instructor. Tarafau will be taking over Lall's duties with the newest trainees."*

Lizzie was surprised at this. Why Tarafau and why was a "Guide" working as what amounted to a P.E. teacher? It didn't make a lot of sense to her, but she imagined it might have been a relief for him. She knew he wasn't housed at the training center. She was pretty sure that at the end of his duties each day he went home to his family.

Then it dawned on her. Amenia was expecting a child. Perhaps this was to allow him to spend time with his family, awaiting the birth?

Liliath continued. *"Each of you have been assigned a counselor in addition to your current guides and will be meeting with them later today. All of this is indicated in the individual briefings on your tablets. For now, you are dismissed, with the exception of your scheduled counseling meetings, for the remainder of the day to allow you to read your briefings and prepare yourselves."*

The entire pod gravitated immediately to "our tree" and without speaking sat and pulled out their tablets to read. The silence was broken only by an occasional sigh or soft exclamation as they each read the detailed information about the next steps in their agent journey.

Lizzie's eyes flew over her new schedule. It seemed to be focused on two main things with only three of her professors.

Her science and technology lessons would continue with Meta, with a focus on gate tech and the ethical considerations of sharing technology—when it was allowed and when it was discouraged or not allowed at all.

She would be increasing her time with Liliath regarding mental defenses and also additional lessons with Reloi to expand her mental abilities and test their limits.

If she had designed her personal curriculum herself, she couldn't have found lessons more to her liking. She had gone from skeptical tolerance to enthusiastic anticipation when it came to her mental training. And, of course, continuing her training in the physics and theories related to gate travel and the interactions between dimensions were beyond what she had hoped for when she had accepted Gaston's offer for "hands-on" science training.

According to the briefing, Tarafau would continue as her guide, but he wouldn't be joining her again until she had completed these final units of study. This suited Lizzie just fine, as she liked the idea that he would be able to be present for the birth and early days of his newest child.

"What did you get?" Gi asked after she had finished perusing her own schedule.

"Science, tech and mind training. Sounds a little simple, considering our past course schedules."

Gi nodded and trilled a laugh. *"You don't really think we're going to get off that easily, do you?"*

Lizzie chuckled. *"No, not really. I think, if anything, it's going to be a lot more intense; and we won't be diluted into an entire class, so they will be focusing entirely on us individually, which, based on past experience, might be more than a bit uncomfortable. However, at least I got things I'm interested in. What did you get?"*

"I'm going to be working with Fin and Baird and Lulindu. I think they are sending me full-on down the diplomacy path. Not sure what to make of that, but I think I'll enjoy it."

"You'll be so very good at that!" Lizzie exclaimed wholeheartedly. *"How many times have you settled disputes within the pod with none of us thinking any worse of you? You have a talent, I think. And for you, it isn't just about the words you say, but the emotion and empathy you project. I expect great things from you."* This last was said with great tenderness on Lizzie's part, as Gi had been the first to become more than just another podmate with her.

Next to them, Minth sighed. *"Looks like my work with Meta will continue, working on tech to free me from my limitations so I can do more within the Alliance than just be a liaison for my people. Also, I'll be working with three Alliance scientists on an idea I had about the effects of various types of power on the gates. They also want to see if I am sensitive to undiscovered gates, a mental talent. If so, my dimension will become much more useful to the Alliance in the future."*

"That sounds amazing!" Gi enthused. *"I can hardly wait to hear what comes of that."*

Minth ducked his head, somewhat embarrassed by Gi's enthusiasm. He had always been one of the quieter members of the pod and often took criticism a lot more comfortably than praise.

Geln, like Lizzie, was going to be focusing on mental disciplines with Liliath and Reloi and also continuing in diplomacy with Baird and Fin.

The rest were each pursuing a schedule tightly related to their various strengths, and surprisingly each of them seemed satisfied with their new schedule.

Chapter 9: A Concerted Effort

(Jenny hadn't touched her lunch, and the soup Lizziebot had set on the side table by her reading chair had gone cold by the time she looked up from the journal. There was still so much more to read, even though she noticed the entries had become farther apart in time. Skimming forward, she realized that Lizzie had become so absorbed in her training and adventures that the narrative had become much more like a series of short stories than a day-by-day account.

She understood how that could be. Her own journal didn't get written in on a daily basis, only when she was catching her breath in between adventures. She still had about half of Lizzie's journal yet to go, and one more complete one. She was about halfway through her recovery time and was anxious to finish.

She took her soup into the little kitchen and warmed it back up in the microwave, marveling at the technology she had become used to, compared to what Lizzie had experienced previous to her involvement in the Alliance. The idea of going from wired phones, no computers and black-and-white television to the tech she knew was so abundant in the Alliance environment must have been overwhelming, although Lizzie never admitted to it.

She took her mug of soup back to the living room, glancing at the clock on her way out of the kitchen. She had a good four hours before suppertime.

She sat down and eagerly found her bookmark and began to read...)

Lizzie once more floated in the water beside Reloi in the large pool in the admin building basement. The water was warm, and her eyes were closed, the soft bluish light of the pool room filtering gently through her eyelids.

She was supposed to be focusing on creating REM sleep, but other thoughts kept intruding. Earlier today, Liliath had observed that she seemed somewhat unfocused. It was true. Her mind kept flashing ahead. This was all leading to something, and the future loomed before her, misty and unknowable. She couldn't help but think that her future held things both promising and ominous, and at any particular time, the path she chose next might lead her into things that no amount of training could prepare her for.

"What is going on with you today?" Reloi asked gently. He wasn't impatient or upset, but she could hear concern in his mind voice.

"I guess I'm a bit anxious," she replied simply. *"I'll get back on track. Give me a minute."*

He didn't reply but waited patiently. Lizzie focused on her breathing exercises. Each calm, deep breath raised her slightly up and down in the water as she floated there. She concentrated on hearing her breathing and the rhythmic beat of her heart, and finally she found herself with Reloi by her side in front of the bank vault door.

"Let's go to the park," Reloi said cheerfully. "I think the sunshine will be good for us today."

She opened the vault door and preceded him out the double doors of the library. She noticed the doors had become larger, more likely to accommodate a dragon than before. Outside on the stone steps, the lions guarded the entrance to the treasury of knowledge she was so fond of.

It was a beautiful day. Reloi's mental-self strode alongside her. In this environment he was as tall as Lizzie and slender, but not skinny. He looked to be in the full blossom of youth and health. And yet, although he was pleasant enough to look at in this form, she knew when she thought of him, she always saw him in his corporeal form and surprisingly felt like she preferred him that way.

His real form didn't feel unusual or out of place for her. He was Reloi, and that was how he was.

They found a place next to the little pond, and Reloi pulled a blanket out of his MDP and gallantly spread it on the ground for them to sit on.

They sat for a while in silence, just taking in the quiet calm of their surroundings. Then Reloi said, "Listen."

"What? I don't hear anything."

"Yes, you do; you just don't know it yet," he assured her.

So, she listened. She wondered, was this like the music? At first there was little to hear. Water lapped gently on the shore of the pond, and somewhere a bird twittered. There was no breeze and none of the traffic sounds you might hear in a city park.

"Deeper," he encouraged. "Listen deeper."

"I don't understand, Reloi. Deeper how?"

"Stop worrying about hearing with your ears. Listen to the sounds your ears can't hear."

Lizzie shook her head slowly. How could it be a sound if you couldn't hear it with your ears? But she made a concentrated effort to close out the sounds she could hear with her ears. Then it came to her... of course! She wasn't actually hearing any of the sounds in this place with her ears, after all. They were all part of the mental place she had created. Were there potentially sounds she didn't realize she had created; much like some of the shops in the town?

Many of the shops were still a mystery to her. She didn't remember ever giving any thought about placing them around the little town square, but they were there. She looked around her. What was there in these surroundings that might make a mental sound instead of an audible one, and what would that potentially sound like to her "mental ears"?

As requested, she refocused, excluding anything that she could hear with her ears. At first it just seemed like a murmuring, like hearing a conversation through a closed door. Like using a magnifying glass to clarify some blurry text, she continued to focus more intently. Perhaps if she reached out?

She tentatively sent, *"Hello? Can you speak to me?"*

There was a slight pause in the murmuring, then, *"Who is this? What do you wish to know?"*

"I am Lizzie. I am listening. Who am I speaking to?"

"We are many and different. I speak for all here. I am what you would call a "tree," although that is a very short word for what I am. How do you come to hear us? This is unusual and requires some thinking about."

It took Lizzie a moment to form an answer. A tree? Speaking to her? Obviously, this was something her mind was making up. How could it be possible? Of course, this was only possible in this REM state.

"I am learning to use my mind to communicate. What can you teach me? I am used to verbal speech, and this is new to me."

"You are of flesh. I am of bark and sap and roots. We experience life in a different manner. You are fleeting. I remain and watch the fleshlings come and go. You wish to learn of root and branch? These teachings go deep. Return here when you can, and I will tend you like a sapling."

One of the benefits of mindspeech was that the mind translated conversations like this not only into words, but feelings and intent. Lizzie felt age, wisdom, and kindness from this tree.

"Do you have a name that distinguishes you from the other trees in this park?"

"I am Wind Dancer. When the wind blows, my leaves and branches careen to its whims. I greet you, Lizzie. I can see buds of wisdom and shoots of intelligence in you. I believe we can benefit from

future association. Please come again to sit in my shade, and we will learn together."

"Thank you, Wind Dancer. I would love to do that. I am new to these ideas and concepts, and I am anxious to learn."

"Very well, Lizzie. Together we will sprout new ideas and will bear the fruit of wisdom."

At that moment, Reloi broke in. "Lizzie we must return. Our time is up, and you need to get dressed to meet with Meta soon."

Lizzie looked up at him, standing beside her, his hand extended to bring her to her feet. She saw behind him the ancient spreading oak and wondered if she could still speak to Wind Dancer without that focus, now that she had made a connection.

"Wind Dancer, I must go. I will return. Thank you for your kind offer to teach me."

"Lizzie, I will look forward to seeing you again."

Reloi grinned. "You caught onto that much faster than I expected. I think you will find that something has shifted in the range of your abilities."

"Thank you, Reloi. I find that I am no longer the girl I was, and the changes are happening faster than I can keep track of. What will I be, by the time I have completed my training?"

"You will be no more than you began, in a way. The thing is, the potential has always been inside of you, waiting for you to discover it. Each new layer of you that is exposed during your life will only make you more you than you were before. I am grateful for my opportunity to aid in that transformation."

Lizzie nodded, not knowing what to say, and then found herself bobbing up and down in the pool once again, Reloi beside her with his beautiful smile, the corners of his violet eyes crinkling as he observed her.

"Thank you, Reloi," was all she could think to say as they exited the pool and retired to the dressing rooms to prepare to leave. As she toweled off and dressed, she pondered the words of both Wind Dancer and Reloi and wondered what in her life she had done to deserve such a rich and unusual opportunity. She vowed fervently to do everything within her power to be sure she merited the investment her trainers and the Alliance had made in her.

Chapter 10: Composing

(Jenny was very cognizant that time was flying by and that she would be devastated if she didn't finish her aunt's journals before she had to go back to full duty.

She marveled at Lizzie's newfound ability and wondered how it would apply to her future agent missions. At this point she realized that she still had a lot to learn about her own mental abilities and vowed to somehow fit more training into her duties.

It seemed obvious that, in the short time she had been given to receive training, she hadn't even begun to scratch the surface, even though the others seemed to think she had advanced beyond their expectations.

She was trying hard not to be envious of her aunt, and in the logical side of her mind she realized that although her own journey hadn't had the richness of deliberate instruction her aunt had received, she had already learned and grown so much despite, or maybe because of, her difficult entry into the Alliance. She sighed, determined not to be negative about her situation. After all, she had gotten Chidwi and Burt and the Mookookie out of it, hadn't she?

She turned the page...)

"...But why?" Lizzie asked Meta plaintively. "Many of these advancements would mean so much to the people of my planet. It isn't like they are weapons or anything."

Meta sighed, fingering the long silvery braid that almost seemed to glow against her blue-tinged skin.

"*One of the most important things we do as agents of the Alliance is to maintain the balance between positive influence and interference. Sometimes the difference is a very fine line,*" She sent with a sad smile. "*Each dimension, each culture, grows into their calling, their purpose, in small steps. This is why the first several years as an agent you will spend your time in dimensions that are already members of the Alliance.*

"*As you have observed, every culture you have experienced so far, including your own, is a balance between positive and negative, advanced and even primitive, in reference to not only their technology, but their philosophies and cultural norms.*

"*It is instinctive to want to protect and nurture and sometimes to correct what we observe to be potentially destructive or negative in any culture or even in the people we know, based on our own experiences, but we have to be careful. There is so much we don't know, even when we consider our home worlds.*

"*Experience teaches us that each culture has its own place and purpose in the multiverse and that forcing advances or introducing new tech seldom accomplishes what we had intended.*

"*The multiverse is vast, beyond the ability of any of us to measure in any meaningful way. Relatively speaking, intelligent beings are comparatively rare amongst them. I believe there is a purpose to all things and that each and every intelligence has a distinct role within the tapestry of creation.*

"*But to answer your question, each one of us is on a unique journey suited specifically to what we can bring to that tapestry. There are appropriate times and places for judgment and sharing to come into play, but in the wide scope of things, it is not our role to stand in judgment of any other culture or to interfere with their natural growth. Our duty is to stand as a protector between those who would impinge on the rights and liberties of others with the intent to do harm and those who are incapable of defending themselves.*

"We treasure the diversity of the multiverse and advocate for the need and right of every culture to advance at their own pace, based on their own desires and abilities, as long as that doesn't mean trespassing on the rights of others.

"So, sometimes we must hold back, even within our own cultures. This can be difficult, but it is necessary."

Lizzie nodded, but she still yearned with all of the depths of her heart to see Earth reach its potential. After finally coming to grips with her own inadequate knowledge and understanding, her one remaining frustration was her feeling that, by sharing much of the science she was learning, Earth could become the paradise she had envisioned.

"Take for example the research being done in Switzerland," Meta continued. *"Unlimited power and food could easily become common among your cultures. However, would it? Your Earth is divided and segmented and often unsettled with warring factions each taking advantage of another's resources.*

"Would that change if this technology was available at this time? Would the technology change the greed and powermongering that is currently such an issue among the people of Earth? Or might one culture try to use the technology to force others into compliance with their will?

"If they come across the technology with their own research and diligence, we will not attempt to stop its use, nor will we move in and quell any conflict that may result from it. It is not our role to determine the destiny of your planet or any other. This is non-negotiable, and you must comply if you truly wish to help your people. From what I hear from Switzerland and Sanglarka, many of your scientists are already opening up theories and practices that will eventually give you the progress you desire; but be aware that circumstances may not change as radically as you hope.

"Probably the biggest advances any culture makes is by changing attitudes and behaviors, rather than the level of technology they enjoy."

Lizzie considered this. She thought of her visits to Geln's and Gi's planets, which were relatively low tech, and how happy and contented the people there seemed to be.

She knew from her conversations with her podmates that no culture had found perfection, nor was every problem solved by technology, such as on Mang's planet, which was modern and advanced beyond even the Alliance headquarters city that had so awed her when she had first experienced it.

As she left the admin building for her pod and first lunch, her head was buzzing with everything she had done in her coursework today.

First, Liliath and working with Ynni on what Reloi and Tanata had showed them the previous week. This had been pleasant, and she felt that the bond between her and Ynni was widening in new ways.

Second, her time with Reloi in the pool and the new concept of listening to things that her ears couldn't hear. And finally, her session with Meta, where she had finally expressed her frustration with the slow progress of her own people.

Out of all of this she realized she had taken some unexpected steps forward; and yet she somehow knew she still had far to go before she was ready to take on a position in the Alliance where she would eventually be independent and responsible for the outcome of her actions.

As she neared her pod, she noticed several of her podmates seated under their tree, chatting in mindspeech, evidently about something funny, as several of them were chuckling.

"What's so funny?" Lizzie sent, smiling to see Gelns' broad grin. She had been so worried that they wouldn't recover easily from the loss of their third, but they had explained to her that he wasn't gone in a true sense of the word, but merely temporarily separated. It amazed her that so many of the different cultures she had encountered had a very firm concept of an afterlife.

"Mang just got his first intern assignment to a planet that is extremely low tech and rural. He feels like somebody made a mistake. We told him he will be better for it. He's not so sure." And Geln chuckled again.

"Oh, come on, Mang. It won't be so bad..." Lizzie began, but he groaned.

"They don't even have running water," he said, ever fastidious. *"Evidently some of their legends and myths have beings similar to myself, so I can go among them without too many questions. I'm going on a gate survey, so it may only be a few months, but I still think they got the wrong person."*

"We all knew our assignments wouldn't necessarily be to our liking, moving forward," Gi chimed in. *"It makes me wonder where we'll all end up and how often we'll even see one another."* And she sighed, not quite so amused at that thought.

"Speak up," Lizzie said, as she noticed a kind of mental murmur. *"Your thoughts aren't clear."*

"Who are you talking to?" Mang sent, irritated. *"I'm hearing everyone clearly."*

Lizzie shook her head. *"I guess it's nothing. I just keep hearing a kind of mumbling, and I wasn't sure how that was possible with mindspeech."*

"I don't hear anything besides us," put in Geln.

Lizzie heard Geln clearly, but she still heard the murmuring undercurrent. *"Is this a prank? Come on, who is making that mental sound?"*

They all looked puzzled.

"Can you hear me now?" a soft mental voice said. It didn't sound like any of her podmates' mental voices.

"Who is this?"

"You call me 'our tree' if that's what you mean. My name is Beam, or at least that's the short version. I've been singing along with your

concerts for a long time now and was hoping you would play again today."

Lizzie was stunned. Was she really having a conversation with a tree outside the REM state? What had Reloi done to her?

She looked around at her podmates who were staring at her as if she had suddenly sprouted a second head. *"I am talking to our tree,"* she sent sheepishly. *"I have evidently gotten a new layer of mindspeech and can hear what the tree is saying."*

"The tree is saying?" Mang's mind voice had a tone of wry amusement. *"Now who's playing a prank?"*

"No, really! Our tree's name is Beam, and it is speaking to me. Ask Reloi about it the next time you see him. I can hear him. He says he has been enjoying our concerts and likes to sing along. I know it sounds crazy, but believe me it is no more insane to you than it is to me."

"They can't hear me?" inserted Beam. *"You are the first being here who has ever talked to me before. I just thought you all considered me beneath you to want to speak to me. It never occurred to me that it might be you were all just incapable of hearing me."*

Her assembled podmates were all looking at her curiously, unable to hear Beam's reply. She spread her hands helplessly, returning their looks with a shake of her head.

"I'm not sure how to deal with this. I don't have a point of reference as to how to link this into our tree time. But Beam seems to enjoy our presence and our music, so I don't see where it needs to change anything. So, Mang, are they giving you any special equipment for your assignment, or will you have to manage with native facilities?"

Mang sighed vocally, shrugging his shoulders. *"Evidently there are some bits of tech disguised as familiar objects I will need to use in the survey, but other than that, I will be roughing it in a way I've never had to do before. Even when we spend time out in nature on my planet, we usually have many conveniences available to us to make it more enjoyable and less primitive. I'll be doing some training with Lall in woodcraft and how to live without the things I'm used to."*

"It will be all right, Mang," sent Geln sincerely. *"You are strong, and you learn quickly. It can't be nearly as bad as Professor Baird's lessons on controlling our facial expressions. That nearly made us crazy."* And they both wiped their brows as if wiping away sweat.

This made them all laugh, and Lizzie was amazed to hear Beam join in with a mental chuckle. She realized that even if they couldn't hear Beam, he had been hearing them and understanding their mindspeech all along. It was almost like she had just added another podmate to her team.

What would this mean to her future endeavors as an agent? How would this new ability influence her future assignments? Would she now be bombarded with conversation from every plant she encountered? As these thoughts ran through her mind, she found herself only partially listening to her podmates continue the conversation. What had Reloi done to her?

Suddenly she realized that Ynni hadn't been participating in any of this. Lizzie reached up to her shoulder and patted Ynni's small hand that rested on her neck.

"Ynni, can you hear the tree? Can you talk to Beam?"

"Ynni has always been able to hear Beam and talk to him. We were wondering why you did not join in our chat. He likes all of you very much."

"Does your tribe chat with trees as well?"

"Indeed we do, and always have done as long as we can remember. All living things have a voice, if you know how to listen. I am glad you have learned to do this."

Chapter 11: Melodies of the Heart

(Jenny found herself wishing that when she had flipped ahead in the journal, she hadn't found so many gaps between future entries, although she also realized that these journals represented nearly sixty years of adventures in the multiverse.

Chidwi was draped, completely relaxed, on the back of Jenny's chair. She reached up the hand that wasn't holding the cup and patted the tiny hand that hung near her ear.

Chidwi stirred and sat up, stretching. "Jenny needs to take a walk," she chided gently in mindspeech. "Chidwi can come? I will turn off my reflection and be very quiet," she continued in a virtuous tone.

Jenny smiled at that and agreed, carefully setting the journal on the table nearby. She took the now-empty tea mug into the kitchen and sent to Lizziebot and Tidbit, "Chidwi and I are going to take a walk. Back in a bit."

She went out her front door to brilliant sunshine, with a few puffy clouds in the distance near the mountains. Living in the foothills in L.A. afforded an amazing view of the city below from various vantage points between houses along the loop as she did her usual several circuits.

As she passed Elias Mensch's house, she noticed a car in the driveway and the "Sold" sign being taken down by someone who was obviously the real estate agent.

"I noticed the house was for sale," she mentioned to the lady in a trim grey business suit and white blouse. "Has he moved far?"

"*You could say that,*" *the woman said wryly.* "*He passed away a few weeks ago. He had declined severely when his dog got sick and died a few weeks before that.*"

"*Oh wow, I've been out of town. I had no idea. I know he really loved Cinder and was getting on in years, but didn't know either of them were sick.*"

"*Actually, the dog got ahold of something, they think it was some spoiled meat when he escaped the backyard and was roving the neighborhood. Might have been a dead squirrel or the like. But Elias had been ill for the past year, just didn't tell people about it. He was, as you may have guessed, not a very sociable person.*"

"*I don't guess he was always that way. I hear he and his wife were good friends with my aunt. I'm just next door.*"

"*Well, I guess there is only so much pain some of us can handle,*" *the woman said, her face softening.* "*At any rate, the folks who bought the house are looking forward to updating it and moving in during the next few weeks.*"

"*I'm out a lot. Hopefully I'll get a chance to meet them when I'm home next. Thanks for the info. Did Elias have any family nearby?*"

"*Not that I'm aware of. He and his wife didn't have any kids and, as old as he was, I'm guessing a lot of his relatives aren't around anymore. At any rate, they're still trying to figure out if he had a will or anything. The money from the sale of the house is going into probate for now.*"

Jenny bowed her head. She felt Chidwi's invisible hand patting her cheek from her perch on her shoulder. "*Well, thanks again.*" *And she moved off.*

Re-entering the bright living room, she noticed that Tidbit was sprawled on the sunny window seat.

"*I guess you already know that Cinder and Elias are gone,*" *she remarked, not sure why this was affecting her. She felt sad, even though she hadn't known Elias very well, only seeing him from time to time on her walks through the neighborhood as he walked Cinder (or more accurately, as Cinder walked him).*

"Yes, I knew; but I didn't feel like you needed anything else to worry your mind at the moment. Lizzie would have been sad to see him go. He wasn't always quite the curmudgeon he had become since losing his wife..." he trailed off, evidently reminiscing about former times. "Cinder wasn't all that bad for a dog, but sometimes his attitude needed a little adjusting, and I was happy to oblige." His tone seemed amused.

"I don't know if there are many left in the neighborhood, besides Bob and the lady next door, who even remember Lizzie. All the more reason for me to finish reading these journals," Jenny added with a sigh.

"Indeed, I'll let you get on with it. As you see, Lizziebot has left you a snack."

"I'm getting so spoiled, and it's a good thing I'm walking. After all of this, what my dad would call 'feeding up,' and I'll be putting on weight."

"I promise you the Alliance will work it back off of you if you do. Get back to your reading. Chidwi, want to go watch the koi?"

Jenny felt her little companion jump happily from her shoulder, knowing that she and Tidbit would have a happy time perched in the yew tree from one of the branches suspended over the koi pond.

Lizziebot had laid out some celery stalks stuffed with peanut butter and decorated with raisins. Her mom had called this "ants on a log," and it was a favorite snack along with a tall glass of iced mint tea. Jenny pulled the journal over onto her lap and opened to the bookmark...)

Lizzie was struggling with her newfound ability to listen to plants. It turned out that bushes, flower beds, and even the grass all had something to say if you listened hard enough. Within a week of discovering this new method of communicating, she realized that learning new things gave her new responsibilities and presented new challenges.

She wasn't particularly excited about this, as her plate was feeling particularly full to be going on with. After all, she still had one-on-one lessons that were becoming more and more intense, as well as the anticipation of her first guided internship in an as-yet-undisclosed dimension.

She had noticed that her podmates were also showing signs of stress and overwhelm. Geln was often heard muttering aloud in stereo in his own language as they did their morning run, and Gi hummed a lot, which for her might as well have been muttering. Mang's normally impassive face seemed to have developed a twitch between his brows, a furrow appearing frequently there, something they had never noticed in him before.

And the rest were all exhibiting various versions of this. It was like the anticipation of a coming storm.

Lizzie's mental sessions focused on only two things these days. She had discovered she could, with great focus and concentration, affect physical objects with her mind, but without the grace and ease she admired in Reloi. Also, both Reloi and Liliath were concentrating on removing any barriers between her and Ynni, as well as teaching her how to filter out unwanted mental attention from the shrubbery.

Therefore, it was almost a shock when Liliath called the entire pod into her office at the end of a grueling week to announce that they would be reporting once again to the outfitters that day with their guides to equip them for their next task, their very first guided agent assignment.

They would be having a bit of a "going away" party at the dining hall this evening, and all would be setting out over the next few days to their assignments.

"Each of you have performed admirably in this final round of classes. This doesn't mean that your training is complete by any means; but from now on, most of your training will take place in the field most suited to your strengths. You will return here between intern segments, but I can't guarantee that those returns will coincide with one another.

"*This, however, does not mean you need to lose touch with one another. As you know, your tablets are equipped with messaging capabilities, as each of them are tuned to the frequencies of satellites that have been put in place in orbit around most of the dimensions that have gateways. This means you can send and receive messages freely, although every message is highly encrypted for security's sake. Each of your podmates have been included in the contacts list on each tablet.*

"*I hope this eases some of your concerns about your coming assignments. I know you have grown close to the other agents in your pod. At some point, we will get you all together to celebrate your award of full agent certification.*

"*As the faculty and staff of the agent training facility, we wish to congratulate each one of you for your diligence and performance so far in your training. You are dismissed to lunch and then to the outfitters.*"

As they filed out of the admin building in stunned mental and vocal silence, it dawned on Lizzie that she was at another huge turning point. She felt, as if from a distance, Ynni's tiny warm hand gently massaging the back of her neck.

"*Lizzie will do well. Lizzie has Ynni. Lizzie has Tarafau. You have worked hard. Now you get to work harder.*" There was almost a twist of humor to this thought, and Lizzie finally smiled. Wasn't this what she wanted? Wasn't a challenge what she had yearned for, what seemed like ages ago, sitting fuming in her college classes?

They trooped to the dining hall in continued silence, but once their meal had been served and they had paused in thankful silence before eating, they could finally look into one another's eyes and talk and even laugh nervously about the challenges to come.

"*I will miss our concerts,*" Geln sent. "*I hope where they send me they will have music. I know some cultures like my own don't have anything we would recognize as music, though. I didn't know enough to miss it before.*" And they sighed.

After they had eaten, they headed just one door down the path to the outfitters. Instead of the one stern being who had originally outfitted them, there were ten outfitters lined along the long counter that separated the warehouse from the entryway. Each of the guides were standing across from an outfitter waiting, apparently patiently, for their charges to arrive.

Lizzie went to Tarafau's side with a welcoming smile. *"How is Amenia?"* she sent.

"She is coming along nicely, and the fetus is healthy. I have made arrangements during your assignment that you will be allowed to come with me to greet my infant daughter. But for now, we must not keep the outfitter waiting with our chat," Tarafau grinned, his catlike fangs showing white in the brightly lit warehouse.

Lizzie laughed and turned her attention to the being before her. To her surprise, it appeared to be a robot. *"Hello?"* she sent tentatively.

The robot sent back. *"Greetings. I am Blit. I have your current MDP inventory. For this assignment, we need to add only a few things. During your assignment you will doubtless acquire other things, either things you have purchased or gifts from the native inhabitants. Your contract says that you may keep anything you are given that is not specifically intended to be given to the Alliance. If you are given tools or any technology beyond the level of your native dimension, you may not share or expose it to any being on your planet. Is this understood?"*

"Yes."

"Then please touch your finger to this device," it said, placing a one-inch cube on the counter in front of her. For one silly moment Lizzie thought it looked a lot like one of the cubes on a game board. She complied, and there was a soft buzz.

"Very good. Your DNA imprint is on record that you heard and agreed to these requirements. Non-compliance will result in potential dismissal as an agent, as well as a complete mind wipe of any and all

things related to your time with the Alliance. Your memories will be replaced with alternate memories matching your cover story, and it will be as if you were never part of the Alliance.

"The equipment issued to you, or whatever is left of it after any assignment, will be yours unless the time comes when it might be needed for use in your duties."

Blit bent and moved several canvas containers onto the counter between them.

"This is a replacement for your current medic kit. Please extract the medic kit you were originally issued from your MDP, and we will exchange."

Lizzie did so, noticing that the new kit was nearly twice the size of the old one. Its blue wavy symbol representing health and life made its purpose clear.

"We have updated your tablet with new training on the use of every item in the kit. I highly recommend that you take time early in your assignment to study this.

"Now this," he sent, pointing to a larger canvas bag in grey tones and touch-sensitive fastenings, *"is your emergency housing kit. Inside is a self-building housing unit fit to hold ten beings of about Tarafau's size, so it should be adequate for most uses. You may replace your current camping gear at this time."*

Lizzie complied, removing her camping gear and handing it to Blit, and touched the MDP to the large canvas bag. She watched it shrivel and be absorbed into the little band and asked no questions, assuming that instructions for its use was also included on her tablet.

"We have also included about a month's supply of a variety of emergency rations in this container suitable for your species." Blit handed the smaller canvas bag to her, and she dutifully installed it in her MDP, thinking with a grin of her own stash she had acquired while at home for her break.

The counter was empty, but Blit bent again and, several at a time, he brought up gallon containers of water. By the time she had installed them all, she knew she had enough water to manage for a month or more. How amazing was this technology that allowed her to store so much without incurring any weight at all? She knew that the storage capability of the MDP was thought to be nearly limitless.

Once more Blit reached beneath the counter and brought out one more canvas bag rather like a duffel bag. *"The last thing for your supplies is appropriate clothing to your measurements. Each culture has its own mores and fashions, as you have learned in your classes. The clothing in this bag is appropriate to the place you have been assigned. I will leave it to your guide to brief you.*

"In the future, you will be outfitted at main Headquarters for other assignments. We wish you well at the first of hopefully many successful projects."

Lizzie thanked Blit and looked on either side of her. Some of her podmates had already exited, having completed their equipping. Others were still in earnest mental speech with their outfitters, their guides hovering to one side. Tarafau steered Lizzie out of the building into the light of the two suns.

"Shall we find a place to sit so I can brief you on your assignment?" he asked with another catlike grin. *"I think you might need to be sitting down..."*

They strolled over to the pod. To her surprise, Reloi was sitting on the grass under the tree in his chair, a welcoming smile on his face.

"Lizzie, let me introduce you to your liaison with the citizens of Grild, Reloi Chid-Wei."

Reloi grinned up at them, obviously in on the joke. *"Surprised?"* he queried, a mischievous glint in his eyes. *"I knew you wouldn't be expecting this. Tarafau had his turn. This time I get the honor of introducing you to my people. It's a very different environment, and this should get your feet wet, as far as diplomacy is concerned.*

"Grild is not much like your Earth. I think time with us will help answer many of your questions as to how and why members are chosen for full inclusion into The Dimensional Alliance.

"Tarafau has requested that we make a short visit to his planet so that Ynni can visit with her younglings, and you can touch bases with his family. Evidently, they are very interested in your progress. When Amenia is ready to give birth, you will again visit there for a short time; and at the end of your term as an Alliance representative on my planet, you will get a break to visit your home world.

"Any questions?" He cocked his head as he was wont to do and for a moment, Lizzie pictured Gaston in that exact posture and couldn't help but grin, even though the shock of this announcement hadn't yet quieted.

"I'll have plenty of questions, as you well know, once this has sunk in a bit. But for now, I guess my only question is, when do we leave?"

"In the morning. Tonight, you will be celebrating with your podmates, and I want you to be well rested before we begin. This is a rather poignant event in your agent training, and we want you to have every opportunity to get a bit maudlin and somewhat silly with your pod family."

Pod family. That expressed very clearly how she felt about these ten beings who had become such a staple of her life. She found herself wistfully hoping that she would never completely lose touch with them. But she knew the multiverse was vast, and their assignments would potentially take them to places so far away, and for long periods; it was very likely that for some of them, this evening might be the last time they would get the opportunity to come together in person for any length of time.

That evening, as they gathered after supper under their tree, they were all in high spirits. A sense of adventure was reflected in each face as Lizzie gazed around this circle of comrades. The memories tied to each smile, each chuckle or, in Gi's case, melodic outbursts, were like little treasures she was determined to hoard in the deepest niches of her heart.

As it turned out, Lizzie wasn't the only one who had prepared to bring gifts to her podmates. It was like some alien version of Christmas as each one, nearly simultaneously, began to extract packages from their MDPs, setting them on the grass in front of them.

There was much *oohing* and *aahing* as the various gifts were distributed, but probably Lizzie's favorite moment was when Geln opened the two gifts from Lizzie, twin mbiras, one for each. The light in their eyes as they looked up from the cases in their laps was beyond expressing in mere words for them or for her.

"We will make music!" And they simultaneously opened the cases and plucked a few keys, the tones ascending blithely into their midst.

They all tested their tablet connections by sending notes of thanks and encouragement to one another, each of them acknowledging receipt to ensure that no one had been missed. To their delight, Lall, Liliath, and all of their instructors had been included on these lists of contacts.

Finally, they concluded their celebration with a traditional concert, Geln delightedly joining in, almost unconsciously blending their harmonies with Lizzie, Ynni and Gi's spontaneous compositions. There was a new addition for Lizzie, however. It turns out that trees could sing, something Lizzie never would have supposed.

She had always considered the sound of rustling leaves as a breeze busily brushed them as musical, but now she heard through her new mind connection a deep melodious crooning, very similar to that of the linklings. She found herself wishing she could allow the rest of her podmates to experience this new expansion to their musical communion.

This was one of the greatest gifts she had received from her training, the extension of her mental gifts that allowed her to communicate with living things she had never realized had a voice. She was excited that the next stage of her adventure would allow her to learn more about Reloi and his people. She couldn't help but feel that learning about his origins would clarify what it was about him that attracted her so much.

None of her pod got much sleep that night. They gathered in the training area to continue sharing and anticipating their coming assignments. The mixture of slight apprehension and growing expectation had increased their adrenalin to the point that sleep was out of the question.

The following morning, there was much hugging, even by Mang, and many promises to stay connected. Her podmates all left to the gateroom, but for Lizzie and Reloi, with Ynni and Tanata on their usual perches, it was as simple as Tarafau putting one large hand firmly on each shoulder as they faded out of pod building to the street in front of Tarafau's home.

Chapter 12: Grace Notes

(Jenny looked up with a start as Burt came in from the gateroom down the hall from the living room. He grinned at her sitting there, her feet tucked under her with the heavy journal in her lap.

"You didn't hear me?" he asked shaking his head. "I know Lizzie's stories must be fascinating, but I never expected to see anyone able to sneak up on you with your razor-sharp hearing and catlike reflexes."

Jenny rolled her eyes. "I think you must have me confused with someone else."

"Never. There's only one like you, Jenny." And the twinkle in his eyes softened. "You look like you're feeling pretty well. I know you're impatient to get back to work and we definitely need you, but I'm glad you're taking this break. I'm afraid that defeating the government of the Insenium was only an important first step. The list of conquered planets and dimensions is much longer than we realized. Evidently this has been going on for much longer than anyone could have known, and it didn't just start with them.

"So, for now, just keep following doctor's orders and get your strength up. Tidbit informs me that you have been getting in several walks a day now, and you're starting to get a little restless. I'm glad you have the journals to keep you busy."

He knelt next to her chair and kissed her on the cheek. "I worry that you're spending so much time during your sleep cycle coordinating things, however. As I understand it, even though you're sleeping, the quality of rest isn't the same as when you are just having normal dreams."

"I'm fine. I'm not doing half of what I wish I could. I promise that I will stick to the regimen they have given me. I don't want to give anyone a reason to keep me home for any longer than the original three weeks. I only have a week and a half to go. I hope to finish the journals by then. Lizzie was so much more than I realized, even after hearing everyone tell me about her. I only hope to be half as good as she was."

"Not to worry, my warrior maiden. You are definitely related to her, as I think you will discover. Have you gotten to me yet?"

"No, silly. I'm still in her agent years. I think her guardian days are in the third journal."

"Okay, then. I'll let you get on with it. I wouldn't want you to miss out on such an important event as my meeting with Lizzie," he said with a chuckle. He leaned across her and hugged her, careful not to rumple the pages of the journal, and kissed her with such fervor that her toes nearly curled. "Just to be sure you don't forget me," he said with a grin.

"I'm going to confab with Tidbit for a bit, and then I'm off to work. Be good."

She nodded, breathless, and sighed as he went out to the patio to hang out with Tarafau and Chidwi. She turned the page...)

Amenia was busy with something in the kitchen when they came down the stairs to the area that encompassed the roomy kitchen and a generous family room divided down the middle with a long table and chairs enough to seat eight.

She cried out happily in Daringi and then in mindspeech. *"Welcome! So glad to see you and Reloi, Lizzie!"*

Reloi had descended the circular stairs easily in his hover chair and now sat at his ease, smiling up at them all.

Amenia gave first Lizzie and then Reloi enthusiastic hugs and then turned to Tarafau, her eyes alight. Reaching for his hand, she placed it gently on her round belly. *"She dances for you,"* she sent tenderly.

Lizzie almost felt embarrassed at witnessing this intimate moment, but as if Amenia sensed this, she approached Lizzie and reached for her hand. As Lizzie's hand was positioned at the top of Amenia's belly, she felt it ripple and bobble rhythmically. Her own eyes wide, she looked into Amenia's face and sent, *"Wow! Does it hurt?"*

Amenia laughed heartily, holding her tummy with both hands. *"No, Lizzie, it doesn't hurt. It is a joyful feeling. Perhaps someday you will know for yourself. Soon enough, she will be where all can see. For now, it is she and I, united and one. But I love to share her movement with those close to me. I didn't mean to startle you."*

Lizzie was a bit embarrassed by her outburst. She had no experience with these things. She hadn't been around for the pregnancies that bore her nieces and nephews and she had never spent any time with an expecting mother, so she had no context.

"Let's go to the grove," Amenia continued with an amused smile. *"There are other little ones who would like to greet you all."*

She led the way to the outer door. Halfway to the back of the yard, just before a broader layer of trees, was the family gathering place with a firepit surrounded by benches and a few chaises. This had been one of Lizzie's favorite places in her first internship.

As they neared the back of the yard, Lizzie realized that there was a soft crooning issuing from the trees in front of them. Ynni hopped from her shoulder and sprinted on all fours towards the sound. Several pale green linklings scampered down from the trees nearest the fire pit area. There were adults about Ynni's size, and in the forefront were Ynni's twins. To Lizzie's surprise, some of the adults had linkling infants clinging to them.

Ynni's little tribe could now be described as exactly that. What had started as just Ynni, the sireling of the twins, and Ynni's sister had now multiplied to several linkling couples, as well as some apparently in their adolescent stage in addition to the infants. Lizzie couldn't count them, as they weren't exactly standing still.

They had gathered around Ynni, crooning and squeaking excitedly. Ynni's twins were cuddled one in each of her arms, and Lizzie felt a pang, realizing the sacrifice Ynni had made to stay with her.

"They have become a part of us," Amenia sent gently. *"Ynni has blessed us in a way we never thought possible before. The linklings are good neighbors and make a peaceful place even more so. Several of our friends have asked permission to have linklings settle on their land. The council is still considering how to do this without causing environmental issues.*

"The linklings themselves don't really present any obvious threats to other species or crops, but our council has always stayed on the side of caution in these things.

"As there are already five intelligent species on our planet, we must consult with all of them, as is just. For now, having a small tribe in our little grove is acceptable and was approved, as you know, before we brought additional linklings here."

Lizzie nodded, unsure how to respond. Reloi hovered in his chair beside her. *"Was this your doing?"* he asked, a bemused expression on his face.

"Not intentionally. It kind of just happened, sort of like with Tanata. Ynni bonded with me before I realized what was going on. And the tribe, well, I don't think it was so much an accident, as much as I just wasn't in on the plan until it was already too late to do anything about it. I definitely can't take any credit for it, if it turns out to be something good. This one is all on Ynni."

Reloi laughed, his eyes crinkling. *"I'm not sure what I'd do with more than one Tanata. He can be quite a handful, so to speak."*

Lizzie continued to be impressed with the way he made light of his physical condition. He seemed to take it for granted that others would look past it and, for the most part, they did. A lot had to do with his own attitude about it, she decided.

The frolicking linklings paused almost in unison. *"Lizzie will be busy for a little while?"* Ynni inquired.

"Of course, Ynni. I'm sure you want to spend some time with your little ones, and I would love to just sit and talk with Amenia, Tarafau, and Reloi. Enjoy your time. I'm not sure how long Tarafau was planning to stop here..." She paused, looking at first Tarafau, then Amenia, the question plain on her face.

"I thought we would spend the night, then go to the Apex for a couple of hours tomorrow, if that would be okay with Reloi," Tarafau answered, nodding to Reloi.

"That will work just fine for me. I've often wondered about this place. Only a few of us in the Alliance even know it exists. I promise not to give anything away to anyone, but I know a few have intimated to me that we all have much we could learn from your people," Reloi sent back. *"If you have room for me to camp out at your house, I would love the opportunity."*

Amenia beamed at Lizzie and Reloi. *"It will be a pleasure to have you both. Lizzie already has a room, and we have another that will work for you, even with your chair. In the meantime, I thought I would bring us out a bit of a picnic so we can enjoy the antics of the linklings and the scent of the new blooms in my flower bed."*

They all agreed wholeheartedly with this plan and, after Amenia waved away Lizzie and Reloi's offers for help, she and Tarafau walked back to the house while Lizzie settled herself on her favorite chaise and Reloi parked his hoverchair nearby.

Ynni scampered over to them. *"Can Tanata climb? He is welcome to meet my family if he would like."*

"*I can climb a tree as well as any,*" Tanata chimed in. "*I would like that very much. They look like nice trees.*" And the little lizard-like creature hopped down from Reloi's shoulder. He had been quiet through the entire exchange so far, and he seemed to be such a natural part of Reloi that Lizzie often forgot he wasn't just an appendage.

Reloi smiled and nodded and the two went off, Tanata running on all fours, his tail straight out behind him. He kept up easily with Ynni, and when she led the way up the tree he followed with no difficulty, as if he had little stickers on his feet.

"*So, here you are. I'd say you're beginning your adventure, but from the looks of it and what I know of you so far, your adventure has already had a pretty interesting start. Moving forward, what do you think you want to do? I know you're interested in the sciences, but now that you've nearly completed your training, where do you think you want to go from here?*" Reloi asked as Lizzie leaned back into the chaise with a sigh.

"*I can't really say. I do know I don't want to stay on as a trainer, and I'm not sure I want to have to work under cover much, although I know a lot of us will be doing that sort of thing. I'd like an assignment that allows me to learn a lot of new things and will still be of use to the Alliance. I was thinking that a liaison for an established dimension with known gateways might be interesting.*"

"*Hmm... I suppose it might. You'll get the opportunity to try a number of things during your various assignments. Your relationship with Ynni definitely puts you in a position to work that way. And then there is your music. As I understand it, you aren't a trained musician, but a natural one. There are a number of cultures that prize music; and even some, like where your podmate Gi comes from, who actually use music as a form of communication.*"

"*That would be interesting, for sure,*" Lizzie agreed. "*If I could combine those things in a useful way, I might enjoy that, but when it comes down to it, it's still about what the Alliance needs, isn't it?*"

Reloi considered her question, but before he could answer, Amenia and Tarafau approached laden with trays filled with food, plates, and utensils. The aroma should have warned Lizzie they were coming, but she had been deep into the conversation with Reloi.

The trays were unique in that they had little legs that extended from the bottom that turned them into small tables. Plates were passed around followed by a moment of silence before eating and then each of them helped themselves to the roasted vegetables and bud crawlers, salad, and a crusty homemade bread that was one of Amenia's specialties.

Reloi caught Tarafau and Amenia up on the discussion they had been having.

"I think you'll find that each new episode in your training builds on the strengths you acquired in the previous one. No two assignments will be the same. And in your case, this means you won't have a chance to get bored, something I know is vital to your personal mental health." Tarafau sent with his catlike grin.

"Lizzie is like the flowers in my garden," Amenia put in, her eyes twinkling and her smile warm, *"She soaks up every bit of light and nutrients to bloom beyond anyone's expectations. She will never stop growing or blooming as long as she is exposed to the things she so craves: learning and new experiences."*

Lizzie barely contained the urge to blush. She wasn't sure how much of this was teasing and how much was praise, but neither made her feel very comfortable. She was much better at handling criticism, as this was how she treated herself.

Reloi nodded his head. *"I don't think you will have a moment to achieve boredom at any time in the future. The one thing of which I can assure you is that you are more likely to feel newly challenged with every unique culture you get to experience, and you will sometimes feel more like you're barely keeping up. That's not necessarily a bad thing, as long as you don't allow it to stress you beyond your strength."*

Lizzie was beginning to feel somewhat like she was a particularly interesting sample under a microscope. She ventured a change of subject.

"How long have you been an agent, Reloi?" she inquired, thinking that might take the focus off of her.

"Me? It's hard to put it into Earth years... perhaps maybe thirty of your years? Relative time is one of the great difficulties of dimensional relations. We have yet to create an accurate way to coordinate all of the dimensional times. Unlike the time zones on a planet, for instance, each dimension has a difference in the way the clockwork meshes.

"For instance, I have no idea what time of day we will arrive on my planet from here. We will go from here back to the agent training gateway and on to my planet from there. Tarafau's planet is such an anomaly in the whole pattern of dimensional travel that we have to make some specific exceptions even to come here at all. His people and their interesting capability for interdimensional travel without a gate is deliberately a well-kept secret.

"And, unless I am mistaken, theirs is the only member of the Alliance without any discovered gateways. If they ever decide to engage in deep space exploration, they may discover a gate planet in their dimension, but for now, they make a major exception to the rule."

Tarafau nodded. *"I don't see any of our scientists going much farther in space exploration any time soon. It appears that they have enough to go on with just exploring the various mysteries of our own planet for now. The little bit of initial exploration we have done didn't seem to give enough benefit to make it worth expending the time, effort, and resources necessary to go much farther."*

"I agree. Oftentimes we reach out too soon," Reloi said, turning to Lizzie. *"I look forward to exposing you to some new possibilities to enthrall your thirsty mind."*

She started to retort but couldn't help turning to see what was going on in the grove. She realized that not only could she hear the enthusiastic crooning of the linklings up in the boughs of the trees, but also the murmuring song of the trees, a gentle descant to the delight of the tribe at their reunion.

"*I'm enjoying the song of the trees,*" she commented to Reloi, changing the subject, "*but I was wondering, how do I turn it off? I mean, I like being able to talk with plants and trees, but I think it could be distracting at a critical time. Is there a filter or an off switch?*" She realized this sounded a bit whiny, but it was a definite concern for her that so far, Liliath had not been able to help her with.

"*There are techniques you can use,*" Reloi reassured her. "*It's one of the things you will get an opportunity to practice during your time on my planet, as you will see....*" And he trailed off somewhat mysteriously.

They enjoyed watching the linklings frolic with their new friend, Tanata, for a bit and then Lizzie found herself yawning.

"*Typically, new interns find themselves a bit worn out at the end of their first day, as they got nearly no sleep the night before. Let's go get settled in, as we have a lot ahead of us in the morning,*" Tarafau said as he watched Lizzie cover her yawn with her hand.

"*Sounds good to me.*" Reloi agreed. "*Every good soldier knows to grab sleep and food when and how they can. Not that I've ever been a soldier, but agents often feel like one.*"

Lizzie was happy to close the door on the room Amenia had set aside for her on her last visit. No sooner did her head hit the pillow than she fell into a sleep so deep that she didn't even remember dreaming.

She awoke to sunshine streaming in through the window that looked out over the garden and the sound of Amenia humming to herself down the hall, as she went to prepare their morning meal.

Reloi was already up and dressed, and Tarafau looked as if he had also had a good sleep. As they ate breakfast, Amenia noted that today was a festival day and that the Apex would be very busy, so the sooner they got themselves together and left for the walk over the hill, the better.

Lizzie was delighted that Amenia had set out a new outfit for her, similar to her own. The gathered skirt and lightweight blouse were in deep tones of blue, which Amenia told her set off her blue eyes perfectly.

She didn't usually wear dresses, something that had distressed her mother to no end, but the long swishy skirt was comfortable and didn't restrict her movement. Sandals out of her MDP set it all off very well.

Amenia's outfit was a complement to her own, deep browns and golds to set off her dark hair and amber eyes. She looped one arm into Lizzie's as they walked along the path that led over the hill to the magnificent view of the city stretched out on a plain between them and a large mountain range. At the nearest edge of the city stood the large pyramidal structure, much like a small mountain itself.

The Apex was nearly a mile on each side, much larger than any of the pyramids on Earth. Rising higher than any skyscraper in Earth's largest cities, it housed what was almost a city in and of itself.

Reloi was impressed by the huge solar collector that was supplemented by the mirrored outer walls and windows that supplied not only the Apex with all the power it needed, but also most of the surrounding countryside with its energy needs.

He was fascinated with what the Daringi had done with this one structure and told Lizzie that the inventiveness of the intelligences of the multiverse never ceased to amaze and delight.

"I think you will begin to see that there are many ways to adapt life to the existing environment, some more successful and enjoyable than others," he told her as they feasted on bud-crawler stew after perusing the goods in the marketplace.

After lunch they met with local leaders who already knew and liked Lizzie. They mentioned the linklings in their discussion, as

Ynni had obligingly turned her reflection on during the meeting. They were interested in Tanata and even wondered aloud whether or not there might be undiscovered beings on their own planet who might become similar companion creatures.

Lizzie explained about the common practice on Earth of human and domestic animals as pets, something unknown in the Daringi culture or any of the known intelligent species on their planet. Afterwards, Lizzie found herself worrying about whether this was some type of cultural pollution and whether it somehow was contrary to the agreements she had made.

When she expressed her concerns to Reloi, he admitted that there were some grey areas in the agreements, but that a certain amount of sharing of cultural norms between member dimensions was nearly unavoidable.

"For instance, the introduction of music to Geln's people. It was not intentional, but it was unavoidable that he would be exposed to new ideas during his training. Who knows what ripples this will make in their culture? Since this isn't exactly technology, it doesn't really violate our statutes. That being said, sometimes ideas are more powerful and can have far greater repercussions than any technological advances can begin to generate."

Lizzie pondered this during the remainder of her day at the Apex, mostly ignoring the rest of Reloi's tour of the facility. She had spent a great deal of time there during her internship; and although she had always been somewhat in awe of the ingenuity of the Daringi people in creating this great complex, she found herself once again absorbed in the question: when was cultural cross-pollination problematical, and when was it actually beneficial?

When all was said and done, it really came down to the judgment and discretion of the agent involved. She realized at that point that no amount of training would prepare her for that. It would come with experience, and there would be times when she might make a mistake that could have more impact than she could imagine.

When she had bought the mbiras for Geln, she hadn't considered the effect it might have, but by that time, the damage, if there was any, had already been done, as Geln's exposure to the music on Gi's planet had opened their mind to possibilities they had never considered.

Lizzie then began to wonder how her coming experiences as an agent might change her in ways she didn't expect. Already she had learned so much. And was feeling a new connection to her family and experiencing true friendship perhaps for the first time in her life.

They returned to Tarafau's home in good spirits and once again gathered by the little grove so Ynni could say her goodbyes to her tribe and her adorable twins. Lizzie once again felt a pang as she realized how much Ynni was giving up to be her companion.

After hugs were exchanged all around and Amenia had held Lizzie's hand once again to her belly as the babe wiggled inside, she sent, *"Lizzie, you will return soon to meet her in person. We think of you as one of ours and she should meet you early on."*

"Thank you, Amenia. I look forward to it, even though I'm not really very good with children."

"I think it's one more thing you will grow into, Lizzie. Take good care and return safely."

Amenia hugged Lizzie and then Reloi and finally Tarafau, beaming up into his eyes. *"Be good, Papa Cat, and take good care of our Lizzie."*

Tarafau hugged her back and, placing a large hand on Reloi's shoulder and Lizzie's, they faded from the Daringi planet into the training area of the pod at the agent training center.

Chapter 13: Prelude to a Fugue

(Fascinated, curious and feeling like she was getting to the center of something important, Jenny knew she couldn't pause in the narrative. She absently sipped the dregs of her mint tea and turned the page...)

As the three of them entered the gateroom, there was no one there to see them off. This, after all, was a normal occurrence at the agent training center. All goodbyes had been said and all counsel given before she had left for Tarafau's dimension.

They stepped through the seemingly ordinary doorway into bright light and what appeared to be a transparent dome about fifteen feet in diameter looking out onto a desolate landscape. Lizzie had often imagined the moon to be barren and lifeless, but this went beyond anything she could imagine. As far as she could see, the glistening white sand stretched in undulating patterns perhaps created by wind; she doubted they could have been made by any living thing, as she couldn't imagine anything surviving in such a place.

Reloi noted the look on her face. *"It's striking, is it not? But take heart, no one lives out there. There is little atmosphere and all of it is toxic. This is the gateway station, the only one on the planet in which any living thing could survive. As you can see, only a few beings can be in the station at any given time, so the likelihood that we might be invaded by another dimension is pretty slim, unless the invaders had technology beyond anything we are able to currently imagine."*

Lizzie looked around her. Besides the plain metal hatch they had just come through, there was only one other thing in the dome. On the opposite side of the transparent tube was another smaller structure, also tubelike, with what appeared to be five seats with straps dangling from the seat backs.

Reloi nodded towards the door leading into the tube. *"Have a seat and strap in, and tell Ynni to hold tight onto you,"* he directed, gliding along behind them as they complied. He settled his hover chair in a space between Tarafau and Lizzie and, using his kinetic ability, he leveraged similar straps on his chair to strap himself in thoroughly. Lizzie noticed that Tanata crept into the opening of Reloi's collar and disappeared under his shirt. Simultaneously, Lizzie felt Ynni's prehensile tail wrap around her arm and felt both tiny hands reach around her neck. Lizzie had no time to wonder about any of this, as Reloi made a high-pitched *squeeing* sound much like a dolphin, and the tube slid down below the floor of the dome and then flipped upside down!

This definitely beat anything she had experienced so far in her training. As soon as the tube had flipped, she realized that the rock walls surrounding the transparent tube immediately began to appear to fly by at a rapid rate. She remembered reading *Alice in Wonderland* and found herself thinking, *"Curiouser and curiouser,"* as they continued to hurtle along for what seemed like a long time.

No one spoke, and she realized she was clutching the arms of the seat so hard that her hands hurt, but as they continued to travel this way, her grip loosened, and she began to simply wonder what was happening. She was pretty sure Reloi wouldn't deliberately put her in any danger, but that it might have been nice for him to have explained what was about to happen. But, remembering his mischievous nature, she realized he was probably enjoying her discomfiture.

Slowly, she felt that something was changing. Although they didn't slow in their journey through the tube, she started to feel a strange lightness, as if she was now floating in her straps with no weight at all. This lasted for only a few minutes, at which point she slowly was drawn back down into her chair, and she felt Ynni settle lightly onto her shoulder once again. Although she knew the tube had not changed direction, she now felt as if she was upright in her seat.

She felt her hair fall back again onto her cheeks and forehead, and a pull as if in an elevator rising at high speed. Just when she thought they would continue up (or was it down?) this rock tunnel forever, the tube began to slow noticeably, and above them the darkness brightened.

"Wow, that was definitely an 'E-ticket,'" Lizzie sent. Both Tarafau and Reloi looked puzzled. Evidently mindspeech couldn't quite translate this idiom. *"It's a saying on Earth when something is a lot more umm... interesting or exciting than you expected. It's hard to explain. What just happened here?"*

"I'm sorry. I should have explained," Reloi replied somewhat sheepishly. *"We don't live on the surface of the planet. We are deep underground, and up and down are reversed here. What you felt as we descended was the shifting of the gravitational pull from outside gravity to inner gravity, otherwise known as centrifugal force. We live in the hollow core of our planet, as you will soon see. Very different from what you are used to.*

"You can remove your harnesses," he continued, nodding toward the hatch in the tube, which had opened automatically.

Lizzie was surprised at how bright it was, considering where they were. It appeared as if there was a sun in the sky above them (or was it below?), and she looked around in awe as she stepped out onto a platform that led into a public park. People strolled on paths between manicured lawns and under what could only have been ancient trees, based on their height and the size of their trunks.

The color scheme was a little disconcerting, however, as instead of green, the foliage mostly seemed to be a deep purple, and the sky was almost golden, as just before sunset or dawn on Earth.

The people were humanoid in shape, as Reloi had told her they were when they first met. They were a pale people with light colored hair in varying shades of silver and white, and either violet or blue eyes.

She shot a glance at Tarafau to see his reaction. He seemed calm but interested. No shock there at all. Of course, with his many years as an Alliance agent, he had probably seen things much more unusual than this.

"Come, and I will introduce you," Reloi sent cheerfully, and Lizzie realized that some of the people out here weren't strolling but gathered in a group to the side of the tube, looking at them all expectantly.

Like Reloi, their large eyes were expressive and seemed to be welcoming as they waited calmly for introductions.

"Councilors, allow me to introduce you to Tarafau Bane and Lizzie Japhet, members of the Dimensional Alliance. Both are agents sent here to learn about our culture and to extend a hand of fellowship to our people. Are we ready to receive them?"

The question seemed to Lizzie like a formal request, rather than as casual as his tone suggested.

A woman with silver hair that nearly glowed in the light, and who was dressed in lavender pants that fluttered around her ankles and a matching tunic, stepped forward with a warm smile on her face. *"Reloi, we greet you and our guests and stand ready to offer hospitality and welcome to you all. We rejoice at your return and hope to make new ties to the representatives of the Alliance."*

She held out her hands, one to Tarafau and one to Lizzie, and they took them. Looking at first one, then the other in turn, she sent, *"It is truly a pleasure to meet you and your companions. If you come with us, we will meet in the pavilion nearby. It is a peaceful place and congenial to happy conversation."* And she released their hands, gesturing for them to walk with her.

The others in the group smiled and nodded and they went off, less than a hundred feet down the path to a gazebo-type structure which had been furnished with chairs similar to the folding lawn chairs Lizzie was familiar with. The chairs had been placed in a circle about the inner perimeter of the pavilion.

As they each took a seat, she noticed they had left a space for Reloi's hover chair as well. The provision to accommodate his chair seemed to be a matter of course.

Being seated in a circle like this gave Lizzie an opportunity to scan the faces before her. The majority of them appeared to be female. They were tall, she noted, much like her own height, and tended to be slender, almost willowy in build.

Although she had thought at first the shades of hair were about the same, she realized that there were many varied shades of the silver and white, some verging on grey and others nearly so white as to be blinding, like snow at noon on a clear day.

The woman who had seemed to be the leader of the group stood and faced their guests. *"Welcome, Lizzie, your companion Ynni, and Tarafau, and we welcome back our dear friend, Reloi,"* she sent with a smile. *"I am Nedai, the chief councilor of the people's commission. It is our understanding that you have come as an apprentice agent for the Dimensional Alliance. As such, we will be granting you access to all of our councils, our libraries, and institutions of learning. Reloi has consented to be your guide in this. Do you have any questions?"*

Obviously Reloi had briefed them on the nature of their small party and their purpose. Lizzie was surprised to realize they knew about Ynni and had included her in their greeting.

"I really don't know enough to ask any questions at this point, Nedai. I am grateful to get the opportunity to learn about your culture and more about my role as an agent and liaison for the Dimensional Alliance. I am excited to learn more about how you came to settle the inner core of your planet."

"Then we shall get you started as soon as may be. Reloi has sent ahead with your physical requirements regarding food and accommodations. Each of several representatives of different areas of our world are represented here today. We will take it in turns to host you and your companions during your stay here.

"In the meantime, we will celebrate Reloi's return and allow you to meet and experience the joy of our people. The people of Grild will welcome you and, for a while, you will be one of us. Not all things are joyful, but today we will begin with joy and move forward from there."

She then walked over to Jenny and held out her hands to raise her from her seat, then did the same with Tarafau. She then touched her forehead with the fingertips of her right hand and then gently repeated the gesture to touch Lizzie's forehead. Then the same with Tarafau. And, to Lizzie's surprise and Ynni's delight, she repeated the gesture with Ynni.

The rest of the company stood and, one at a time, they repeated the little ceremony, each with a brilliant and sincere smile, looking into their eyes as they did so.

Reloi sat there grinning at the look of delighted puzzlement on Lizzie's face. *"In your culture, I believe they shake hands. Here we do differently for the same reasons. This gesture is a signal of welcome and commitment to be kind and to always give of the mind and heart."*

"Thank you, one and all," Lizzie said, a small quaver in her mental voice. *"I feel welcome and cherished. I look forward to getting to know*

you better." And with no prompting, she went down the line of the representatives of the Grildites, repeating the gesture to each one, Ynni copying her, and Tarafau following in her wake with the same greeting.

Nedai grinned at her as she finally reached the beginning of the circle of her comrades. *"You will do well, Lizzie of Earth. Already we begin to see why you were chosen. Now let us depart to feast and celebrate your arrival."*

Nedai led the way out of the pavilion down a stone walkway lined with flowers that looked a lot like dandelions only several times larger and taller. As Lizzie walked beside Reloi as he glided along in his chair, she felt no shame looking about her avidly at the beautiful but alien surroundings.

She felt like she had arrived in a deep valley surrounded by massive mountains, but as light poured down from above, it didn't seem shadowy or foreboding. They strolled along and, as they did so, Lizzie noticed that although she could hear the soft murmuring of the local flora in the background when she took time to notice, she heard no birds and felt no breeze. The foliage around her was still.

They arrived at a broad boulevard. It was now obvious that where they had met in the pavilion was part of a city park, but not a city like any Lizzie had seen before. The buildings were low, and the only traffic on the street was either people on foot or small hand-drawn carts or wagons. Those milling to and fro down the long street nodded to one another or waved and hailed others they saw.

The buildings were low, seldom more than a single story, made of either brick or mortared stone. Through large glass-paned windows, Lizzie could see displays of goods which indicated that many of the buildings were probably shops. At the base of each window was a flower box filled with colorful blooms of various kinds, none of which Lizzie recognized.

Even with the conversations of people on the street, it was relatively quiet compared to any city Lizzie had ever visited. Her companions conversed in low voices in their musical language, which sounded lisping and filled with more vowels than consonants.

Her hostess, Nedai, kept up a stream of mindspeech as they walked, pointing out buildings of interest and managing at the same time to greet people verbally as they passed.

"Once you are settled in, I will be happy to introduce you to the various establishments that serve our people in this, our main city. We call it, Encashara, which means 'first home' in our language. There are now many settlements throughout our inner world, but this was the first place we fled to when the outer world became uninhabitable," she explained as they walked.

"Doubtless, this is a relatively small planet compared to many you will encounter in your duties. My son, Shemin, is also an agent of the Alliance. Whenever he is home, he entertains us with tales of his travels. You have much to look forward to. It is probably well that you begin here, as our culture is simple, not so complicated as many you will yet encounter. Ah... we are here," she said, gesturing to a door that seemed no different from many others, except it was in one of the largest buildings they had encountered so far.

She led the way through, and she and Lizzie were followed by the rest of the group into a well-lit lobby of a sort, its shiny floor appearing to be some sort of marble veined in patterns of black, grey, and silver.

At one end was a long, wide hallway lined with occasional doorways with glass doors. As they passed down it, Lizzie looked into many of them, noticing they were offices very similar to the kind she would have expected in any administration building.

At the end of the hallway stood a set of double doors that swung open at their approach, and they passed through into what looked a lot like the city hall at home. At the far end was a slightly raised dais with two long tables set about four feet apart facing the semicircle of rows of chairs where a few people were already seated. After they passed down the center aisle that sliced through the arc of chairs, Nedai gestured to a seat at one of the tables.

"Get comfortable," she sent, sounding amused. *"The niceties must first be observed, and then there will be feasting and entertainment to honor you as a guest. Don't get too used to it, however, as after tonight you are no longer a guest but will be a working part of our community."*

Lizzie hoped that the intention of the remark was as jovial as it seemed, but perhaps her hostess had not meant it all that much as a joke. This was fine with her. Welcome banquets were all well and good, but she had come here to work. So, she nodded to Nedai and sat and watched the hall begin to fill up. The rest of her party had filled the remainder of the chairs behind the tables, with Reloi in a space that had been left for his chair.

It seemed obvious to Lizzie that all had come in what her dad would have called "their Sunday best." The style here for both women and men was flowing and loose-fitting garments in a wide range of pastel colors. It was like watching a flower garden bloom before her very eyes. As the chairs filled up, the murmur of sibilant voices susurrated through the hall, not loud, but definitely not a whisper. Evidently, these were just not a loud people.

For a moment she found herself wondering if they sang at all, and what their music would sound like. If their speech was any indication, it would be like listening to the breeze talk to the trees by a burbling stream. Her thoughts were interrupted, however by Nedai's rising from her seat. The sound of the crowd was silenced as if a knife had sliced it off, and all faces looked attentively and respectfully to the front of the room.

Nedai stood and, spreading her arms wide as she gave a brilliant smile, she said (interpreting her speech into mindspeech as she spoke aloud for Jenny, Ynni, and Tarafau's sakes), *"Welcome one and all. We are here today to greet our guests from the Alliance. They are Lizzie Japhet of Earth and her companions, Ynni and Tarafau. They come here that we may exchange ideas and culture and to strengthen our friendship and ties with the Dimensional Alliance.*

"We also welcome Reloi home. We have missed his insights, his wisdom, and his unusual sense of humor." This was said with a mischievous smile in Reloi's direction and was greeted with a nearly unanimous chuckle from the crowd. Evidently Lizzie wasn't the only one who appreciated Reloi's spontaneous mischievousness.

Nedai nodded appreciatively and went on, *"While Lizzie is here, it is important that she sees both sides of our culture, the serious and the potentially whimsical. Treat her as we would any of our young adults. She is thirsty for knowledge, and we will happily share what we know, but it is also important she understands the things in our lives that bring us joy and make us smile."*

Lizzie was startled by this pronouncement. She hadn't considered that she would be doing anything but working and honing her skills in diplomacy, science, and Grildite society. It sounded a lot like Gaston's insistence early on in her training that she take regular breaks and socialize with others.

"In a moment, we will adjourn to the multipurpose room to be fed and entertained. But for now, would Lizzie like to stand and introduce herself? I will be happy to translate from mindspeech to our language for you."

Lizzie was not really prepared for this invitation, and she almost declined, but she remembered her training and nodded, arose, and stood beside Nedai.

Her mind raced. They had practiced this during training many times, and Lizzie had never quite achieved the fluency or the natural calm developed by her podmates. But she plunged ahead, knowing that these kinds of experiences were one of the reasons she was here.

She straightened herself, beginning by panning her eyes across the room as she had been trained and taking a deep steadying breath. *"Thank you for your warm welcome."* She paused as Nedai began to speak in the Encasharan language next to her. It was a bit disconcerting, but she moved forward anyway, trying to block the sound of Nedai's voice from her mind as she spoke.

"This is a new experience for me, as I have never lived inside a planet before; and as I continue my training, I realize this could be one of the experiences that will always stand out in my mind. I look forward to making new friends and learning new things. I hope to be a creditable representative for the Dimensional Alliance. I don't want to keep you from the upcoming feast, so I'll keep it short. Thank you."

As she sat back in her seat behind the table, she realized her heart was pounding. Giving oral reports in college had never been her favorite thing, and for a few years she usually concluded her report by excusing herself to the restroom to empty her stomach. But the group before her were tapping their fingers on their legs, which she hoped was their version of applause.

Fortunately, her stomach behaved itself, and in a few moments, she was calm again. Tarafau reached out a huge hand to cover her own on the table and nodded respectfully. She heard Reloi's mental voice comment, *"Well said."* And she looked down the table to see him smiling encouragingly.

Nedai then spoke again. *"Thank you, Lizzie. Let us now adjourn to our meal and entertainments."*

In near unison the crowd stood and began to exit what Lizzie thought of as the council room. Those seated at the table waited until the room was nearly empty and then stood and followed the crowd down the long corridor to where it branched to the right. At the end of this shorter hallway was another set of double doors.

These led into a large dining hall. There were tablecloths on all of the long banquet tables, and all the chairs faced the dais. On every table were flower arrangements and table settings not much different from what Lizzie was used to at home, except she didn't recognize any of the flowers.

The table on the slightly raised dais was set for the same number who had been on the dais in the council room. They seated themselves in the same order; and as soon as all had taken their seats, Nedai rang a small crystal bell in front of her. As the bell chimed, what appeared to be an army of women with trays held high over their heads proceeded into the room in what was almost a graceful dance.

The guests applauded and Lizzie joined in. Ynni crooned in delight from her perch on Lizzie's shoulder. On every tray were beautifully presented dishes of what were probably vegetables and fruits native to the planet, some cooked and some raw. On every table, the various dishes were arranged in rows, each dish looking more enticing than the last.

At this point Lizzie was grateful for her agent training and their coaching in etiquette. She didn't immediately reach for a dish but paused to watch and see what happened next.

But, similar to any Earth family at a Thanksgiving feast, each of the guests reached for a dish in front of them, took a portion and passed the dish to the person next to them until every dish had been sampled. Lizzie politely took a little of everything. There was no meat in evidence. Lizzie decided not to ask about it, but to save her questions about it to ask Reloi in private.

She found, to her delight, that all of the food was delicious. Ynni sampled happily from Lizzie's plate. *"Food is very, very good,"* she sent with a mental feeling much like the purr of a contented cat.

"This is all delicious," Lizzie broadcasted in mindspeech to the group. *"I look forward to learning about food production in such a unique planetary environment."*

"We will be giving you a tour of our city and the farming community starting tomorrow. We want you to feel at home here during your internship. You need to be sure to get plenty of sleep as we go, since we plan to keep you very busy," Nedai replied.

Lizzie grinned. *"I was hoping you would. I couldn't have wished for a better first assignment. This is beyond anything I expected."*

Nedai nodded. *"We think we have some interesting insights to offer you. We also would love to learn more about you and your culture. I know that some tech conversations are carefully restricted, and for good reason, but I would love to learn about your art and music and history when we get time to talk. In the meantime, I want you to feel welcome; and be forewarned, we don't intend to make this too easy for you.*

"I hope to keep you challenged and give you many opportunities to practice your diplomacy skills as well. Reloi has told us you have a lot of potential to make a real difference in your time as an agent. The Alliance has been a great resource for us in the past, and we are happy for the opportunity to give back as we can."

"Thank you," Lizzie replied, grateful that mindspeech allowed her to enjoy the new tastes of the banquet placed before her while she could carry on a genial conversation. *"I can hardly wait to get started."*

"Tonight, we play, and tomorrow we promise to wear you out," Nedai said with a wicked grin that reminded her of Reloi. *"Your agenda for the next few weeks will be intense, but hopefully also enjoyable."*

For the rest of the meal, Lizzie just soaked up the ambience and enjoyed the various entertainments provided by her hosts. There was dancing, reminiscent of the hula she had seen at a luau she had attended in her senior year of high school. The swaying motions of the dancers were mesmerizing, and it seemed apparent that the movements of their hands were significant to the lyrics of the songs they danced to.

There were some acrobats who performed, as well as with jugglers. It reminded her somehow of the royal feasts she had read about in medieval history accounts. She definitely felt like a foreign dignitary, which made her hope she could live up to their apparent expectations of her.

By the end of the evening, she was definitely ready to be escorted out of the dining hall to their peculiar applause, tapping fingers on their legs, which was nearly silent, a kind of murmuring sound. All were smiling and some bowed to her. Nedai led her out of the building and down the street to a kind of single-story apartment building.

Lizzie and Tarafau were shown to a little two-bedroom apartment with what might have been a little kitchenette and bathing facilities. It wasn't large, but it was definitely better than her dorm room had been in college.

"We'll come by in the morning to take you to breakfast, and then we'll get started," Nedai said as she moved to leave. *"We'll stock your kitchen with food once you decide which kind you like best, so you can potentially prepare food for yourselves eventually.*

"Make yourself at home. I imagine you both have had an eventful day and will be glad for your beds. If you need anything, you can push that button near the inside of your door. Lighting can be extinguished by waving your hand twice in front of any lamp."

"Umm, I was wondering. Your 'sun,' the bright light in the sky, doesn't go down at night. How do you differentiate between night and day?"

"Ah yes, you are used to living planet-side. All windows in all homes have special blinds that darken a room when needed. See here," and she walked over to a window at the end of the sitting room. There, she pulled on a cord by the window, and the blind descended to cover the window. The edges on either side were hidden between long slots they slid down, which sealed out any light.

"I'll leave you to it, then," Nedai said.

"Good night and sleep well," Reloi added with a smile. *"We have adventures to pursue tomorrow. See you then."*

Tarafau and Lizzie wished them goodnight. After the door closed, and after saying the same to one another, they each retired to their sleeping quarters. It had been a very long day.

Chapter 14: Song of Light

(Lizziebot cleared her AI throat to get Jenny's attention. It always tickled Jenny to see the little humanlike behaviors that Bob had programmed into his sidekick bots. Fidget was more like a teenage kid than an AI programmed by an expert programmer.

"Ahem," Lizziebot said, her AI face in a wry smile. "You need to get out and take your walk, orders from the healers. Burt told me I'd be in big trouble if I didn't get you out of that chair and out into the open air."

Jenny sighed dramatically and put the journal down on the side table, carefully marking her place. "I'm just so fascinated by all of the things you did as an agent trainee. You know I never got the chance to experience any of these things."

"Lizzie programmed me with her memories, but I cannot respond to your emotion as I am sure you would like. I do know it was her intent to connect with you on an emotional level as well as to give a historical account of her various experiences," Lizziebot replied. "Now you need to get out there and walk. I observe you are getting better, but you won't fully recover if you don't follow the advice of your doctors."

"Okay, I get it. I'm moving." And suiting words to action she headed out the door. As she exited into the front yard, she noticed Bob's son, Chris, out mowing the lawn. Chris had been assiduous about caring for the house and yard and made for a nice neighbor. He waved and continued his work, and Jenny waved back with a smile.

The neighborhood was quiet, as most people were out working at their various occupations this time of the day and the children were all in school. As she walked around the loop, she considered the impact that Lizzie's life and adventures had created in her own life.

She marveled that she had merely scratched the surface so far and realized the time Lizzie spent on Reloi's planet must have been very important to her, as she had noticed that the journal entries were closer together now, but earlier and later entries were more like summaries, less detailed and farther apart.

She was anxious to get back to the journals since her short medical leave would be over way too soon, at which time she would be plunged fully back into the conflict between the Alliance and the Insenium. She knew Lizziebot was right; she needed to get back into shape. And these daily walks and the nutritious meals Lizziebot had been preparing for her, along with the supplements recommended by the Alliance physicians, were vital.

In the meantime, she felt like reading Lizzie's journals were somehow also part of the healing process. Not only was she learning a lot more about the training she had missed out on, but she was also realizing that her aunt's experiences were just a sample of the vast training and organization necessary to run such a huge program. She was gaining respect for the mission of the Alliance and insights into how her role as the Gatekeeper of the Alliance impacted the unimaginable multiverse.

Wrapping her head around the sheer magnitude of it all was nearly impossible, and she knew she would never fully comprehend it. But she was beginning to understand that she didn't have a lot of time to grow into her calling, so she was determined to finish reading the journals.

At night while she slept, she usually mentally checked in with both Sanglarka and Alliance headquarters to stay abreast of current events. For now, however, they continued to encourage her to limit the time she spent mentally keeping up with events, as she didn't get as much out of her sleep when she was connecting across dimensions.

Of course, she also had a short mental date with her husband, Burt, by their special little inlet pond on the Merced River, each night, even though they couldn't be together in person as often as either of them would have liked.

During Lizzie's walk, Chris had finished the lawn and gone back into the house. Lizzie entered into her sunny living room to discover Tidbit ensconced lazily in the window seat, with Chidwi snuggled close beside him.

She went into the kitchen, grabbed the drink and the snack Lizziebot had already prepared, and retired with anticipation to her cozy chair, picked up the journal, and opened it to the page she had bookmarked.)

As Nedai had promised, the week that followed the warm welcome she had received was fast paced. They started with a tour of the city itself. Her first impression didn't imply that they were very high tech, but she was soon disabused of that notion. It turned out that perhaps the only way Reloi's people had survived the decimation of their planet was their advanced understanding of geology, biology, and physics.

They had been a space-going people, but they had to choose between exploring the universe and survival. The decline of the ecology of their world had been gradual at first, but when it became apparent that they could not slow the erosion of the environment, they knew they had to do something desperate.

Their space program had produced no hope for a livable planet to transfer to, so they had to make hard decisions. Turning inward, they discovered, to their astonishment, that their planet was hollow at the center; and after exploring it, they realized they could potentially survive inside the planet.

Colonies were established, small at first, mostly populated by scientists and farmers. The two issues that needed to be resolved were light and establishing a workable ecosystem.

Solar energy was abundant on the surface, so huge solar farms were established on the surface, circumnavigating the globe, so that at any point or at any time, there was a constant flow of solar energy to pull from. Vast systems of energy transfer were created leading from the surface to the planet's interior.

An interior satellite was suspended in the exact center of the inner core, giving light to every single potentially colonizable space. The only drawback was that this meant there was no darkness, no cycle between night and day. They had to change the way they calculated the passage of time.

By the time they were ready to transport the remaining people to the interior, they realized a few things:

First, that the majority of the animals native to the planet had either expired or would take up too many resources to bring along. Cattle and animals they had previously relied on for food would not be viable in their new environment.

Second, much of the technology they had relied upon for transportation and industry would be incompatible with an enclosed environment, as there was no way to get rid of the potential pollutants they would induce.

And finally, since they would have to subsist largely on farming, the status of those who could produce food was elevated beyond that of the bureaucracy or other notables.

A surprising number refused to make the transfer and perished over time, along with all of the flora and fauna of the planet, as water resources dried up and the air became unbreathable.

At the point Lizzie came to them, however, they had long since adjusted to their environment and had a thriving community that was noticeably well-organized and peaceful.

Her hosts explained to her that the few vehicles she saw on the street were powered by a combination of solar battery power and physical exertion by the passengers. Unless they were traveling long distances, most preferred to walk.

Water was abundant, streams both above ground and below provided water enough for both farming and consumption. Their purity was strictly enforced. The lessons of their past had changed how they appreciated their environment.

City streets were clean, and everyone seemed to be busy at some task or another most of the time; but all took time to pause and enjoy interacting with one another. The lessons they had learned had been hard.

As they toured, Lizzie was told their history. They had been and continued to be an advanced society. Much of their technology had been at a higher level than that of the planet where the Alliance had their headquarters. But at some point, they had been so intent on new technological advances that they had neglected the planet.

Waste and pollutants generated by production of consumer goods and technological discards had poisoned much of their water source and the air they breathed. At one point it had become necessarily fashionable to wear designer air purification units strapped to every back. As time went on, they could no longer deny the fact that their planet was dying.

All farming was done indoors via hydroponic systems, and all of the larger animals had long since become extinct. In the meantime, a small corps of scientists had been quietly working in the background. When they realized there was no hope for the planet to recover, they split into two groups.

One group focused entirely on the idea they might find another planet to colonize, so they focused on space exploration and the technology that would allow them to find and explore new options.

The other group turned inward. The seas were drying up, but where did the water go? What other options did they have? Ironically, it was a writer of fiction who came up with an idea that eventually saved them. This writer had written a story long ago, describing an inside-out planet where the people lived in the planet's core.

At first most scoffed at the idea. No one had ever delved deep enough into the crust of the planet to completely understand what that might look like. There had been myths about their planet's being hollow, but the majority of scientists had discounted it as the wild imaginings of creatives and dreamers. However, one scientist and an engineer had gotten the backing of some curious entrepreneurs and had begun delving deep into the planet.

The project took years and was popularly mocked and derided by the majority of the people, most of whom were still going about their business, unwilling to admit that the planet they lived on would eventually no longer support life.

Then two things happened that radically changed their attitudes. Small volcanoes began to emerge at the edges of their shrinking oceans, obscuring the already severely compromised atmosphere and decimating the remaining plant life.

At the same time, the venture to bore into the planet finally hit what at first seemed to be just another air pocket. As the cavers explored it, though, they discovered not just an air pocket but what other scientists had considered a mythological place. Their planet was indeed hollow.

All of a sudden, every scientist, engineer, and the general populace were now focused on one thing. How could they make this a viable alternative to roasting and strangling in their decaying world?

So, for many years they planned and worked, delving multiple tunnels deep under the surface. Once a preliminary colony was established, they began to work through the multiple challenges that would need to be overcome to make the interior of the planet livable for the dwindling number of survivors of the now rapidly decaying world.

It was a race against time; and when at last the remaining colonists arrived as the final refugees, they realized a lot of things would need to change, starting with the general attitude of consumption and how to balance a comfortable lifestyle and the primary need for survival.

Once they had put the solar farms in place, equidistant from one another along the equator of their planet, and had figured out how to suspend the satellite-type star from the center of the interior, they had set about creating well-planned communities that could take advantage of the abundant resources within the planet's shell without compromising the environment. Learning to balance their current needs with their future needs had become one of the main studies of their scientists and engineers.

Lizzie toured the farms, noticing a distinct lack of farm animals that she would have expected to see on an Earth farm. In place of land animals, enough freshwater fish of various kinds had been preserved and stocked in the various ponds and streams. They told her that when they had done this, they were amazed to discover many distinct varieties of fish already living in this underground environment. They also realized that they could replenish the natural richness of the soil, so long untilled for farming, with the remains of the fish they harvested to add protein to their diets, replacing the use of cattle and other meats from their life above ground.

In addition to the traditional farms, nearly every building in every community had a basement similar to the basement in the Swiss observatory that housed the Swiss gate on earth. Aquaponics, so new to Earth science, was a matter of fact and daily living on this planet. Every home, apartment building, or business within every community created a continuous food supply not dependent on weather or soil conditions.

Reloi's people had learned from hard experience to take a mindful approach to survival, and in the process, they had reduced much of the stress found in other societies. They never lacked for power, water, or food.

Weather was not an issue. Because there was nothing resembling wind within the confines of their world, water simply condensed as dew that naturally watered the plants. There was literally no sky here. This made the landscape more than a little surreal.

No blue sky. No clouds, only the light above. There was no horizon to speak of. It was like living in a valley with the sun always high overhead at noontime. You couldn't see the land that hung above you. The light was too bright for that. It had to be, in order to thoroughly light such a vast area.

Of course, the distances were such that it didn't feel claustrophobic, just very different. The nearest curve of anything you might call a horizon was so far away as to be nearly unnoticeable. Although the ground gently curved upward in every direction around the hollow core, it felt as flat as any prairie might from wherever you stood. Low hills broke up the landscape to make it feel almost normal, until you noticed the difference in the sky.

As strange as that was, it was the people she met who fascinated Lizzie the most.

One of the first things she had noticed about Reloi was his gentle nature. It seemed that this was a common trait among his people. The outcome of surviving such a great common catastrophe was that they had changed their priorities and shifted their attitudes.

They had used their technology to reduce the need for stressful occupations and to lessen the impact of their daily living on the environment. It was readily evident that they had learned some hard lessons. Many millions had perished in the long running devastation of their outer planet. Many generations after the last of them had fled to the interior, they were still earnestly seeking and finding new ways to be more responsible.

As Lizzie continued her tour, with Reloi as her guide and Tarafau also attending, she began to feel anxiety for her own world and to wonder how she could somehow effect changes there before something as catastrophic befell Earth, and how she could do so without compromising her oaths to the Alliance regarding non-interference.

She began to wish with all her heart that she could figure out a way to create some urgency in the nations of Earth, starting with her own country. Her initial conflicts began to reemerge with vigor and her mind raced. She knew she would have to consult with Liliath at some point to reconcile herself to what was allowed and what was not.

Despite her personal conflict, the days she spent in her initial tour were peaceful and enjoyable. She was delighted as the different communities shared music, art, and various performances with her as an honored guest. More and more, she gained an appreciation for why Reloi was who he was.

At one of the towns they visited, she finally got an opportunity to meet Reloi's parents and siblings. It was a sort of family reunion, as Reloi hadn't been home in several years. They welcomed Lizzie, Tarafau, and Ynni joyfully and kindly.

Reloi's mother took Lizzie under her gentle wing almost immediately, as if they had been neighbors for years. She very much reminded Lizzie of a next-door neighbor she had bonded with in her junior high school years. The woman had no children and so had adopted the children of her family like a favorite aunt.

As Reloi had told her when they first met, his family didn't pander to him as if he were an invalid. Instead, they seemed to expect him to manage most things on his own. Of course, there was the fact that his kinetic abilities sometimes allowed him to do things others couldn't. That being said, he hadn't developed those abilities until long after he had left home to become an agent of the Alliance.

Lizzie tried to imagine him going through the training she had just completed, and she was amazed at the determination and fortitude it must have taken for him to not only complete his training but to be considered a valuable agent in the Alliance hierarchy.

"He was a delightful little boy," his mother confided to Lizzie as they sat digesting a wonderful meal. *"He would never quit, once he had decided he wanted to do something. My husband and I decided early on to give him as normal a childhood as we could, and he didn't disappoint us. Of course, he is also extremely stubborn and not easily turned, once he decides on something he wants to do, even if it isn't always in his best interest."*

She glanced at him with a mischievous grin. *"The stories I could tell...."*

"Oh please, Mother, don't. There are some things Lizzie definitely doesn't need to know."

She laughed and shook her head. *"Perhaps she should be forewarned about you?"*

Reloi shook his head vigorously, nearly knocking Tanata off of his shoulder. *"Come on, Mother! Really? You know I'm just an angel in disguise...."* And he grinned winsomely at the two of them. *"Lizzie? A little help here?"*

Lizzie and his mom laughed at his distress, and he rolled his eyes in despair. Lizzie felt Ynni quivering with her own peculiar little chuckle that sounded a lot like a burbling brook. Evidently this type of teasing was not unknown among the linklings.

At that point, Reloi's dad came in from the kitchen with something that looked a lot like a tall gelatin confection molded with curlicues and swirls of what might have been whipped cream.

Lizzie found herself as much surprised at the similarities between such widely separated cultures as the differences.

The appearance of the dessert distracted them all from Reloi's mother's discomfiting revelations. But the give and take among Reloi and his family felt familiar and comfortable, so much like what she would have expected in any Earthly family gathering.

They had accepted Tarafau into the family circle as well. Reloi's dad especially seemed to enjoy swapping stories with the big man, and they bonded almost immediately, as if they had known one another for a long time.

They later said their goodbyes with regret as they continued their journey, but Lizzie hoped she would be visiting them as often as possible during her internship.

Chapter 15: Intermezzo

(Jenny was startled when Chidwi leapt up onto her shoulder. Chidwi had been frolicking in the garden, as she often did when Jenny was reading.

"Jenny, your tummy is unhappy," Chidwi sent, sounding a lot like a mama scolding her child. "You haven't eaten your supper. I know reading about Lizzie and Ynni is nice. You are learning many things. But Lizzie and Ynni would be upset with you if you made yourself sick by not eating. Come. Eat supper on the patio in the open air. Breathe. Remember breathing?"

Jenny blushed and marked her place, taking care not to damage any of the delicate yellowed pages. It occurred to her that Chidwi had gotten some instructions from Burt about her. Although she knew this was for her own good and they cared about her, it still was a bit humbling to know that she needed such care.

She certainly was intensely absorbed in reading the journals, even more so now that so much depended on her and her future decisions. She felt that the one way she could continue her training while recuperating from "the shout" was by vicariously experiencing Lizzie's journey as an agent and a gate guardian. Perhaps at some point she would have enough experience on her own, but for now she was entirely dependent on the experience and understanding of others around her.

Her own recent history had taught her that she might not always have the benefit of easy contact with her advisors in every situation, however, so she was anxious to move forward as quickly as she could in her training, even if it was mostly "on the job."

She obediently followed Chidwi out to the patio, where Lizziebot had laid the little table with a salad, a sandwich, and her favorite pink lemonade, still cold, with condensation running down the sides of the glass.

As Jenny sat there and watched Chidwi perch herself on the opposite side of the table in front of a bowl of fruit and raw vegetables, she sighed. As was her habit, she took a moment of silence to show appreciation for the meal that was laid before her and for the many blessings of her life.

And despite all of the adventures she had personally experienced so far, she did indeed feel blessed. Despite a lot of pain, uncertainty, and the fright she had gone through in the short time since she was first handed the keys to the little house on Infinity Loop, she had still gotten so much out of it.

She and Burt had found one another. She had many great and faithful friends and colleagues. She had connected with Tarafau and his family on a very personal level. She had become great friends with Bob, her "bonus dad," as he called himself. In fact, she realized that despite all of the seemingly negative things she had been through, she was actually much better off than she had been.

And then there was Sam. Such a sad outcome to what Jenny once thought had been a friendship so close that she thought of Sam as more like a sister than just a friend. True, in the end, Sam had done the only thing she could think of to redeem herself; and Jenny knew, via Miriha, that Sam had felt deep remorse before she had sacrificed herself to destroy the evil Gall. Nevertheless, she couldn't help to continue to mourn the loss of her friend on both levels.

Now, as she ate her lunch, with Chidwi munching delicately and happily across from her, she couldn't help but wish that at least that part of her adventure had been different.

"Jenny is sad, but she is loved. The sun is shining, and Sam is only continuing her journey in a different dimension. Jenny wants Sam to be happy, yes? Sam is moving forward to her own happiness, and someday Jenny will know this."

Jenny cocked her head. "You understand these things much better than I do, Chidwi. How is it that your people know so much?"

"Linklings are born with good thoughts and good memories. We hear the minds around us and we are given the memories of our past parents and their parents down marches of time. Humans must learn these things. We are born with them. You will know when you are ready and when you choose to remember."

Jenny shook her head. She often felt like Chidwi was so much wiser and smarter than she could ever be, even though she was extremely meek and humble in her approach to Jenny.

Chidwi chuckled her giggly little laugh. "Jenny is smart. Jenny is good. You will see. Chidwi chose Jenny because we need one another. You will see..." she repeated, and Jenny couldn't help but smile.

As she finished her meal and collected the plates and utensils to take into the kitchen, Chidwi sprang up onto her shoulder, crooning happily to herself.

Jenny stopped and stretched, realizing that Chidwi had advised breathing and that she hadn't done her breathing exercises at all today in her rush to get back to the journal. So, she sat cross legged on the floor, settled into a relaxed position and breathed, taking herself deep into her REM state. By the time she came out of it, she did feel much more rested and energized.

She got back into her chair and picked up the journal, feeling much better prepared to find out what happened next.)

Lizzie placed the little seedling gently into the slot with soft rubbery sides, taking care to be sure the tiny roots were properly submerged into the nutrient solution. A long row of these extended down the planting room. Reloi worked across the planter from her.

"How often do you do this?" she asked, noticing how his seedlings seemed to float of their own volition into the slots in front of him. She really wished she could get the hang of the whole mind kinetics thing he was trying to teach her.

"Except in planting season, the plants generally only need weekly tending, mostly checking for those things that are ready to harvest. Of course, this kind of farming eliminates the need for pest control or weeding.

"Planting season for each type of plant varies. For instance, some vegetables like the leafy kind used in salads are harvested a leaf at a time at need. Some need to be harvested monthly or weekly, and often we do sequential planting that spaces a planting a few weeks apart to give a continual supply of a particular vegetable that doesn't keep well.

"Generally, the way we do things means we don't need much in the way of preservation or refrigeration, as we nearly always harvest the vegetables directly from the aquaponics to the kitchen.

"Obviously, some things, such as fruiting trees that require more space and need to be in soil, have their own planting and harvest times. Those things still need to be preserved, most often dehydrated or freeze dried for out of season use."

Lizzie nodded. She found the planting a peaceful activity, allowing her to enjoy the atmosphere of the plants at different stages all around her while allowing her mind to engage in other things.

This had become part of her morning routine. Ynni perched happily on her shoulder, crooning softly to herself, something she tended to do when contemplating things, she didn't always share with Lizzie.

As they completed their task and moved up into the hallway of the apartment building leading to Lizzie and Tarafau's apartment, they met Tarafau coming through the main door from the outside. He had gone out to help with a detail that had been clearing an area just outside the town for a new school building. It appeared that the town was growing, albeit somewhat slowly compared to what Lizzie had seen on Earth.

"Workout and then showers," Tarafau sent. They all trooped into the community room of the apartment, a place where the occupants could engage in various recreational activities or just sit and talk or read. This time of the morning, the room was usually vacant as the other occupants were engaged in work and school activities.

The outer edges of the room held furniture arranged for conversation groups while the inner part of the floor was empty, a perfect place for Tarafau, Lizzie, and Reloi to do their breathing exercises and then for Tarafau and Lizzie to do their quarterstaff forms. They didn't spar here, as Reloi's people were pacific and wouldn't have understood the need.

They did go out and do a jog around the town square afterwards. By the time they had returned, showered, and dressed, it was still early in the day. They had a meeting with the supervisors of the educational system today, something Lizzie had been looking forward to.

Ynni and Tanata had evidently become good friends in the short time they had been here and now chittered to one another, somehow having overcome the need for mindspeech. It was funny to see them, both so very different from each other and so accepting of their differences. Lizzie found herself wishing the citizens of Earth could learn that one important mindset.

When they were ready to go, Ynni and Tanata resumed their usual perches on Lizzie and Reloi, and the four of them, along with Tarafau, set out to meet with what Lizzie kept thinking of as the "school board."

They arrived on a very interesting campus. Somehow Lizzie had expected it to be much like her college campus at home, but every age range seemed to be accommodated here. From the youngest children (what she might have thought of as nursery school) up to students who seemed to be obviously more the same age as Lizzie, and even some students who appeared to be well past middle age.

They walked into the administration building, which also housed a gymnasium that doubled as an auditorium. The few offices at one end of the large building didn't seem to be very exclusive or impressive. The office they were escorted into looked a lot like Professor Cormier's little office, only slightly larger, enough that they all could find chairs around a conference table.

There wasn't a lot of shine or polish, but the furniture was well made and looked like it was fairly old, worn by much use.

The man and woman who greeted them were dressed in the usual flowing garments she had seen on nearly every resident of the town so far. Lizzie had to guess that the work clothes of laborers and farmers were probably a bit more utilitarian.

"Greetings," the male sent. *"I am Glath, and this is Beleen. We are honored to have you here, Lizzie, Tarafau, Reloi, and friends. Today you will have an opportunity to see what we are doing to educate and help our people progress and hopefully to survive. I am sure you will have many questions, but I ask you to hold them until we finish the tour."*

"We would ask you to sit," sent Beleen, *"but we have a lot to see today and want to give you plenty of time to meet the students and see the full range of our facilities. This is important, as your first assignment as an Alliance intern will be to teach some classes in those things that are allowed by the Alliance precepts."*

Lizzie was stunned. *Me? Teach? What?* She was grateful for her training in keeping her emotions concealed, for she was sure, if she had not been paying attention, pure shock would have shown on her face. Ynni sent her a mental chuckle, and Lizzie almost swatted at her for it.

Their hosts gestured back towards the door, and they proceeded immediately out of the admin building across the campus to another building obviously housing classrooms.

The first class was of the nursery level, but to Lizzie's surprise, there were not just a couple of nursery teachers, but several young people of varying ages interacting enthusiastically with the little ones. Some were reading to a circle of entranced listeners seated on a carpet. Some were building with blocks, and others were playing some kind of game that involved a lot of jumping up and down and giggling.

"We have found that one of the best ways to thoroughly learn something is to teach it to someone else. For the most part, our teachers take it in turns to instruct directly and then to supervise other students as they teach in small groups the various disciplines."

As they stood there, one of the little girls looked up from her blocks, looking directly at Lizzie. She jumped up and ran full tilt at Lizzie, her arms outstretched as she leapt up into Lizzie's arms, throwing her arms around Lizzie's neck and wrapping both legs around her waist. Lizzie had opened her arms reflexively at the last second as she realized what the girl was about to do. Now she stood, frankly dumbfounded, returning the enthusiastic embrace.

Ynni had jumped down from Lizzie's shoulder, chirruping in surprise, and the rest had just laughed at Lizzie's surprise and delight.

"Izzie!" the little one said aloud. Then in rapid mindspeech, *"We knew you were coming. We practiced your name. Did I do it right?"*

"Very well done. And what is your name?"

"I am Ephreni. I have five annuals now. We are glad you are here. Will you stay with us for a very long time?"

"I will be here for a while, and then I must return to my own home. But thank you for your welcome. It makes me happy to be here with you." And to her own surprise she knew she meant that sincerely.

She set Ephreni down gently, looking into wide violet eyes and noting that her hair was so white as to be nearly transparent. Other than that, she could have been any Earth child of five years old. Lizzie looked around her in astonishment. This was very different from any Earth school she had ever experienced or heard about.

"Would you like to help us show Lizzie the rest of the school, Ephreni? It can be your lesson in Socials today," Glath sent.

Ephreni beamed the kind of smile that can only be generated by the pure and honest soul of a child. *"May I? That would be wonderful!"* Then to Lizzie, *"Would that be all right with you?"*

"Of course, Ephreni. I would like that." Lizzie replied, impressed with the courteous question from such a young one.

Beleen gestured for them to follow her out the door into the hallway. As they emerged, a classroom appeared to be exiting a few doors down the hallway. Lizzie hadn't heard any bells ringing nor noticed any other classes leaving their rooms. She asked about class schedules, having forgotten about holding her questions to the end.

But Beleen answered her calmly. *"Classes are taught in a modular fashion with breaks in between modules. These breaks are determined by the instructors. There is no firm schedule, with the exception of the midday meal and the beginning of classes in the morning. The only time you will see all of the students out and about at the same time will be when we do a joint activity, usually once every week."*

Mindspeech interpreted week as a division of time periods, but not necessarily seven days, as on the Earth calendars. In the case of this planet, a week was the vague equivalent of nine Earth days. There were five weeks in their equivalent of a month. Tarafau's planet was similar, but with 8 days in a week and 5 of their weeks in a month. And in both cases the days varied in length.

Lizzie was sure there must be some way of coordinating all of these time differences in some kind of usable reference format. She made a mental note to ask Tarafau about it when she got the chance.

As they walked down the corridor, they entered what seemed like another random door. This room was something Lizzie recognized immediately as a library. Books (actually rolled scrolls) lined shelved walls, and many students sat at tables and in random chairs reading and writing quietly. It seemed to be a common theme among every culture with a written language to collect stories and reference materials in a public place.

Of course, not all people in any given culture had access to massive libraries such as the fabled Alexandria library, extending those privileges to only a few scholars and government officials. Lizzie had noticed, however, that cultures that made learning accessible to all citizens seemed to thrive in ways that those who restricted learning did not.

She looked around in awe, realizing that in a way she was restricted by her lack of understanding of the language these books were written in, and she began to understand how much her own literacy meant to her. She vowed, when she had time to spend on Earth, to use some of her resources to make literacy more accessible to more people in more places.

"Every school in every town in our planet has a library such as this, and even the parents of students and other citizens have access to every book we have on our shelves," Baleen explained, seeing Lizzie's longing look.

Sure enough, as Lizzie continued to look around, she realized, to her surprise, that some of those she had thought were students were actually mature adults.

They didn't pause here as much as Lizzie would have liked to, but she noticed the library had a space devoted to small children and some who looked to be of preschool age were sitting in a circle on the floor listening with wide eyes as an adult, dressed a little more colorfully than most of the adults Lizzie had met so far, told them a story with wide gestures and animated facial expressions.

They went from classroom to classroom, pausing to listen and watch the various activities for different age groups. Some of the classrooms looked almost typical of what Lizzie was used to at home, but she discovered that those classrooms were used only for studying individually, not for instruction. Students circulated in and out of these classrooms as needed at any given time.

As they paused in front of the admin building before viewing the Physical Education areas, Lizzie asked, *"And what do you expect me to teach here? I have no teaching credentials worth mentioning."*

"Credentials? What does that have to do with teaching? We have no dedicated or professional instructors here. Everyone in the community takes a turn, a month at a time, to teach here. Each brings with them their own experiences, skills, and wisdom. We teach not only thinking and basic skills, but life skills that will be necessary regardless of their future vocation," Beleen remarked, her eyes widening. *"It is not so on your world?"*

Lizzie shook her head, almost embarrassed to admit it. The way Beleen had put it, it seemed so obvious that this was the way to do it. Lizzie could see that each way had its merits, and she still had nothing but respect and gratitude for the professional teachers in her life.

They all tramped to the large, cleared field behind the school where people were working out. Some were playing a game with a large ball about two feet in diameter, rolling it back and forth with hands and feet in some kind of maze-like pattern cut into the sward. Others were doing what looked like a construction project, assembling the framework for a building.

"What is that?" Lizzie asked, pointing at the construction project. It reminded her of a rather expanded version of woodshop classes from her high school.

"They are building muscles, improving motor skills, and learning the rewards of effort and persistence. At some point, the walls they are constructing will be taken to a building site and assembled into a usable structure; a home or shop or other building needed by the community.

When it is done, they will be invited to the dedication of the building as one of the contributors."

Lizzie didn't know what to say. This was so very different from what she had expected. She could see where some of these principles could be very useful and effective if some of the educational communities on Earth chose to adopt them. And, since this wasn't technology, perhaps it would be okay for her to share them at some point with someone on Earth who had some influence.

Reloi, who had been somewhat subdued during the tour, now spoke up. *"I was thinking perhaps you could teach them something about your music, Lizzie. Also, I think they would enjoy interacting with Ynni and learning about the concept of a close-knit tribal community."*

"Music teacher? Me? I only doodle on the mbira, Reloi. I know practically nothing about music theory."

"Ah, and do you think that is so necessary? Perhaps you can teach them how to feel the music. Perhaps you can teach them to do as you have done. Obviously, making music isn't dependent on classical music training; otherwise, how would you have created such a loyal following in your concerts under 'our tree'?"

Glath's nearly transparent eyebrows shot up. *"Music? Our students would love this. Could you give us a sample?"*

"Play here? Now? I don't have my instrument with me." Lizzie fibbed, not wanting to extract it from the MDP in a public place.

"Then perhaps we will do a gathering tomorrow early on. It may inspire the students in their later classes," Beleen said, and as if she knew this was somewhat embarrassing to Lizzie, she continued with a mischievous glint in her eyes, *"I'm sure it will be instructive, regardless of your own opinion of your skill level. Remember that the role of a teacher is to expose students to new ideas, not to decide what they choose to do with the information you give them. Who knows where this may take some of them in the future?"*

"Yes, please!" Ephreni sent excitedly. *"Please will you play for us tomorrow?"* Her bright eyes peered earnestly into Lizzie's in a way that Lizzie could not say no.

"All right, I will. But I cannot guarantee how it will be received. I am myself only a musical doodler, as I said. I will do my best."

"Which is all any of us would ever expect from you or any other being," agreed Glath. *"Now that we have shown you the main areas of the school, I am sure you have questions, and we hope we will have answers for you. Let's adjourn to the picnic area where our culinary students have prepared a lunch for us, and we can relax and speak freely."*

He gestured to a young man who was waiting his turn at a game they were playing. *"Hefen, please escort Ephreni to the garden. I believe her classmates are tending the new shoots today."*

Ephreni looked a little disappointed at this, but she obediently followed Hefen away, turning to wave one more time to Lizzie with a sad smile. *"See you tomorrow!"* she sent before she turned to follow.

They walked down a short path and around the end of the building to an area that was populated with many tables, similar to any picnic table you might find on Earth, except that they were low and there were no benches or chairs. Instead, like Lizzie had seen at a Japanese restaurant in L.A., there was a space dug out under the table in which to put your feet. Obviously, they would be seated on the ground.

One table was already laden with a variety of dishes of the typical fare she had come to expect here, mostly raw foods consisting of vegetables and fruits, with some crackers Lizzie had become fond of, alongside every plate and a glass of water. At one end of the table was a tray set up like all of the other table settings, intended, as Lizzie saw, to sit on the arms of Reloi's hover chair.

The arms of his chair usually served well to hold a tray or desk when he was interacting with his tablet or reading. In this case they made a perfect platform for the food tray.

Once they had all seated themselves around the table, there was the usual moment of thankful silence, and then they all enjoyed the small feast that had been prepared for them.

"This was prepared by students?" Lizzie asked as she drizzled a light vinegary sauce onto the cooked portion of vegetables on her plate.

"Indeed. The students are actively engaged in running the school under the supervision of teachers and teacher helpers. They also help keep the school clean, work in the gardens inside and outside that provide their meals at the school, and assist the teachers of their younger classmates. The purpose of the school is to prepare them mentally, physically, and materially to live successful, productive, and creative lives," Beleen explained.

Lizzie thought about this. She knew that most educational institutions on Earth thought they were doing the same thing, but now she wondered again, if maybe some adjustments of how education was perceived and implemented would make a difference, especially for the full spectrum of different needs she had seen during her school years. This appeared to be designed to flexibly adjust the curriculum to suit the needs of the students.

"I was impressed with the way you allow the students to teach one another. I've seldom seen that in the schools where I come from. I know I could have learned a lot by teaching the things that came easily to me to those who were struggling with the same concepts. I think it would have also allowed me to connect with other students better. I was always ahead of my classmates and felt somewhat isolated throughout my school years.

"Has it always been this way in your schools, or is this some kind of advancement in education?" Lizzie asked.

Glath frowned for a moment and said, with an audible sigh, *"I wish I could say it had always been this way, but alas, it took the major disaster that led us to the core of our planet to allow us to see a better way. When we first arrived, there were no schools. We were too focused on just surviving.*

"We discovered that our young could do much more than we had realized to contribute to their communities, including caring for the younger ones and learning trades they never expected to pursue.

"Many parents began to teach their children separately and then started to combine lessons with other families. The current system evolved from the lessons we learned as a community. At present, almost all education within the planet operates in a similar way.

"It has decreased competition among our children and encourages teamwork. It also means that the entire community contributes to the success of our schools; no student is ever charged for their education, as even the students contribute in one form or another. Vocational training is accomplished through an organized apprenticeship program on several levels, up to journeyman and mastership.

"We try to expose our students to a wide range of skillsets, as well as courses in the arts taught by artisans in the community they live in, to allow them to make intelligent decisions as to what to pursue as contributing adults in their communities."

Lizzie nodded her head in agreement. That had been the one major irritant in her own educational experience. The fact that she couldn't get hands-on experience in the things she already had studied on her own and advance at her own pace had been a constant frustration for her.

Lizzie observed, *"I can see that much good has come from the disaster, even though I know it must have been horrible to have experienced at the time. Even, with the little I have been able to observe, so far, it appears that the changes you have made as a culture under difficult circumstances, have been, on the whole, beneficial to all of the survivors. It appears you are on a good track to thrive in your current circumstances. I am looking forward to learning more about your people and I hope I can contribute in some small way."*

"And now," Beleen sent, rising gracefully from the table and holding out a hand to Lizzie to help her up, *"I think we need to allow you to go on to the next briefing on your agenda, Lizzie. There is much to see. Can you be here tomorrow morning to introduce yourself to the student body and do a music demonstration for us?"*

"I will be happy to," Lizzie replied, although just the thought of playing in front of the entire student body made her a little weak in the knees.

"Thank you, Beleen and Glath," Reloi put in, levitating the tray from his chair to the table below. *"We appreciate the tour. It brings back wonderful memories for me. We look forward to tomorrow, then."* And after one and all did the finger touching gesture that was the equivalent of a handshake, they headed out to the street to move on to the next appointment.

Chapter 16: Music of the Heart

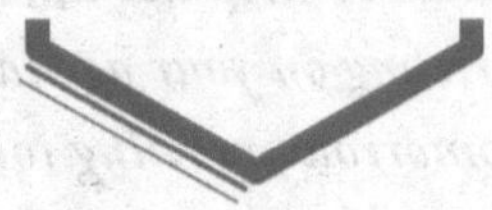

(Jenny lowered the journal into her lap, noticing with a smile that Chidwi had curled up next to Tidbit on the window seat, both of them basking in the waning sunlight. Jenny was beginning to realize more fully that she was building a family here in her little house on Infinity Loop, not to mention all of the many beings who had become an intrinsic part of her family circle... beings from all over the multiverse who had made such a huge difference for her.

She thought about Liliath and Cornelium, her two draconic friends, about the several Mookookie who were like little brothers and sisters, about the Groga family who had taken such gentle care of her after her accident during the rebellion on the Inseni planet, and about her loved ones who were all either gate guardians, agents of the Alliance, or blood relatives. In addition, she had acquired more family members by being adopted into Tarafau's family and then by Bob, who had offered to be a bonus dad.

And then there was Burt, the love of her life. It still came as a complete surprise to her that she had found him in this otherwise somewhat bizarre adventure. Every time she thought of him, a silly grin found its way onto her face. As newlyweds, their situation was definitely peculiar, since most of the time they only saw each other in Jenny's nighttime mental forays out into the dimensions.

Their favorite place to meet was still that little inlet on the Merced River. Jenny wasn't even sure if it was even there anymore. It had been a memory from Burt's childhood, but it made a romantic background to their nightly meetings. Funny how it all seemed so real to them, though.

Now, through the journals, seeing Lizzie going through some similar things, she realized how much more they had in common than she had ever expected. Reading the journals had proven to be an eye-opening experience. She found it difficult to put them down and felt an increased urgency to finish reading them before she was drawn back into the intense conflict ahead.

She felt she would finish this journal before the end of the week, if she continued to focus on it. And hopefully she could complete the third journal before her final week of recuperation was complete.

The intel she was receiving during her nightly check-ins with the Alliance told her that she couldn't afford even a single additional day beyond what the healers had required her to take, to allow her to recover from her episode with "The Shout."

She wasn't sorry she had made the decision to use it, but it had taken so much more out of her than she had expected. To be fair, however, Liliath and Miriha had both warned her of the dangers of this particular mental power. Historically, it had been used seldom over a range of hundreds of years. Few could even attempt it successfully, and more than one who had attempted it had either died or been permanently damaged by the outcome.

She had noticed there were many differences between her own abilities and Lizzie's. She recognized that each of them had learned much of what they knew how to do with their minds under very different circumstances, and intense need seemed to be the determining factor to acquire those skills.

Taking another glance at Tidbit and Chidwi, she picked up the journal, excited to read about Lizzie's concert for the school in Reloi's planet.)

The rest of the day had been taken up with a tour of a weaving craft cottage, which, of course was fascinating to Lizzie. It felt very familiar, as she had noticed the art of weaving seemed to be foundational in most cultures.

In it had been a number of huge looms that were turning out yards of fabric of various types, but there was no automation in evidence. Men and women of various ages operated the looms, using hands and feet to rapidly move the heddles and shuttles back and forth. The clackity-clack of the movement of the looms was like the beating of many hearts.

When she arrived home that evening, the rhythms of the looms were still echoing in her mind. Once again, she reminded herself of how much she owed to Gaston and his unusual training program. She still carried the frame loom she had created at that time in her MDP, along with some weaving supplies.

What would she be doing right now if she hadn't taken Gaston up on his offer? She shuddered, thinking of day after day, sitting in classes on subjects she could have taught from the front of the room, bored to tears by the suffocatingly slow pace of instruction. She knew she still would have had years of boredom ahead of her before she would have been allowed actual hands-on experience in the sciences.

And here she was, deep into an internship that would eventually allow her access to the entire multiverse and its diversity. She was experiencing sciences beyond anything yet dreamed of by Earthly scientists; and she was allowed not only to study them, but to actively participate in them.

Yet, she could also now appreciate the innovation of simple things, like the tools of the weaver's trade, due to the early projects Gaston had given her when testing her for the qualities that would be necessary in her occupation with the Alliance.

She discovered feelings she had never anticipated prior to her time at the Alliance agent training center. She found herself bonding with those feelings and beginning to feel at home amongst them.

Reloi's people were generally hospitable and welcoming to Lizzie and Tarafau and Ynni. When she had revisited the school to do a demonstration of her "doodling" on the mbira with the aid of Ynni's crooning descant, she had been received with enthusiasm. The enraptured looks on the faces of the students, ranging in age from what she would have thought of as kindergarten to students who might have been in junior college on Earth, made her wonder if there was more to her musical ramblings than she had supposed.

Afterwards, they were full of questions, and she had allowed some of them to actually handle the mbira and finger the keys. They were delighted to be able to pluck out some basic tunes and experience the connection between the instrument and their musical instincts.

"Is it magic?" one enthusiastic child had asked mentally, her violet eyes wide.

"Sometimes it feels like it is," Lizzie answered in agreement, *"but it isn't really magic."* And she had explained how the resonating chamber in the mbira made the sounds created by plucking the keys loud enough to hear. She demonstrated how each of the keys, by its length, made a completely different sound and how they were arranged in steps to allow one to choose the right notes to make a song.

One of the instructors had even asked to borrow the mbira with the idea of potentially creating a similar instrument.

She privately sent a query to Reloi about this, and he had reassured her that the mbira would not have been considered a restricted type of tech and that it would be allowed for her to accede to his request. So, she had lent Arpen, one of the cultural instructors for the middle year students, her mbira.

She did not display or play the kareena, the instrument Tarafau's people had given her, however. First of all, she had no idea how it worked, so she didn't feel it was appropriate in this situation. And secondly, she was sure the tech was beyond anything she had seen in this culture.

After the week of tours was finished, she was told it was time for her to meet with the council and receive her instructions and assignments for the remainder of her time in the planet. It was interesting to Lizzie how quickly that "in" had replaced the idea of "on" the planet.

Each day, as she went from town to town and met with the people who lived inside their planet by necessity, she felt more like the horizon tilting upward and the bright light that emanated constantly from the interior of the planet was normal. The fact that day and night were not discernable based on the rising and setting of a sun no longer made her feel uncomfortable.

At the beginning of every day and in the evening before retiring, Tarafau, Reloi, Lizzie, Ynni, and Tanata routinely got together for their breathing routine and then advanced mental exercises based mainly in Lizzie's inner mental world.

Afterward, she and Tarafau went through the forms for the quarterstaff, although they didn't spar. Lizzie could have gone through them in her sleep at this point, she was sure.

Before lunch they would go on a walk through a park or down a country lane, but the exercise was hardly needed, as most of Lizzie's assignments involved her working alongside people in various vocations. It turned out that a major part of her assignment by the council was for her to give them an unbiased evaluation of how the populace felt about their life in general and what needed to be done to improve their future, based on her experiences.

Lizzie had been stunned that something that important had been put into her hands. After all, in her culture she was just barely an adult. Nevertheless, with the encouragement of Reloi and Tarafau, not to mention the quiet confidence of Ynni, she agreed to make her best effort.

It had surprised Lizzie how adept all of the denizens of Grild were with mindspeech. Liliath had once told her that mindspeech didn't come naturally to all beings, but it was a fairly widespread ability in the multiverse. On Grild, they varied from speaking aloud to mind-speaking, shifting gears unconsciously from one to the other, depending on the conversation and who they were speaking with.

It was nice, then, to both hear them speaking aloud with one another and know she could still participate in the conversations, as Reloi was an adept simultaneous translator from his language into mindspeech.

She almost felt guilty that she was enjoying her "work" so much. It felt almost like a vacation from all of the intense work and study that had preceded this assignment.

It wasn't all work, but play was a part of this culture. At the end of a productive day there were many recreational activities, where communities gathered together to eat, sing, dance, and perform for one another. Lizzie had been glad she had lent her mbira to Arpen, deciding it was more pleasant to enjoy and show appreciation for others' performances than to perform herself.

Ynni was a favorite among the Grildites, especially the children, as she happily participated in their frivolity, especially the dancing and singing. Each week, they spent time in a different community and discovered that each had stories, songs, and dances that were unique to that area.

It seemed like the first month flew by, Lizzie going weekly to the council to report her observations and each time receiving a new assignment to a new community. She had discovered that although many of the older citizens were still adapting to the new environment, having been small children at the transition between surface and interior, the younger adults and children seemed content with their life.

Reloi's people typically lived somewhat longer than Earthlings, what Lizzie guessed to be the equivalent of a couple hundred years, on average. They had told her that their lifespans had been extended considerably after transitioning to the inner core, a phenomenon that still puzzled their lead scientists.

They visited several construction sites, marketplaces, and farming communities and attended community events. The farming communities were considerably smaller than Lizzie had expected. This was because nearly every home had a basement aquaponics unit, and most of the decorative plants around their homes and businesses served two purposes: to beautify the area, and to produce some kind of food or useful herb.

In each place, Lizzie had an opportunity to work alongside Grildites of all ages and vocations. Before she knew it, a Grild month had flown by. The longer she stayed there, the more she began to see the complexity of the task laid before her as an agent of the Alliance. It became very clear to her that her first responsibility was to get to know the people she was serving, and the best way to do that was to serve with them.

She didn't necessarily like every Grildite she met. Like Earthlings and other beings she had interacted with since joining the Alliance, they were all unique and displayed the full range of emotions and quirks you might expect.

A particularly grumpy teen she had worked with on a construction project seemed to think he was being inflicted with the most arduous tasks, more than anyone else on the project. He was sure he was being singled out. From Lizzie's viewpoint, it didn't appear he was doing more than anyone else on the crew, but he spent as much time murmuring and complaining as he did working.

His co-workers simply ignored it. It was obvious that they were used to his attitude and simply worked around him without reacting.

So, Lizzie said nothing, although she was itching to give him a sound talking to about his attitude.

She met creatives who spent part of their time working at some practical task and the rest of their time creating beautiful gardens, participating in community art projects, and performing arts of various kinds.

She was nearly at the end of the initial part of her internship when Tarafau woke her up one morning with a big catlike grin on his face.

"It's time for you to take a break. Amenia will be giving birth any time now, and she was hopeful that both of us would be present for the event. We'll only be gone for about a week, and then you will begin the other side of your apprenticeship, engaging actively in the affairs of the Grildite council. Get your things into your MDP and we can go. We'll breakfast at my house," he sent.

Lizzie rubbed her eyes and turned to Ynni, who was already up and jumping up and down excitedly. *"Go now? See family? Yes! Let's!"*

Lizzie couldn't help but smile. She realized that Ynni had been away from her babies for what must have felt like a very long time to her. She hadn't complained once, but Lizzie knew that no mother could be away from her children for long without regret. It was evidence of the strong link between them that she had opted to leave her little ones with their dad and aunt and the small tribe now inhabiting Tarafau's grove, in order to support Lizzie in her task.

Reloi met them just outside the apartment building. He smiled at them, perhaps a bit sadly, and sent, *"I don't want you to hurry your visit, however. when you return, we have much to do, as your active work with the council will begin from that time forward."*

"Thank you, Reloi. I will miss you and all of your people." It surprised Lizzie that she really meant this. She had grown to feel great affection to these beings who had seemed so strange to her in the beginning.

She reached out two fingers and touched his cheek, the customary greeting here, realizing he could not return the gesture. But Tanata reached out a tiny hand and touched two little fingers first to his cheek and then Ynni's. Ynni repeated this, and Tarafau put a hand on Lizzie's shoulder and Reloi and Tanata evaporated from her view, to be replaced by the yard in front of Tarafau's home.

Ynni leapt from Lizzie's shoulder to disappear around the house to the backyard, where her small tribe and her little ones waited. Lizzie laughed. She knew the linkling's longing had built up to a nearly fever pitch in the few minutes it had taken Lizzie to prepare to leave.

She and Tarafau entered into the living room and proceeded down the spiral stairway to the main living area, where Amenia stood behind a kitchen counter, stirring a pot of something that smelled like a hearty stew.

Her face lit up and she dropped the spoon into the pot with a happy cry. *"You are here! I was beginning to wonder if your assignment would cause you to miss it."*

As she rounded the counter, Lizzie saw that her belly preceded her. She walked with the typical waddle of a pregnant woman who was near to term.

She first gently hugged Lizzie and then turned and snuggled into Tarafau's muscled arms with a sigh. Tarafau bowed his head over hers and closed his eyes for a moment, a small tear trickling from the corner.

"I would never miss this for anything other than a major catastrophe, and perhaps not even then. You know that, my wife. We will be here for the birth and for some time after. Of course, Lizzie will need to return to her duties at some point, but for now, we will take a break and just enjoy what comes next," he sent.

Lizzie was surprised that he didn't make this mental comment private, but she presumed that part of this message was intended for her. Even then, she felt a bit embarrassed, as if she had intruded on a very private moment.

Amenia turned her face towards Lizzie, her smile glowing like a sunrise. Her long wavy brown hair, burnished with gold, was accented by large sea-green eyes, which often changed color to amber like her husband's, and her expressive eyebrows now arched inquiringly. *"Have you eaten yet?"* she sent. *"I have made a green drink for us to break your fast, and we also have a vegetable stew simmering for our afternoon meal. The rolls are about to come out of the oven. Sit, both of you."*

"If you show me where everything is, I can serve us," objected Lizzie. *"Should you be doing all of this so close...?"*

Amenia laughed, her tummy shaking and rippling with her mirth. Her eyes crinkling with amusement, she sent, *"My dear, my mother gave birth to me out in our vegetable garden. We don't pamper ourselves while we await a birth. I promise you this is no trouble. Please be seated."*

And, following Tarafau's example, she seated herself on the other side of the counter and meekly allowed Amenia to wait on her. The green drink that they typically had for breakfast was tasty and satisfying. Lizzie's nose, however, was much distracted by the aromas of baking bread and the bubbling stew as she finished her drink. She herself was not much of a cook, generally only doing as much meal preparation when she was on her own as she needed to in order to survive. In her time in the Alliance, her mealtimes had always been prepared by someone else, and she had been well fed. She had gotten used to eating well-prepared meals and began to wonder if maybe at some point she might want to learn to be a better cook.

Amenia and Tarafau chatted amiably in general mindspeech as they ate, catching up with one another's latest adventures. It must have been hard for them to be apart at this tender time, and once again Tarafau gained new respect in Lizzie's eyes for his dedication to his role as an Alliance guide and to her own ongoing education and protection.

"Shall we go out and greet the linklings then?" Amenia sent when they had all finished their breakfast. *"Ynni's little ones are coming along well, and it will be fun for them to see you."*

Lizzie agreed with enthusiasm and, after cleaning her mug and leaving it to dry, they all walked out into the sunny yard surrounded by the grove of trees.

Lizzie went to her favorite chaise, and Tarafau and Amenia settled themselves on either side of her. As if this had signaled the opening of a stage curtain, a crooning mass of linklings streamed down several trees all at once. The tribe had grown, with several new little ones, and as they encircled the chaises, Ynni came forward with her own scampering beside her.

"They have grown so much!" Ynni exclaimed, her chin held high and pride shining in her huge blue eyes. *"You would like to hold them?"* she inquired; her head cocked to one side.

"I would love that," Lizzie sent, stretching her arms wide to invite the little linklings up onto her lap.

They were so soft and so tiny, about half the size of Ynni and as light as if they almost had no weight at all. She had noticed that Ynni never seemed to be much of a weight even as she perched on her shoulder wherever they went. Her little ones almost seemed like they could float away.

Lizzie knew that Ynni was strong and sturdy. She had proven that more than once, but now Lizzie wondered if their bone structure was of a potentially different material than human bones, dense yet extremely lightweight.

There was so much she still didn't know about her little friend, and she began to think she had been very naïve to think she would ever have all of her questions answered. Every time she got one answer, a dozen more questions seemed to occur to her.

That being said, she was beginning to realize that there was so much more to life than what had ever considered. Her experiences in the Alliance were shifting her attitudes and sensitivities in a new direction. Slowly, she was beginning to make connections with the beings around her, caring more about others than she had done previously. And for some reason, that stray thought brought Reloi's face to her mind.

As she cuddled the little linklings on her lap and stroked their downlike chartreuse fur, she found herself wondering why she felt so connected to Reloi. The soft and kind look that was on his face when he had faded from her view now stuck in her head like the tune of a catchy song on the radio. She just couldn't get it out of her mind.

And now, watching Tarafau and Amenia passing looks back and forth, catching each other's eyes and smiling contentedly, she began to guess the intensity of the love they shared and suddenly felt a pang of loneliness.

She watched Ynni, gamboling happily with her loved ones, and noticed Rinn, reaching over to Ynni from time to time, lovingly patting her arm. Sympha, Ynni's sister, had since birthed babies of her own, and she and her sireling cuddled them joyfully. Several of the other linklings she had not yet met also had younglings, and all were obviously happy, crooning their delighted tunes that somehow seemed to effortlessly harmonize with the sync that could only have been developed with close ties.

As she sat there absentmindedly stroking the baby linklings, she felt tears begin to drip from her eyes for no reason she could think of.

Ynni scampered over to her, leapt up on the chaise, and reached up to touch the tears. *"Lizzie is sad? Lizzie not be sad. Lizzie is loved. Lizzie is with friends. New one comes, and it is a day of joy. Please do not be sad, Lizzie."*

The gentle pleading of Ynni brought fresh tears. What would she do if she ever lost Ynni? Right now, even though she felt accepted and connected to the beings that surrounded her here in the bright sunlight, she felt more than a little lost. And yet, the logical side of her mind could find no reason.

She sat up straighter, wiped her eyes, and gave gentle hugs to the little ones in her lap. *"I'm okay, Ynni. I don't know what came over me. I'm just being silly. I'm so sorry. Don't worry, I'll be all right."* She changed the subject. *"Mina and Gil have grown a lot. They are so sweet. I'm sure you have missed them while we have been gone. I hope in the future we will get to visit more often."*

Ynni shrugged her little shoulders, looking deeply into Lizzie's eyes. Lizzie knew Ynni was not fooled, but answered her, *"Mina and Gil are good little ones, and they are well cared for by family who love them. Lizzie has family who love her also. We can be joyous. And the new one comes."*

Lizzie nodded and looked over at Amenia, playing happily with a cooing little linkling, a twinkle in her deep green eyes. But it became evident that Ynni was not making a general statement, as all of a sudden Amenia's eyes went wide and her hand gripped her belly.

"We should make preparations. Our daughter is coming. She is rather insistent, as a matter of fact. I don't think I should move. Tarafau, you know what to do."

Tarafau nodded and ran to the house. Lizzie was stunned. They were going to have the baby here? Right now? In the middle of a field near a grove of trees? What about the hospital? What about a doctor or midwife?

"Should I do something, Amenia? Shouldn't you go to a hospital?"

Amenia shook her head. *"Tarafau knows what to do. This is not a medical condition. I'm just having a baby. Birthing is the most natural thing any woman can do. Tarafau has aided me in the birth of our older daughter and both of our boys. This daughter should be no different."*

Her mental voice was calm and her face serene, not even tensing as her belly rippled in a gentle rhythm beneath the light sundress she was wearing.

Tarafau returned immediately with a stack of towels, a clean sheet, and a small blanket that appeared to have been prepared well in advance for this very purpose.

"She will be born in the sunshine," he commented as he helped Amenia arrange the sheet under her on the chaise. He set the towels and blanket aside on the chaise next to her.

"If you would like to help," amended Amenia, *"you could stand behind me and give me your hands. It will help me when I am focusing on letting her out from her confinement. I know you have a firm grip, and that will work well as Tarafau guides her out into the world."*

All Lizzie could do was nod. What if they had delayed their return even an hour? Who would have helped Amenia? Her concern must have shown on her face. Amenia sent, *"Many of us give birth on our own. It is so nice to have you both here at this exciting time. It is so much nicer to be surrounded by those who care about you during a birth. Even the linklings are helping."* And she gave a tinkling laugh.

Lizzie noticed that the tone of the linklings' crooning had changed. It was soft and flowing, feeling very much like a lullaby. They stood in a semicircle around the chaises, holding hands and crooning, with their eyes raised to the sky.

Amenia's laugh turned to a grunt, however and she squeezed Lizzie's hands, not hurtfully, but firmly. Lizzie gripped her in return, trying to stay focused on helpful thoughts. *"You are strong,"* she sent. *"Your baby is healthy. We are all here for you."*

Amenia was breathing evenly and intentionally in the breathing patterns that Lizzie recognized so well. Tarafau kept up a soothing litany in their verbal language, and Lizzie was amazed at the quiet rhythm of the experience, like a mutual heartbeat.

Suddenly there was another being, another mind in the space where they all existed as one. The mind didn't have any words, only feelings, and Lizzie was surprised that she could sense this. In the past, mind speech had simply been a tool for translating speech into an easier way to communicate. But now, it was as if she was receiving more than words. It was feelings translated into concepts. Concepts like "light" and "warm" and, to her delighted surprise, "love" spilled into her mind as this new life separated from her mother.

Lizzie never noticed the cutting of the cord or even the change in Amenia's breathing. She was still mentally inside herself with the little mental voice that was being expressed from a newly minted mind.

Therefore, it was almost a shock when Amenia's mental voice intruded into her thoughts. *"Lizzie, would you like to hold Elizabeth?"*

"What? Who? Elizabeth?" she stammered mentally in return.

"Tarafau and I wish to name her with your formal name, if that is all right with you. She has a similar spirit, I think."

"I'm stunned, Amenia, and honored. Yes, I would like to hold her for a moment, although I don't have a lot of experience with babies."

Tarafau smiled, his amber eyes glittering in the sunlight. He gently passed the baby to Lizzie. It was a little awkward at first, but he helped her position her arms to cradle and support the tiny head, and suddenly it just felt right.

She looked into the green eyes, so much like her mother's, and the solemn little face looked up at her. Lizzie had no words, could think no discernable thoughts. All she could do was feel, deeply feel, the intense closeness, the gentle, innocent acceptance of this little one. Once again, the tears came, but this time they were tears of overwhelming peace and joy.

How could such a tiny little being, newly come into the world, have such an impact on her, she wondered. Awestruck, she looked up at Amenia. *"Thank you,"* she sent, *"Thank you so much. I have never felt so honored and humbled at once."*

"It has been and continues to be an honor to have you as a part of our family, Lizzie. Tarafau has often told me that despite your struggles and the times you don't agree with one another, he feels you are a daughter he would be proud to call his own. It is his hope, and mine, that she will grow up with your many strengths of character. I feel like you have yet many interesting and potentially difficult challenges ahead of you, but that you have the strength and integrity to meet them."

Lizzie didn't know what to say to this, so she looked back at Elizabeth. She almost didn't notice when Ynni hopped up onto her shoulder to also view the baby with great interest.

"Little one is beautiful like her mother," Ynni commented as she crooned gently to the baby.

"I don't understand, though," Lizzie sent to them. *"I thought labor preceding birth was a long, protracted and painful process. It looked like this took you only a few minutes, and you didn't seem to be in pain at all."*

"Of course, it wasn't as short as you may have thought. My body has been preparing for the birth for a few weeks now, gently positioning the child and building up the necessary hormones. I have also been active physically throughout the birth, strengthening the necessary muscles to allow my body to do the work to move the child through the birth canal.

"In addition, the breathing exercises make a huge difference in focusing on things other than immediate pain. For some, the birthing process can be very uncomfortable and sometimes painful, I am sure. I have never had that problem. You will find, as you continue to hone your mental skills, that you will also be able to control fear and pain to some extent. Some of us are better at it than others."

Lizzie considered this. Again and again, it came to her that diversity was one of the most consistent rules of the multiverse. Even on any single planet, no two beings were identical. Even Geln, her podmate, a joined mind being, had some variations in thought patterns and even facial expressions that indicated his/their feelings.

As she continued to gaze into Elizabeth's eyes, she felt an unexpected surge of emotion; mixed gratitude, awe, and affection for not only the drowsy infant in her arms but also all of those who had propelled her on this journey and given her the opportunity to experience so much more than anything she ever thought possible.

Elizabeth's eyes began to droop closed, and Lizzie sent to Amenia, *"I think she needs to sleep. Will you take her?"*

Tarafau helped Amenia to her feet, his eyes glistening with as yet unshed tears. He reached down to Lizzie to take the baby and place her gently in her mother's arms.

"You are welcome to either come inside or stay out here," sent Amenia gently. *"It appears you are thinking deeply and may need some time."*

"Thank you, Amenia. Yes. I think I'll stay out here with Ynni and her tribe for a bit. So much has happened in such a short time, and my brain is buzzing."

Amenia and Tarafau left together, his arm protectively around her as they escorted Elizabeth into their home.

Lizzie sat for a moment, just watching the linklings play with one another on the lawn between the arrayed chaises and the grove of trees that had become their home.

And where is my home? she mused to herself. She had no permanent place at Alliance headquarters. Even the pod building that was reserved for her and her podmates was temporary, as they would no longer be able to call it home once they received their final official certification as genuine Alliance Agents.

Of course, Gaston had told her that her little apartment at his lab would always be there for her, but it still was nothing she could consider permanent. She had barely left a mark on it. Anyone entering it would not be able to tell that anyone had ever actually lived there.

Would it be her lot to never have a place to call her own? She wasn't sure how she felt about that. About the only stable place she could think of right now was the place she had discovered in her mind through her mental training with the Alliance. It seemed to her that perhaps that would have to do for now.

The sun was gentle on her face, dappled slightly as it shone through the grove. The play of the light was mesmerizing, accented by the soft and contented harmonic crooning of the linklings around her. And as if that had triggered something, as a sleepiness fell over her, everything seemed to fade from her view, and she found herself in the park of the little town within her mind.

She strolled along the flower-bordered path towards the gazebo by the sparkling pond in the center of the park. She could see someone standing quietly, his back to her on the raised dais of the gazebo. Whoever it was, he was dressed in a formal-looking white suit.

She glanced down at herself and to her amazement saw she was wearing a simple white dress, conservatively cut, that ended at mid-calf. Her hand went to her neck and beneath the agent's necklace with its infinity symbol was a short string of white pearls that swooped just above the slightly scooped neckline.

She frowned. This was nothing like anything she had ever had in her wardrobe. The closest thing to it had been a party dress her mother had made for her when she was twelve and went to her first junior high school dance. After that, she had confined her wardrobe to blouses, shirts, and pants, with an occasional skirt, as she really didn't care much for dresses.

But here she was, dressed up and approaching someone who had also done the same. As she drew closer, she realized that his head was devoid of hair, and an unexpected feeling of anticipation began to build within her, somewhere between her heart and her stomach.

When she was nearly there, he turned to face her, his face wreathed in a tender smile. His spiky silvery eyebrows were raised happily, and his violet eyes danced with what could only be described as pure joy.

He held a hand out to her. She had only seen him thus in her mental world. But somehow it had never mattered much to her that his natural form didn't include arms and legs. She could have accepted him either way, and she knew she had not understood her feelings for him, because they had been new to her, and her heart seemed to swell within her.

As she approached, she mirrored his gesture, reaching out to him in a way she had never done before, her hand being only an extension of her heart.

As their hands touched, he said to her, "I wish we could have had many, so many, years before this. I wish I had been given eons with you, an eternity to be two hearts knit into one, beating in sync beyond the bounds of time and space, life and death. You have brought light into my life I never thought possible. Can I possibly hope you feel the same?"

Lizzie didn't answer right away. Gazing into his amazing eyes, she wondered how she had ever not noticed how her feelings had been growing. There had been no romantic encounters, no dates, no tender conversations. He had never brought her flowers or gifts. She had never spent hours doodling his name on random pieces of paper like many of her friends in school had done. And yet, working alongside him in his native world, meeting his people and his family, seeing his kindness and his wisdom and surprising sense of humor had been working some kind of magic unknown to her.

"I am new to these feelings," she confessed shyly, but still looking into his eyes. "I am also somewhat confused by them." His spiky eyebrows knitted in concern. She rushed on.

"I'm not saying I don't feel more deeply for you than I realized, but I'm not sure how to respond. And why now, when we are so far away from each other?"

He smiled, an ironic twist to his mouth. "I wanted to tell you as a 'whole' person, and there was no time while you were in Grild. Also, I admit that I was concerned I might embarrass you and that it would make working together awkward. This way, you can have some space between now and when you return, to consider."

"Wait," Lizzie said, suddenly understanding what he was saying. "I thought maybe I was dreaming this or making this up. Is this real? If so, how are you doing this?"

"Ah, something I hadn't revealed and that few people know. I discovered this about the same time I developed kinetic abilities. I can communicate across dimensions. Since I had connected mentally to you previously, I have the 'coordinates' to allow me to reach you wherever you are physically. Although that's not an accurate word. Coordinates is a simplistic concept on a dimensional level. But it works for this conversation.

"No one I've talked to can explain to me how this is possible. Evidently it is a rare, almost unheard of, ability."

He blushed. "I don't think it works both ways, unfortunately. If it is uncomfortable for you, I won't do it again, and you need not answer my question immediately. I don't wish to pressure you, and it may even be inappropriate, since we work together, for me to say anything about it at all, but I realized when you had left that I could no longer restrain myself."

Lizzie shook her head and then smiled up at him, for in this state he was taller than she was. "I'm not offended, just a bit surprised. I simply had never considered anyone would ever care for me in this way. I'm not exactly a loveable person, after all."

He laughed out loud. "You? Unlovable? Who has ever told you that was the case? Show them to me!"

"No, nobody ever actually said that to me. I just always assumed…"

"Well, I hate to say it, because you are almost always right but, in this case, you were dead wrong. Absolutely and completely, utterly wrong." He opened his arms to her and she nearly dove into them. He cradled her head on his chest with a sigh.

"I wish I could do this when we are together, hold you in real arms like this."

"If we were together in person, I would do it for both of us. Your physical uniqueness has nothing to do with how I feel about you."

"Ah… so you *do* feel something for me!" he said with a delighted chuckle.

"I suppose I do," Lizzie replied with wonder in her voice. "I really think I do. But this is a little much to take in all at once, especially since I don't think I've ever been through this before. Can you come again to see me? Especially since I can't return the favor.…"

He laughed again, delight in every feature of his face. "I think I can manage it, but only if you really want me to."

"I think I really do," she replied shyly. "I'm sure I really do," she said more assuredly.

He leaned forward and kissed her briefly on her forehead. "As you wish." And with that, the vision disappeared, and she found herself looking once again into the dappled sunlight in Tarafau's grove.

Chapter 17: Finding Resonance

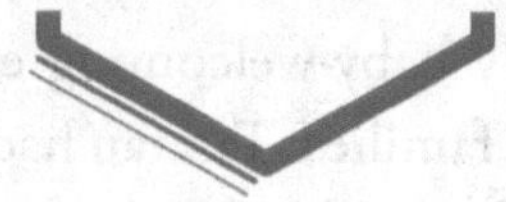

(Jenny wiped her eyes on her sleeve, glad there was no one in the sunny living room with her. She had known Lizzie had never married and had often wondered if Lizzie was just one of those people who didn't make those kinds of connections.

Before getting to this point in the journals, she had been convinced she had been right about that. Somehow, she kept forgetting that during this stage of Lizzie's life, she was about the same age as herself, perhaps a bit younger. And hadn't it taken her what felt like forever to find Burt?

The revelation that Reloi could do a version of what she did herself was a bit startling as well. Of course, he hadn't had the same need for it as she had, but it was incredibly romantic to her to note that he had chosen to use his talent for communication across dimensions distinctly for the purpose of connecting with Lizzie.

Remembering her own dalliances with Burt by the little pool on the Merced River and where it had led them as a couple, she smiled through her tender tears. In the quiet of her home, she eagerly turned the pages to uncover the mystery of why no one seemed to remember this thing about Lizzie, or if they had, why she had never been told about it. And why hadn't she known about Reloi's talent?)

Tarafau had told Lizzie before they had begun their internship in Grild that when the baby was born, he would be taking her to stay with him and Amenia for at least a week's break. It had been understood by the Grild council that this would be the case. At the time, she had been looking forward to it somewhat; but since her first long-distance mental communication with Reloi, she now felt restless.

It wasn't like there was nothing to do. She did her usual mental and physical workouts with Amenia and Tarafau, played with the linklings, and attended various Daringi events. She had gotten to participate in the family baby-welcoming event with Tarafau and Amenia's boys and their families. Tarafau had confided to her at one point that they also had an older daughter who was currently away on a mission of sorts, but was out of reach of any communication, so they were glad to have Lizzie there, symbolic of the daughter who was absent.

What had sounded like a reasonable break when Lizzie had first agreed to it, now became a bit of a burden. At this time, she could think of little else than returning to Grild to continue her internship. Not only had she become very engaged with the people in Reloi's planet, but she now yearned to return to be with Reloi, face to face.

Although she enjoyed their time together on the mental plane, it could not replace the need she felt to be with him in the real world. At first, he had only appeared to her in his imaginary state of a complete body with healthy limbs, but eventually she had requested that he come as himself, the way he really was.

She remembered with fondness the tears that had glimmered in his startling violet eyes when she had made that request and he had instantly transformed, hoverchair and all, into the Reloi she had come to care for.

During the day throughout the seemingly endless time at Tarafau and Amenia's home, she found her mind drifting to him and to the culture that surrounded him that she had grown to respect and delight in.

How can this be? What is happening to me? What can possibly come of this? Since when are you a silly love-struck child with nothing better to do with your mind than to day dream about a man whose origins are so alien from your own? What would your parents say about this?

But she had no answers for any of these thoughts. All she knew was that any time her mind was not fully engaged with people in active conversation, she found her thoughts drifting once again to Grild.

Even watching the linklings play or caring for Elizabeth while Amenia cooked or cleaned didn't seem to consume her as it normally might have. If anything, she found herself feeling wistful, noticing the close ties between the linklings or Amenia, Tarafau, and their newborn.

It startled her then, after one of their usual morning mental training sessions, when Amenia sent to her, *"What is troubling you, Lizzie? There is a melancholy aspect to your mental voice these days. Perhaps it would help to talk to someone about it?"*

"I'm honestly not sure. Something is changing inside me, and I don't completely understand it."

"Like what? Is it the baby or has this been coming on for a while?"

"I don't think it's Elizabeth, although she could be part of it, I suppose. It's just that there is something I can't stop thinking about, and it's beginning to wear on me. It might be a good thing, but there is so much more to it than it seems on the surface...." Lizzie trailed off.

"Ah.... I see. What is his name?" Amenia sent with a gentle smile.

"Pardon? His name?"

"This is about a young man, unless I have read the signs amiss. Am I wrong?"

Lizzie sighed and rolled her eyes. *"How did you know when I don't even know for sure myself?"*

"You're not the first young lady I've seen like this. Your eyes seem to stay wide in surprise. You seem nervous for no particular reason, and you seem to spend a lot of time staring off into space. You're distracted in a way that is not normal to your personality. In short, you are either

infatuated or in love; but either way, the signs are unmistakable." And she chuckled at the surprise on Lizzie's face and the shake of her head.

"Me? In love? Jiminy Cricket!"

"It's not fatal, my dear Lizzie. Most of us survive it."

"No," Lizzie countered. *"I'm a scientist. I'm an agent! I can't be in love. I have things to do!"*

Amenia didn't just chuckle now. She laughed heartily, wiping her eyes and holding her sides.

Lizzie didn't know how to respond to this. She just sat there and stared until Amenia laughed herself out. When she finally paused and caught her breath she sent, *"I'm sorry. It's just that love is one of the few things one hardly ever plans for. It happens, and then you deal with it. Nothing you can do can prepare you for it. It defies all the logical impulses and rational timelines you may have made in the past, and it will affect your future for the rest of your life."*

"It's... it's Reloi! He's been visiting me every night since I've been here, mentally, saying such things I never thought to hear from a man. Nothing untoward or inappropriate, I assure you," she added quickly. And the rest just rushed out in a stream of thought. *"It's just that he has come to care for me deeply. We talk about things that are important to each of us, and he is a good listener. We both think very much like one another and believe many of the same things, even though we were raised in cultures completely alien to one another.*

"He is worried there is a conflict between how he feels and his role as my instructor, and he knows there is a huge difference in our ages, but I don't feel that this should be a problem if we care for one another. And I do care for him. It's been coming on for a long time, since we first started training together at the agent training camp.

"He also worries about the fact that he has no arms or legs and how that might potentially disgust me. But I don't care about that. I just find any minute not in his presence as a wasted minute that I can never

recall. Oh, Amenia! What am I to do? How can I ever figure this all out?"

And then, Amenia's arm was around her shoulder, and she held her close while Lizzie wept. What seemed a long time later, she dried her eyes and sat up, realizing Amenia's shirt was wet with her tears.

"I never used to cry! What's happening to me? First, my Alliance apprenticeship, and now this. I'm turning into a big old crybaby!" Lizzie sent, distressed that she could be so very weak.

Amenia smiled and gave her another one-armed hug and sent, *"You're growing up. Tears aren't a weakness when they are genuine. It's just stress leaving the body. Now, here's what you and I will do. First, this is between you and me. Tarafau isn't here, and we don't need to say anything to him, although he would completely understand, if you decided to tell him.*

"Second, you will go take your shower and dress nicely, and we will take Elizabeth out to the Apex, as it is time to get her some new clothes, since she will soon grow out of most of the things I had prepared for her. Then we will eat lunch and watch some of the performers. Then we will see. Off with you! It will all work out, one way or another, but in the meantime, let's just do what good friends do."

And this they did. Amenia put Elizabeth into a sling-like carrier that snuggled the baby on her chest, leaving her hands free. It was made of bright multicolor cloth that was both lightweight and strong. It coordinated well with her choice of a loose-fitting tunic and skirt of bright matching colors.

As they walked along in the sunlight and crested the hill overlooking the valley that housed the Apex, Lizzie reveled in the view. The crystalline top of the huge pyramid sparkled like a jewel in the sunlight.

During Lizzie's initial internship there, she had made many friends in the community, and so it was enjoyable, as they walked towards the Apex along the wide boulevard, to greet and be greeted by various beings going about their daily lives. The Daringi city was a hub for the many varied intelligent species on their planet, and each of them had a different language, so the common tongue was actually mindspeech, a thing for which Lizzie was grateful.

Once in the Apex, Amenia guided them through the various market shops, searching for some larger clothing for her daughter and chatting the entire time in mindspeech with Lizzie as they searched for just the right little outfits for the beautiful little baby girl.

It surprised Lizzie that it actually lifted her spirits and, for several blissful hours, she was able to distance herself from her fears and doubts concerning the status of her relationship with Reloi.

They had a sumptuous lunch and watched performances of various types from the balcony that overlooked the marketplace. All in all, by the time they walked back home, Lizzie was glad to retire to the grove to visit with the linklings.

She had purchased some fruit to share with them that Ynni particularly enjoyed, and they gathered happily around her as she leaned back in her favorite chaise facing into the trees. It was comical to see Ynni solemnly doling out the fruit, overseeing her tribe to be sure that every member received their fair share.

Afterwards, with full tummies and happy tastebuds, they danced and frolicked together, the males sometimes wrestling with one another in mock combat and the females chittering at them, egging them on to greater efforts.

Ynni scrambled up onto her lap, looking intently into Lizzie's face. *"Lizzie is better? Ynni worries for you. You miss your friend, Reloi, and yet something in your mind is rejecting his offers of love and kindness. Ynni does not understand. How can you think both things?"*

Lizzie chuckled at her puzzled expression. *"Humans are strange that way, I suppose, Ynni."* And she sighed. *"Am I being silly? I didn't realize I could be such a coward, but I'm actually afraid of getting distracted by a close relationship and attached to someone who then becomes a new responsibility. I don't know how to put it any clearer than that. It wasn't until I became involved in the Alliance that I ever felt any real closeness to the people around me.*

"Even my family are not as close to me as I would like—or, I should say, I'm not as close to them as I would like to be. They've never neglected me or been anything but loving to me, but I was always locked into my head, driven by curiosity and the need to 'know' things; how things worked and what I could do about that."

Ynni threw her furry arms around Lizzie's neck, crooning to her as she did to her little ones. She stroked the back of Lizzie's hair and sent, *"Lizzie is not lacking. Lizzie is growing, becoming more of herself. This has always been there, in your heart, dear Lizzie. Let it grow. Be who you are, because who you are is marvelous to me. This is why Ynni linked to you from the beginning. This is why our link will never break."*

Lizzie felt her heart warm at Ynni's words; and so, when Reloi joined her again that night after she had retired to her room and settled herself in her bed, she realized she had also settled her heart. Perhaps there was room in her life, after all, for the love he offered so freely.

Chapter 18: A Thread of Melody

(Jenny heard the door to the gate office open and close in the hallway. She carefully closed the journal, still stunned by this aspect of her aunt's life. She almost felt like she was intruding on something intensely private.

Bob, Burt, and Merv strode purposefully into the living room, their faces, somber.

"What's happening?" she exclaimed, placing the journal back in its place on the side table next to the remains of her lunch. At the same time, Tidbit strolled in through the open patio door, Chidwi at his side, as if they had been summoned.

The three of them sat side by side on the couch across from her, while Tidbit and Chidwi both leapt up onto the window seat waiting expectantly. Jenny assumed Chidwi had read their minds as they had come into the house and had alerted Tidbit. For a moment no one spoke.

"The main Inseni planet is in a complete uproar. One of the remaining generals has apparently taken over for Gall, and there is a major, very bloody housecleaning going on, not only on the planet but on several other planets that are currently held by the Inseni. It appears, based on our communications via the Mookookie still on the planet, that they are planning on a raid and re-capturing of the Groga," Burt reported, Merv and Bob both nodding in gruff agreement.

Jenny gasped, and Chidwi jumped from the window seat and laid a soft gentle hand on Jenny's leg before scampering up onto her lap and finally up to her shoulder, where she perched, one soft hand on the back of her neck.

"I assume the council is on top of this?" she asked hopefully.

"Of course, and we could have waited to give you the news when you did the next update, but we felt you might be able to handle it better if you had some actual support. I promise you action is being taken, but you needed to know, as Gatekeeper, that there will be intense and constant use of the gates, even more than usual, even with everything we have been doing to prepare for the rescue of the Insenium-infested dimensions already planned," Burt assured her.

"Maybe I should cut my recuperation time a little bit short? I'm feeling much better. Honestly, I am."

All three of them shook their heads in unison.

"Absolutely not," Bob interjected vehemently. "The healers at headquarters are adamant that you need this time, and we agree. Even when you come back on duty, you will need to be careful with yourself. No one in living memory has ever survived 'the shout,' and they don't want to take any chances with you."

"No, don't give me that look," put in Burt. "This isn't negotiable. Besides the fact that we all care about you, your continued survival is key. No one else has the abilities you do, that allow us direct instantaneous communication across dimensions, and that will be critical to any chance we have of ever defeating the Insenium. Besides," he continued with a mischievous grin, "Chidwi would miss you...."

Jenny shook her head in defeat. "Okay, guys, but now what happens?"

"The council will brief you when you mentally check in tonight at your usual time. They will continue to keep you up to date, as normal, and they will still need you to do some mental check-ins with various parts of the team once a day unless there is an urgent need for something more pressing. As Burt said, the reason we came to tell you now in person was more for moral support than anything else," Mervin insisted.

"We have a little time," Bob broke in. "Maybe some lemonade or root beer out on the patio? We do need to get back soon. Cornelium will be fuming if I'm gone for too long. And Merv promised to look over our calculations for—" he paused and cleared his throat. "Well, nothing you need to worry about at the moment. So, root beer or lemonade?"

Merv and Bob both looked a little sheepish. Obviously, the reference to "calculations" was a slip of the tongue. Burt stood and reached for her hand and, holding hands, Jenny led the way out while Bob and Merv rummaged in the fridge for the drinks.

It was a pleasant interlude, and Jenny was happy for the small talk and general catch up with these three who had become fast friends. It was good to see Bob in his element. And of course, she couldn't get enough of holding Burt's hand while each of them held their drinks in the opposite hand. She found herself feeling deep sympathy for her aunt. What might take the place of hand-holding with someone who had no hands?

After they had finished their drinks and Lizziebot had cleared up after them, hugs for all ensued, Burt kissed Jenny with gusto, and they left back through the door in the hallway to each of their assignments.

As she returned to the living room and settled into her reading chair, she contemplated what an amazing thing a hug was. She, like Lizzie, hadn't been much of a hugger before she got involved in the Alliance, but now it was a comfortable and friendly thing she had begun to take for granted.

Her life had changed so radically in the past year or so that she wasn't even sure she remotely resembled the young woman who had inherited this incredible house and all of the things that went with it.

As she opened the journal, even more than before she began to empathize with the changes Lizzie was going through and to relate to her obvious confusion about them.)

Lizzie was surprised to find that newborn babies, apart from being cute and cuddly, were actually kind of boring. Elizabeth pretty much did three things: she ate, she messed herself, and she slept. Since Amenia did most of the care of the baby, Lizzie found herself spending more time either working out or playing with the linkling tribe.

She had taken out the amazing kinetic instrument one day by the grove and had started to play, letting her mind drift back to those days under the tree by the pod as she and Gi had begun their spontaneous concerts to the delight of her podmates and the other agent trainees.

As she did so, the linklings gathered almost immediately around her, crooning in complex harmonies along with her "doodlings," as she called her extemporaneous musical wanderings. It set her to wondering, as she continued, how the linklings managed to do that. After all, she wasn't playing from any sheet music or creating a song from memory. Her tunes were random and created entirely from her feelings at the time.

Then, she remembered that day on Gi's planet where all speech was actually musical notes and how they were never cacophonous or clashing, but always harmonized.

It came to her, as her little voicestra of crooning linklings continued to anticipate her musical wanderings, that all linklings could read minds; and even though she wasn't consciously creating the tunes she was playing, they could feel the notes in her head as she played.

Astoundingly she also realized that, although Gi had never mentioned it, to some extent she and her people must have had similar abilities. It was the only explanation she could think of that would allow their intricate and perfect harmonies. No wonder Gi was so quick to pick up on her impromptu little concerts and why the three of them had made such amazing music together.

Suddenly she noticed there was another chorus of voices in her mind singing in breezy, breath-filled tones along with her and the linklings. It was the trees and plants around her! And one booming mental voice sent to her, *"You caught us, little sister! We have been listening in for a while now and could no longer resist the urge to join your joyful sounds."*

"I hope it wasn't disturbing you. I just missed it so much, and I miss my friends and our tree," she sent back timidly.

"Not at all, not at all! Please continue, and we will make music of light and wind and green things, together with your music of heart and thought."

And so, they did. Lizzie couldn't have said how long they swelled the chorus of glad and beautiful voices, but she almost jumped when Amenia's mind voice sent to her, *"We thought we might eat outside today. We don't have you here for much longer, and it is obvious the grove is dear to you. Is that okay?"*

"Oh yes! Sorry, I didn't notice you until you spoke. I guess I got a little carried away."

For the next week before she and Tarafau were to depart for Grild, they took all of their meals outside with the linklings and the joyful trees, the evening concert becoming a new tradition in the grove, just as it had been at the pod.

And every night during that time, before she would go to sleep, she would spend time with Reloi. They didn't do much, mostly just chatted about people they both knew, both from the training center and Reloi's community. It became more and more comfortable for them to just talk about seemingly inconsequential things, a friendly chat while strolling through the little park in Lizzie's mental village square.

They found things to laugh about while Tanata and Ynni frolicked in the background. She now often also spoke with the tree she had first contacted, what seemed so long ago, who had taken an interest in the goings on of the humans who had the unusual gift to speak with the plants around them.

It actually surprised her, therefore, when Tarafau ended their meal one evening with, *"We'll be leaving in the morning. I'll travel back to visit Amenia weekly. During that time, I will be leaving you on Grild under Reloi's supervision.*

"We are nearly to the end of your internship there, but you still have at least a couple more projects to work on with them as they are getting ready for a closer relationship with the Alliance. A number of their young people will be training as agents and in other Alliance responsibilities. They want your help in preparing for this."

"That sounds interesting, for sure," Lizzie replied with some enthusiasm. *"I'm pretty much already packed."*

They spent one last evening entertaining the linklings. Ynni already knew, of course, without Lizzie telling her, that they would be leaving, and her tribe gave her a rousing going-away party, complete with acrobatics and their own composition in addition to Lizzie's now traditional concert.

That night, before going to bed, as Lizzie did her mental exercises, Reloi appeared in their usual meeting place, his eyes bright and a huge smile on his pale face shining with the huge full moon that now shone above Lizzie's mental village.

"I can hardly wait to see you face to face again," he said softly. "We've all missed you, but no one more than me."

Lizzie sat beside him on the park bench, one hand on his shoulder. "It will be good to get back to work with your people. I've begun to feel quite at home there, even if there is no actual night or moon or stars to look up to. I thought it would be fun to enjoy a moonlit evening together before I get back to the constant brightness of your inner planet.

"Tarafau says we will just transport our way into the apartment building instead of going to headquarters and using the gateway. I think I will be glad of that. The sight of your outer planet is so very sad."

Reloi agreed. "I have to get used to it all over again every time I go to headquarters or visit another dimension in my travels for the Alliance. But it is home to me and my people now." He sighed. "We'll have to go back to mindspeech, at least in the daytime, once you're back. I will miss being able to speak directly."

"It's okay. We'll be together for real, and that will be worth it all. Perhaps I will get better at your language, and that will make it easier."

"They have been talking about assigning you a language instructor; I guess that means me, if you don't mind."

"Mind? Hmm... let me think about it. Of course, I don't mind, silly."

"Well, you'd better get some sleep. We have a rigorous schedule planned for you starting as soon as you get here."

He faded from her mind space with a cheerful wave.

Next morning after breakfast, they went out to the grove to get Ynni and say goodbye to the tribe, whereupon Amenia, with Elizabeth cooing in her arms, hugged first Lizzie and then Tarafau.

Ynni threw her furry arms firmly around Lizzie's neck, and Tarafau put one of his massive hands on Lizzie's other shoulder. Amenia, smiling and waving surrounded by the linkling tribe, faded from view. Immediately they were in the little apartment on Grid. Seated in his hover chair, Reloi grinned expansively, and Tanata hopped up and down excitedly on Reloi's shoulder.

"Welcome back!" he sent cheerfully. *"Are you ready to get to work?"*

"Hello to you two, too!" Lizzie sent back ironically. *"So nice of you to let us catch our breaths."*

From his expression, Reloi knew she was teasing. *"Tarafau, what are we to do with this young lady? So cheeky! Actually, if you don't need to put some things away, they are waiting not very patiently in the conference room for you two. I think they have done all they can without getting some feedback from the Alliance. After our meeting, they were hoping you could take some messages to Alliance headquarters to expedite matters?"*

Lizzie looked inquiringly at Tarafau, who nodded. *"Sure, we can do that. I was kind of hoping we'd be here for a bit longer...."*

"Not to worry. It will only be for a day or two while the Alliance council makes a few decisions about our situation. I believe I will be traveling with you, if that's all right?"

Tarafau nodded with a grin. *"I think we can manage it."*

"Then it's decided! Let's hop over to the council room and get the details out of the way, and we can get right on it. The sooner we leave, the sooner we can return."

As Reloi had said, the council had pretty much wrapped everything up in a neat package for the Alliance council regarding stepping up their original agreements. Every Alliance member dimension was issued special tablets that allowed cross-language communication. One of these had been filled with all of Grild's requirements and the resources of personnel they were offering to the Alliance.

The guardian of the single Grild gate would be managing the movement of the various people involved, to and from the Alliance, so they would need to stay here to mind the gate. This was why Lizzie, Tarafau, and Reloi had been chosen as go-betweens for these negotiations until a better, more permanent communications system was established.

Part of the agreement was that the Alliance would launch an orbiting satellite from the dead planetary surface with special communications tech that would allow them future, more convenient interaction via the Alliance communications network.

Lizzie liked the sound of this, as her internship would revolve around facilitating all of it. This meant she would be able to stay on Grild a bit longer than she had thought she originally might have done.

Within less than an hour, the council was bidding Lizzie, Tarafau, Reloi, Tanata, and Ynni goodbye from the pavilion at the park as Tarafau put one large hand on both Lizzie's and Reloi's free shoulders, with their little friends clinging carefully to them. As they faded from view, Lizzie found herself in familiar surroundings.

Tarafau had transferred them to the inside of her pod building on the training grounds. They exited and walked to the admin building. Entering Liliath's office, they found her in a discussion with two of Lizzie's instructors, Lulindu and Meta. These turned in their seats and smiled a welcome while Liliath gestured to them.

"Come in and welcome! We were actually just talking about you, Lizzie. I understand your internship is going well? Lall is waiting with an Alliance hovercar for you. Reloi's usual arrangements, of course. Perhaps you can stop in on your way back for a chat?"

"I would love that!" Lizzie enthused. *"It is strange not to be on my way to classes, to be honest. Nice to see you all."*

As Liliath had said, Lall was waiting in the parking area in a hovercar adapted to receive Reloi, chair and all, and soon they were whizzing down the road that led to the city, glass buildings rising impressively before them. It was so different than either Tarafau's home or Reloi's, or even Lizzie's native Los Angeles. She had visited many of her podmates' home planets, and none of them had even come close to this experience.

Once again, she marveled at the diversity of cultures and what they created, all filling most of the same needs but in so many different ways. And to think, she had only scratched the bare surface of the many places she would see and cultures she would experience in her life as an official agent of the Alliance.

They had been told early in their training that their assignments would vary in length and intensity, and now Lizzie found herself hoping that her time on Reloi's planet would be extended. Working alongside them and participating in their various activities, including spending time in their schools, had made her feel a part of what they were trying to accomplish.

As they pulled up to the large glass headquarters building with its massive double doors large enough to accommodate even a dragon with ease, Lizzie wondered if it would be inappropriate for her to ask the council for an extension on her assignment. She wasn't sure she could pluck up the courage, but she would hope for an opening to do so. It wasn't like they would fire her for it, she thought with a nervous chuckle.

When they went up the steps to the large doors, the guards at the front told them to go straight up to the private council room, as they were expected.

Lizzie experienced a swoop in her stomach that had nothing to do with the ride up in the huge elevator. For the first time she realized that she was now performing in the role of an Alliance Agent. True, she was just an intern, but the responsibility for this assignment was hers.

Tarafau may have been her guide and Reloi a representative of his planet and a fully certified agent himself, but even as an intern, she had been chosen to be the spokesperson for the group. She thought back on all of the oral reports they had given in her classes at the agent training center and all of the oral reports she had given in college, and all of a sudden, she felt herself unprepared and inadequate to the task.

Ynni patted her cheek gently. *"Lizzie knows what to do. Lizzie has studied and has paid attention to many details that will be important. Ynni knows you can do this thing."*

It's a little like having my own Jiminy Cricket, she thought with a sigh, the difference being that no one could hear anything Ynni said to her if she didn't want them to. She deliberately straightened her shoulders and lifted her head in the posture Lall had taught them when facing a difficult opponent. She composed her face and focused. Even with her stomach roiling, she would move forward as if she knew what she was doing. Otherwise, what were all of those cubes games about, after all? And that made her smile, if only briefly.

The birdlike receptionist waved them in as they exited the elevator and nodded towards the doors that led into the private council chamber. She had been there only once before.

Gleph and Linaa, the dual headed Chief Councilor of the Dimensional Alliance, stood as they entered. The other two councilors, Khol and Bern, remained seated, or at least Bern did. With Khol and his many tentacles and octopus-like body, it was hard to tell if he was seated or not. His single large golden eye was fixed on Lizzie. Bern's fuzzy round body was resting on what looked like a low cushioned stool, his legs bent underneath him and, as usual, there were no discernable eyes or ears.

"Welcome, delegation from Grild," one of the heads of the Chief Councilor said, although Lizzie couldn't tell which. Both heads were looking attentively at her and since she had only heard them speak once before, there was no way to tell their mind voices apart.

"Thank you, Chief Councilor," Lizzie replied in her most businesslike tone. *"We come to present you with the information you requested from the people of Grild. They have worked hard to create a document with all of the numbers and requirements their people have as they come to add their strength to the Dimensional Alliance. They wished me to convey their sincere desire to be a valuable asset to all of the good work we do here."*

Lizzie had memorized this part of her presentation, but from here on out, she was on her own. She held the tablet out to the Chief Councilor, and they took it solemnly.

"You may tell them that we appreciate their efforts in behalf of all Alliance members. In your opinion, how can we best help them in return?"

Lizzie knew this was a test of sorts. They had addressed her and not Reloi or Tarafau. She took a calming breath and responded, *"They are a very self-sufficient people, Councilor. They have done amazing things with the resources left to them. I would say that the communications satellite and any allowable technical help with it would be a good thing. They have to be very careful about any mechanical devices that could potentially pollute their contained atmosphere, so they do so much of what is needed by hand. That being said, they have come up with some ingenious tools to help them work more effectively; and, I think, if left to their own devices, they may come up with potential technologies that no one else has thought of."*

She paused and looked at Reloi. *"Wouldn't you say so, Agent Reloi?"*

She thought her use of the formal title surprised him just for a moment, but she remembered that he too had gone through the agent training, for none of the surprise showed on his face. She and he had discussed what needed to happen for his people, going forward, and he seemed to agree with her that they had been progressing quickly enough.

They had long since gone past the survival stage and were now in a growth and improvement stage that would do well for them if they just continued to work together.

"Lizzie is correct, Chief Councilor. We really only wish to be of service to the Alliance. Despite our unusual circumstances, we are making great progress at a doable pace. The few helpers you have requested will not affect our development and may, at some point after Alliance training, be a great asset to us."

The two heads of the chief councilor nodded in unison. Lizzie could see a slight flush on Reloi's face, as if he was relieved by their reaction. She had always only ever seen him poised and self-assured.

"In that case, my councilors and I will download these documents to our records and go over them this afternoon. Tomorrow morning,

we will give you the tablet back with any further instructions we may have for your people regarding the satellite connection and use of the communications network. We will also send techs to install the necessary equipment at a central location within the planet and train your people in its proper use. If there is nothing further, Tarafau will escort you all to the guest suites, where you may relax until we call you in the morning."

Lizzie was a bit surprised at the abrupt dismissal, although the mind voice of Gleph or Linaa, whichever it was, did not seem curt or rude. Somehow, she had thought there would be more in the way of discussion or further instruction or, at the very least, an inquiry about the progress of her internship.

Nevertheless, her party turned back and went through the door to the massive elevator. When they had all entered, Tarafau addressed the AI attendant, "Guest suites." And the doors closed.

They got out on a level Lizzie had never visited before. The first and only time she had ever been there, it had been in and out of the council room, where she had been transported directly to the agent training center. Tarafau led them down a long, wide, tall hallway lined with doors spaced about thirty feet apart. He paused between two doors across from one another and sent, *"Lizzie, this door has been programmed for you,"* and pointing to the other, *"and this is for Reloi and me. To enter, simply touch the yellow square next to the doorknob with your palm. It will react to the DNA in your skin."*

Obediently, Lizzie placed her palm on the yellow square next to the door handle, and there was a click. She turned the knob, and a small gasp escaped her lips. This was no pod barracks accommodation or a cheap motel. The large room was twice the size of her entire apartment at Grild, which was already larger than her apartment above Gaston's lab had been.

The outside wall featured a large picture window with what might have been damask curtains of a light beige. There was a small kitchenette, a conversation area with a couch and a couple of very comfortable-looking overstuffed chairs, and two doors on one side of the room that Lizzie guessed were probably a bedroom and a "personal hygiene station," as Reloi's people called a bathroom.

She turned to Tarafau. *"All this for me?"*

"These are the non-designated temporary guest quarters. Once you are a certified agent, you will be assigned a shared apartment with another agent. At some point, if you have a lot of business with headquarters, you will be assigned a permanent apartment. There are several floors in the building authorized for this purpose. For instance, Miriha has her own assigned apartment, as does Liliath."

She entered the conversation area and sat down on one of the chairs. *"So, what do we do while we wait?"*

"Now that you have activated the ID at the door, we can go down to the dining room and get something to eat. Let's activate Reloi's and my room. After we eat, we can do some exploring in the city."

Reloi had no palm to touch to the yellow pad, but he grinned at her, and his hover chair rose to the level of her shoulders. He then pressed his forehead to the pad and the same click responded. He kinetically turned the knob. His and Tarafau's suite was almost exactly the same as Lizzie's, but there was an additional door on the opposite side of the room, presumably going to a second bedroom. Having successfully registered the room, they went downstairs to eat.

It was evidently not a usual lunch or suppertime, so the room wasn't crowded. Various types of beings were eating, and many were in obvious mental conversations. Some, however, were chattering away in various interesting languages that included clicks, hums, and in one instance a kind of quiet yodeling.

Lizzie had been prepared to eat something native to the area, but she was amazed to discover that even Earth foods were included on the menu. Evidently, the Earth guardians also attended events at headquarters often enough that they kept a supply of Earth foods on hand. There were even some of Ynni's favorite fruits and vegetables for her and Tanata.

Now they had an opportunity to catch up, and Lizzie and Tarafau spoke of Elizabeth's infant antics, Lizzie's trip to the Apex, and her concerts with the linklings. Reloi told some funny stories about some of the construction projects where they were trying some new things.

All in all, it was pleasant to just sit there and eat and chat, especially since Lizzie assumed that, when they returned to Grild after meeting with the council in the morning, there would be so much to do that quiet interludes might be few and far between.

When they had finished their meal, they went down in the elevator to the main lobby and out the huge double doors onto the street.

"There are some interesting shops in this direction and a park within a few cross-streets from here." Tarafau told them. *"Let's take a look."*

Once again, Lizzie was struck by the diversity of the population of the city where the headquarters of the Alliance made their home.

"Many of the agents and military have permanent housing for their families here in the city and the outlying areas," Reloi explained as they made their way down the street amongst many others. She noticed that most of them walked rather than using the hover cars they had arrived in.

"The hover cars are generally for transporting people from outside the city," Tarafau said, when she asked him about it. *"It's simply traditional to walk and interact, a pleasant activity, when so much of the business of the Alliance can be so serious and admittedly a bit disconnected from what is familiar and comfortable."*

Lizzie could see that this might be important and had to confess to herself that she was enjoying just walking out in the open air without the significant traffic, noise, and congestion she might have seen on a typical street in Los Angeles.

They peeked into shop windows and even entered a few that had interesting displays of art or technology. Lizzie would have liked to buy one of the paintings that reminded her of Geln's art style, but she knew she had no permanent place to display it. Geln's painting still resided safely in her MDP.

They wandered through the vast park, noting the interesting birds and other small animals that wandered freely throughout the trees and bushes. Lizzie, when she focused on it, could hear the murmur of the trees and other plant life but chose not to interact with them. She had been happy to learn that she could basically turn this particular mental talent off and on at will. It would have been terribly distracting to have plants constantly whispering in her thoughts.

They took their time, wandering and chatting, and Lizzie was grateful that, if nothing else, she wasn't sitting around waiting for things to happen.

At one point, they paused to sit on a park bench with a view of a lovely little pond. Ynni and Tanata went down to the water to splash and play with one another.

"I think they're becoming good friends," Reloi remarked as they watched their little companions' antics. *"I'm glad they get along so well together."* And he looked into Lizzie's eyes significantly. *"It would be horrible if they didn't like one another."*

"Indeed," Tarafau put in, *"It would be like arguing siblings... an annoyance and one more thing a couple has to deal with."*

Lizzie inwardly winced at the word "couple." Was it that obvious? Or had Amenia told Tarafau about Lizzie's dilemma? Certainly not. Of course, not. She wasn't sure she wanted everyone around them to see the burgeoning romance between her and Reloi.

Although, if it went the way she thought or hoped it would, it would be obvious soon enough.

Back at headquarters, they returned to the dining hall after having worked up an appetite in their wanderings in the city. Once again, they had a pleasant meal.

Afterwards, Tarafau said, *"The main council is meeting in the atrium in about an hour. I thought it might be interesting to see what they're dealing with today. I don't think you've had an opportunity to attend a session before, Lizzie?"*

"No, I can't say I have. I think it would be instructional. What do you think, Reloi?"

"Certainly. I haven't been to a general session in quite a while, since I started working at the training center. It will be good to catch up on what's happening."

They headed off to the atrium, a beautiful combination of an indoor courtyard with various plants and even a small pool and waterfall and a council room set up to accommodate a lot of different types of beings. The council room reminded Lizzie of the meeting hall of the U.S. House of Representatives, although it was several times larger.

There were seats reserved for visiting agents, in addition to those intended for the elected councilors and delegates from the various member dimensions.

They sat in their appointed seats and, as they were early, watched the seats fill in around them with more variations on intelligent life than Lizzie had heretofore seen. She tried to hold in her memory the amazing scene set before her. She noted that Liliath sat with a draconic delegation and that several of her agent training instructors were also seated in the crowd.

These meetings were open to anyone who wished to attend, and Tarafau informed her that the meeting was also broadcast via the Alliance communications network to member planets throughout the Dimensional Alliance. When an issue required a vote of the members, votes were taken electronically via the clever tablets issued to all Alliance member officials. All Alliance members across dimensions, as well as the thousands of Alliance member delegates, could attend these meetings without having to even go through a gateway to do it.

The Alliance communication network relayed messages via the satellites installed around nearly every gateway planet. These satellites, like the one which would be installed on Grild, were comparatively minuscule but powerful, allowing nearly instantaneous communication directly through the gateway portals. Because the messages didn't have to traverse in real space time, there was almost no time lag between the transmission and reception of a message.

Not only could they send messages composed of text or numbers, but photos and video were also possible. Once again, she found herself wishing that Earth had such amazing technology. She was certain that, if the people of Earth could communicate with such incredible speed, it would solve so many problems.

The susurrations in the audience ceased as if cut off by a knife as the Chief Councilor and the two companion councilors entered the raised dais by a door at the back. All in the audience stood in respect and then, at a gesture from the Chief Councilor, resumed their seats.

Fortunately, Lizzie had been forewarned that this would happen, and she was glad. She would have been terribly embarrassed had she been the only one to remain seated, not that many would have noticed, as vast as the crowd was that filled the auditorium.

The Chief Councilor greeted all of them: *"Welcome, one and all, whether here in our council or joining us throughout the multiverse via the Alliance network.*

"We are pleased to welcome our guests as well, students, agents and other interested parties. We hope this meeting will be instructive and will help you understand the work we are engaged in."

The two heads swiveled, taking in the delegates and guests. With a wave of their hand, a large screen appeared above their head facing the audience. It wasn't like a screen in the movie theaters Lizzie was used to. It had no physical presence; rather it seemed to float above them, semi-transparent, a picture of a planet on it that was so three dimensional that it almost seemed that the planet had actually invaded the room.

Lizzie felt it was familiar somehow, and beside her, Reloi gasped.

"This is Grild, one of the newest fledgling members of the Alliance. It has only been a few centuries, depending on how your culture views time. They have since encountered issues they are resolving and have met all requirements for full membership, even during severe trials of their own ingenuity and perseverance.

"At this time, we wish to extend them and their dimension the additional benefit of the Alliance communications network. They have committed the required number of potential agents and military conscripts and currently require no special aid from the Alliance, except training of their techs to operate the satellite communications network.

"All in favor, please indicate."

Immediately the screen above them began to show numbers flashing up on the screen in two columns. One was the affirmative and the other the negative vote. There were almost no negatives. The number in the positive column was growing at such a rate as to almost be a blur as the number continued to grow.

Beside her, Reloi was grinning like a schoolboy with a new toy. *"I had no idea they would be doing this tonight,"* he enthused. *"I somehow thought it would happen after we left with our instructions. This is amazing. Thank you, Tarafau, for including us in this."*

"I had gotten the message from the Chief Councilor while we were in the park. I'm glad you can both be here for this. This is actually a rare bit of business in the council these days. There are so many hoops that have to be jumped through to prepare a culture for membership that it is rare to witness it solidified in this way."

"The vote, as it stands, is nearly unanimous," said the Chief Councilor as the numbers slowed down on the screen. *"We can assume that we will move forward. I will be notifying them in the morning regarding our decision.*

"In other business, we want to thank all of those who generously contributed to the assistance of the Inladian dimension during their worldwide pandemic. Thanks to the combined efforts of the scientists from various dimensions, they have nearly eradicated the virus that had killed nearly half of their population.

"We are grateful to have been able to stop this plague on this gateway planet with your assistance. Also, they send their thanks for your help with food and other necessary life-saving supplies and equipment.

"We will now open the floor for various delegates who have registered to address the assembly."

The remaining meeting was enlightening. Lizzie had studied Dimensional Alliance laws as part of her training, but it was only cursory, considering the age of the Alliance and the complexity of dealing with such diverse cultures throughout the multiverse. It had required so many exceptions and amendments as to make it a lifetime study to even begin to scratch the surface.

Delegates stood on the dais, front and center of the arc of the seated assembly, and through mental projection and facial expressions (when there were faces involved), laid out proposals and requests, many of which Lizzie did not fully understand. Often their presentations were highlighted by pictures and video on the floating screen that had obviously been prepared in advance to enhance their effectiveness.

At the end of each of five presentations, the floor was open for discussion. Not all measures were voted on, as many were simply informational and not necessarily a request for action on the part of the council.

At the end of the meeting, the Chief Councilor stood and dismissed them to the atrium for a short reception in which they could meet the representatives of Grild and continue discussing the issues raised in council that evening.

They found themselves unexpectedly in one of the most bizarre reception lines Lizzie had ever experienced. Once, when she had won an award for a scholarly paper on the effects of gravitational pull in the solar system, Lizzie had been accorded the honor of being featured in a reception line, but it had been nothing like this.

Lizzie was grateful once again for her training in guarding her facial expressions, as she felt she would have otherwise stood there with her mouth agape during most of the time they stood there, alternately shaking hands, fins, or tentacles, or engaging in other cultural greeting rituals with the varying beings that came to congratulate Reloi and to encourage Lizzie with wishes for continued success during her internship.

Tarafau, in his role as guardian, stood slightly behind her, mentally coaching her as each of the new beings presented themselves before her, something for which she was incredibly grateful.

Almost all of the delegates made over Tanata and Ynni, both still perched happily on the shoulders of their companions. It turned out that linklings, because they were native to the planet that held the Gatekeeper, were not only well-known throughout the multiverse, but well liked. The fact that Lizzie was linked to one seemed to give her additional credibility.

Tanata was a bit of a novelty, however, as his gate planet was not yet a member of the Alliance. Reloi grinned when answering questions about how he had met his little friend, and the story was told multiple times to an appreciative audience.

Reloi himself was the center of attention, and Lizzie was gratified to see how well received he was, even in his physical state. He had elevated the hover chair to allow him eye-to-eye contact (when there were eyes to look into), and Lizzie marveled at his self-assurance and poise in what for her was a difficult and unnerving experience.

By the time the reception was over and they had headed up to their rooms, Lizzie was so exhausted she only took off her shoes and, fully clothed, she lay on her bed and dropped off to a dreamless sleep.

Chapter 19: In a Minor Key

(Jenny found herself reminiscing about her first reception at Alliance headquarters and remembered the same feelings of astonishment and wonder at being the unexpected center of attention.

It was late. The twilight had long since dissolved into night, and Chidwi was fast asleep on the window seat. Tidbit had gone out for the night, as Jenny knew, to secretly visit his home and to return by morning like any cat that had been out prowling all night.

She decided she couldn't quite leave her reading yet. She knew she would be chided for not getting to bed at a reasonable hour, but she just couldn't help herself.

She had her suspicions about where this relationship with Reloi was headed, and she was so hopeful to see her aunt experience the same joy she had with her Burt.

She turned the page.)

The next morning Lizzie woke to a mental nudge from Ynni. *"Lizzie awake? Lizzie must prepare for the day. Much to do!"*

She yawned and stretched, looking with dismay at her rumpled clothing. She hadn't even made the effort to turn down the covers of the bed. She headed to the well-designed bathroom, showered and dressed, removing her clothing from her MDP, carefully putting her dirty clothes into the designated spot reserved in her MDP for laundry.

As she dried and fluffed her auburn hair, looking in the mirror, she realized she was due for a haircut. Normally a dry and fluff was all she really needed for her hair to fall into her customary style, but she knew if she didn't get a haircut soon, she would have to resort to styling it, something she didn't relish.

By the time she had gotten herself completely together, Tarafau knocked on her door. She left the apartment and followed Tarafau and Reloi down the hallway in silence after greeting them with *"Good morning."*

Reloi and Tarafau also looked contemplative. They rode the elevator to the council room and were greeted by the receptionist. *"You are expected."* And she waved them through to the double-door entrance to the chamber.

Inside, all three councilors were seated on the dais. The Chief Councilor rose to greet them but did not gesture for them to sit. Instead, he handed the tablet down to Reloi and said, *"We won't keep you. In the gateroom, you will encounter your tech support agent. She will travel with you via gate to your planet, instead of Tarafau's method."*

Lizzie found herself wishing that they were using "Tarafau's method," as she dreaded the trip down the tube from the planet's surface.

"After the satellite is deployed, one of the things the tech will also be assigned to do is to search the interior of your planet for potential additional gateways. This research could be very enlightening for our gate scientists; and if any are found, with your permission we will be sending scientists to study this and potentially establish connections to the Alliance gate network. Any questions?"

They all shook their heads.

"Then we will bid you farewell. Lizzie, in two months you will report temporarily to the training facility. Assuming the council on Grild is satisfied you have met all of the requirements, at that time you will receive your certification, along with the rest of your podmates."

"Thank you!" Lizzie exclaimed, her excitement and confusion plain in her face. *"I had no idea I was so close. I will return as promised."*

With that, the three of them turned to leave.

"One more thing," the Chief Councilor said from behind them. *"Tarafau, you will also need to be in attendance, as an assignment is pending for you at that time."*

Tarafau nodded and they left to descend to the basement, where they met up with the tech. To Lizzie's delight, it was Meta.

"There won't be a new agent class coming through for another few months. By that time, I should have Grild sorted out and be ready to go back to teaching," she said, a mischievous glint in her eyes. *"You can't seem to get rid of me, Lizzie."*

Lizzie grinned back. *"That's fine with me, Meta. I may get an opportunity to work with you some, but I think they have some other projects in mind for me."*

They stepped through the gateway into the little domed room that looked out on the desolate landscape of outer Grild.

This time the topsy-turvy ride down the tunnel that delved deep into the planet's crust wasn't so disconcerting. It was a long ride, however, and the change from one direction of gravity to the other didn't seem any less jarring. When they arrived at the welcome station at the bottom that was now the top, a delegation was waiting with smiles on their faces.

"Welcome home!" they sent in concert. And indeed, Lizzie did feel like this was a home, albeit a temporary one. She was beginning to really relate to the Grildites and felt comfortable in her surroundings here, as unusual as they may have seemed in the beginning.

Reloi introduced them all to Meta and explained what she would be doing for them. He handed the tablet to one of the Grild councilors. They proceeded to the apartments where Lizzie and

Tarafau were residing and introduced Meta to an apartment of her own with a single bedroom, only a few doors down from theirs.

Unlike Lizzie's initial formal reception, they set to work immediately. After issuing Meta the keys to her apartment, they all went to the building that was assigned to the tech team. Meta had her own office in the building, and there was as extensive a lab as the Grildites could provide, with plenty of space for Meta to install her own equipment.

The team of four Grildites was waiting in the lab area of the office when they arrived. Reloi introduced them.

"Meta, these are Nenn, Armir, Linga, and Lell. They will be your team. They are some of our top scientists and are completely at your disposal. They will have no further duties until the system is completely functional and we have trained other support staff."

Meta nodded to each as they were introduced, and Lizzie was awestruck at how quickly she got down to business.

"I will need access to the surface at some point. Is there breathable air?" Meta asked Nenn, who seemed to be the most senior of the four.

"We cannot go outside of the dome without protective clothing, as not only is the air toxic, but the heat at most times of day is dangerous. I would like to suggest that we erect a temporary shelter for any work we need to do outside the dome," Nenn answered. *"What kind of work will we need to do on the planet's surface?"*

"I have some equipment that needs to be erected on the surface to launch the satellite. The satellite is very tiny, but in order to attain escape velocity to reach orbit, a fairly large launcher needs to be set up." Meta informed them in her usual calm manner.

"When will that arrive?" asked Lell.

"Actually, it is already here, just in storage." And Meta indicated her MDP.

They all stared as she invoked a metallic sphere about the size of a volleyball from her MDP. Lizzie remembered her own awe when she first experienced this incredible bit of alien technology.

"*This*," she sent, "*is our little satellite. The remainder of the launching equipment is in here.*" And she tapped the seemingly innocuous bracelet on her wrist. "*We will be setting it up outside, once we have the satellite properly tuned and all of the reception equipment is set up here in the lab.*"

The expressions of the assembled techs were almost humorous. It was obvious they were excited, and Lizzie could relate. Her first ventures into alien tech had made her feel so much like a kid in a candy store that she knew these techs would probably not sleep much for the next few weeks as they were introduced to the equipment and science that would make this all work.

It was clear that no additional introductions were necessary, and Reloi gestured with a grin and a head nod towards the door to Lizzie and Tarafau. "*I think we can go now.*"

Meta and the four techs were gathered around the little satellite, obviously in focused conversation not directed to the rest of them and seemingly oblivious to anyone else in the room.

As they left the office, Reloi sent, "*Let's head over to the admin building. We're about to get some new assignments, and I think we're going to be just as busy as Meta and her new team.*"

Sure enough, when they sat down with one of the council members in a semicircle of chairs, she stood and addressed them, spreading her hands in greeting.

"*Lizzie, you and your companions have impressed our citizens with your willingness to work alongside them and learn about our culture and our needs. It has been requested that you spend more time in our education system. The administration of our largest school feels that there is much you can teach our instructors, as well as interacting with the students themselves.*

"We would like you to do some inservice training for them. The administrator of the school system will sit down with you to plan out a curriculum and create a syllabus that we can use as a template for future training when your time with us is finished. Education is key to our continued survival within Grild; and of all the things you might do for us, this may be the most significant.

"Also, the music instructor you lent the mbira to has found craftsmen to reproduce your instrument, and he would like to consult with you about that. Very few of our musical instruments survived the migration from the surface. The small size and minimal resources necessary to reproduce them in large numbers makes the mbira ideal for musical instruction, not to mention it will make instrumental music more accessible to our population on an individual basis."

Lizzie was dumbfounded. On Earth, to be given such a position would have required, at minimum, a bachelor's degree and teaching certifications. At the least, she felt underqualified and certainly overwhelmed, especially since she had no formal musical training.

Nevertheless, she nodded her assent, which made the rest of them smile. She could imagine that both Reloi and Tarafau knew about her self-doubt, but that they wouldn't let on in front of any official. She had a feeling that later they might tease her about it, however, when they were in a more private setting.

And that was how she found herself thoroughly engaged with the administrators, teachers, and students of the large school they had originally visited what seemed like a very long time ago.

Arpen was happy to involve her in his master plan to use the mbira as the key piece to musical instruction in Grildite music. Long before they had migrated into the depths of Grild, they had developed a music notation system that he was now adapting to the note structure of the little instrument.

And, with the encouragement of Reloi, Tarafau, and Ynni, Lizzie found herself up to the task of creating a credible syllabus for the teachers within the community. She had been unconsciously evaluating the educational system on Earth for most of her life and so had much more to say about it than she may have previously thought.

Evenings, she and Reloi spent time together after dining with Tarafau. Tanata and Ynni generally found things to interest the two of them, and Tarafau used that time to visit Amenia and Elizabeth on his home planet, fading in and out within the walls of the apartment.

So, she and Reloi had a lot of time to spend together. Some days, instead of eating in the dining hall in the admin building, or one of the little restaurants in town, they went and spent time with Reloi's family.

His mother was always happy to have them both, and Lizzie started to look forward to spending time with his family.

One day on a break, while strolling through the park where Lizzie had first met the council members of Grild, Reloi guided them to a private little area shaded by trees and where they could barely see the more open areas of the park.

"Lizzie, are you happy?" Reloi asked, looking deep into her eyes, after she had seated herself on a tree stump padded with moss.

"Yes, I am. Why do you ask?" she responded cautiously.

"I was wondering if you would be interested in making your internship here a more permanent assignment once it is complete. You don't have much longer here, as you know, at which time you will become a certified agent. Not all agents wander the multiverse, you know."

"No, I don't think I realized that. I thought agents usually traveled widely. Of course, I haven't had my final briefing yet," she admitted.

"Well, some agents become guides, some are even promoted to Gate Guardians, and sometimes they are given long-term assignments. Anyway, I was wondering, if you got that kind of assignment here, for instance, if that would disappoint you."

"I actually hadn't considered it, to be honest. I didn't even know it was a possibility. Why do you ask?" And for a moment, she wasn't sure if she wanted to hear his answer.

He gazed into her eyes, his expression soft and maybe a little sad—or was it anxious?

"Lizzie, I know we have known each other for a relatively short time, and there are definitely some things to take into consideration, but I have made no secret of how I feel about you. Is there any chance you return those feelings at all?"

The hopeful and yet despairing look on his face would have been comical, if Lizzie hadn't known it was heartfelt and sincere. She knew the specific thing he was referring to wasn't her agent status or her career, but his lack of arms and legs. She knew that, although the Grildites didn't make a big deal about it, he was still very aware of the one thing that kept him separate from them, regardless of their kind acceptance of his circumstances and the respect with which they treated him.

"Reloi, I have almost no social skills. All that I do have, I only developed during my time training as an agent. I have little experience with human relationships, much less, alien ones." She paused, watching his face as she spoke, both hopeful and despairing, his silvery brows furrowed in growing consternation. She hurried on.

"The feelings I have for you are very new to me, but I think I can honestly say they are deep and true. Your physical differences mean nothing to me. Never think they do, even for a moment. I don't know where this will lead, but I do want to spend more time with you and with your people, if the Alliance will allow it. I'm not sure that's the answer you were looking for, but for now, it's all I can tell you."

Reloi's face had softened to a gentle smile, his brows unknitting, and the light reappeared in his eyes. *"It is enough. It was more than I hoped for. If I had hands and arms, I would like to hold you in them.*

If I had legs, I would love to dance with you, dance for you. My heart is happy to be patient, knowing you care for me even a little."

Lizzie returned his smile and, to the surprise of both of them, leaned forward and kissed the top of his smooth head. *"Let's see where it takes us, shall we?"* she almost whispered into his ear. *"If you can be patient, that will be enough, and time will tell."*

They sat there in companionable silence for a while, and then they returned down the path back towards the school and the work they had committed to.

And work they did. Day after day, Lizzie and Reloi and Tarafau, with Ynni and Tanata happily tagging along, met with teachers and students. Tarafau taught them principles of discipline and teamwork. Reloi taught them perseverance and to be proud of their heritage and to learn from past mistakes. Lizzie taught not only the basics of the use of the mbira, but also the principles of how to learn new things.

She had noticed over the course of her high school and college years that one of the skills most lacking in the majority of students was how to study and learn new things; how to use resources such as the library or their own logic and diligence to obtain what they needed to take what they learned to the next level.

So, she instituted a new course with a well-laid-out syllabus, training the teachers as well as the students, so they could become more personally responsible for their own education.

In the meantime, Arpen had enlisted craftspeople from many different areas to create mbiras with resonant and strong keys made from a bamboo-like plant that grew wild all over Grild. Within a month, he had enough instruments to begin what was shaping up to be a small mbira orchestra.

As Lizzie threw herself into her endeavors, she felt more and more satisfaction and fulfillment than she had ever had in any of her studies up to this point. She realized that perhaps teaching was the one expression of learning she had neglected. She had never pictured herself as a teacher but began to see that all of her questions had given her the impetus that had led her to this point.

Time seemed to fly by so quickly that, before she knew it, there was only one week before she needed to return to the Alliance training center for her certification. Either this final week of her Grid internship would be extended to become a future assignment, or her time here would come to an end as she was assigned elsewhere.

She prepared all of her students and the teachers she was working with for her departure by making sure she had left behind documentation of everything she had done, encouraging them to move forward and improve on what she had begun by adding their own insights and experience into the courses of instruction she had created.

And during all of that time, every evening, when she wasn't working on paperwork and reports, she and Reloi went walking in what she had come to think of as "their park." Even the trees of the park had begun speaking to her familiarly, calling her by name. Some days the two of them just sat together, gazing out onto the small pond, simply breathing, Lizzie with her hand on Reloi's shoulder, in place of holding hands as most couples would have done.

After that first timid kiss on his forehead, Lizzie had felt closer to him; and when he looked into her eyes, she was no longer uncomfortable with his intense and obviously loving gaze.

On breaks, they still visited with his family, and his mother and father had greeted her each time with kind enthusiasm. His siblings seemed to have begun to take for granted that when Reloi came, Lizzie came with him; and they chatted comfortably with her at mealtimes and in between, speaking of their work or schooling and joking with them both.

And when Reloi and Lizzie announced that she would soon be leaving, with no idea of when or if she might return, his mother insisted on making a celebration of their time together. *"We will all hope with a unified heart that you will return to us, Lizzie,"* His mom said, both hands resting on her shoulders and looking up into her face sincerely.

"Thank you, Lydian, but you needn't make a big fuss. I already have felt very welcome in your home, and I will never forget your kindness," Lizzie replied, meaning every word of it. *"I have felt very much a part of your family."*

"As was our hope," agreed Reloi's dad, who looked nearly identical to Reloi except with all his limbs in place. *"You will always be welcome here."*

And so, the final week passed, with Lizzie, Reloi, and Tarafau spending time with the council and looking in on Meta and the goings on in her lab.

They had already erected a workspace on the planet's surface after having fully calibrated the satellite to the receiving equipment. They would be establishing the launcher and would soon launch the satellite.

Meta promised to keep Reloi informed of their progress, knowing Reloi would gladly pass on the information to Lizzie in their nightly meetings of the mind. Like Lizzie, Meta was impressed by this unusual talent in Reloi.

Finally, after more than one going-away party by the schools, Reloi's family, and the Grild council and community, it was time to go. It was a surprisingly simple thing. Tarafau gave Reloi and Lizzie time alone, taking Tanata and Ynni with him into the hallway.

"I will stay in touch," Reloi sent to her. *"Save some time each evening for our little chats."*

"Of course," Lizzie replied, knowing that had she been using her voice it would have been a bit husky. And then she did something on impulse that once again surprised them both. Leaning towards him in his hover chair that was raised to her eye height, she put both

arms around him and hugged him tightly, then leaning back only far enough to see into his eyes, she kissed him full on the mouth.

It may have lasted days or weeks or only a moment, for time had seemed to stand completely still, but for the first time in her life, Lizzie felt something stir inside her that was beyond anything she had ever previously imagined.

She knew she loved him, utterly and completely, and that this kiss was the beginning of something beyond time and space, beyond the boundaries of any dimension in the multiverse. There were no words. The understanding passed between them faster than the speed of light and stronger than the force of gravity on any livable planet.

When they pulled apart, Reloi only nodded. *"I will live on that until you return."*

Lizzie knew a promise had been made between them, even though nothing more was said.

Tarafau knocked and then entered the room. He took in the two faces before him. Ynni and Tanata scampered in and alighted on their respective companions without comment.

"Are you ready?" was all Tarafau sent to Lizzie and Reloi. Lizzie could only nod.

"Goodbye," Reloi sent, his face alight with hope. *"See you soon."*

Once again, Lizzie only nodded. Tarafau put his huge hand on her shoulder, and Reloi's hopeful face faded from view.

Chapter 20: Resonance

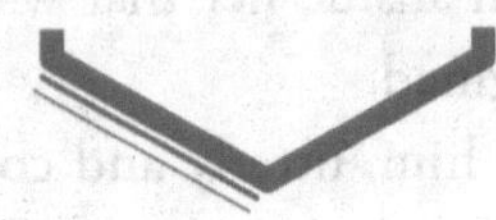

(Jenny sighed as she gently closed the journal. She had a feeling there was so much more to this part of Lizzie's story, but for now she felt she could sleep with this scene in her mind.

With a little over a week left before her recuperation was due to end, she felt an urgency to finish this journal so she could begin the next one. Lizzie's adventures had been enthralling, and yet she knew that she would be coming into the picture herself as she continued with the next journal.

Like Lizzie, she would be spending time in her mental world with someone she loved as soon as she went to bed. She could relate to how hard it was to care for someone so much and be separated by necessity. She always looked forward to her visits with Burt at their little pond by the Merced.

They seldom met in Jenny's fortress, because for Jenny that represented her work in the Alliance and held little or no romance for her.

Since Jenny's wedding, Chidwi had appropriated the window seat as her bed and was already fast asleep. Tidbit had already left by the cat door that Burt had installed next to the french doors that led out to the patio.

As she headed to bed, she stopped and stroked Chidwi's little head, and the linkling stirred only slightly in her sleep.

The next morning, she awoke to bright sunlight. How late had she slept? She was jealous of every moment lost in reading the journals and was a bit put out that no one had gotten her up. But once again she remembered their protectiveness of her recuperation and sighed.

After she had showered and dressed, Lizziebot was already in the kitchen preparing her nutritional shake.

Jenny took her shake off of the counter as soon as Lizziebot poured it into the glass and carried it into the living room, setting it on a coaster on the end table next to her reading chair, and carefully opened the journal to the bookmark.)

Lizzie and Tarafau walked from the basement to Liliath's office to report in before going to the pod building. As usual, Liliath was stretched out on the huge dragon-sized chaise, a book in her hands. She looked up and smiled.

Lizzie still felt goosebumps whenever Liliath smiled, the ghost of every dragon tale she had ever read still conditioning her to respect that mouth full of fangs. She had seldom seen Liliath angry but could testify that it was not something she would ever want to have directed at her personally.

"Good. You are all here but Reanni. The rest of your pod will be heading to the dining hall in a few minutes. I think you have time to set out with them if you hurry. So glad to have you back. The reports from the council through Reloi are very good, and we will discuss this later. For now, go get some food, and enjoy catching up with your podmates."

As they headed out of the admin building, Tarafau sent, *"I'm going to go have a chat with Lall. Some of the things we were doing at Grild will interest him, I think."*

Lizzie nodded. She moved forward briskly, excited to finally get the chance to see her podmates and hear about their adventures. She knew they had each been assigned to diverse situations requiring them to use their unique talents as they pursued their internships.

She didn't have to enter the building. There, under "our tree" were her podmates, obviously engaged in enthusiastic mental chat;

and as she neared, Gi looked up and saw her approaching, and every head turned in her direction.

They were all there except Reanni, the two Geln grinning with delight; Negoth, with his self-assured smile; Linlin, her hair squirming excitedly even though her face was as placid as ever; Mang looking commanding but with a welcoming look in his green eyes that contrasted so sharply with his magenta skin; Feth, short of stature and the sun glinting off of his shiny bald head; as the much taller Mang, with a mischievous look in his brown eyes; Minth, in the special insulated suit he had received before he had left for his internship; and Ben, bright green with blue and yellow spiky hair, his chin tilted up in his usual arrogant manner but with as close to a smile as Lizzie had ever seen him.

A mental chorus of *"Lizzie!"* greeted her, and she ran the rest of the way, taking it in turn to hug them all, even Minth, who was now safe to be close to, due to the new technology that had created his special suit.

"We were about to go to the dining hall. We understand that Reanni has been delayed, but we're hungry," Geln said jovially. *"Shall we go?"*

They all nodded and headed around the corner to the lane behind the pods that led to the dining hall.

As they trooped in and sat at their usual table, Gi reached up and patted Ynni. *"How is our little mama doing?"* she sent.

"Ynni and the younglings are well. Our tribe thrives in the grove near Tarafau's home."

"They imported some additional linklings from Miriha's planet," Lizzie explained at Gi's puzzled look. *"There are now nearly two dozen of them. They have taken over the grove and even help with the landscaping, to Amenia's delight. It is amazing to see her, with her baby in the sling on her chest, surrounded by willing and helpful linklings, crooning as they work."*

"How has your internship been going?" Gi then asked with a chuckle. *"I understand you got Grild? That has to be interesting, living inside a planet instead of on the surface."*

And from there the conversation was a mish-mash of each one of them sharing their experiences on so many disparate and unique missions. From what Lizzie gathered from the conversation, each internship had indeed been designed to take advantage of the unique talents, experience, and skills of the one assigned.

She found herself hoping for some quiet time with Gi, as she thought that only she would appreciate her experience with the change in her relationship with Reloi.

All of a sudden, her reverie was interrupted when everyone at the table broke into laughter. She chuckled, even though she had obviously missed someone's joke.

"I understand that in the morning we will be debriefed on our internships; and assuming we pass the muster, the next day we will be installed as official agents. There will be a ceremony and a celebration. As soon as they do that, we get a two-week leave to visit family and then it's on to work," sent Linlin in her flat mental voice. *"I had hoped for a little bit longer leave time than that."*

Most of them nodded in agreement, but they had all been instructed in the beginning that it was likely they would be put right back to work with very little time off. Regular breaks would happen, depending on the assignment. The commitment they had made with the Alliance meant they wouldn't see a lot of their families or friends from what they now considered a former life.

"It's a good thing, then, that we can all look forward to something new and exciting, right?" Negoth put in. *"I joined up for adventures. Who knows where we'll get sent next?"*

"I'd kind of like to go back to where they sent me this time," Mang sent. *"I've gotten to do some really interesting work, and the beings I*

work with are stimulating to be around, highly intelligent, and really diligent."

Which started a conversation about the pros and cons of getting an entirely new assignment versus returning to the place where they served their internship. The opinions in the group were split nearly in half, as far as those who would want to return and those who would prefer the excitement of a dimension previously unknown to them.

If Lizzie hadn't still had the last moment with Reloi fresh in her mind, she realized that the former Lizzie would have actually wanted to move on to a new assignment, not because she hadn't enjoyed her time on Grild, but to further her quest to know and learn more about the multiverse.

For now, knowing there was nothing she could do about it one way or the other, she decided to just get through the coming couple of weeks and hope for the best.

The rest of the day was spent catching up. By mutual agreement, they had a nice little concert under the tree. By the time it was lights-out, Lizzie had a feeling she wasn't the only one who couldn't seem to fall asleep.

That next morning, they all got up, did their usual workout with Lall, showered and dressed, and went to breakfast. There was little chatter and Lizzie suspected she wasn't the only one going through her report to her instructors in her head, trying to prepare for the unknown and hoping she wouldn't be rejected or sent back into training without getting certified.

As they left the dining hall, she realized that she was instinctively doing her breathing exercises as they walked towards the admin building. As they entered the double doors, their instructors were all lined up facing the entrance, even Meta, who Lizzie had thought was back at Grild.

Fin stepped forward, the shortest of them, his brown eyes twinkling. *"I see you have all mastered your facial expression training. However, I remember standing in your place many years ago and how nervous I was. Let me assure you that it won't be nearly as scary as you are making it in your minds. Each of you have been assigned a room for your debriefing, and your instructors will be filtering in and out to speak with you about the reports we have received.*

"There will be a short break in between each review to allow you to catch your breath. The debriefing won't take but a few hours, after which you may all go to eat some lunch and then return here for your final briefing in the same room as your debriefing. Following that, you may take a break until later today, when we will all assemble to issue certifications and celebrate our new agents.

"Understood?" He scanned the faces in front of him. All of them nodded. He then led them down the corridor, stopping at different doors and pointing to each one of them and gesturing for them to enter in their turn.

Lizzie was next to the end, with only Geln left, standing patiently together. As she entered the room, only about ten paces square, she noticed the only furniture in the room were two chairs facing one another. She sat, despite the feeling she would rather be pacing the small confines of the room.

Almost immediately, Lulindu entered, a tablet in her hand. The contrast of her light green skin and the long teal robe she customarily wore was striking, and her dark green eyes were serious as usual.

"I must say I am impressed with the reports we have received from Tarafau about both your internship on his planet and your work on Grild. I don't have a lot that needs discussion, but I do want to encourage you to hold to the non-interference ethics of the Alliance. I know in the past you have had issues with our firm stance on avoiding tech-pollution of the various cultures, even your home planet. I understand your concerns, but it is a fine line we walk.

"What would you say was your favorite part of the internships you have served so far?"

And so it began. Each of the instructors seemed to be satisfied with her performance on both Tarafau's planet and Grild, and each of them emphasized something she had learned from them in their own course of instruction.

They each also paid attention to the part Ynni had played in her internships and how the two of them had used that companionship to great advantage. More than one of her instructors stressed what an asset Ynni could be in Lizzie's future assignments.

Baird was particularly interested in the work she had done at the school and the introduction of the mbira to that culture. He reassured her that this was not cultural pollution. It was understood both by the Alliance and the member planets they dealt with, that agents would bring with them new ideas and outlooks that would potentially impact the new culture they were interacting with. They just weren't to share advanced technology that was unknown to the worlds they visited, unless they had the express permission of both the Alliance Council and the host member world, nor to interfere or give opinions about local politics.

The satellite technology that was being installed for Grild was an example of that kind of agreement. The sole purpose of the satellite was to allow instant communications in the case of an emergency and to allow council members to vote on issues and to stay up to date on any decisions made by the council or news that pertained to Alliance membership.

Lizzie's interviews were pleasant and not the grilling she had expected. Before she knew it, she was heading to the dining hall with the rest of her podmates. The mood was a lot lighter than it had been, but most of them still weren't sure they had passed muster; only that the first part hadn't been nearly as stressful as they had expected it would be.

Following lunch, they trooped back to the admin building, once again feeling the stress begin to build. They each returned to the little rooms they had started in.

To Lizzie's delight, Meta was the one to attend her for her briefing. Since their initial training at Sanglarka, Meta had become more than an instructor. Lizzie thought of her as a friend. Their mutual interest in science and technology had created a strong bond between them, and their personalities were similar enough that they often completed one another's sentences, especially when they were in the throes of discovery.

"Well, Lizzie. After these final interviews and taking into consideration the reports from both internships, we have come to the conclusion that you are ready to be certified as an official agent for the Dimensional Alliance. This means, assuming you accept the commission, your life will be mandated by the assignments you receive from the Alliance council. This means that, although you always have the option to make choices within each assignment, based on your training, experience, and the help from your guide, you have agreed to answer to the council in all things and to accept their assignments or any changes to a current assignment. Do you agree to this?"

Lizzie countered, *"You mentioned a guide. I thought that was only during my internship."*

"Ah, yes, well, every agent continues to travel with a guide for the first full year after certification. Consider it a kind of safety net. In this case, Tarafau would continue to be your guide. So, do you agree to these conditions?"

"I do. Do you know where they will be sending me?"

Meta raised her eyebrows mischievously, *"Now that would be telling, wouldn't it? You won't find out for sure where you are going next until you return from your two-week leave. For now, you are dismissed until we meet again this afternoon for the awarding of agent symbols and our celebration feast. I'm excited for you, Lizzie. I see amazing things in your future."*

She stood and, as Lizzie copied her, reached forward and gave her an enthusiastic hug, something she wouldn't have expected from any of her other instructors.

"I'm very glad I got to be the one to tell you this," she said, her eyes sparkling with enthusiasm. *"I hope we get many opportunities to work together over your career."*

"And I, too," Lizzie agreed, as they walked into the hallway. *"I have learned so much from you, and I really enjoy the time we get to spend together, even though it hasn't been a lot lately. How is the satellite project coming? Will you be launching soon?"*

"I expect we will launch sometime in the next few weeks. The conditions on the surface of the planet make the work moving forward slower than I had hoped, but I have a great team, and they will get the job done."

Lizzie left the building with a happy heart. Gi was already waiting for her under the tree, as they had all agreed before going in that they would meet there to celebrate or commiserate, depending on the outcomes. She was grinning, and Lizzie knew without asking that she had also passed.

She couldn't imagine that any of them wouldn't pass. She had a lot of faith in the skill and intelligence of her podmates. So they sat there and greeted every one of them as each of them arrived, affirming that they too would be looking forward to the ceremony and the celebration.

Once again, they did one of their impromptu concerts in celebration of their accomplishment, and it was glorious to join in harmony with Gi and Ynni and the tree; and to Lizzie's surprise and delight, Geln took out their mbiras and joined in. They basked in the glow of the bonds of friendship they had created over the course of their training. Lizzie felt a little wistful, however, when she realized that she probably wouldn't get many opportunities to spend time with these good friends over the coming years.

Indeed, after they were sent off to their various home planets for their leave time, they would spend the very last night in the pod building they had been assigned to. From that time forward, they would be reporting directly to the Alliance headquarters building and staying in guest quarters there as needed. It would only be by chance that they would meet there.

She was encouraged when she remembered she could still keep in touch via her tablet, something she wasn't generally very good at. She made a personal vow, however, that she would try to take a moment every week to contact her friends. She also knew she would have to be more diligent about staying in contact with her own family. The Alliance had given agents of non-member dimensions access to a system that would allow her to appear to be sending regular mail to family members and Gaston, something she had not taken much advantage of.

This reminded her that she needed to contact Gaston and let him know she had passed and that she would be returning to visit him soon and to make arrangements for her to go home to visit her parents and siblings.

As they continued to hang out under the tree, they began to notice that the outside dais was being assembled in front of the admin building. When it was complete, a musical assembly call went out over the loudspeakers that could be heard throughout the training complex.

They had been told that when they heard that, they were to seat themselves on the dais and wait for the ceremony to begin. Obediently, they all arose and brushed any grass or leaves off of their clothing and, along with the other trainees who were heading to the space in front of the dais, trooped to ascend the dais steps.

Liliath and the instructors were all already assembled and seated in their places, and some of them nodded to their students as they took their own seats. True to their training, none of the anxiety or excitement Lizzie knew they were all feeling showed on their faces. She thought wryly that Baird must feel very proud of them at that moment.

There had been only the sound of the crowd milling around, finding a good vantage point, as the majority of the trainees, even those who spoke the same language, generally used mindspeech by habit. However, even those small sounds cut off abruptly when Liliath rose to her full height and the instructors all stood.

"The entire purpose of the training each of you is pursuing in this facility is to become certified agents of the Dimensional Alliance. It is a long and difficult road, and each of you can begin to appreciate how fulfilling it must be to finally achieve that aim.

"Each of the trainees on this dais have fulfilled their assignments with honor, completing the training and their internships in a manner to make us proud of their accomplishments. We foresee that each of them will be a tremendous asset to the Alliance, and their future service will allow the Alliance to move forward with confidence that we will fulfill our mission to protect the multiverse from those who would use the gateway network to oppress and take advantage of their neighbors.

"As we call their names, each will rise and line up on the dais to stand before you. When all are standing, we will applaud them as the instructors fasten their badge of office around their necks. Each of these have agreed to the strictures and responsibilities of an Alliance Agent. The donning of the infinity symbol that represents their certification is a sign of that covenant."

One at a time, beginning with Geln, Liliath called their names. Facing the vastly diverse crowd of trainees, Lizzie realized that they were looking up at the new agents with a certain awe and hope for the future time when they too would stand to receive this honor.

As the last one stood and faced them, there was a loud cheer interspersed with hoots, shouts, and some sounds that were completely alien. However, the mental shout that went up simultaneously was in unison and also mentally deafening and enthusiastic.

A shiver went up her spine when Baird stood before her and presented the golden infinity symbol dangling on a chain for her to see up close before he reached behind her and fastened it on her neck.

"As you have been instructed," he sent directly to her, *"this symbol can be removed only by death, retirement, or by a member of the high council. It is a commitment for a lifetime. Welcome, Agent Japhet. Kudos to you for your accomplishment, and thank you for being such a great representative of the planet and universe we both love."*

It touched her that Baird, one of the few Earth representatives she had met so far at the Alliance since she left Sanglarka, was the one who gave her the symbol of her office.

"Thank you, Professor O'Flaherty," she sent. *"Erin go Bragh."*

He grinned. *"Aye Lassie, you've got it right."*

He turned and went on to Gi, who stood there with her chin up, spine erect. Watching out of the corner of her eyes, Lizzie remembered how her first impression of this good friend was that she was stuck up and overly impressed with herself. Of course, she had learned that this was strictly a physical trait of Gi's people and not an indication of her attitude. This was one of her first lessons in the importance of not judging the beings she met based on their outward appearance.

Once again, a private mental conversation appeared to occur between Baird and Gi and Lizzie saw her face light up with whatever he said to her. Once the necklace had been fastened around Gi's neck and the professor had moved on, Gi reached out and grabbed Lizzie's hand. *"Congratulations, Agent Lizzie."*

"Congratulations, Agent Gi." Lizzie returned with a grin, no longer trying to hide her emotions from her face.

When the ceremony was complete, Liliath once again broadcast to the entire assemblage, *"Welcome, new agents, to the Dimensional Alliance. We will celebrate in the dining hall with a feast and a reception. You are dismissed."*

Once again, a shout went up from the crowd, and they all turned to head to the dining hall. None of the new agents on the dais hurried off just yet. Their professors and Liliath were each shaking their hands and praising them, and there was much hugging and congratulating amongst these podmates who had made it through a more difficult than usual training.

As Geln approached, Lizzie hugged them both at once. *"We will miss your brother,"* she sent to them, *"And we honor him."*

One of them held out a hand. In it was a gold infinity symbol, without a chain. *"They gave us this to honor our brother. We will give it to our mother, and it will be cherished as a family heirloom."*

Lizzie couldn't help the tears that escaped down her cheek, but she smiled and nodded. *"It has been an honor for all of us to know him, and he will never be forgotten."*

And with that, they trooped off to enjoy the feast and prepare to depart the next morning to their various leave destinations, each knowing that this could possibly be their last evening together, each resolving to enjoy every minute of it.

Chapter 21: Point and Counterpoint

(Jenny only skimmed Lizzie's brief account of her visit with Gaston and with her parents, and the celebration at Sanglarka, knowing somehow that something significant was about to happen.

Something inside her wasn't sure she really wanted to know what happened next, but she also needed to know in a way that was somehow visceral.

Her own introduction to her key had been almost a side note with no major ceremony. Her friend Sam had fastened it about her neck, and Miriha, in the privacy of her office, had activated it. Tarafau had been there, but it had been no momentous occasion. She did envy her aunt somewhat to have been able to celebrate with her fellow trainees and her instructors.

The closest thing she had been given in the way of training was the preparations she had experienced in Sanglarka, and the mental training with Liliath and Amenia. She still felt inadequate to the task before her.

For now, these journals were very instructive, and she felt she might be a little better prepared, having vicariously experienced Lizzie's account.

She turned the page.)

Lizzie stood in the gate room with Gaston, facing the door that led to the Alliance headquarters gate at the top of the hill overlooking the city.

Gaston grinned. "Well, Agent Japhet, may I be allowed to give you a little going away gift as you prepare for your next adventure?"

"Of course, Gaston, thank you. But I have nothing for you. I didn't know... I didn't expect...."

He laughed and patted her arm. "Not at all, not at all! There are no protocols for this kind of thing, and you spent enough of your allotment on gifts for family members and our associates at Sanglarka during your leave. Your visit was gift enough for me. To think, you made it and did so with honors! I feel very vindicated in my choice of you as a prospective agent.

"You have done Earth proud! Every single gate guardian is happy to have you as a representative of our dimension. Until Earth is officially vetted as a knowing member of the Alliance, we have very little representation among the good and the great. Your success has made me feel very full of myself, I can assure you!"

He chuckled again. "It is a small thing, not even new, but I thought somehow you might like it; and when you wear it, you will think of me."

He held out the hand that had been behind his back. "This belonged to my wife. I always enjoyed it on her, and you remind me of the self-assured attitude I always admired in her. Anyway, wear it in good health."

In his hand was a grey wool beret. "Your heritage is French, after all, like mine. And this will look good on your saucy new haircut."

Lizzie blushed for a moment in embarrassment. One of the first things she had asked Gaston to do for her was to get her an appointment with a stylist to get her hair cut, which had gotten shaggy and shoulder length. It had been very uncomfortable for her and required much more attention than she was used to having to give to her appearance.

She took the beret from him and put it on her head. "No, like this," he said, adjusting the hat so it perched jauntily to one side. "Now you look like the two best ladies I have ever known."

Lizzie reached forward and hugged him fervently. "Thank you, Gaston. I will treasure it and wear it any time it is appropriate. It isn't like the agents have a uniform, only the symbol," and she self-consciously touched the little symbol at her neck.

"Funny, no one at home even noticed I was wearing it, and they all know I never wear jewelry."

"Ah, yes, avoidance technology has been programmed into it, along with your DNA and designation. The eyes of anyone not specifically looking for it will just skip over it and dismiss it from their mind," Gaston said with a smile. "I'm guessing your mind was wandering when they talked about it during your training."

"Possibly," Lizzie said, somewhat embarrassed. "Well, I suppose I need to go. There is supposed to be a hover car waiting for me at the bottom of the hill. I don't want to keep those guards waiting."

He hugged her one more time, and she turned and went out the door to exit through the water-like gate shield onto the platform that overlooked the valley that accommodated the capital city of Dimensional Alliance headquarters.

She took a deep breath of the fresh air, so different than Los Angeles, and headed down the hill. As expected, the two guards with a single eye in the middle of their foreheads were there to greet her. More than one hover car waited there. Lizzie assumed it was because her podmates would also be reporting to the Council today.

By the time she arrived in the reception area in the headquarters building, she was unsurprised to find several of her podmates waiting apparently patiently.

"*Have a seat,*" the receptionist sent. "*There are three more expected any time now.*" Her tone implied that they would be weighed in the balance if they showed up even a minute late.

Lizzie sat and greeted them. *"So, this is it,"* she sent. *"Is it just me, or is it hot in here?"* She pulled at the collar of her blouse, hoping her sweat wouldn't be taken as a sign of nervousness.

But before anyone could answer her, Geln and Minth exited the elevator into the room.

"The council will see you now," announced the receptionist, gesturing towards the doorway with her head, her wing, and her hand.

Obediently, they all rose and went through the huge double doors where the council was assembled in front of the dais to greet them.

Chief Councilor of the Dimensional Alliance, Gleph and Linaa, greeted them, both heads smiling and beckoning them forward to a semicircle of chairs before them. His councilors, Khol of the planet TKZ in the Invi dimension, and Bernviniarcusa, who went by "Bern," was from the planet Liftzi in the dimension of Gul stood beside him. It was hard to tell if they were smiling or not, but they were mentally sending approval towards the group of new agents.

"For the purposes of security, your new assignments have been loaded to your tablets, and we ask you not to reveal them to anyone unless you have approval from your guide, who will be aware of the strictures of your assigned dimension.

"You will go from here to the basement of this building to logistics, where you will receive the necessary equipment, clothing, and any supplies needed for your specific assignment. After that, you will proceed to the headquarters gate, where you will meet your guides. I'm assuming you all are packed with any necessary personal things?"

They all nodded somberly.

"Then we congratulate you on your first assignments and welcome you into the society of Alliance Agents. The symbol you wear around your neck is more than a badge of office. It also gives you access to any gates a Gate Guardian will allow you to go through. In some cases, they

may be programmed temporarily for unlimited access, but that usually only happens in the case of an emergency or disaster situation.

"Do any of you have any questions for us?"

They shook their heads in near unison.

"Then you are dismissed. Fair well, and return with honor."

The group turned on their heels and departed without a word. Lizzie could sense that she wasn't the only one who felt the meeting was a bit abrupt.

In the basement, they found the outfitters area, and each of them went to a separate counter and presented their tablet to a clerk, who accessed the assignment information, checked that it matched with their own data, and then proceeded to hand them packages. Lizzie found that they were each being given private mental instructions for their bundles. Hers was quite small, compared to some of the large packages that were being handed to some of her podmates.

"Since your assignment is not changing from your previous internship, you are already mostly supplied. In this packet is your personal emergency beacon, which will connect with any Alliance communications satellite, even from within a planet such as your situation indicates."

Lizzie was careful to keep her face placid, but inside she was jumping up and down like a kangaroo. She couldn't believe she had gotten her wish to stay on Grild.

"In addition, there are a few sets of workout clothes, such as you are already accustomed to, and additional ration bars for an emergency. You already have a three-month supply of potable water and all of the necessary equipment for an extended camping scenario. If, at any point, you have other needs we did not expect, you can requisition them through your tablet via the Alliance communications network, which I understand is currently being installed on Grild."

Lizzie nodded as she installed her supplies in her MDP. *"Thank you,"* she said.

The clerk smiled and sent, *"Good luck on your first real assignment, Agent Japhet,"* and turned to the shelves behind her to get the next package for another order ready.

As Lizzie turned for the door, she heaved a great sigh. *"Wow,"* she thought, *"This is it. This is real, and I am an agent of the Dimensional Alliance."*

She and the others headed down a long corridor to the gate room. There they were greeted by their guides and the headquarters Gate Guardian.

The guardian was humanoid, tall, and apparently female. Seeming to have no ears she did have golden eyes and long, sunshine-yellow hair that draped to the back of her knees and was as fine and transparent as silk fibers. She was dressed in green breeches and a matching long-sleeved, flowing, satiny tunic.

"I am Tul, the guardian of the headquarters gate. Line up and in turn hand me your tablet, and I will lead you to the gate of your assigned dimension and hand your tablet back to you. Please install the tablet back into your MDP before you enter the gate. Understood?"

Lizzie watched as her podmates, one at a time, handed their tablets to Tul, waved goodbye to the group, and left with her to disappear down the impossibly long hallway. Tul then returned and repeated the process. Lizzie was one of the last to depart.

Gi had turned to her before leaving and gave her a one-armed hug. *"Stay in touch when you can,"* she sent and with a wave headed towards her assignment with her guide, Minga, a stout, short woman with black hair shorter than Lizzie's and a broad, toothy grin that never seemed to fade. Gi had told Lizzie that the smile was not a smile at all. Her teeth were always bared, and the corners of her mouth permanently turned up.

Lizzie looked up at Tarafau, standing beside her, his massive arms folded across his chest. His face was calm and his eyes were serious but not grim. He knew where they were going, and she thought he may have actually been looking forward to continuing their work with the Grildites.

When Tul returned and held out her hand, Lizzie was relieved. When she had discovered they were going back to Grild, the first thought that came to her was of a bald shiny head, spiky silver eyebrows, large violet eyes, and the smile that he reserved just for her.

As much as she had enjoyed being the aunty who came to visit with amazing gifts to spend time with her family, as nice as it was to see Gaston and to visit with the Gate Guardians at a special party given in her honor at Sanglarka, and as amazing as it was to spend time with her podmates, when it came down to it, now she felt like she was really going home.

How ironic that she hadn't found such deep feelings until she had traveled clear across the multiverse to a dimension far, far away. She stepped through the door Tul indicated, after retrieving her tablet and putting it into her MDP. She immediately found herself, Tarafau and Ynni standing inside the crystalline dome on the planet's surface, and there were Reloi and Tanata in Reloi's hover chair, smiling happily at them.

She noticed, not far from the dome, two small structures that hadn't been there the last time she had been here.

"The construction site and the launcher," Reloi mentioned, noticing her glance outside. *"They will be ready to launch sooner than expected. Meta and her team have been working day and night to get it in place as quickly as possible."*

She hardly even noticed the ride down the chute to the inner surface of Grild. She just couldn't stop smiling. She was truly home, and she was looking forward to digging in and getting to work.

There was no ceremony for her this time. They headed to the council room, and Lizzie was welcomed back as if it had been taken for granted that she would return. They had several reports from the school waiting for her and told her that there would be a meeting later that day with the administrators of the educational system for the entire planet, as they wanted to institute the program she had established in the first school she had worked at planetwide.

This suited Lizzie just fine. She still hadn't checked her tablet for the details of this assignment. She had been afraid it would be only a few months and wasn't sure she wanted to know, but the council was behaving as if she would be there permanently.

She happily threw herself into continuing her work with the schools on a much larger scale, and she was invited to participate in general council meetings every couple of weeks.

More and more often, she spent time with Reloi's family, happily engaging in their unique games and family activities. His mother and father welcomed her gladly every time she visited, and they often had long discussions about the raising of Reloi, a both gifted and physically challenged child. Those conversations often embarrassed Reloi, who made light of his parents' praise and blushed furiously about their recounts of his childhood mishaps, often created by his own stubbornness and his unwillingness to submit to his condition.

Lizzie's feelings for Reloi continued to deepen the more she knew about him, both his gifts and his failings. They didn't always agree about everything, and sometimes she found his advice a bit annoying. They continued to work on Lizzie's mental exercises as if she were still an agent trainee. Her affinity for plants was, according to Reloi, a rare gift and she was also beginning to get the hang of basic kinetic abilities.

As she traveled through the lusher areas of Grild, she would find herself in conversation with large trees, flowering shrubs, and sometimes even the coarse blue-green grass that was abundant nearly everywhere that other plants weren't growing. The one thing about Grild that was strikingly unique was that there were no deserts there and nothing that you might think of as a mountain, although there were many low hills and deep valleys throughout the countryside.

The Grildite roadways were simple affairs. Not many were paved, and most threaded through the landscape, taking only as much space as necessary for heavy foot traffic or manually pulled carts. Lizzie was grateful for well-designed boots, which had become her favorite footwear, as they visited various schools and apprentice co-ops throughout the planet's lush interior.

By the time she had been there about three months, she truly felt at home. Every new day gave her new opportunities to make a valuable impact on the Grildite culture. The use of the mbira as a common instrument continued to grow. The little project to create mbiras for what was initially a small group of students was fast becoming a small industry, providing jobs and a brand-new apprenticeship program sponsored by the school system.

It had never occurred to Lizzie when she had first introduced the mbira to that small group of students that something like this would have grown out of it. This also made her realize that even the initially smallest action can sometimes have a widespread effect on a population, reinforcing what Lulindu had been trying to teach them about why the Alliance was so intent on their policy of selective intervention into any of the cultures they interacted with.

Ynni had become a favorite with the Grildites, especially the children. She always was given a part to play in any of the instruction or presentations they gave and was a big hit with all, including the instructors. From time to time, both she and Tanata would play out some of the learning scenarios. These proved to be especially memorable to all concerned.

Ynni and Tanata had become fast friends and seemed to know when Lizzie and Reloi needed some privacy. At those times, they would scamper off to engage in their own conversations and play.

"They're probably discussing all of our foibles," Reloi commented one day as they watched them go to the edge of the little pond, engaging in mental conversation, nodding or shaking a head and

sometimes laughing together. *"I'm sure it's probably a relief for them to discuss our shortcomings without fear of hurting our feelings."*

"Not that Ynni is very shy about discussing my failings to my face," Lizzie chortled with a grimace. *"She doesn't hesitate to let me know when she thinks I need to fix my attitude or that I've made an error in judgment."*

"Yeah, I get that from Tanata all the time. He seems to think I need to be more upfront with you, for instance."

"Upfront? How? I wasn't aware you were ever less than honest with me."

"Um... well..." he sighed. *"It's just that... Lizzie, I love you. I fell for you almost from the beginning. When we were student and mentor, I felt it would have been inappropriate for me to approach you about it, but now that we are on equal footing, it has become harder and harder for me not to tell you this.*

"I think now it has been more about being rejected than anything, and I apologize if this makes you uncomfortable. I fear it might affect our friendship for you to know my true feelings, but... well... there it is."

He looked into her face, searching for anything that would give him a clue as to how she felt.

"Oh, Reloi, don't look at me like that. I could never reject your honest feelings for me. But let me confess that I too have been holding back for a long time now. Even with all of the difficulties a romantic relationship would present for me at this time, I want you to know that I love you and as more than a friend. I'm not sure where we go from here, but..."

And she leaned into him, put her arms around him and kissed him on the lips for the second time, but this time it was no impulse. She had wanted to do it every time she looked at him. His face was the face that had come to her mind again and again while she had been away to finish her certification. His was the face that intruded on her thoughts while she had spent time with her family. She had dreamed about kissing him. About holding him in her arms though he had no arms to wrap around her.

As they finally drew apart, there was delighted amazement on his face.

"I have little to give you, Lizzie Japhet, agent of the Alliance, but what I have I offer you. I don't know the customs of your dimension, but here, if you wish to make a relationship permanent, we register with the council and wait for six months before a relationship can be sealed in marriage. Lizzie, will you wait with me for six months so we can be together officially? Will you grant me the supreme gift of becoming my wife? I promise you my faithfulness beyond life and death."

Lizzie had always thought it was a bit corny when the heroine in a romantic story said, "This is all so sudden!" but now she understood. Nevertheless, she answered, looking deep into those violet eyes framed by the expressive silvered spiky eyebrows that she would have found so alien in another time, another life.

"Yes, Reloi. I can think of nothing that would bring me greater joy." And seeing his gratified smile, she kissed him again, several times.

When they next visited the council, they submitted their request for a nuptial agreement and then announced it to his parents. She realized, regretfully, that she could never tell her own parents. The strictures she had agreed to when she had become an Alliance agent didn't allow it. But his parents rejoiced wholeheartedly and were delighted that she would soon become an official part of their family.

Lizzie had also communicated with the Alliance to confirm that this marriage would not be against the agreements between dimension member planets. She discovered, to her surprise and delight, that she was not the only one who had fallen in love with someone from a different dimension and that, although these arrangements weren't common, they were not against any of the articles of the Alliance.

At this point, her work on Grild became even more satisfying as she realized she was about to connect with the Grildites in a new and more committed relationship. This definitely had not been on any of her imagined lists of what she might accomplish as an Alliance agent. Now she began to think of the Grildites as "her" people.

She found herself counting down the months and began to wish the Grildite "month" had been more like Earth months. A Grildite month was six Grildite weeks long, each week divided into 10 days.

The first few months were a curious mixture of satisfying works that took up most of the "days" in Grild, not defined by the rising and setting of the sun, but by a time system developed by the Grildites that mimicked the days and nights they had been used to before retreating to the inner core of their planet. Days were typically closer to thirty-eight hours of earth time, which she had measured by an app in her tablet designed to measure time in whatever was "normal" time for that particular agent.

So, although she was kept busy and got to spend lots of time with Reloi, his family, and the friends she was making amongst the communities where she worked most often, she wished fervently for the time to speed by so she could finally be officially Reloi's wife.

They went on two kinds of dates. On the one hand, they enjoyed visiting the various parks in whatever community they were working in at the time. These visits during the day were happy times. They discussed future plans for building a home of their own, a traditional process once their bill of marriage was finally official, and spent hours designing it in stages.

Typically, on Grild, each home was begun in the most basic format: living space, one or two bedrooms, a kitchen, a basement to house the family aquaponics, and hygiene facilities. As families grew, additional rooms were built on. This preserved resources and kept land space mostly wild or used for the little bit of farming that supplemented all of the aquaponic systems used by each family in Grild.

Lizzie could see that this was a good system for preserving resources and allowing for reasonable growth in what seemed a very limited environment. And she took great delight discussing all of the possibilities with Reloi, including ways to make all aspects of the home accessible to him. It was true that his mental kinetics gave him an advantage that paraplegics on Earth didn't have, but Reloi's mom had given her a lot of ideas on how they could make their home much more comfortable for him.

She sometimes reflected on what her family would have thought of her choice of a mate. She knew they would have been kind to him, despite his physical condition, but she could picture her mother advising her to think carefully before she made a lifelong commitment to someone with physical limitations. As far as the alien humanoid thing, well, that obviously might be an issue.

As they made their preparations and continued their work in the Grild education system, Lizzie found she was more content than she had been at any previous time in her life. Interacting with both the teachers and the students had become a true joy, and she even found herself looking forward to the council meetings, where she had become a true member of this prestigious body.

In council meetings, she was able to contribute in ways that earned her the respect of her fellow members. She found that they often asked her opinions of things that had nothing to do with her assignments in the educational system.

All in all, she found herself blessing Gaston, who had seen her potential and had taken the risk of proposing this new course of action to her. His unique method of testing her for the necessary attributes of an Alliance agent, his kindness, and his encouragement had prepared her well for the training.

Chapter 22: Dissonance Descends

(Jenny felt the joy bubble up in her. Joy for Lizzie's journey and gratitude that it had led to her own experiences. Like Lizzie, Jenny had found satisfaction, usefulness, friendship, and love in her new life as a Gatekeeper that she might not have known otherwise.

We pass it on, don't we? she asked herself, as she turned a page, eager to see what happened next.)

Lizzie listened with delight to the little concert being performed by a small mbira orchestra at the main school where she had first begun her teaching experience. The young faces of the performers were ecstatic as they focused on the beautiful music that Arpen had composed especially for her, a salute to what she had done for all of the students on Grild.

The music seemed to reflect the peaceful and pastoral life of the Grildites, flowing like a gentle gurgling stream and then soaring as high as the constant light in their internal sky. As they concluded, she rose to her feet and, along with the others in the audience, applauded enthusiastically, a smile on her face that she could not have hidden even with Baird watching her.

"Excellent! Amazing! That was truly beautiful!" she enthused. *"You have obviously been working hard to master this new instrument, and it shows in your performance today. Thank you so very much."*

Arpen stood with her, his eyes shining with unshed tears of joy. *"Thank you for what you have done for us, Lizzie Japhet. We have titled*

*this, 'Ode to Lizzie' and hope that you will accept it as our first attempt
to do justice to your teaching."*

Lizzie blushed to the roots of her hair. She had never been very
good at receiving compliments and this was more than a little over
the top for her. She just ducked her head and nodded.

At a signal from Arpen, the students stood and gently placed
their instruments on their chairs, then one at a time came forward
and placed two fingers on Lizzie's forehead and then on Ynni's with
a sweet and sincere *"Thank you."* By the time the twenty-person
orchestra had filed past her, Lizzie had tears streaming joyfully down
her face, and Ynni was crooning happily.

Reloi hadn't been able to be there for the concert, but she could
hardly wait to tell him about it. Just before the concert had started,
a messenger had come to him with an urgent request from Meta to
report to the lab immediately. He had told Lizzie not to worry, he
would attend to it while she went to the concert that these young
people had been preparing for her for weeks.

She exited the auditorium surrounded by the others who had
been in the audience and the students who had participated. She
felt a gentle glow surrounding them all, a connection of spirit that
felt more permanent than the mountains that surrounded the Los
Angeles basin where she had grown up.

As they spilled out onto the large lawn square in front of the
school, she noticed Reloi, speeding towards them on his hover chair,
a look of concern on his face. She hoped he didn't feel guilty that he
hadn't attended the concert. That would be like him. As he slid to a
stop before her, she started to tell him that she understood why he
had missed this important event, but the look on his face stopped
her before she could utter a word.

*"You must come with me. Tarafau and Meta are waiting. No time
to explain,"* was all he said. Even his mental voice sounded breathless

and reflected the distress on his face. His silver eyebrows were knitted together hard, as if he was experiencing physical pain.

Lizzie only nodded and rushed off with him, without a word to the confused people that surrounded her. It wasn't easy keeping up with Reloi; and the farther they went, the more concerned Lizzie became.

Had something happened to Tarafau? Was there something wrong with the satellite? She had attended the official launch and it had been successful as far as she knew. This was the first time since their people had retreated to the inner planet that something had been launched into their orbit.

Lizzie knew that when they had launched, they had been required to adjust the trajectory because there was some space junk from their previous attempts to go into space. Perhaps some of that junk had caused a problem? But, if so, why would they be consulting her? She knew very little about this level of engineering. Earth was only just now talking about sending humans into space.

They ran into the apartment building. Lizzie's agent training and the fact that she continued to do her run every day, as well as all of the walking that everyone on this planet did, had conditioned her to the point that she wasn't even out of breath, but her heart raced. This couldn't be good. Reloi hadn't sent a single word to her since asking her to come.

As they entered the room, both Tarafau and Meta looked up from their mental conversation. Their grim faces told Lizzie to brace herself, but she still couldn't imagine what was happening that could be so urgent.

"Okay. What is this all about? You're scaring me," she said, trying to keep a plaintive note out of her mental voice.

It was Meta who spoke. *"Jenny, as you know, our satellite is more than just for communications. And the security protocols require it to scan a large radius to determine any threats to the communications system or the planet it orbits around.*

We have only had the system up for a short time, and only in the last day or so did we finally do our first scan. And we found... we found..." She stopped, shaking her head as if it was too overwhelming to say. She gulped, looking straight into Lizzie's eyes. *"... an asteroid on a collision course with this planet. An asteroid so large that when it hits, this planet will be demolished, with nothing left behind but a huge asteroid field devoid of life."*

"When will it hit? Can we evacuate the planet? Surely, we can get them all through the gate if we organize quickly." This was all Lizzie could think to say. Her agent training had included strategies for a number of emergency situations, but this was beyond anything Lizzie had been taught.

"We have only three days. There is no possibility the council can save everyone in that amount of time. The Alliance will open several gates for evacuation and be prepared to aid the refugees when they arrive. But, since there is only a single usable gate, we will be able to save only a minority of the population.

"The council is reaching out to people in family units, a few at a time, and giving them no time to gather any supplies or anything to take with them. They are trying to keep it as organized as possible to prevent panic, which would mean we could save fewer rather than more.

"You, Ynni, Tarafau, and I are being recalled, and we will travel via Tarafau's special talent to one of the reception centers to help organize the refugees from that side. This is your assignment as an Alliance agent and is nonnegotiable." And she shot a meaningful glance towards Reloi, who only nodded, restraining his emotions with all of his might.

Lizzie's head swam with conflicting ideas and emotions. Her assignment? Nonnegotiable? *"And Reloi?"* she asked, fearing the answer she already expected.

"I must remain, my Lizzie. I cannot abandon my people in their need. I think you already knew that. I will come to you, if I can, but first I need to help as many of my people escape this awful calamity as we are able. You understand?"

Without embarrassment she flung her arms around him, sobbing and nodding and whispering in her tiniest mental voice. *"I understand, but Reloi, I need you. Please, I want to be with you. We are going to be married! I am torn between my commitment to the Alliance and my commitment to you and to your people. These are my people too, now!"*

He leaned into her embrace and replied in the same tone, *"That will never change, my Lizzie. There is no time, no space, and no circumstance that can ever truly separate us, but we must both do our duty; and I know you enough to know that you will do yours always, with all your heart."*

"Ynni, take care of her for me, please?" he said, looking up at the tiny face peering at him from her shoulder. Lizzie noticed that Ynni and Tanata shared a look, and they nodded at each other.

"Ynni will always care for Lizzie, brother Reloi," she affirmed with a somber shake of her head. *"Always."*

"Then you must go. We need you to be at the main reception center as soon as possible. My people know you and that will be a calming influence in such an unanticipated disaster. Take care of them, my Lizzie."

Then, looking up at Tarafau. *"She will need you now more than ever,"* was all he said, and understanding seemed to pass between them that was more than words could express.

"Goodbye, my Lizzie," he said. And she kissed him, a long kiss and embrace that enclosed her entire heart in it.

Before anything more could be said or done, Tarafau transferred her and Meta as Reloi's loving face faded from her sight.

They appeared in the basement of the agent training center and were promptly directed to a gate that led to the main reception center. From there, the refugees would be redirected to several welcoming dimensions who would help them with needed supplies and housing until the Alliance could find a place for them to create a settlement for the Grildites that would become their new home.

When they arrived at the main reception center, they were briefed on the procedure. As new groups came in, usually five to seven at a time, Meta, Lizzie, and Tarafau would greet them, and one of them would escort them to the gate of the satellite reception center they were assigned to. Their names were taken down and added to a list that meant that different families would be able to find one another and know their status. They divided the responsibilities for the refugees, with Lizzie actually greeting them at the gate, Meta registering them for future reference, and Tarafau escorting them to their next gate.

One of the things that surprised Lizzie was that the Alliance was making a true effort to comfort these distraught people. Small children were given stuffed toys to cuddle and sweets to distract them. The adults were briefed kindly about next steps, and all were treated with respect and gentleness.

Most of them came out of the portal with eyes wide and often weeping. This generation of Grildites had lived in peace and relative prosperity and had never experienced violence or disaster. But Lizzie knew they were made of strong stuff, having been pioneers of a kind, building a new society and life in small steps. She knew they were hard and willing workers. She felt confident that those who escaped the calamity looming over their planet would survive this and eventually thrive.

She recognized many of those who came through the portal and received many hugs and sincere thanks as she helped them go to the next step. There was about ten minutes between each transport, and the most the tube could hold at a time was seven, if small children sat on their parents' laps. With only three days to evacuate as many as they could, the gate would be operating day and night until the very last minute.

Lizzie calculated that at most they could save maybe eight thousand people on a planet with nearly a million people living on its interior. She often found herself weeping with the few who came through, but she refused to take a break, only nibbling on a rations bar between transports when she could and sipping at the water bottle she had been given by one of the other workers at the gate.

There were very few quiet moments during her labors, and by the second full day without sleep she finally succumbed to the offer of a cot in the other room. Both Tarafau and Meta had already taken short sleeping shifts and were back at work.

When she finally lay down on the cot, only sheer exhaustion kept her from reviewing the shock and distress she had felt constantly since that moment in the little apartment in Grild.

When she faded into sleep, she didn't dream, but to her joy and astonishment, Reloi visited her, appearing in the little park in the town square where she had lived.

"This was the first moment your mind wasn't occupied with more important things, my Lizzie. We are continuing to evacuate as quickly as we can, while avoiding panic as long as possible." His violet eyes looked at her with concern. *"You are working too hard,"* he said, reaching for her to take her into the arms of his mental body. *"Please take care of yourself. There are others there to help as well as you."*

"But I can't stop. Not until we have saved every one of them it is possible to save," she replied, her face nestled into his chest. *"They are my people too. You saw to that. They would have built an epic society and would have been a strong and positive influence in the multiverse."*

"We have rebuilt before. We will do so again. You will see. I know you will always watch over them. They will need your help and your

advocacy. The Alliance spans so many multitudes of cultures that it will be easy for them to get lost in all of the work the Alliance does. I need to know that my angel will watch for them.”

“You know I will. And you will too. We will do it together. You will see. It will happen,” Lizzie replied, with a confidence she didn't really feel, *“together.”*

“Together,” he agreed. *“Whether from this dimension or the next.”*

Lizzie wasn't sure what he meant by that, so she just nodded, still snuggled against his chest.

“I must go back to work,” he said after a long moment. *“I will visit you on your next sleep break. Thank you for being you. Thank you for caring for my people. Thank you for loving me.”* And without waiting for her to respond, he faded from the mental connection and Lizzie drifted into deep sleep.

When she awoke, she felt somewhat calmer and was rested enough to take an extended shift, continuing the work with a will, remembering all of her amazing experiences with the Grildites. She could only hope that even if they could not save them all, they would save as many as they could.

All day and late into the night they worked, realizing that the literal deadline was looming nearer and nearer and nothing could stop the ticking of that countdown. Of course, no one could predict it down to the very last minute, but even if they knew, they would desperately continue to work and wait, long past the time when the catastrophe was going to descend on Grild.

At the point of impact, there would be nothing more they could do. Between the earthquakes and the streaming in of the toxic outer atmosphere, there was only the one gate, and it would be completely inaccessible.

She knew that the council's decision to keep most of the people in the planet ignorant of their impending doom had to have been a hard one. On the one hand, advance notice would have given them time to mentally and spiritually prepare for death but would have inevitably created panic and would have made the orderly evacuation nearly impossible. On the other hand, Lizzie was sure that survivors' guilt would probably be intensified when those who escaped realized that they had been given a chance that the rest had not.

As she continued to greet more of the refugees in a constant and consistent stream of tired, scared, and disoriented people, she noticed, in family units, she was surprised to learn that the relief she felt as each group stepped through the gateway never lessened. Each time it drew close to the ten-minute interval, she tensed up, hoping against hope that yet another family would emerge; and each time when they did, she heaved a huge sigh and went through the routine with Meta of getting them registered. But she immediately tensed up again, once more watching the clock, on edge and worried.

By the time she was told unequivocally to take a break and get some sleep, she was so exhausted that she was asleep almost before her head hit the pillow on the little cot in a corner of the aid station.

Immediately, or so it seemed, she was there in the park with Reloi, looking into his big violet eyes and wishing she could just hold this moment forever, never leaving this spot, never looking away from his face.

"It is close," he said, reaching to stroke her hair. "We may be able to get another couple hundred through the gate. The populace who do not yet know about it are calmly going about their daily lives. It seems a bit unreal; and yet, it's all about to explode like a star going nova. According to the satellite, we have less than a day."

Lizzie could not speak. He pulled her into a hug, and they just stood there, being together. Lizzie didn't want to move, didn't want to speak, didn't want time to move forward, but finally she said, "You're about to do something heroic and selfless, aren't you? You're about to give your place to someone else, probably a child."

"I don't know about heroics, but it makes sense to give my place to someone who has more time to live and to grow, and I would see no parent have to make a choice of which child to leave behind just so I could leave and be safe.

"I want to be with you more than anything else in the world... in the multiverse, but we don't always get what we wish for." He sighed and continued to stroke her hair as if comforting a child.

"I will not give up hope until there is no choice, Reloi. Perhaps there will be an empty space on one of the trips up to the surface before time is up. I will hang onto that; but if not, your love is the only love I will ever wish for. I will love children and family. I will love my fellow beings, but the love I feel for you is one of a kind and could never be duplicated or replaced. Marry me. Marry me now."

He pulled back, looking deep into her eyes. "I will say the words even though we have no one to officiate. Will that do? Will you say the words?"

"I will. Say them now and I will be as content as I am able to be."

"Lizzie Japhet, of my own free will and choice, I would have you as a companion and spouse throughout life and beyond, committing life and light to our companionship. Will you, of your own free will and choice, take me, Reloi Chid-Wei, as a companion and spouse throughout life and beyond, committing life and light to that companionship?"

Even in her sleep she felt the tears trickling down her cheeks. "I will, with all my heart," she replied, her mental face alight with a smile to match his.

"Then I get to kiss you!" he exclaimed happily, and did so fervently. In this mental state, she felt them lifting from the grass beneath their feet, suspended in a column of light so intense she could see it through closed eyelids.

As they settled gently back to the ground, he whispered in her ear, "I love you, Lizzie Japhet."

"You mean, Lizzie Chid-Wei," she retorted.

"Ah, yes. It is your tradition to take the name of your husband. We do not do that here. Girl children receive their mother's surname and boy children the father's surname. But for formality, we use the hyphenated version of the two names. So, as a Grildite bride, you are still Lizzie Japhet.

Nevertheless, you can do as you will. Regardless, you are now my bride and ever will be. This one thing I can give to you as I would have, regardless." And he kissed her again.

"I cannot give you a honeymoon, as Earthlings call it. I can't even give you many more minutes of my time, as I am being called away. I love you. I have given Tarafau a token for you of my everlasting affection."

Suddenly, both Tanata and Ynni were there, and Lizzie knew they were there to support her and to comfort her as Reloi then faded from their little mental park that had meant so much to her for such an agonizingly short time.

She awoke with tears streaming down her face in a mixture of joy and deep sorrow. She couldn't just lie here. Only throwing herself once more into the rescue effort would give her any comfort now. Ynni was there, crooning softly and patting her arm.

"Come on, Ynni," she said flatly. *"We have work to do."*

They worked, bringing more and more refugees through the portal while Tarafau and Meta got them processed and sent through the other portals to the refugee camps that had been hurriedly set up by the Alliance on willing member planets. In addition to the refugees pouring through the portals, various agents were streaming through, their MDPs filled with food, supplies, and self-erecting tents normally used for the military.

In addition, healers and other medical personnel and support staff were being sent in between each new group of refugees, to ease the burden of caring for all of the now impoverished Grildites.

Lizzie could begin to see the benefits of being a full member of the Alliance. Although the Alliance would never have interfered with a war between conflicting factions on a planet, they evidently were happy to lend aid in situations like these where the inhabitants could not help themselves.

Then came a moment when two things happened at once, the one thing Lizzie had been both dreading and expecting. As she felt an urgent touch on her mind from Reloi, a family came through panting and wild-eyed.

Simultaneously, she herded the family through the portal, handing them off to Meta almost mechanically and then sank to her knees as she felt an overwhelming flood of love and warmth diffuse through her mind and heart. *"My Lizzie, my wife. I will meet you again in a new dimension at a future time. Do not despair. The most destructive force in the multiverse cannot destroy our love."*

"Forever. We made a vow. I love you, my husband. Watch for me." And then he was gone.

The family she had shepherded through the gate was babbling in the Grildite language. Lizzie, tears streaming down her face, calmed her mind and reached out with mindspeech. *"You are safe,"* she told them. *"We will see that you are cared for."*

The mother, one child on her hip and hands on the shoulders of two older siblings looked up at her. *"We could see it. Like the sun itself had come loose of the heavens, streaking directly towards us as we stood in the dome next to the portal. The gate guardian shoved us through without a word. We did not feel or hear the impact, but we are sure it happened within less than a second after we came through. There were still families waiting in line in front of the ascending tube, and they are lost! Lost, lost, lost.... All... lost...."*

Lizzie couldn't even mindspeak to the woman. She could only put her arms around the shoulders of the weeping woman and her husband, weeping with them for the hundreds of thousands of those they had not been able to save. And for her dear Reloi, who stayed on to the end, saving all he could, who took a moment before their destruction to reach out to her, his wife, with one last love note.

Chapter 23: Requiem

(Jenny looked at the tear-stained page of the journal through her own tears as she came away from the movie that Lizzie had created in her mind. It had been so vivid, as if she herself had been experiencing it.

The beautiful crescendo of the love story that Lizzie had never told anyone still resonated in Jenny's mind, overlain by the horrific catastrophe that destroyed so many whom Lizzie had loved and served with a happy heart. She couldn't begin to imagine the pain that Lizzie must have felt, and yet no one who had ever told her tales of her aunt had ever hinted at such a tragedy in her life.

Now she knew why Lizzie had never married, or at least that no one had ever known of the marriage vows she had made with Reloi. Lizzie had remained true to those vows, not even caring that technically she was a widow and could have found romantic love again at some point. For her, there had only ever been one, and that was enough for her.

Jenny thought about Burt; and as usual when she thought about him, her heart swelled, and she felt warm all over. She hurt for Lizzie that she had never had the opportunity to be with her dear Reloi as Jenny was with Burt.

Even though they didn't see each other as often as she would have liked, it wasn't much different from when her dad had been in the military and had been sent on assignment, leaving her mom with her and her siblings until he returned. Her mom would never even acknowledge the possibility that her dad would not return, but Jenny had known once she was older that her mom was always so relieved when he did come home.

She finally understood what that must have meant to her mother back then, especially now, with this multidimensional war looming over them all. Even when Jenny was back in action, she and Burt wouldn't see much of one another other than their nightly mental date at the little pool by the Merced River. But she also knew that in wars, things happen that were unpleasant and unexpected.

There weren't many pages remaining in this journal, and the next one waited in the box in her MDP. She would finish the journal today, and tomorrow she would pick up the third journal, focusing all of her attention on finishing before her release from her medical leave and her return to her duties as the Gatekeeper for the Dimensional Alliance.

She wiped her eyes, took a deep breath, and turned the page, Lizzie's words once again creating a vivid motion picture on the screen of her imagination.)

Lizzie placidly watched the linklings playing quietly in and out of the trees of the grove behind Tarafau's house. She couldn't raise any enthusiasm for the frolics of the furry little green creatures. She felt numb, distant, beyond any emotion.

How had she entangled herself in romance, in loving anyone this much? And yet, she couldn't bring herself to regret loving Reloi. Kind, gentle, funny, strong and intelligent, he had captured first her interest and her intellect and then her heart. This was a person worthy of her love and respect and beyond. She knew without reservation that he loved her in the same way.

After the last family had come through the now-demolished Grildite gate, she had almost mechanically done everything she could to help the relief efforts of the Alliance, visiting the refugee camps, speaking with the Grildites, who were often people she knew and had worked with during her first official assignment as an agent of the Alliance.

And she was still an agent. That hadn't changed. Instead of going back to Earth, as she had been told she could while she awaited reassignment, she chose to return to Tarafau's home with him. Amenia had welcomed her, assuring the healers at the Alliance that she would use her own skills as a talented caregiver of the distressed and depressed to help Lizzie heal from the shock of the disaster on Grild.

She had known that going back to Earth would only make her feel more disconnected than ever before. She couldn't seek comfort from her family. There was no way they could understand what she had gone through, especially since she couldn't even tell them why she was feeling as if she had been cut adrift from life.

The trees in the grove had been immensely comforting as she tried to process all of these deep feelings. One old tree in particular, who styled himself as "StarSinger," had often made an effort to speak to her; not about the disaster, but about common things like birds and sunlight and the beautiful sky rings that showed clearly even in the daylight on this planet. He was a joyful soul and always had something encouraging to say.

This gift, Reloi had given to her. He was the one who had opened her mind to the voices of growing things around her. One more reason she missed him. Now, every time she interacted with a growing thing, she would remember him with a grateful heart.

Tarafau and Amenia came out with little Elizabeth, who had grown so much during the months Lizzie had been away on assignment. She was a sweet baby, already pulling herself up on any available piece of furniture in preparation for taking her first steps. Her crown of curly black burnished with brown hair and her cheerful nature were comforting to Lizzie, but even as she held the baby or played with her, she found herself wondering what her own babies with Reloi might have been like.

She had never pictured herself as a mother, motherhood being so very far from anything she had been focusing on. But now she found herself sometimes envisioning herself holding a little one on her lap, telling them stories or tucking them into their bed at night with a kiss and a hug.

Elizabeth held out her chubby little arms to Lizzie as they approached, and Lizzie responded by reaching out to her. Amenia placed her into Lizzie's arms with a smile. She cooed and snuggled onto Lizzie's chest with a happy sigh.

As soon as Tarafau could make eye contact with Lizzie, he said, *"We got a communication from the Alliance today. Liliath wants you to report tomorrow to her office. They have an assignment for us. She recognizes that you may not feel up to it but thinks it will be in your best interest to get back to work."*

Lizzie just nodded, running her fingers through Elizabeth's curls. She had known it was coming. She had been at Tarafau's home for a couple of weeks.

Ynni had hopped up onto the chaise as soon as Amenia had handed Elizabeth to Lizzie. Ynni loved the little girl and couldn't resist coming near to croon to her, laughing when the little one reached out to her. *"We are leaving? Soon?"*

"You could stay here for a while if you prefer," Lizzie sent, sensitive to the joy Ynni always expressed when she could be with her family. *"I could always come back and get you later."*

"Ynni goes with Lizzie. Always."

"I thought you would say that," Lizzie replied with a wan smile. *"I just wanted to give you the chance to stay if you wanted to."*

"Tribe is happy. Little ones are happy. Ynni will go with Lizzie."

"Well, that's settled then," Tarafau sent with a smile. *"I didn't think there was much chance you would persuade Ynni to stay, not when we are off to do some good in the multiverse. Let's take a day at the Apex to do any last-minute shopping, and then we'll roast some bud crawlers*

and have a last little concert before we settle down to sleep. We'll leave first thing in the morning, so be sure to pack your MDP tonight before you go to bed."

Amenia reached for Elizabeth, who shook her little head and started to pout when Amenia was insistent. *"Lizzie needs to get ready, Elizabeth. You can play with her more in a minute,"* she said, grinning at her daughter and shaking her head. *"You're going to miss your Lizzie, aren't you?"*

It was as good a distraction as any, Lizzie decided. A day at the Apex was always a treat; and even with the shadow that seemed to follow her around every day since the Grild tragedy, it was pleasant not to have to focus on what came next.

True to his word, after a day of shopping and entertainment at the Apex, greeting many beings Lizzie had become familiar with during her initial internship on the planet, Tarafau purchased some fresh bud crawlers, and they had a fine barbecue out in the grove with the linklings frolicking for the delighted entertainment of Elizabeth. After that, Lizzie took out her mbira, and she and the linklings gave a fine concert, the trees and flowering bushes that surrounded them adding a beautiful descant that only she and the linklings could hear.

She remembered how surprised Ynni had been when she had discovered that before Reloi's instruction Lizzie had not been able to "hear" the rooted life around her. Evidently this was a common trait among the linklings, one of the reasons they made their homes in the branches of trees. The trees were not only a home, but companions.

The stars had come out and the rings were vibrant in a dark sky by the time they finally said goodnight to the linklings and went to their beds.

Lizzie dreamed; and instead of the nightmares she had been experiencing nearly every night since the disaster, she dreamed of walking down a flower-lined path toward a country cottage, similar to the house Reloi's family had lived in. Reloi's arm was around her waist, and he no longer hovered in his chair beside her, but strode next to her with strong legs. He was slightly taller than her, and a sideways glance told her he was content.

"This will be our home, when you are ready to come to me," he said, turning to her to clasp both of her hands in his to look directly into her face. *"Hang on, my darling wife. I am in a good place. You will yet do much good. I will be waiting for you until your work is done."*

As he kissed her fervently, the dream faded, and she was in her bed in Tarafau's house, and the sun was peeking from behind the curtains at the window.

As she sat up, she mentally shook herself to full wakefulness, almost wistfully looking back at her pillow. But she felt somehow strengthened by that brief contact, even if it was only a dream. She would make Reloi proud. She would move forward. She dressed and went out to face her future.

After breakfast and warm goodbyes, she, Ynni, and Tarafau looked one last time at Amenia with Elizabeth on her hip, and he put his hand on her shoulder.

They hurried from the basement of the admin building. Lizzie didn't want to spend more time near the gateroom than necessary. Her recent memories of that place were still much too tender.

Liliath was waiting for them in her office and looked up from the tablet in her huge, clawed hands. When she wasn't agitated, she was shaded from blue to green down her long, scaled body, her large green reptilian eyes usually calm with large black pupils. Lizzie knew from experience that when she was angry or agitated, the colors shifted from the green and blue to deep crimson and purple, and the dark pupils narrowed to slits.

She rose and came forward to greet them. Even as long as Lizzie had known Liliath, this was still a bit intimidating. However, she had met few beings in her experiences in the Alliance who were kinder or more encouraging to everyone she interacted with. Liliath had been an incredible mentor to Lizzie throughout her experiences, as she trained for her current full agent status.

There was something amazing about dragon hugs, Lizzie thought as Liliath enfolded her in her huge arms, gently pulling Lizzie close to her very warm body. When she released her, she lowered her head on her long neck to Lizzie's eye level and sent, *"Your path so far has been rougher than any agent in recent memory, Lizzie, but you are strong, and your strength is needed. Will you continue to serve?"*

"I will, Liliath. I won't lie to you, I can't say I feel as confident in my abilities as you seem to, but I will serve as I promised. That much I can do."

Liliath drew back, returning to her chaise, and gestured to them to sit. Lizzie realized that the dragon hug had included Ynni, still perched on her shoulder, and wondered how that experience had affected the little linkling. She would definitely want to talk to her later about that.

Lizzie and Tarafau sat in chairs facing Liliath, and she wasted no time. *"We have a unique assignment for you that requires your specific talents. The planet, Fanilia, a long-time member of the Alliance, has a rare condition we do not often find on inhabited member planets. Their populace has a particular and perhaps peculiar view of what we call 'science.'*

"They also have a very different relationship with their plant life, as they communicate directly, much as you do, with the ability to mentally interact with all growing things. The agent that has been serving them for several years has served well and faithfully but does not have your particular ability. We will be transferring him to another position.

"They are expecting you and will be ready to greet you when you come through their gate today. This particular culture is very advanced, but not in a way that is obvious at first impression, for reasons you will understand as you interact with them.

"Lizzie, I know your inquisitive mind and that you will take delight in discovering these things for yourself, so I will not spoil it for you, except to say that your tablet has been loaded with as much background information as we have on record, which you can read at your leisure. Your initial relationship with them need not be obscured by all of that, however.

"I urge you to allow this to unfold naturally, as any new friendship must. You can study later. You will have time. I hesitate to ask, knowing you as I do, but do you have any questions?" This last was sent in a wry tone and Lizzie noticed that Liliath's mouth was twisted in a toothy grin.

Despite herself, Lizzie grinned back.

"No, Liliath, I actually don't. I'm beginning to learn that not all questions have answers and that I can be patient while I work things out for myself."

"Ah, our Lizzie is maturing quickly among us. Then, if there is nothing else, I will let you and Tarafau take your leave. I hope and expect that the time you spend among the Fanilians will be enlightening and that you will be a true asset to the Alliance there."

"Thank you, Liliath. I'll try to make you proud."

"Lizzie, you always do." Liliath responded warmly.

At that, they took their leave and headed back down to the basement. The Gate Guardian nodded as they came through the door to the gateroom and gestured towards the long corridor full of doors. Quite a way down the seemingly endless hall, he stopped, indicated a door, and waved them through.

Lizzie wasn't sure what she expected, especially since Liliath had emphasized that this was an advanced society, but the gate opened out to what she could only call a jungle. Dense foliage allowed sparkles of sunshine to create intricate patterns on the ground before them. The security field was simple, similar to the one in front of the gate on the hill above headquarters. It was a thin, transparent, silvery sheet they passed through without any unusual sensation.

Waiting in front of them was a delegation of humanoids who could have been from Earth, with the exception that their skin was green, dark enough to almost be black. All of them had long, plaited, black hair. They were tall, nearly a head and a half taller than Lizzie, and very slender, what her mother would have called "willowy."

Their eyes seemed to be uniformly a bright blue with large pupils, Lizzie assumed because of the shaded light of the surrounding vegetation. They were dressed in brightly colored clothes wrapped about them like an Indian sari or a Polynesian sarong, their legs bare below the knees. They were barefooted, but this did not detract from the dignity of the way they held themselves, erect and yet somehow graceful.

Per instruction by Tarafau, Lizzie held her quarterstaff, evidently because this was a formal statement of her office as a qualified agent of the Alliance. She felt a little sheepish about it but had complied.

The foremost of the gathered Fanilians smiled and held out a hand in welcome. "*We greet you, Lizzie Japhet of Earth, agent of the Dimensional Alliance, and your fellows,*" he sent formally. A dim echo from all around her said, "*We welcome you, welcome, welcome....*"

"*Thank you. I am happy to be here.*" And with a slight shock, Lizzie realized she really was happy to be there, something she had not expected.

"*I am Galauph, speaker for the overtribe and wielder of the power. My companions are Dangi, Ninka, and Jou. Each is a tribe leader, and they assist me in all things. The plantlings who surround us greet you as well. Over the coming years, you and your companions will meet and spend time with many of them. Your predecessor did not have the gift of hearing or sending to our plantling citizens, so we look forward to growing, learning, and joining with you in the magic.*"

Lizzie had no idea what the whole "magic" thing was about, but it came to her mind something Gaston had said once, quoting one of the scientists of the Alliance, "Magic is only science we don't understand yet." Perhaps the word magic was their word for science?

She nodded her agreement and sent, *"I'm looking forward to it."*

"Follow us, and we will escort you to the lodge where we will establish you in your dwelling and begin to introduce you to those with whom you will labor amongst us," Galauph sent, and motioned for them to follow.

They walked down a worn footpath that wound through the trees. The path didn't appear to have been made by clearing the trees out of the way, but more like it had just been worn over long years to its present state.

As they walked, Galauph continued the mental conversation. *"The little one who perches on your shoulder. Who is this honored one, and does it have the gift?"*

Lizzie almost blushed. She had been so taken aback by her new surroundings that she had neglected to introduce her companions. *"This is Ynni, a linkling from far away. She does have the gift of speaking with plantlings, as well as all other beings."* Lizzie deliberately left out the other gift of the linklings, of being able to read the minds of those around them.

"And this," she sent, pointing to Tarafau, striding along beside her, *"Is Tarafau Bane, a Daringi. He is my guide, as is traditional for the first year of an agent's service in the Alliance. He does not have the gift of speaking with plantlings, but he is adept at mental communication and is a helpful and wise companion."*

She hoped her belated effort at introducing her companions was adequate. Tarafau just grinned at her and nodded approval and Ynni was gently patting her cheek, something she often did when trying to calm Lizzie.

"Welcome, Ynni and Tarafau," was all Galauph said in reply. *"We are always gratified to meet new and interesting beings. Our relationship with the Alliance is an old one, going back to nearly the beginning of the discovery of the gateways."*

The path suddenly opened out onto a clearing surrounded by many buildings of several stories. These weren't exactly skyscrapers, but they were well constructed with many windows glistening in the bright sunlight. The sky, now that they could see it, was a brilliant amethyst blue. Lizzie had gotten used to the idea that not all dimensions she had visited had the same blue sky and green trees as her home planet, but in this instance, she could almost feel at home.

It took a moment for Lizzie's eyes to adjust from the abrupt transition from semi-dark jungle to the brightly sunlit square before her, but she looked around her in delight. Gathered in the square was a large group of Fanilians, looking like a flock of colorful birds. There was a wide white smile on every face as they turned towards the group emerging from the jungle path onto the sward.

Lizzie noticed that more than one carried long staves in their hands, long as they were tall. To her surprise, most of those who carried a staff were apparently female.

Galauph raised his hands, palms towards the crowd, returning their smiles. *"My people, come and meet our new agent and her companions, Lizzie Japhet, a linkling by the name of Ynni, and Tarafau Bane, a Daringi from far away. You will get to know them over the coming months, as many of you will be working closely with them on several ongoing projects.*

"You should know that Lizzie has the gift of relating to plantlings, as we do. One of the benefits I wish to extend to her is to increase her magic through instruction with our greatest wizards. For now, I will lead her and her company to their dwelling amongst us in the main lodge and then we will feast and celebrate. Are we agreed?"

A shout went up and a mental call, *"We are agreed! Preparations are made."*

Galauph nodded happily and, leaving the assembly, led Lizzie and Tarafau to the largest building centered at the top of the square. It was four stories tall and appeared to be sheathed in a dark stucco. They went through a single wide door that slid aside as they approached.

Inside, they were greeted by what could only have been a robot. *"Greetings new agent."* And Lizzie's jaw dropped. A mechanical construct with mindspeech? She had only seen this before at the Alliance outfitters at the training center.

"Hello," she sent in response, still confused.

"Allow me to introduce you to Glim, one of our robotic assistants," Galaugh said. *"Not all of our mechanical friends have his ability to communicate mind to mind, but we have given some of them this talent. His magic is limited but useful, as you will see."*

Lizzie found herself somewhat uncomfortable with the continued reference to magic but remembered Liliath's counsel and kept the questions now blooming in her head for later.

Galauph gestured ahead to a caged lift similar to some Lizzie had seen on earth, the elevator completely open to the room it faced. They entered, and Galauph pushed a button with a character on it Lizzie assumed indicated the floor they were going to. Lizzie memorized it and mentally requested Ynni and Tarafau to do the same.

The lift stopped on the third floor and opened out into a long hallway that felt familiar, like any large hotel she had ever visited. Spaced about thirty feet apart were doors on either side of the long hallway that ended on both sides with a large picture window that looked out on the square on one side and some more buildings on the other.

Galauph stopped in front of two facing doors. *"This,"* he said, indicating the one on his right, *"is Lizzie's apartment. And this,"* he said, gesturing to the one on his left, *"is for Tarafau. You will find all you need within. Please place your hand in the center of the door in front of you."*

They complied, and he said, *"Now the door recognizes you. Now each of you place your hand on the opposite door."* They did so. *"Now each of you may have access to the other apartment for emergency purposes. These were the apartments of the past agent and his guide, who was kind enough to remain with him during his entire service with us."*

Lizzie turned the ornate doorknob and entered the apartment where she would be spending perhaps many years on this planet and nearly gasped.

The room was dominated by a large sliding glass door that led out onto a wide balcony that gave a breath-taking view of the jungle canopy. Its gauzy curtains undulated slightly, since the door stood partially open. The furnishings were as rich as any in a deluxe hotel suite, upholstered in fabric similar to velveteen in lush dark maroon. The carpeting was plush.

The room was divided into a small kitchen and dining area and a posh sitting room. There were shelves lining the walls to accommodate any books she might have brought with her. It was obvious she would be able to make the space her own, something she had not often done since joining the Alliance.

On the wall were tapestries depicting scenic vistas and natural panoramas of wildlife and plant life. Galauph gestured to a door on one side of the sitting room. This led to a bedroom suite, complete with a room for bathing and personal hygiene. The bed seemed enormous after her time as a trainee, about the size of a queen-sized bed on Earth, with bedposts and curtains to draw around the bed at need.

There was a walk-in closet that led to the bathing room, and on one side of the closet were more than ample shelves for her folding clothes and anything else she wished to store there. Stacked on one of the shelves were linens and blankets, as well as toweling and cloths for her bath.

"It is amazing!" she exclaimed once she had caught her breath. *"I had not expected anything half so grand. Thank you."*

Galauph smiled in appreciation, mirth obvious in his large blue eyes. *"You are very welcome. If there is anything you need, you can simply come here,"* he sent, leading them back through to the sitting room and indicating a small, rounded metal disk similar to the call bell on the registration desk of a hotel. He touched the top of the disk, and it didn't appear to do anything.

"Anytime the bell is pushed, someone in the service cadre will answer soon after."

Lizzie wondered if it had been temporarily disconnected or if he might even be pulling her leg; but before she could ask him about it, a light knock came at the door.

"Come," sent Galauph, and a tall man in more subdued clothing came in and nodded to them. *"This is Sneel, one of the servers in the lodge. Most of the time, when you call, he will be the one to answer."*

Sneel nodded again. *"Sneel, this is Lizzie Japhet and her companions, Tarafau and Ynni. She is our new agent from the Alliance, and these will be her living quarters as long as we are blessed with her presence. Tarafau will be taking the quarters across the hall."*

"Nice to meet you, Sneel," Lizzie sent. *"Thank you for your help."*

"Happy to serve, agent Lizzie," he sent in return, then nodded at Ynni and Tarafau. *"And Ynni and Tarafau. Welcome to your new home."*

"Thank you," Tarafau sent at Sneel's nod in his direction.

"You may go now, Sneel. Thank you for your prompt attention," said Galauph in polite dismissal, and Sneel left with a smile and a nod. *"At*

this time, if you wish, you can take some time to settle into your quarters before the greeting festival." There was a question in his mental voice, but Lizzie looked at Tarafau and shook her head.

"*No, thank you, Galauph. I think we would like to get to work. We have not been tired by our short journey from Alliance headquarters, and I would prefer to stay busy, if that is all right with you. Perhaps you can show us where we will be working and introduce us to some of those we will be serving with?*"

Galauph nodded, only slightly raising his dark eyebrows in surprise. "*As you wish. And you, Tarafau?*"

"*We are eager to learn more about your people and the community we will be working to serve, Galauph. I agree. None of us need time out to rest right now. There will be plenty of time to settle in later.*"

They left down the hall to the lift, descended, and went through the automatic door to the square, which was being transformed. In the short time they had been inside the lodge, around the perimeter booths had sprung up that were festooned with streamers and banners, evidently indicating their purpose or perhaps their origin. The various people bustling about seemed cheerful, and the air was filled with many conversations in their verbal language which had a similar rhythm and tone to the Polynesian languages on Earth.

Next to the lodge was another large building of only three floors. Once again they entered through automatic doors that led into a small lobby with long hallways radiating out in three directions. Galauph led them down a hall to the right of the lobby, to one end and through an open door into what was like every reception area Lizzie had ever seen. There were chairs ranged around two sides of the room for people waiting for appointments and a desk with a male Fanilian seated behind it, with a welcoming smile for them as he looked up from a stack of tablets he had been perusing, similar to those used by the Alliance.

"Greetings, Mil," Galauph said with an answering smile. *"Are the others available for a short meeting before the greeting festival?"* he asked.

"Indeed, I think they were hoping you might bring them beforehand. Please enter."

They went on through a door to the right of the desk into what might easily have been a boardroom in an executive office on Earth. Around the large table made of something shiny that did not seem like wood, sat eight Fanilians, all dressed in the typical Fanilian wardrobe.

Introductions were made around the table. Dangi, Ninka, and Jou were there, as well as five others, each person, male and female, nodding respectfully as their names were given to Lizzie, Ynni, and Tarafau. Lizzie knew she probably would need to be reminded of them when next they met, but Ynni had a nearly photographic memory, so she knew she would be able to count on a mental nudge if she forgot by then.

Lizzie was impressed that in every instance, Ynni was accorded as much respect as either she or Tarafau had been. Evidently these people didn't judge a being by their size or appearance. She knew that many she met had treated Ynni more like a cute and interesting pet than an intelligent being, someone Lizzie depended upon for her wisdom and her many abilities.

"I was hoping to get an idea of what I might be doing in your service," Lizzie asked, when she was invited to ask questions of the group.

She was informed that the Alliance council had told them about her work with the Grildites, and they were particularly interested in the work she had done for their educational system. They also hinted that once they had introduced her to the plantlings on their planet, she would be using her skills for a special project that they would introduce her to at that time, but that there was so much to it, there was no time to discuss it here and now.

Galauph explained to her that he was the Speaker and these were the "elders" of the tribes. and their function was to advise and consult with the Speaker for the overtribe, their term for the combined tribes all over the planet.

Galauph then looked up at what appeared to be a clock on one wall with unknown symbols on it. *"It is time. Let us go and celebrate!"*

They streamed out of the boardroom, beckoning to Mil to follow, and out they went.

The square was once again thronged with people in colorful costumes, and rhythmic cheerful music came from a group at one end of the square on a dais. Many were dancing boisterously, hips swaying with hands raised above their heads, waving back and forth to the time of the music.

Someone grabbed one of Lizzie's hands and another grabbed Tarafau's, pulling them into the dance. It took Lizzie a moment to get over the shock of being made part of the dance, but the music was compelling and to her delight, she watched as Tarafau with a grin on his face joined in enthusiastically. Ynni jumped from her shoulder and, for a moment, Lizzie was concerned she might get trampled by the revelers. But then she saw that Ynni had paired up with a small girl in brilliant reds and yellows and was dancing delightedly with the little one, holding tight to her hand.

There was no ceremony to it. One moment they were dancing, the next they were escorted to low tables that had been set up at the far end of the square. They were invited to sit on the ground at the table, where they were served an excellent meal of vegetables and fruit, as well as what she thought might be some kind of fish in a creamy sauce.

She had been assured by the gate guardian before they had gone through that there was nothing for her to worry about as far as the food the Fanilians eat, so she hadn't been sent to logistics to pack anything special. Lizzie also knew that while she had been on Earth for her leave before her first assignment, she had stored away some of her favorite foods, just in case; most of it was still stored away, as she had eaten well on Grild and had not had any problems with any of the native food there.

Table conversation had revolved around different ones introducing themselves and what they did, and asking her questions about her life as an agent.

After the meal, there were many entertainments, as well as strolling around the perimeter looking at the wares displayed at the various booths. Before they began, both Lizzie and Tarafau were given net bags with handles and told that they could take anything that interested them, and the overtribe would reimburse the vendor.

Lizzie soon realized that each vendor would have been offended if she had not taken at least one of the trinkets, bits of clothing, including some of the beautiful sarongs or foodstuffs offered, so she tried to keep her "purchases" small. Tarafau picked out some things he thought Amenia might enjoy, and soon both of their net bags were bulging, each time leaving behind an exultant vendor.

By the end of the evening, Tarafau and Lizzie both were ready to retire to their apartments. After many *goodbyes* and *thank-yous*, they headed to their beds ready to get a good night's sleep before the coming day, which Lizzie suspected might be as jam-packed as any day at the Alliance training complex.

She was right. In the coming week, by the end of each day she was ready to fall into the comfortable bed in her apartment, Ynni collapsing equally tired on the pillow next to hers.

There was evidently a lot more to this agent thing than she had supposed. She remembered all she had learned during her months on Grild, and now it was like learning all over again. She began to understand why her insatiable appetite for learning qualified her for her position as an agent for the Alliance. Each new assignment would require her to learn a completely new set of rules of etiquette, customs, cultural norms, and history.

And despite the fact that she relied mostly on mindspeech, she began to realize that she was picking up words and phrases in the Fanilian language. All in all, she was kept so busy that, although she still missed Reloi fervently and still mourned for the Grildite people, those feelings were softening; and, more and more, she was able to remember all of the good times she had there.

She began to hope that she would become as engaged and at home in Fanilia as she had been in Grild. In a way she also feared it, as she didn't want to ever feel the loss she had felt for Grild again. Nevertheless, she set her mind to what she called "hope mode" and threw herself into serving the Fanilians as heartily as she had the Grildites.

Chapter 23: Fantasia

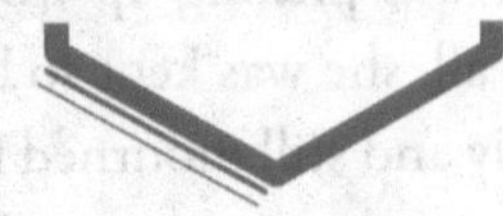

(Jenny scanned the pages left in the second journal. She was nearly to the end of this middle piece of the puzzle that was her Aunt Lizzie. At this point, she felt sure that she would be able to finish the third journal as well, as long as...

She heard a stirring in the hall and looked to her left to see Bob emerging alone from the gate office.

"Well, hello! Back so soon?" she called to him, and he answered with a wave and a grin.

"Just popping in to make sure you're eating, sleeping, and exercising, per your doctor's instructions. Merv is busy with a new trainee in the lab, and right now I'm in waiting mode. I don't like waiting."

"It's funny you should say that. According to Lizzie, it was one of the things she hated the most."

Bob chuckled. "Yep, that's our Lizzie," he said shaking his head. "She always had something to read, just in case she would have to sit around, which wasn't often. Even though I didn't know anything about what she did with the Alliance, it was always clear to me that she preferred being busy to twiddling her thumbs."

Jenny thought for a moment. "Bob, did Lizzie ever say anything to you about someone named Reloi?" She guessed she probably hadn't, but she needed to know.

"Reloi? Really? Yes, but I don't know who that is. It's only a name she mentioned just before she passed in that hospital room. I had no idea

who or what she was talking about, or at least I could only guess. It was someone she cared about?"

"Yes, it was. Tell me. What did she say?"

"Nothing much. She had just opened her eyes for the first time in days. First, she looked at me, almost as if she was looking through me, then she shook her head and sighed. Then she said, not much louder than a whisper, 'Ah, there you are, Reloi. I'm ready for my honeymoon.' And she let out one last breath and was still. I knew she was gone."

Bob's eyes filled with tears. "Why honeymoon? I had to conclude Reloi was someone she had cared for long before I knew her."

For a moment, Jenny couldn't respond. Her eyes were tearing up, and the lump in her throat kept her from speaking. Bob waited patiently, nodding with understanding.

Finally, she said. "Reloi was the husband she never got to live with, the love of her life and an alien she met while on assignment for the Alliance. She could never tell anyone about him, only wrote about him in the journals she had hidden away from everyone but me."

He walked over and knelt beside her chair, putting an arm around her shoulders. Chidwi, who had been lying on the window seat across from her, leapt down and hurried over to put one hand on her knee, looking up into her tear-blurred eyes and crooning.

"I can see why these journals have been so important to you. Someday when we have time you will have to tell me about them."

"I'll do you one better. When I am finished with them, I will have Lizziebot scan them into digital format in the original handwriting and load them to your Alliance tablet."

"Oh, wow!" he said, his salt and pepper mustache twitching into a smile. "That would be amazing, thank you! In that case, can I tell Merv and Burt you are being a good girl and doing what you're supposed to do, so you can get back to your reading?"

She hugged him. "Yes, please, Bob. That would be great. Give Merv a hug from me, will you?"

Bob cocked his head and then shook it. "Me, hug Merv? I think you'd better do that yourself the next time we're here, which should be in a few days, as there are things we need to discuss. Liliath hinted we might bring you into headquarters a little early for a short meeting before your recuperation time is finished, but that's for later."

He hugged her one more time, got up and turned, and headed down the hall. He went through the door to the gate office with a wave and a grin, a tear still sparkling on one cheek.

Jenny wiped her own face as Chidwi scrambled up to sit on the back of the chair behind her, one hand resting lightly on the top of her head. She opened the book to the bookmark in the final pages of the journal.)

Lizzie strode along with Tarafau by her side, Ynni in her usual perch on her shoulder. It was between the morning and evening rains. Nearly every morning and a few hours after sunset, it rained in a short torrential downpour of warm rain. Getting caught out in it generally meant you would be soaked to the skin, but she hadn't seen anything remotely resembling an umbrella.

Whenever the Fanilians were out in it, they simply stood there, faces upturned and joyful. They didn't exactly worship the rain, but more than just accepting it, they rejoiced in it. Generally, most of them timed their work outside around the downpours, so it didn't really affect them much. What it did do was to create a lush, rainforest environment.

As she thought back over the past several weeks, she once again found herself in awe of the opportunity she had been afforded by her commitment to the Alliance. This was so far beyond anything she had ever expected to experience. While it was true that her first experience as an agent had been traumatic, she had begun to realize that even that had been enriching to her life.

She wouldn't have traded the time she spent with Reloi and his people for anything she could imagine, even if it meant taking the pain of her loss away.

Once again, she found herself in a position to make a difference, and the benefits were beyond anything she had ever imagined, even during her agent training.

She had been able to go on many a field trip to various villages and towns during her time on Fanilia and had met many unusual creatures. She had engaged in many long conversations with plantlings of many types from trees to shrubbery, even something resembling a large mushroom the size of a truck tire.

At one point they had gone to one of the large lakes that looked more like an ocean to Lizzie. One of the first things she had noticed was that the sand that lined the beaches was incredibly sparkly, catching the light of the sun and sending it back spectacularly. The entire shoreline for as far as she could see was lined with this fine glittering sand.

"What is this?" she had asked one of the native women who was preparing to go into the water to swim, tucking her sarong up and knotting it to leave her legs free for swimming.

"It's just sand, just gravel. If you don't remove your shoes, it can get inside, and it rubs on your feet," she sent disdainfully. *"It is everywhere, all up and down the waterways throughout the world. Worthless for anything but maybe sandbags."*

Lizzie had shaken her head. She thought she knew what it was and was flabbergasted at the wealth this one sandy beach represented.

"Do you think anyone would mind if I took some? To analyze for my studies?"

"Take as much as you'd like," she had said, amused by the strange request. Lizzie could almost hear the mental shake of her head at the odd alien woman and her unnatural curiosity.

Lizzie had waited until her friends had waded into the water to splash and play and had extracted from her MDP a few empty sandbags with a shake of her head. These were part of the supplies that were a normal inclusion in every agent's emergency kit. Only good for sandbags, was it? So, sandbags she would make.

All of the villages and small cities nestled within forests and took advantage of natural clearings or rocky areas to build structures from a hardened plant similar to bamboo. It was caulked and covered with a stucco-like substance that dried as hard as rock. Some few buildings were constructed of large bricks made from the same stuff as the stucco. These were then painted in bright colors, which made each building stand out against the greens and browns of the surrounding vegetation.

They were on their way to visit one of the more prominent tribes that contained a major schooling center. The Fanilians, like the Grildites, had created an all-inclusive schooling system that included every age ranging from what would have been called a nursery school on Earth to advanced collegiate studies. The complex was huge, larger than any of the universities Lizzie was aware of at home.

Unlike Grild, the Fanilian system was stratified into age and skill levels. In that, it felt very similar to what Lizzie had grown up with. One of her responsibilities on Fanilia was to help institute some of the learning and teaching protocols she had helped develop while working in Grild.

The first month had been interesting, to say the least, as Lizzie was treated as if she were a vetted authority on education, something she definitely didn't feel qualified for. And she was absolutely unprepared for the odd attitude of the Fanilians about what she thought of as science. They had created and freely used advanced technology, including the use of robotic servants, instant communications, and medical advances utilizing the herbs that evidently grew wild in the forests throughout the world.

But they viewed science as something mystical and called it magic. Most of the scientific protocols she had grown up with were still in use by the "wizards" of Fanilia, but their processes were also shrouded in practices of hand motions, spells, and incantations that they felt were necessary for the "magic to work."

Lizzie was once again grateful for Baird's insistence that the agent trainees learn to control their emotional facial expressions. It was a struggle, some days, not to roll her eyes or shake her head when a "wizard" professor carefully explained the incantation that must be uttered while doing a simple scientific process.

The concept of magic didn't interfere with their ability to create complex advanced technology, however, and Lizzie began to understand the importance of not judging another culture by her own cultural norms.

This morning she had gotten an urgent summons from the head of the school, and she and Tarafau had set off right away to see what the problem was.

The person named Laval, whom she thought of as the dean of the college, was waiting for them, his long plaits hanging down the front of his colorful wizarding robes, different from the sarongs the common people of both genders wore. They looked similar to the togas of the ancient Greek philosophers, with five long silken cords dangling from one shoulder indicating the high level of this scholar.

From his facial expression and the clasped hands in front of him, constantly twisting as if he were washing them vigorously, she could tell he was agitated, something she hadn't noticed in him in any of their previous meetings.

"Come," he said waving them into the building. *"I am so glad you made haste. This could be very bad."*

Lizzie's gut clenched. Not again! The last thing she needed after months of spending time with these people and getting to know them was another disaster!

They entered the dean's conference room and sat down.

"How can I help you?" Lizzie intoned, hoping her anxiety didn't show either on her face or in the tone of her mental question.

"The magic is dying!" he exclaimed, putting his head in his hands, then looking up at them with panic on his face, *"The Great Tree is in peril, and we will lose everything!"*

This startled Lizzie, and for a moment she repressed a laugh. The magic dying? What could that possibly mean? And how, in all creation, could she and Tarafau do anything about this? But Ynni put one hand softly on her cheek and sent, *"Listen, Lizzie. Listen with your heart. There is more here than you think. Remember that they are not you. They speak differently, they think differently. Listen before you speak."*

Lizzie barely stopped herself from gritting her teeth. But she knew that Ynni knew things she didn't know. The innate ability of the linklings to read minds had helped her more than once in her role as an agent beginning in her training.

"Please explain. I want to help you, but I need more information. Take a deep breath and organize your thoughts. If I can help you, I will," she sent, leaning forward and assuming an intent listening posture.

He sighed and straightened in his chair. *"I sometimes forget you do not fully understand our ways. Your own magic is so strong. Please forgive. I will try to rephrase my request.*

"As you know, our society has become dependent on the magic assistance all around us. From our mechanical servants to our communications, even how we cook our food. The origins of the magical force that makes all of this work are ancient and derive from our relationship with the plantlings. All life exudes a magical force, and the plantlings that surround us are the source of all magic.

"As with other beings on Fanilia, the plantlings have a principal chieftain, the Great Tree, or, as we call her, Bonwen. Her influence extends to all living things on our planet. She has been not only a guide to all, but the source of the power that exudes from all other living things. She was the founder of our houses of learning, and as the

head of this main house, she communicates with me. It is one of the responsibilities of my office."

And he unconsciously reached up and stroked the cords laying on his shoulder.

"During the morning rain today, she reached out to me more powerfully than I have ever felt her. It was a cry for help. It was not clear, but she said there is an inimical force that is preparing to attack her and that may have the ability to harm her, and in that process will harm us all."

He paused, looking hopefully at Lizzie, then at Tarafau. *"We have not had conflict of any kind on Fanilia in living memory. I understand that your culture and that of your guardian have an understanding of such things? I need you to discover the source of the conflict and advise us as to how to prevent the destruction of all that is important to our survival."*

Lizzie sat back, stunned and more than a little confused. How was she supposed to "prevent the destruction of all" that was important to the survival of Fanilia? Her magic? She wanted to laugh. She wanted to cry. Once again Ynni's mind touched her own.

"You have more to yourself than you believe, my Lizzie. I sense the fear that you may find yourself in the middle of something like the catastrophe of Grild, but, if I understand Laval's mind correctly, what we will need to do is within our reach. Request a retinue of helpers and agree to serve. You are not alone. Ynni is here. Tarafau is here."

Lizzie looked into Laval's troubled face, maintaining a calm outward appearance. *"We will do what we can. We will need to assemble some of your people who are experienced in woodcraft; strong ones who can help us navigate the forests so we can discover what must be done. Is there any way you can connect me to Bonwen, so she knows we are coming and what our mission is?"*

Laval heaved a deep sigh of relief and his fingers stopped ceaselessly scrubbing themselves. *"I was hopeful. Yes, I am a trusted wizard of Bonwen. Give me your hand."*

She extended her hand, and he took it in both of his hands, one on the back of her hand and the other on her palm. *"Close your eyes and breathe slowly,"* he instructed.

She did so, and he began muttering softly in his language. She instinctively fell into her training, breathing as if to enter her own mental space as she had done so often with Reloi, Liliath, Tarafau, and Amenia. She didn't have to even think about it anymore.

Nearly immediately she began to hear a mental conversation, softly at first and then clearly. *"Oh, great Bonwen, allow me to introduce you to one who is worthy and wise, who seeks to aid us in our time of need. Lizzie Japhet is an authorized agent of the Dimensional Alliance. Wilt thou speak with her?"*

The mental voice that replied reminded Lizzie of the breeze through the forest canopy; soft, melodious, and almost a whisper. *"Laval, I thank you for your devoted service. I will indeed speak with this one. Agent Lizzie Japhet, I sense your magic is indeed strong and your heart is true. I also sense companions. Will you give me their names?"*

"Hello, Bonwen. My friends are Tarafau Bane, a Daringi as well as my Guide. Ynni is a linkling bonded to me. They have many important skills that help me to do my task. You are far away from here, as I understand it. How is it that you can communicate by mind from such a distance? I have only ever known one other being who could do this."

"Ah, Lizzie. I am what I am. I have no understanding as to why I was created as I am. I remember the first stirrings of life on this planet and have watched over all from my beginning. I sense that there was a time of existence before I first sprouted from the rich soil of Fanilia, but those memories are dim. You are yet young, but I sense a power in you that is different than my own or any on our world.

"Please come to me and help me defend our world from this new threat."

Once again Lizzie found herself wondering how in the world she might have any skill or talent that could make a difference in what sounded like another crisis beyond her control and that the native creatures of this planet obviously thought was beyond their ability to cope with. But it wasn't in her nature not to try, and now curiosity sprang up in her mind, driving her to find a solution to what might be unsolvable.

"It appears that this is indeed urgent and might take some time to resolve," she sent to all, *"in which case we should set out as soon as possible. How long will it take to assemble a group of about a dozen, to equip them for travel, and to get us where we need to be as soon as possible?"*

Laval seemed a bit taken aback by her businesslike manner and quick agreement. She felt like he had expected it to take some stronger persuasion. But it wasn't in her nature to hesitate when action was needed. And she would do almost anything to avoid another situation like she had experienced in Grild.

"You will not have to trek through the forests. I will arrange for transport, and I have a cadre of wizards from the school who are strong physically and in the power who will be glad to accompany you and your friends. They can be ready to leave before the evening rain. The transport can take you and your company to within a day's walk to the valley of Bonwen. There is an inn there that will be prepared to take in your company for the night, and you could start out immediately after the morning rain, if you would like."

It was obvious that Laval had already given this considerable thought while he had waited for her to arrive this morning. Lizzie simply nodded. *"Then let's do this. Tarafau, Ynni, and I are already prepared to do whatever is necessary, as we carry all of our supplies with us,"* and she tapped the MDP meaningfully. The Fanilian wizards were aware of the device, having hosted more than one Alliance agent over many years of their membership.

They did not possess such technology, and Lizzie was surprised at their restraint. They didn't ever ask her about the magic that made the tech, which was good, as Lizzie wasn't sure if she understood it herself.

Laval nodded in return and stood. By the look of concentration on his face, Lizzie assumed he was summoning his wizarding team.

It seemed to take no time until they were ushered to the flat paved roof of the fourth floor of the main college administration building, along with the wizards assembled to take part in their quest. There, Laval touched a button that stood on a post closest to the edge of the rooftop. There was a whirring sound, and panels slid aside in front of them. To Lizzie's surprise, a platform rose up with what appeared to be a small, very sleek airplane with short wings and no propellers. The windows on the side of what Laval had called a "transport" indicated that the little plane would seat over a dozen passengers, not counting the pilot.

As the floor beneath the plane came level with the rooftop with a hydraulic whine, a door in the side of the plane opened out to become a short stairway leading into the plane.

A Fanilian popped her head out of the little door. *"Come aboard. We can proceed when you are ready!"* and she ducked back inside the little craft.

Laval turned to Lizzie. *"Fortune go with you, friend Lizzie. All here will be faithful and support you. We await your return with hope."*

It sounded formal to Lizzie, and she replied as best as she knew how. *"We will do our utmost, friend Laval. We honor your trust."* This seemed to be the right response, as Laval seemed almost relieved and waved them all towards the aircraft.

It was like no airplane Lizzie had ever flown on. The engines made almost no noise as they fired up; and instead of being propelled forward as she had expected, they lifted almost gently into the air for about a hundred feet before moving, nearly soundlessly, suddenly and rapidly forward.

So much of the technology in their culture was subtle, and they seemed to avoid the more obvious things like wheeled transportation as on Earth and much of the things Lizzie had grown used to during her time with the Alliance.

There were no flashing signs, no blatant machinery or anything loud enough that you couldn't easily speak over it. They had nothing like television or radio, despite their sophisticated communications tech. On the surface, they lived very simple lives. Something as advanced as this aircraft, moving as softly as a bee or hummingbird with such speed through the air, appeared to be an anomaly to the seemingly humble way of life she had become used to among the Fanilians.

They arrived at their destination in about an hour. During the flight, Lizzie and Tarafau took the time to introduce themselves to the members of their team. It was nearly equally split between men and women. Lizzie had noticed, that unlike the Earth of her time and in times past, there seemed to be no bias between what women and men were expected to do in their society.

Women did indeed tend house and raise children, but they also worked in nearly every type of vocation they chose. Generally, they would work in a part-time capacity while raising a family and transition to full-time status as their children left home to pursue their own vocations. Lizzie had also noticed that household chores did not seem to be solely assigned to women in this culture, but families worked together in everything from meal preparation to cleaning.

They landed with only the slightest bump on the rooftop of the inn at which they would be spending the night. As they deboarded, the staff waited calmly to invite them in. They were each led to their rooms and told there would be a meal prepared and ready in the dining room on the first floor when they had stowed their things.

Lizzie had to be impressed with the arrangements that had been made so quickly for her team and once again wondered if there wasn't some actual "magic" at play here. The thought made her brain itch. She had a hard time even considering anything outside the realm of science. She knew some things in life had always seemed unexplainable by the science they already understood, but she held to the idea that if you couldn't measure it in some way or discern it by your senses, any other explanation was unlikely or at least due to ignorance.

During the meal, she asked the head wizard, Delile, to explain what they would be doing the following day. She knew there would be a hike involved, but that was as much as she understood.

Delile seemed reluctant to explain much. *"It's just that there is so much we don't understand. The being we know as Bonwen is ancient beyond recorded history, and her magic is powerful and seems to nurture the entire planet in a way we don't fully comprehend. I know the multiverse is broad and filled with powerful magic, and the magic as we experience it on our planet is minuscule by comparison.*

"As needed, we will wield what magic we have to support you, but we still don't know what we will encounter when we get to the Great Tree."

That was about all Lizzie could get out of her with the exception that the terrain they would be crossing was hilly, and in some places the undergrowth in the forest made passage somewhat difficult. However, all of them assured her that they would be able to get there between rain showers, and that all of them were capable of making the trip without too much trouble.

They had all come equipped for a long hike, including portable foodstuffs and drinking water. All of the wizards had their ever-present staves and seemed inclined to wear their wizarding robes, regardless of the terrain they would be covering.

Lizzie herself decided on typical Earth garb, a short-sleeved shirt and jeans with her sturdiest pair of boots. She knew it set her apart, but perhaps, in this case, it wasn't a bad thing. She would be easy to pick out among the group as someone different. Her companions had no idea this was considered very casual clothing and didn't appear to take umbrage or think she wasn't taking this task seriously. She guessed they just assumed that this was what wizards wore where she was from.

The next morning, they set out right after the early rain, while the ground was still wet but not particularly muddy. As they walked along at a reasonable pace, she heard mental conversations sweeping up and down the group, mostly casual, but in some cases, discussing one or another wizarding discipline.

As Delile had said, the hike wasn't onerous, just long. They paused a few times at rest areas that had been constructed along the path to eat and drink and rest.

The rest areas always came as a bit of a surprise, usually around a bend in the path, which never seemed to go straight for long. At each were hygiene stations, fresh water to refill water bottles, and sturdy benches that looked well worn, enough for her entire company.

When she commented to Delile at the lack of people they had met on the road, Delile shook her head. *"Not many come this way these days. There was a time when there was much traffic to and from the Great Tree, but I am afraid we have become somewhat lax in our attendance. I fear this may be one of the causes of this summons. We, as a culture, have neglected our roots and origins."*

She shook her head, standing, stretching, and hoisting the pack back onto her shoulders. *"I admit we are dreading what we will find when we get there."*

This gave Lizzie much to think about as they walked along, over hills and through underbrush that had overgrown the path in places. The wizards murmured at this and vowed to send word to the surrounding townships that crews should be assembled to tend the path more carefully.

Finally, they topped a rise that led down a gentle slope into a wide valley. At nearly the center was a sight that made Lizzie and Tarafau gasp and caused Ynni to croon in delight. A tree taller than any redwood or sequoia Lizzie had ever seen, the diameter of the branches extending nearly the length of a football field, stood majestically before them. The density of the forest they had emerged from was the only explanation of why they hadn't seen it before from miles off.

"Greetings, Agent Lizzie Japhet," the breezy whisper of Bonwen came to her. *"Come beneath my branches and we will talk. Welcome all."* Despite the kind words being spoken in mindspeech, the nuances sounded as if the tree were weary.

They approached the tree with something akin to reverence. Lizzie could feel, in a way she couldn't explain by any logic, the vast age of this being and that beside it she was little more than a potentially annoying insect. But Bonwen didn't feel annoyed by them, only tired and kindly.

The tree was projecting something that was tangible in every direction, even skyward, as if a glow that could be felt rather than seen. But her wizard companions looked wary and not at all comforted by this.

"What's wrong?" she asked Delile. *"I thought Bonwen was supposed to be well known to you and that you cherished her for her kindness and the nurture she gives your planet. You are almost behaving as if you were afraid of her."*

"Something is definitely not right," Delile breathed, her eyes wide. *"Something here feels very wrong."*

Suddenly Ynni chirruped concernedly. *"Go back. All go back! Run from under the shade of the branches. It is wrong, so wrong!"*

Lizzie didn't question, nor did any in their party. They quickly retreated to about a hundred feet from the nearest branches.

"Okay," Lizzie asked Ynni when they had paused in the sunshine. *"What do you think that was? And is this why we are here?"*

The wizards all chimed in, speaking at once, denying that the bad feelings under the branches of the tree were in any way normal. It was a confusing jumble, and Lizzie held up her hands for silence. She turned to Delile.

"In your opinion, is it unsafe to go under the branches of the tree?"

"I don't think it is wise for all of us to go," Delile admitted, shaking her head for emphasis.

"And you, Ynni? What are your thoughts?"

Ynni broadcast her thoughts to the entire group. *"This is sickness, but not from within. Bonwen is firm in her mind but may not continue if the cause of this attack is not removed."*

"Attack? I don't see anyone or anything attacking her." Lizzie looked around them in confusion, half expecting to see an army of scary creatures sneaking towards them to do the tree harm.

"They are not coming. They are already here. They have taken shelter up, up, up in the branches. They are intent on consuming her. If they are not removed, she will die. She is already weakening, although she fights it with her whole soul. She knows, if her influence is removed from this planet, that all will perish." Ynni sent a mental picture to everyone of small creatures that were a cross between a spider and a lizard, brown scaly skin but with multiple arms, what might have been numerous red eyes and something that very much resembled antennae protruding from their heads. Their three mouths looked like the suckers on the tentacles of an octopus.

There were thousands of them. Evidently Ynni had been looking up when all the rest of them had been looking forward when they were under the branches of Bonwen. From the pictures Ynni was projecting to the group, the upper branches were completely covered in the creatures, large ones and tiny ones.

"They are reproducing," Lizzie concluded grimly. *"Even with their current numbers they are a threat, and when they have consumed the master tree, they will invade your planet until there will be nothing left in only a few generations. I won't see that happen. I won't. Not if there is anything we can do about it, but how do we eliminate this threat without harming the tree?"*

The wizards around her shook their heads in consternation and disbelief.

"Stop it!" Lizzie was so emphatic it was like a mental shout and brought the entire party to shocked attention. *"Don't you dare give up until we have tried everything,* everything! *Do you hear me? Let's withdraw back to the cover of the path where we entered the valley and think this through. I will expect suggestions from each of you. Do you understand?"*

To Ynni she sent privately. *"Can you read their minds? Can you tell me what their motives are, or anything about them? These people think I'm magic and that I'm going to come up with some amazing spell that will fix this, and we both know I'm no wizard."*

"Ynni didn't have time to probe their minds, and they are very, very different from anything I have ever seen. I must be closer to hear them clearly. But this will be dangerous. They are many and we are few. Ynni did sense they are hostile creatures and would not willingly bargain with us to change their location. Ynni would not inflict them on any living thing, especially a tree such as this. And where would we drive them?"

Lizzie considered Ynni's counsel and, taking a deep breath, turned to the group who cowered on the other side of the breast of the hill that led to the valley. She explained to the wizards their dilemma, then said firmly, *"I want solutions. Assuming we can get these creatures out of the tree without damaging her, where could we send them without causing further damage to your world? And what tools or technology do we have to get rid of them? Remember, I am new to your world. Tell me what my resources are."*

One of the youngest of the wizards in the group, named Trynn, spoke up almost timidly. In her mind's eye, she could see him raising a trembling hand like a student in a class unsure of the answer to the teacher's question. *"Agent Lizzie, we don't have magic to deal with aggressive creatures, but we may have some herbs that can help. There is still the problem of what to do with the creatures if the herbs work. The herbs I speak of grow in this forest. I have seen them along the way as we walked here. I can take some of my fellows and gather them, if that is okay with you?"*

"Are these herbs poisonous?"

Trynn was shocked at the idea, *"Oh no, of course not!"* he protested. *"A potion in the right proportions would put them to sleep long enough to do something with them, to get them away from the tree and keep them from decimating our forests. I'm not sure how to do that part, but I do know how to properly make the potion."*

A middle-aged woman named Nayla broke in. *"I think I know how we can deliver the herbs, if we can get under the tree to the roots, but it will mean the potion must be strong and it may mean that those things may not be the only sleepy ones. It could cause Bonwen to sleep as well, but I'm not sure about that. I don't think it will harm her, but we don't know if the crawly things will become aggressive to us if we go too close to the trunk of the tree."*

"But we still don't know what to do with these crawly things, as you call them, once we have knocked them out," sent Lizzie, thinking mentally out loud as she was wont to do when she was hashing out a problem. And then a new question came to her. *"We don't even know where they came from. Are you sure that none of you have ever heard*

about something like this before? Maybe in a legend or old stories? They certainly didn't spring from nowhere."

Tarafau nodded thoughtfully. *"Lizzie has the right of it,"* he sent. *"Like all living things, these must have an origin, and it must be somewhere on this planet."*

Then it struck Lizzie. *"Not necessarily."* She turned again to Delile. *"How many gates are there on this planet, that you know about?"*

"There are four gates, each with a trained and certified Guardian, Lizzie. What does this have to do with our current problem?"

"What is the closest gate?"

"It is many miles from here. Again, why do you ask?"

"These intruders may not be from your planet or even your dimension. If I remember my gate network training correctly, not every gateway on every gate planet has been found. Tell me about the surrounding area. I need more information. Do you maybe have a map?"

"I have my magic slate," Delile replied still looking puzzled. *"It contains all of the maps made by our best cartographers."*

"Good. We'll need it. Ynni, you and I need to get under that tree again while the rest of the team are scouting out those herbs. Tarafau, we will need your help.

"Each of the rest of you go with Trynn and collect as many of those herbs as you can. Delile, you will find the map of the local area and scan for any and all stony areas within a day's walk from here. You'll be looking for anything that might hide a cave or anything like a cave. Also, any large and sudden dips in the land that might look like a hole. Got it?"

"Yes, but I don't understand."

"Right now, it's best you just focus on my instructions. I think I'm onto something, but I don't want anyone second guessing me for now.

When Ynni, Tarafau, and I return, I promise to explain, if we discover what I think we will. Okay?"

Delile nodded and then shook her head and nodded again. *"Yes, Lizzie. At least I think so. I will do as you ask."*

"Come on, Tarafau. I have an idea, and I'll need your help to find out if it has any merit. You, me, and Ynni. Let's go." She watched for a moment to be sure that the rest were all following her instructions and then turned back to the valley.

Chapter 25: Crescendo

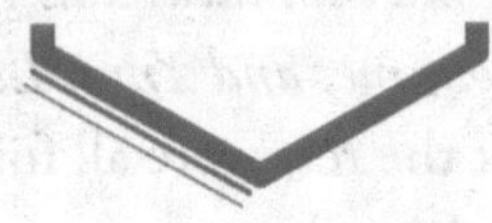

(Jenny looked up only briefly when she saw that Lizziebot was placing a drink and sandwich on the little table next to her chair. She hadn't even noticed her stomach growling insistently.

As hard as her own entrance into the Alliance had been, she was only now beginning to appreciate that maybe she wasn't alone in this. Reading about Lizzie's training and experiences as an agent was beginning to help her understand that her own journey was perhaps not unique, after all; and it made her respect the agents and gate guardians she knew even more. She realized that she didn't even know the tiniest bit about their individual stories.

She resolved to spend more time getting to know the Gate Guardians she was responsible for, once she was back on duty. Between that and the ongoing conflict with the Insenium, she had a lot to do, but she would take a page out of Lizzie's book, buckle down, and get to work.

She absently took a bite of her sandwich and turned the page.)

Lizzie extracted a length of rope from her MDP intended to be used for mountain climbing. She knotted it in an intricate way around her legs and waist, so it would hold her without slipping or putting too much stress in one place if Tarafau had to pull really hard to get her out from under the tree.

It appeared that the creatures her team were now calling "crawlies" had confined themselves to the branches of the Great Tree, content to stay where their food was plentiful.

Lizzie's plan was to get Ynni close enough to sense the minds of the crawlies and see if she could determine something of their origins. She had a theory, but she didn't want to expend too much energy or resources to pursue something that would be ineffective and perhaps stir the crawlies and potentially scatter them. That would be disastrous—perhaps not quite as much as an unexpected asteroid, but either way, it could mean the eventual destruction of Fanilia.

Once she was sure her line was secure and had Tarafau test it, yanking her off her feet several times with an evil grin, she settled Ynni on her shoulder with instructions for her to hang on with all her strength once they were under the leafy canopy.

She put her hand for just a moment into her jeans pocket and touched the smooth stone that lived there all the time since Tarafau had given it to her. The stone was deep red and heart-shaped, with tiny sparkles glinting from within its translucent depths.

This had been the thing Reloi had given him to give to her. He called it a peace stone. It was said by the Grildites that when you stroked it, it gave you courage and peace to do difficult things. It was the only token she had from him, and she was surprised to find that it did indeed calm her and help her to move forward.

With a final glance up at the grim face of Tarafau, she began her tethered walk back under the tree's outstretched limbs. He had objected strenuously to her plan but had acquiesced when she had pointed out that if their roles were reversed, she would be less likely to be able to pull him out than he would to pull her out. Either way, her logical mind told her that to act without more information could be tragic on an epic scale.

Tarafau played out the rope slowly as she walked, keeping a firm tension between her and him. Her flesh creeped as she moved slowly into the shade of the tree, and she felt thousands of eyes fastened on her and Ynni.

Once Ynni patted her cheek to signal for her to stop, she just stood there for what seemed like ages. Ynni generally didn't mindspeak when she was focused on reading the minds around her, so Lizzie could do nothing but wait, focusing on breathing and staying calm, even though she thought she felt anger and fear being projected at her from above.

She heard a rustling and looked up. A number of the crawlies had begun to creep downward in her direction, their eyes glinting when an occasional sunbeam filtered through the leaves. She wasn't sure how they could harm her, as long as they didn't get close enough to attach one of their sucker mouths to her skin, but she didn't want them to consider descending out of the tree, regardless.

"Ynni?" she sent, pushing panic down. She didn't want to interrupt Ynni before she got all the information she could, but...

"We can leave now. Go now!" Ynni sent, wrapping her arms and tail firmly around Lizzie's neck. Lizzie tugged the rope, and Tarafau began to rapidly reel her in so quickly that it was hard for her running legs to keep up. His last yank pulled her right into his arms, and for a moment he held her close to his broad chest.

"Amenia would never forgive me if I let you come to harm," was all he said and then released her when Ynni squeaked. Her tail had gotten caught in Tarafau's grip.

"Well, Ynni? What do we know about the crawlies? How can we remove them? Where did they come from?"

Evidently Lizzie's insistent tone amused Ynni, who grinned up at her and then reported in an equally serious tone.

"Crawlies are, as you guessed, not from this planet or this dimension. A few of them strayed through an open gateway many years ago and didn't know how to return to their home. They found the Great Tree and settled there and multiplied. Here there are no predators to keep their numbers in check.

They have few thoughts other than eating and mating and eating some more. They don't have tribes or even anything we would think of as families. They are not soulless, nor are they completely mindless, but they will react, probably without any kind of strategy or plan except as may be instinctive to them from their original habitat."

"Did you speak with Bonwen? How long do you think she has before the damage they are causing is irreversible?"

"She is weakening, but she is not in danger, yet. She did not ask for our help for herself; but she knows that, if she died, the crawlies would eventually overrun Fanilia and all would perish."

Lizzie considered this. The good news was that she had time, but the bad news was that it wasn't a lot. As she and Tarafau walked back to the crest of the hill and the beginning of the path, Ynni crooned soothingly on Lizzie's shoulder. Lizzie was beginning to see why the Alliance council had told her that Ynni would be a great asset in her duties. It didn't hurt that Ynni was also closer to her than any friend she had ever had, excepting maybe Reloi.

She met with her team, who had set up a camp of sorts just on the other side of the hilltop and were busily preparing the herbs that would be distilled into what Trynn was calling a "potion." She gathered them quickly and relayed Ynni's information to them.

"There is a previously undiscovered gate in the area," she concluded. *"We need to do several things and we don't have a lot of time to do them. First, we need to contact the Alliance and have them send a gate technician to the planet to allow us to accurately locate the gateway. Second, the head Gate Guardian on your planet needs to come here to aid us in the next steps. Third, we will need at least a hundred of your people to come and help us.*

"Even once they are sleeping, the crawlies are too numerous to remove from the tree with only a dozen of us. We will need climbing equipment and some kind of containers to transport the sleeping crawlies in from the tree to the gate, once it is found."

She turned to Trynn. *"How many people do you need to make a big enough batch of this potion to cover the numbers we are dealing with?"*

"I think I can do it with six of us," he said humbly. *"The process is simple. We can have the potion ready in just under a week."*

"How long will it keep and still be potent, in case our other preparations take longer than that?"

"This potion should remain stable for at least another two weeks, after which I can't guarantee anything. We have nearly stripped the forest of every bit of the essential ingredients, so it would take a few weeks to make another batch."

"Thank you, Trynn. That gives us a reasonable deadline, I hope."

"Delile, please contact the university immediately with all of this information and let them know there will be more visitors from the Alliance coming through the main gate. Tarafau, will you please go directly to Alliance headquarters and let them know what we need? Ynni and I will wait here for your return."

Tarafau didn't argue or ask any questions. To the surprise and awe of the rest of the team, he faded out of sight. Delile got out her "wand," a multipurpose device they considered magical, and began to speak to it expressively in her native tongue. Trynn chose half a dozen of his companions and turned back to the area where they were preparing ingredients for the potion.

For just a moment, Lizzie stood there in amazement. She had just given orders to all of these people, and they had rushed to obey. It had never entered her head that she would be placed in such a position of authority, and she wasn't sure she was comfortable with it; but her training in Professor Fin's class had stressed the skill of leadership for a full term. It had not occurred to Lizzie at the time that this skill would ever be one she would actually use. She wondered how he would have graded her first attempt.

She reached up to stroke Ynni's arm, as her little hand rested on Lizzie's shoulder. *"Thank you, Ynni. You were very brave. Thanks to you, we may actually stand a chance to remove this threat, and we probably won't even have to hurt any of these creatures."*

"Whatever Lizzie needs, Ynni will do. We are linked. Lizzie's future is Ynni's future."

With that simple statement, Lizzie was comforted. Finally, she began to understand what it truly meant to be linked to another soul. More than friendship or even a family relationship, this bond wouldn't be dissolved. She could depend on it.

It was a few days before they had assembled all of the various new members of the team; the equipment, including a large cauldron large enough for Tarafau to stand in up to his waist; and the specialists from the Alliance who would help them discover the gate where the crawlies had emerged from originally.

Delile had diligently plotted on the map some areas that might hide a cave or the dips in the terrain surrounding Bonwen's valley. Some small scouting parties had already located them so they could escort the gate specialist and the gate technician directly there. Lizzie was glad they had thought to do this, as it would speed up the process of elimination.

In the meantime, they continued to monitor Bonwen's condition, speaking with her several times a day. Bonwen had begun sending them mental notes on the behavior of the crawlies.

She had observed, for instance, that they all seemed to eat on a schedule based on the progress of the sun across the sky. Nearly in unison they would begin to suck on the bark of whatever branch they were on and continued for nearly an hour. Lizzie had conferred with her about the plan they had devised, and Bonwen had agreed the plan was sound.

But Lizzie still wondered about the application of the potion to the roots of the tree and whether it would have any long-term consequences. The last thing she wanted to do was to solve the crawly issue by killing the tree.

She still wasn't sure how much she believed that the tree was the source of "magic" and life on Fanilia, but her contact with Bonwen had assured her that this was a good and kind entity and that Bonwen truly cared about all of the creatures and plants on the planet.

She opted to go out with the techs to visit the potential gate sites. They carried equipment with them to open the gate when they found it, but probably the most important thing was Egain, the main Gate Guardian who accompanied them.

This man had the tiny gold key hanging around his neck that not only was the badge of his office but also was tuned to gateways, allowing him to access them anywhere on the planet—although it was a two-step process to travel gates in the same dimension, as it had been on Earth.

They had to travel through the Gatekeeper's gateroom to get to any gate on their own planet. This extra step took only an extra minute, as they didn't actually go into the Gatekeeper's office but simply went from one gate into another in the impossibly long corridor in the gateroom. According to her instructors, no one really knew why this was so, but it was how it worked.

His key, whenever he approached a gateway, would warm on his neck, and then the gate techs, via his Gate Guardian authorization, should be able to reactivate that gate and send the crawlies back where they came from, as no one else had likely used the gate since they had come through. The first three sites were nearby and could be visited in a single day, but none of them were gateways.

The following day, they visited two more sites with no luck. Lizzie began to worry. What if none of the sites they had mapped out were gateways; then what? Her stomach clenched at the thought that in order to save Fanilia they might have to destroy the sleeping crawlies. Even though they were inimical to life here, life was life, and she didn't think they were deliberate invaders. They had found themselves in an alien place and were simply trying to survive.

On the third day, with Ynni on her shoulder crooning encouragingly in her mind, they set off to see two more potential sites in a completely different direction than the others they had seen so far.

It wasn't an easy hike. There was no clear path, and they had to navigate with Delile keeping a wary eye on her wand, correcting them whenever they got too far from their objective. And sure enough, the first one was just a large rock with a small opening in it tunneling back, but not even large enough for one of the crawlies to come through. Lizzie wanted to cry. There were only a few more places to check, and just that morning she had noticed how much weaker and how tired Bonwen sounded.

Once again, they set off, often having to clear areas in order to get past the thick undergrowth of the surrounding forest. When Delile announced they had arrived and pointed just beyond the trees in front of them, Lizzie prepared herself to be disappointed again. Stepping around a large tree trunk, she nearly fell into a huge hole nearly twenty feet in diameter and deep enough that she couldn't see the bottom.

The Gate Guardian, Egain, nearly bumped into her as she leapt back. He wasn't paying attention. His eyes were unfocused, and he was touching his key with one hand as he steadied himself on the trunk of the tree with the other. *"It's here,"* he sent with a touch of awe in his mental voice. *"We've found it, but I have no idea how we're going to get to it. It is deep in the bottom of that pit, and I can't tell how deep it might be. Did I mention I'm afraid of heights?"* That last question was nearly a mental squeak and Egain's eyes were wide with fear.

"It's all right, Egain; you aren't going to have to do this alone. We have special equipment, remember? And," she added with a wry twist to her mouth, *"do you think that the magic will fail us now?"*

She felt a little sheepish, using their beliefs as a prod this way, but she would do whatever was necessary to give him the confidence he needed to get this done. Besides, if she substituted the word "science" in her mind for "magic," then it just became the difference in how they each defined a word. They could disagree on the finer points at another time.

She stepped back behind the tree to confer with the four other members of her team and explained the situation, each of them taking a moment to step around the tree carefully to view the hole. It was going to be difficult to set up any equipment on the edge of the hole, as it was surrounded by the boles of large trees spaced, in some cases, only inches apart. The small gap they had stepped through was only large enough for a single person to stand in, and it was the largest space there.

"*Well,*" said Rolin, the Alliance gate tech, after he had viewed the hole, "*we'll need to get some light on the subject first, to see exactly what we're dealing with. Then we'll figure out how to get the thousands of crawlies back home from there. We'll need a way to transport them in quantity from the tree, as well as some way to move them down into the hole. But first, let's see what we've got.*"

Delile extended her wand, but Egain held up a hand. "*Are you also afraid of heights?*" he asked her with a grin.

She lifted her chin challengingly. "*It depends on what you mean by heights....*"

"*How do you feel about climbing trees?*" he returned, unfazed. Lizzie could tell that these two were used to taunting one another good-naturedly.

She looked up at the branches above her. "*Want to give me a boost?*" She had caught on instantly. "*Who's going to look into the hole? Maybe someone should take a photo?*"

Rolin held up a small rectangular metallic thing about the size of a business card. "*I've got it. Lizzie, the photos will transfer magically to your tablet. Delile, as soon as you can cast light with your wand over the hole, I will take several shots.*" Lizzie appreciated the mental wink that had gone along with his words "magically" and "cast," as if he dealt with magic all the time. Of course, as an active and experienced Alliance agent, he had gone through the same training as Lizzie and took it all in his stride.

Lizzie let them get to it. There wasn't room for more than one person to do anything effectively from the gap in the trees. This was something she had to consider as Delile and Rolin worked on getting some aerial shots of the hole.

"*How do you usually transport large amounts of anything long distance on Fanilia?*" she asked Egain after he had boosted Delile up into the tree. This business of having to plan on the run like this, felt a lot like trying to create a parachute with a needle and thread while falling from a plane before you actually hit the ground. She didn't like it, but the time they had left continued to run like the sand in an hourglass, and she feared they might not keep up.

"*It is hard to do this any way except perhaps by air,*" he replied thoughtfully. "*Our hovercraft sometimes deliver large shipments, but generally only that which can fit inside, and I don't see how they could ever land in or around this hole.*" He scratched his head. "*The opening is too narrow, and there is little open space flat enough for it to land anywhere close to here. And we would still have to get the crawlies out of whatever container we put them into from the container into the gate.*" He shook his head. "*I think this might be a bigger problem even than getting access to the gate.*"

Lizzie thought about this. Suddenly she remembered the first time she had seen news footage of a military helicopter lowering a rescue boat to victims of a sinking ship. The boat had been large enough to hold a dozen or so people and had even had a gas-powered engine, so it had to have been very heavy.

"What about this?" And she sent a mental reenactment of the incident to Egain. His eyes widened. *"They were right about you. Your magic is strong. What was that you just sent me?"*

Lizzie realized she had just done something unusual. Generally mental speech was translated into concepts. No one beside Ynni or Bonwen had ever sent her images, much less film footage before. She made a mental note to ask Liliath about it when she finally got the opportunity to speak with the dragon again.

"That was a memory of mine from my planet. Our technology isn't as advanced as yours, but that aircraft is similar, in a primitive way, to your hovercraft. They used something we call a "block and tackle" to suspend the boat from underneath the aircraft. Could we somehow rig some magic that would allow us to do something similar?

"If we could find a container large enough to contain large numbers of the crawlies and one of your hovercraft large enough to suspend it from above, couldn't we lower it into the hole, or at least get close enough to send them down a chute to the gate?"

Egain's eyes lit up and he reached for his "wand." *"Let me call in some wizards who specialize in this kind of magic, and I will see what we can do. It's the closest thing to a solution I've heard so far."*

Rolin returned from the gap and called up to Delile. *"Are you ready to come down, or would you like to hang around up there for a while longer?"*

Her face peeked from between two large limbs. *"Just don't drop me. I've still got a lot of work to do, after what we just saw."*

She cautiously edged out onto the limb and then dangled her feet in the air, slowly lowering herself until her feet made contact with Rolin's hands. She then used her hands to steady herself on the tree trunk as Rolin gently lowered her to where she could step off of his hands onto the ground.

She looked relieved to be on solid ground. Thanking Rolin for his help, she brushed some leaves from her shoulders and straightened her wizard's robes.

Lizzie immediately took her tablet out of her MDP, conscious of the fact that the Fanilians considered this ability to manifest solid things out of apparently thin air magic of the highest caliber. She had to admit that there was a time when she would have also thought it a fine sleight-of-hand trick if she hadn't known there was science behind it. Even the scientists of the Alliance didn't completely understand how it worked.

One more question to be answered, she thought, mentally rolling her eyes.

Rolin had taken several pictures at as many different angles as he could in the constraint of the small gap he had to maneuver from. The light from Delile's wand had been surprisingly bright and showed that the hole was surrounded on every side by the huge roots of the trees around the perimeter of the hole. The roots interlaced in many places; and although the hole wasn't fully blocked, it meant there was not much room for maneuvering once inside it. However, the roots also meant that climbing down into the hole might not be as difficult as it had first appeared.

She showed the pictures to Egain. He frowned and then sighed with relief. *"I think the Alliance wizard and I could manage that with some climbing equipment. It looks like there is support of one kind or another all the way to the bottom. I suppose, if we can rig something hanging from the sturdier branches of the larger tree, we could get started fairly soon. What do you say, Rolin? Ready to do some gate magic?"*

Rolin grinned and shrugged. *"Why not? I don't have anything else on my schedule today."*

Now that they had the beginnings of a usable solution, Lizzie was surprised at how fast the Fanilians began to put the pieces together. Tarafau kept Lizzie abreast of the progress of the various teams created by the Fanilians to handle the many parts of the plan.

One group was constructing a flexible chute out of the fabric usually used to bale straw together after harvest. Another was building what amounted to a cargo container, slightly shorter than the largest hovercraft they had, out of the light but iron-hard bamboo-like wood they used to construct their buildings. The wizards who had originally come with the company were finishing the potion, and another group had come into the camp bearing enough casks to take the potion to the tree when they were ready for it.

It had all been going so well until news came that there had been a casualty among them. Two of them had ventured under the tree to determine the best way to administer the potion to the tree roots. They were on their way out from under the branches when a crawly had dropped out of the tree and landed on the head of one of the pair.

It had immediately attached suckers to the man's forehead. He and his companion ran in terror from under the arching branches. But just before they reached the safety of the outer valley, the man had collapsed, dead. The crawly was still attached to his head, its many legs waving energetically. It was making a gurgling noise, and then it spasmed violently and died also.

His companion hadn't been able to pry the crawly away from his head. They had finally decided to carefully cut it away, to hopefully ascertain what had happened.

"Based on this incident, it seems likely that our blood is poisonous to these creatures. We also don't think this was a deliberate attack. The crawly may have simply slipped off of the branch; otherwise, there might have been more of them," the Fanilian healer concluded after examining both the man and the crawly, and he shuddered. *"The man's brain and head were drained of blood and fluid. This probably*

means they aren't directly dangerous to us, but that it would be unwise not to take precautions against direct contact."

"We have environmental suits that should prevent anything like this from happening again," Tarafau counseled them. *"Did we learn anything while they were under the canopy? Do we know where we need to apply the potion?"*

The companion of the man who had died spoke up sadly. *"Yes, Tarafau. The closest intake roots begin about eight paces after the first large branches appear. Most of the crawlies stay back a bit from the ends of the branches, though. We had only gone a few feet beyond that point when the crawly dropped on Lenn's head. May his transition be guided by the magic to the next good place."*

Lizzie felt responsible, like she should have foreseen this and taken precautions before now, but she still wasn't used to the resources she had available through the Alliance. She felt she had failed them somehow, since they all seemed to look to her for leadership. She appreciated more than ever the practice of pairing a new agent with a guide for the first year after they were certified.

Nevertheless, she had no time to belabor the incident. She thanked everyone for their report; and then, based on more encouraging reports from the rest of the teams, she announced they would put the operation into motion in two days.

None of them got much rest in the hours that followed; with everyone sleeping in shifts, the preparations went on nonstop. They had determined that the best time, based on the eating schedules of the crawlies, would be a couple of hours before the sun rose. They would apply the potion on the entire circumference of the inner circle that the last scouting party had determined would be most effective.

According to the wizards who specialized in plantlings, it would take until the second eating shift for the potion to have spread far enough to reach the feasting crawlies, and at least another half an hour Fanilian time for the potion to put the entire population of crawlies to sleep.

They admitted they didn't know if ultimately the potion would have the desired effect or whether it might in fact be harmful to the crawlies. More than one expressed regret they hadn't known farther in advance to have time to capture some crawlies and run tests, but it was obvious by the state of Bonwen that they had run out of time. It was either take action now or watch her die and see all of the plant life on their planet consumed by the hungry crawlies.

The next morning, by the time the sun was up, the potions team had already applied the potion and returned to the camp. Bonwen had thanked them sincerely and then had sleepily stopped communicating as the potion took hold within her.

Every team was put on alert and stood ready. The first team, before leaving the leafy canopy, had planted a little device supplied by Rolin to monitor movement of the crawlies by tracking body heat. Rolin attentively watched the tiny screen of his little handheld device and finally sent to Lizzie, *"They haven't stirred in a few minutes. I suggest we move now."*

The transport team immediately sprang into action. Nearly a hundred of the crawly harvesters swarmed into the branches within minutes of Rolin's announcement, the rest standing below them with large cloth bags to collect the crawlies as the tree climbers threw them down to them.

One of them was brought into the camp for the wizards to examine. *"It's alive,"* the head healer affirmed. *"It only sleeps, but for how long I cannot say."*

A long line of workers led from the tree to the edge of the valley where the cargo container had been built. They passed bags of crawlies from hand to hand, dumping them out of the bags in through an open hatch and then returning the bags back to the workers under the trees. There was an urgency to their work, but none of them were handling the bags of crawlies with unnecessary roughness, something that Lizzie wasn't sure would have been the case in a similar situation on Earth.

In what seemed like many long hours but was really only about the normal time between meals, the job was done. The tree was thoroughly scoured by those within the branches for any sign of anything foreign, and the hatch of the container was finally closed.

The next stage was to hitch the rigging they had built onto the container to the block and tackle that would finally be attached to a sky hook. Four of the workers would ride the top of the container to the gate site to help balance it and would operate the mechanism that would gently lower the container to rest, one end on either side of the lip of the pit.

Considering none of them had ever done this before and only had Lizzie's little mental movie of the helicopter and the boat to go by, she was amazed at how easy they made it all look. Initially, as the hovercraft began to slowly lift the container up into the air, the container swayed slightly, but the workers, true to their briefing, boldly moved into place to settle it. Lizzie couldn't help but be impressed at the feat, considering how much the container must have weighed with the number of crawlies harvested from the limbs of Bonwen.

The final count, according to the foreman of that crew, had been nearly three thousand, of various weights and sizes.

She was told that the going would be slow, not covering the space nearly as quickly as they would have done when carrying only freight inside. They would have time, if they hurried, to get to the gate site by the time it arrived.

The gate site had been transformed in their absence. The boles of the trees with the exception of the gap they had initially used to access the pit had been wrapped in a weaving of what might have been cloth, turning the encircling trees into a fence around the perimeter of the pit.

From the trees on either side hung rope ladders that extended to the first layer of entangled roots, and lights had been hung on the branches all the way around the pit so that all could easily see into the bottom. Egain and Rolin stood below them on either side of a long cloth tube that extended up the trunk of a tree on one side of the circle. The cloth appeared to be propped open by wicker-like slats.

The upper end of the tube was held in place near the top of the tree by a combination of ropes knotted to the heavier limbs of the tree and also supported by workers who would be attaching the end of the tube to the hatch in the bottom of the cargo container.

The premise was that the workers who had ridden on top of the container would be literally sweeping the crawlies out of the container to go through the hatch and down the tube, which was attached to the gate that the gatekeeper now held open to what they thought was the dimension from which the crawlies had originated.

While all of the other preparations were being made, they had sent scouts in environmental suits into the dimension and reported that the part of it they could see was forested, and indeed there were crawlies in the branches of those trees. At that point they had sealed the gate after attaching the tube to the entrance.

Lizzie wasn't quite sure how all of this worked, considering that in reality the gates didn't have any actual size or shape but seemed to adapt themselves to the visualization of the Gate Guardian in charge of any particular gate. Thus, a gate for dragons would have a different size, shape, and presentation than one for humans, for instance.

There was a soft murmur from the workers in the trees as the hovercraft began to lower the container very slowly down into the center of the gap in the trees. Lizzie's instinct was to hold her breath, but her training kicked in and she began to breathe slowly and mindfully as the pilot maneuvered the container carefully to within reach of those waiting in the tree branches beside the tube.

The tube was attached to the outside edges of the hatch; and with a signal from workers atop the container, the latch was pulled that let the trapdoor fall into the interior of the tube. Lizzie found herself praying, and she heard soft murmuring around her that she imagined were probably spells and incantations by her accompanying wizards.

And then the cloth tube began to wiggle and twitch with the sleeping bodies of the crawlies as they fell down the gradually sloping tube toward the bottom of the pit. Evidently the gate had been reopened, because the tube never seemed to fill but gently undulated as hundreds of crawlies continued to be swept from inside the container.

When they had built the container, they had added a device that resembled nothing more than large push brooms like the janitor in the university had used back on Earth. They swept slowly from either end of the container, meeting finally directly over the hatch. When it had reached the center, one of the intrepid workers from the top of the cargo container jumped down into the top hatch and checked every corner of the container to be sure they had not left a single crawly behind.

Then, as he emerged, he gave another signal to the workers in the trees who began to shake the cloth tube from side to side as if it were a very long giant salt shaker, to move any crawlies who might have gotten stuck on one of the slats that held the tube open. Finally, when it was quite evident that the tube was empty, to Lizzie's surprise, Egain and Rolin stuffed the entire length of the tube into the gateway before closing it.

Rolin then held his little metal device in the palm of his hand and ran it over the area where the gateway had appeared. *"It is locked,"* he broadcast finally to the group. *"We did it. The crawlies are home. Now let's see to Bonwen!"*

The transport ascended slowly to take the container back to the valley. They had decided when they had built it, that after it had been sterilized they would turn it into a place for people to stay when they visited Bonwen; they had vowed they would never leave her so undefended again.

After helping Rolin and Egain out of the pit, they trooped back to the valley, where they found the entire encampment standing around the tree holding hands. At first Lizzie was puzzled. All eyes were on Bonwen, and with a start she realized they were singing. There didn't seem to be any words to the song, but she was informed by one of those with her that this was a song of healing.

She listened for a while, taking in the soothing rhythms and melody. Then, without thinking, she took out the kareena that Tarafau's people had given her what seemed ages ago. She removed it from its carved wooden case and stroked it. It swelled. And responding to her touch and to her mind, the music that she heard around her emanated from it like a symphony orchestra, welling up into every heart, seeping into every mind.

She remembered the times she and Reloi had explored the way this instrument connected with her mind and the musical side of her brain, and the music swelled even more. She poured her entire heart into it. It raised them all on its waves of sound that reached beyond the ears, beyond any of the physical senses.

At one point, what seemed like forever later, she realized that all around her had stopped singing. As one, they stared in awe at her, swaying as if dancing to the great sonata that had been pouring out of her. Like the many times she had done her extemporaneous concerts under the little tree by her pod, she felt a great calm and connection to every being present.

And just like what had happened after she had realized she could communicate with the trees and plants around her, she could feel that every plantling in the valley had joined in, including Bonwen, somewhat weakened but alive and, Lizzie could tell, joyful.

Chapter 26: Finale

(Now Jenny understood, or she thought she did. She and her aunt were connected by so much more than blood. How her aunt had known that Jenny could stand up to similar challenges, she couldn't say; but, somehow, she had recognized a bit of herself in Jenny.

So much was coming into focus and with only a few pages yet to go in the journal, she didn't hesitate to plunge back in, turning the page to read the last words of this second journal before she would move on to the third one.)

For the next several months, Lizzie spent most of her time working with the Fanilians to create a small annex to the main college in Bonwen's valley. The wizards had all agreed that they had been remiss in ignoring the importance of the Great Tree and had grown away from the very roots that had made them who they were.

Much as it had at the training center, by popular demand evening concerts had become a new tradition, sometimes featuring Lizzie with either the mbira or what the natives were calling her "stroker"; but generally, many different musicians, each with their own special presentation, participated with enthusiasm.

Mostly, pilgrimages to the valley were becoming a tradition for newly married couples or those with newborn infants and even wizards who had recently earned their robes. Lizzie, to her surprise and a certain amount of consternation, had become a vital part of the many ceremonies and events that now centered around Bonwen and her wisdom.

Bonwen had recovered slowly over the months following the rescue from her ordeal, and she was gracious and welcoming to the Fanilians, gladly speaking mentally with them whenever they came to her, never seeming to tire of their questions or from their adoration.

Tarafau frequently left Lizzie to her own devices these days, visiting his home for a few days at a time, and Lizzie didn't mind at all. She had become a part of this culture and finally had begun to feel a certain amount of confidence in her role as a representative of the Alliance, although some of the attention she had received due to her part in Bonwen's rescue had been uncomfortable for her.

They often treated her like some celebrity or, at the very least, a dignitary. But, as months passed, she even started wearing the native style clothing most of the time.

Then one day, Tarafau showed up in the small cottage the Fanilians had constructed for her in the valley, appearing from seemingly nowhere, something she had gotten used to. With him he had what was obviously another Alliance agent, due to the tiny infinity symbol that dangled on a gold chain in the *V* of his shirt collar.

"Well, Lizzie, how are things going? Allow me to introduce you to Gar from Fleem. He comes with a high recommendation from the council. You will introduce him to the Fanilians as your replacement. You have a new assignment."

"Just like that? Is this a joke?"

Tarafau shook his head apologetically, *"Actually no, but I had hoped you might take it easier if I just told you straight out. I know you have gotten very comfortable here. You know, as an agent, you can't always depend on staying in any assignment on even a semi-permanent basis, right?"*

"Tarafau!" She noticed that Gar looked a bit concerned at their byplay. *"Sorry, Gar. Nice to meet you. I don't mean to be unwelcoming, but this is a bit of a shock."*

He nodded his head. He was humanoid, tall and lanky, but he reminded her of Meta with a slight bluish tint to his skin. *"I know. You just never know when they will call you to a new place. I'd been at my post for nearly two years and was beginning to wonder if I should buy property,"* and he laughed sheepishly.

"Okay. So how long do I get before we leave?" she asked, looking pointedly at Tarafau.

"You have a few days to get Gar oriented, and then we're off to headquarters. You've done some good work here, and it was noticed that's all I'm allowed to tell you."

The Fanilians didn't take the news very well, although they were nice enough to Gar. Lizzie went to visit Bonwen, and the tree understood. *"I have been for so long. I have been since before all of these. I will be long after these are gone. I wish to thank you for your kindness and your care for me and my world. Touch my bark."*

Lizzie held out a trembling hand and touched the dark, smooth, worn bark of the great tree, feeling like an insect on an elephant. For a brief moment, she felt only the bark beneath her hand, but then a warmth welled up in her like being immersed in a hot spring. She felt, rather than heard, the music of the tree and the love of all living things. Something inside of her came alive, like someone had flipped a switch.

"I cannot tell you what was just instilled in you. You must discover it for yourself, but it is something that was already inside of you that I have brought to the surface. Continue to learn about yourself and what you can do. You are more, Agent Lizzie Japhet, than you ever thought was possible."

Lizzie spread both arms as far as she could reach to either side of Bonwen's trunk and hugged the tree, as much with her mind as with her body. The tears that had hung unshed from her eyes sprang forth from sheer joy and deep affection for this amazing being.

"This has made everything worth it," she told Bonwen. And somehow, she knew that the tree understood it all, her struggle all her life with her curiosity and the dissatisfaction she had felt for her instruction before her time with the Alliance, the struggle she had with her own emotions, and how difficult it had always been to connect with others.

She even thought that Bonwen understood the pain and the joy and the disappointment of her time with Reloi, and somehow a healing greater than she ever thought possible warmed her heart.

"Thank you."

"Return to us when you can." Bonwen told her in parting. *"I understand that your kind can travel the vast distances of the multiverse like walking through a forest glade. Come again and be welcome."*

Of course, the Fanilians couldn't let her go without a feast that doubled as a welcome to Gar. In what seemed like no time, she was walking through the Fanilian gate into the basement of the headquarters building of the Alliance.

As she, Tarafau, and Ynni traveled up in the huge elevator to the private council chamber, Lizzie couldn't help but be a bit melancholy, considering all of the goodbyes she had been through over the last few years, between Sanglarka, the Alliance agent training center, and her various assignments—first as an intern and more recently as a certified agent—and wondered how many times this would be repeated in the future.

They walked into the now familiar reception room and were waved into the main council room by the receptionist.

There, in addition to the Chief Councilor and his two under councilors, was someone Lizzie did not expect.

Gaston turned to look at her with a big grin on his face. "Hey there, stranger!" And he came forward, arms outstretched. Lizzie didn't hesitate—she wrapped her arms around him in a fervent hug.

"Oh, Gaston! How wonderful to see you!" Then, when she thought a second, she said, "Is everything all right?"

Gaston looked a little sad, but only for a moment. "Nita passed away this past week. I will miss her. She wasn't sick, just old. Her heart gave out while she was out hanging clothes. I had tried to convince her we needed one of those electric dryers, but she would have none of it.

But I am well. I hear you have had some adventures and some sadness yourself. We can speak of it later." He turned to the council. *"Sorry, one and all, a small reunion of friends,"* he sent with an apologetic smile.

The Chief Councilor nodded both heads in unison and sent, *"Not to worry, Gaston. But let us get to the business at hand, and then you and Lizzie can have as much time as you would like."*

They turned to look intently at Lizzie, and she realized to her embarrassment that she was the focus of everyone in the room. She let nothing of it show on her face, however, and waited as patiently as she was able for someone to say something.

"Agent Japhet, you have acquitted yourself in your initial assignments as an agent beyond anyone's expectations. You have exhibited talents and abilities far greater than any of us anticipated, including, we think, yourself.

"Your ability to think logically through a problem, your dedication to continuing to learn and expand your abilities, and the presence of mind you have exhibited in two separate events of disastrous proportions have made us think that perhaps you are capable of much more than originally thought.

"As Gaston just said, his situation has changed with the passing of his housekeeper, and he has confided in us that he feels a need to retire

from his duties as the Gate Guardian of the Earth, Los Angeles gate. He wishes to spend the remainder of his life in Sanglarka, where he can continue to associate with his fellow Gate Guardians, but without the ultimate responsibility of the gate guardianship itself.

"You may not realize it, but one of the responsibilities of a Gate Guardian is to choose a potential successor. Gaston didn't choose you just to become an agent for the Alliance. Ultimately, his hope was that you would eventually replace him as the guardian of the Los Angeles gate."

Lizzie couldn't help herself; she gasped, and all in the room smiled. Evidently her shock had been expected.

The Chief Councilor continued, *"Therefore, at this time, we would like to extend the calling of official Gate Guardian to you. Your training as an agent of the Alliance was in preparation for this calling, and you have exceeded any of our expectations. Will you serve now, as a guardian of the Earth, Los Angeles gate? This will be a permanent assignment that you will relinquish only when you, yourself, are ready to retire and have found a suitable replacement. Will you serve?"*

Nobody moved or spoke. Lizzie took a moment to think. A permanent assignment? No more unexpected changes? A chance to reconnect with her family and perhaps to make some friends who wouldn't go away or that she wouldn't have to leave behind for what seemed like forever?

She knew she would still be able to stay connected with her podmates and other agent friends through the Alliance network, and she would love to reconnect with the other Earth guardians who had first introduced her to this amazing opportunity.

"Yes," she said humbly and simply. *"I will serve."*

"Gaston, you may do the honors," the Chief Councilor intoned.

Gaston turned to Lizzie, touching the tiny key that dangled on the chain around his neck, something Lizzie had never really noticed before. She was aware now, after her training, of the Guardian keys, and she also knew they were programmed to give off a signal that made people look anywhere but directly at them unless they were authorized agents or guardians.

As he touched it, he said, "Lizzie Japhet, I hereby relinquish the key of my office to you." Reaching behind his neck, he unfastened the chain; then reaching it around her neck, he fastened it around her own, at the same time removing the infinity symbol that she had never been able to remove before.

With wonder that she knew was showing on her face, she reached one finger up to the tiny key and touched it. Then, Gaston touched it with his own finger, and she felt it warm as if touched by the sun.

"*It is done.*" The statement by the Chief Councilor hung vibrating in the room like a chord on a long fermata. Ynni crooned exuberantly. Lizzie knew her life had changed again, and this time her heart sang with the joy of it.

The End

About the Author:

Reading has always been my passion. Starting in libraries at the age of four, I have travelled near and far via the printed page, from places of ancient history to the stars and beyond. It seemed a natural thing for me to want to write as well.

Being able to go from simple daydreaming and pretending to creating worlds of my own invention has been an ongoing passion and from my teen years I had thought that "someday" I would write books myself.

What happened to that dream? Honestly? Life happened. Out of high school I went into the military. I met my future husband, got married, had children, moved all over the place, including three years in Frankfurt, Germany, had many adventures including clowning professionally, 15 years of broadcast television as a producer/director/show-host, owned more than one business and then went through several major health challenges including breast cancer.

So, what changed? What made me decide to pursue the dream of my teen years? Let's go back a bit...

At about the age of 16 I had started having a recurring dream that pestered me most of my life. Time and time again I would discuss the dream with people I thought were wiser than me and time and time again the repeated answer came, "No idea. I've never heard of such a thing."

At age 63 after having the dream once again I decided that maybe if I wrote it down it might leave me alone. I did so and filed it on my desktop but didn't think of it again until I started hanging out with published authors.

At the end of a recorded interview I did with Mercedes S. Lackey, after I had turned off the recording, I timidly confessed I had often considered writing a book. Mercedes leaned forward in her chair, looked me in the eye and said, "Put your butt in the chair and write!" It was some of the best advice I had ever gotten.

In search of material to write about I stumbled upon that dusty text file about my dream and the rest is history. From it came the science fiction - fantasy series "The Dimensional Alliance" beginning with "The House on Infinity Loop". I am grateful for the events leading up to setting myself upon this path. The series has the word "Infinity" in all of the titles since there seem to be an infinite number of stories I have to tell and I will continue writing them until I transition to the next dimension in some distant date.

To my readers: Never give up on your dream. The first book in this series was published two weeks before my 64th birthday. It is never too late. There are many more to come.

Also by Bonnie K.T. Dillabough

The Dimensional Alliance
Chords of Infinity

The Dimensional Alliance 2nd edition
The House on Infinity Loop
Infinity on Fire
Mirrors of Infinity
Ripples of Infinity

Watch for more at https://dimensionalallianceheadquarters.com.